Anne Wh

In Lily's Books

To Anne,
thank you for making
me feel so welcome in
Swainby.
  God bless you!
    love, Anne

This book is a work of fiction. Names, characters, incidents, establishments or locales are the product of the author's imagination, or are used fictitiously. Any resemblance to actual persons, living or dead, is purely coincidental.

Copyright © 2023 Anne Whorlton

All rights reserved. No part of this publication may be reproduced, stored, or used in any form without the prior written permission of the author, except for the use of brief quotations in a book review.

Edited by Cecile Shanahan and Shirley Enoch
Cover Design by Ken Dawson, Creative Covers
Typeset by Kate Coe, Book Polishers

In loving memory of my parents.

Contents

PROLOGUE	7
CHAPTER ONE	13
CHAPTER TWO	22
CHAPTER THREE	29
CHAPTER FOUR	40
CHAPTER FIVE	49
CHAPTER SIX	55
CHAPTER SEVEN	70
CHAPTER EIGHT	80
CHAPTER NINE	88
CHAPTER TEN	96
CHAPTER ELEVEN	110
CHAPTER TWELVE	119
CHAPTER THIRTEEN	127
CHAPTER FOURTEEN	133
CHAPTER FIFTEEN	144
CHAPTER SIXTEEN	154
CHAPTER SEVENTEEN	161
CHAPTER EIGHTEEN	169
CHAPTER NINETEEN	180
CHAPTER TWENTY	191
CHAPTER TWENTY-ONE	199
CHAPTER TWENTY-TWO	206
CHAPTER TWENTY-THREE	211
CHAPTER TWENTY-FOUR	219

CHAPTER TWENTY-FIVE	231
CHAPTER TWENTY-SIX	237
CHAPTER TWENTY-SEVEN	245
CHAPTER TWENTY-EIGHT	252
CHAPTER TWENTY-NINE	263
CHAPTER THIRTY	273
CHAPTER THIRTY-ONE	282
CHAPTER THIRTY-TWO	292
CHAPTER THIRTY-THREE	302
CHAPTER THIRTY FOUR	308
CHAPTER THIRTY-FIVE	313
CHAPTER THIRTY-SIX	319
CHAPTER THIRTY-SEVEN	329
CHAPTER THIRTY-EIGHT	334
CHAPTER THIRTY-NINE	343
CHAPTER FORTY	356
CHAPTER FORTY-ONE	364
CHAPTER FORTY-TWO	370
CHAPTER FORTY-THREE	376
CHAPTER FORTY-FOUR	383
EPILOGUE	389
Acknowledgments	395
A note on animals and places in this book	397
Jessie's Cinnamon Swirls	398
About the Author	400
Reading Group Questions	401

PROLOGUE

Three months before

Lily Henderson was a lucky girl, or so everyone thought. She was pretty and intelligent, she had a handsome and charming boyfriend, a well-paid job that she loved, a bright red Mini, and a smart little apartment in Oxford that all her friends would have envied her for. That was, if she'd had any friends. As it was, she only had one, Beth, and Spencer of course. Sometimes Lily thought there ought to be more to her life, but most days she told herself she was lucky, and privileged, and therefore had no reason to complain.

Today was her birthday, and Spencer was taking her out — not to any of the fancy restaurants he usually took her to, but to the country, as a special birthday favour. A country girl at heart, Lily had been looking forward to this day for weeks, trying to squeeze in as many of her favourite things to do and places to see as possible. In the end, they had settled for a walk along the Thames Path National Trail between the Gloucestershire village of Buscot and the village of Kelmscott in Oxfordshire. Kelmscott was famous for its connections with William Morris, the founder of the Arts and Crafts Movement. Lily loved his furnishing designs which were so wonderfully rich with flowers, leaves, and birds, and was excited at the prospect of visiting his country home, Kelmscott Manor.

Comfortably settled in the soft leather seats of Spencer's Mercedes SL convertible, Lily watched the countryside slip by with all the clarity that an open-topped car affords and marvelled at every church spire, every manor house tucked away in the rolling fields, and every maple tree that showed the first tinges of red, until Spencer shook his head laughing.

'You really love this, don't you? Tell me, what are you doing in Oxford if clearly you would be so much happier in the country? Being cooped up in a stuffy university library must be hell for you. You should marry a farmer!'

Lily felt the blood drain from her face. She was trying to think of a witty reply, but her mind was blank, and she swallowed back the tears that were forming at the back of her eyes.

Without even realizing he had hurt her feelings, Spencer went on obliviously. 'So, tell me about Kelmscott Manor. I am taking a weekday off to take you there, so hopefully the place is worth visiting. I expect there will be a gift shop, too?'

Of course there would be a gift shop. She would not buy anything though because it would only look as if she expected him to pay — and that was the last thing she wanted, even if it was her birthday, and even if he had the money. Spencer, a successful lawyer, came from a rich family; his parents owned a huge manor house just outside Oxford, and were members of more country clubs than Lily cared to count. Sometimes she wondered why, of all the girls he could have had, Spencer had chosen her, an insignificant college librarian with a builder for a father. But they had been together for over two years now; so she supposed he must love her after all, even if his family did not.

And although he could be such a snob at times, she admired and loved him as she had never loved a man before — if he asked her to marry him today, she was sure she would say yes. There was little chance of him asking, of course, as Spencer had been married before, and had made it clear from the beginning that he would not marry again. Ironically, he was a divorce lawyer ('I have those poor fools sitting at the other side of my desk every day, thank you very much!') and made money from getting people legally separated.

'Lily?' he prompted, putting a hand on her thigh. 'Kelmscott Manor?'

Lily started at the sound of his voice but caught herself quickly. She should not give in to such gloomy thoughts on her birthday. 'Kelmscott Manor, yes … I don't know if there is a gift shop, but the house dates back to 1570, and Morris loved it because of its perfect setting – he said the house 'sat so well in the countryside it was almost as if it had grown up out of the soil'. I'm sorry it is only open to the public on Wednesdays and Saturdays, but as it is my birthday, I thought you wouldn't mind …'

He sighed. 'Of course I don't mind, darling. I was only joking. Forgive me, it was stupid of me to say that, and quite insensitive. You know I would do anything for you, especially on your birthday.'

Although she was not sure about the *anything*, she gave him her best smile, and — for what it was worth — the benefit of the doubt. 'I know you would. And it's very kind of you to take the day off. Oh, look, there is Buscot now, and the sun's just coming out again.'

***

Despite Spencer's initial protest that he was 'a runner and not a walker', they both enjoyed the walk along the river immensely, chatting away and admiring the scenery (although Lily did most of the chatting, and certainly most of the admiring). Much to Lily's delight and surprise, he did buy her two cushions at Kelmscott Manor 'to remember this beautiful day'. She tried to convince him that one would do, but he shook his head in mock seriousness.

'It would not look right with only one Morris cushion on your sofa. Two corners, two matching cushions,' he said and kissed the tip of her nose, 'because I know what a little perfectionist you are.'

'Guilty as charged, I'm afraid — I would probably have come back for a matching cushion, so … thank you.' As she smiled up at him, Lily had no idea how charming she looked with her bright amber eyes and bouncing dark chestnut curls. 'You're my hero.'

They walked back to Buscot following the Thames Path National Trail which led them across two footbridges and a rather muddy field (it had rained for the best part of the last two weeks), that gave them splendid views of Buscot House. Lily happily took photo after photo while Spencer complained that his new boots were getting muddy.

'That's what walking boots are for!' Lily laughed. 'Don't you ever get your trainers muddy when you run? But don't worry, I'll clean them for you,' she promised cheerfully and put her phone away, pointing to the other end of the field. 'Look, there's a yellow waymarker over there. We need to follow that one, or we'll miss the stile. I love stiles, don't you? And kissing gates. Such a shame there aren't any on this walk. You would have to kiss me every time we passed through one!'

'Would I?' he said, arching an eyebrow as he reached for her waist. 'Well, well. I don't need a kissing gate to do that — I can kiss you any time. Just wait until I get you home and …'

Lily tried to relax into his arms as his kiss grew ever more passionate but found that she couldn't. She wanted to walk on. She did not want this day to end. She did not want to go back to Oxford where they would sit in the elegant atmosphere of *The Folly*, eating lobster and lemon sorbet. She would not dare tell him, but she would be quite happy to stay here and have fish and chips at the pub instead, with mushy peas, and sticky toffee pudding for afters.

'Hey!' Spencer had pulled back and was frowning down at her. 'What's the matter? Don't you want me?'

Quickly putting on her sweetest smile, she said, 'Of course I do. Perhaps not right here in the middle of a public footpath …'

She was not sure if she had convinced him, but he took her hand and said, 'Alright then, I suppose I'd better take you home. First dinner, good wine, and then — back to your place — or mine? Yes, back to mine, I have the better coffee machine. And then — mmm…'

***

LATER THAT NIGHT, when Spencer had made love to her and lay with his back turned to her, as he always did, snoring lightly, Lily slipped into the bathroom and sat on the floor, put her head on her knees and wept.

Why am I doing this? Why am I still with him? He doesn't want to marry me, he doesn't want children, he doesn't want a house in the country, he doesn't even want a dog! He does not want a single thing I want. He is not right for me. I am not right for him. We can't go on like this, we really can't.

Tomorrow, she thought when she slipped back underneath the sheets half an hour later, her eyes red and swollen, *I will tell him. I will return his birthday presents and tell him it's over.*

CHAPTER ONE

'Merry Christmas!'

On hearing her friend Beth's cheerful voice, Lily looked up from the e-mail she had just been writing and found herself being presented with a huge Christmas bouquet.

'Beth! You shouldn't have! We said we wouldn't, remember? No presents. That is really unfair, you know, you not sticking to the rules!'

'Yes, well, I know we said that, but Matthew bought me one and I thought I just had to get him to buy you one, too, seeing as Spencer would probably not think of such things — oops, sorry, that wasn't kind. Forgive me.'

Lily shrugged. 'It's okay. We both know what he is like … romantic doesn't suit him.' She looked around for a vase, then decided she wouldn't bother, as she would go home in half an hour. Surely the flowers, if she wrapped them in some wet tissue, would survive that long.

'Matthew always gets me a red amaryllis with a white rose to go with it just before Christmas — the rose symbolizing Baby Jesus, you see — and it has become quite a tradition, I must say. Well — you know how Matthew loves to spoil me.'

Matthew and Beth had been childhood sweethearts,

growing up in the same village and attending the local church with their families. They had got married just over three years ago when Matthew had taken the position of curate in the Cotswold village of Lower Rissington.

Spencer wouldn't dream of buying Lily flowers just because it was 'nearly Christmas' — he just was not the romantic type. He was not the marrying kind either, and why they were still together ... well. She shook her head. She *had* tried to tell him that morning after her birthday, but he had been in such a hurry to go running, and then he had gone to work ... there simply had not been time. And somehow the months had slipped by, and now it was five days before Christmas, and ...

'Are you listening?'

Squeezing her eyes shut for a second, Lily took a deep breath, and blinked. 'Sorry, what did you say?'

Beth looked at her in mock exasperation. 'You were daydreaming again! Lily Henderson, you really are impossible! — Anyway, we're going to have an after Christmas Party on the twenty-seventh. Well, just brunch, really. Nothing big. Will you come?'

'Should I ask Spencer?'

Beth raised an eyebrow. 'If you like. But I'm warning you, there will be mostly very serious Christians who are not a bit interested in horse racing and I don't think there are any athletes among them either — oh, no, wait, there is Simon, of course, who goes running every morning. Absolutely *every* morning. Hannah told me he even went for his run the day they got married. Can you imagine?!' She shook her head, laughing. 'So, yes, he could come and sit next to Simon, I suppose, and then they can talk sports to their hearts' content! You will come then, yes?'

'Of course I will. I probably won't know what to do with myself after Christmas, and the fridge will be empty — did I tell you we are all going up to Yorkshire this year? We're going to spend Christmas at my Auntie Abigail's. Well, she's my great-aunt, really, who lives all by herself on a farm in Rosedale where she used to breed ponies until her brother, who ran the family farm, died some years ago. She gave up the breeding and horse show business after that. Just kept a couple of her favourite ponies and withdrew from the world. Sad really, isn't it? Anyway … where was I?'

Beth was right of course — she *was* a dreamer. *And* a hopeless romantic. It was one of the reasons she was so happy in her job as college librarian: Apart from being surrounded by thousands of books, some of them dating all the way back to medieval times, there was the stillness of the place, the comforting smell of old leather and of course, the view of the beautiful city from her window. She would not want to trade this view for anything in the world. Well, for a cottage in the country perhaps. Or for being a published writer herself one day — not even Beth knew that she wrote poetry and had even posted some of her work on Instagram lately. Not that she would get many people to follow her. So far, there were four.

'Lily?'

She shook herself. 'Yes?'

'You are hopeless,' Beth sighed. 'But I love you, anyway. As long as you remember to come to my Christmas brunch and bring your cheese scones along.'

'I will,' said Lily, already scribbling away in her notebook. '27th December, Brunch at Beth and Matthew's. Bring cheese scones.' She snapped the notebook shut. 'There you go — done!'

'Excellent! Now I must rush — Matthew is waiting outside, and I said I wouldn't be long … We need to go shopping, and we have a little social with our house group tonight. What time are *you* going to finish and leave this desk then?'

Lily glanced at her Radley watch, which had been caught in the sleeve of her cream-coloured blouse, and gave it a little shake to set the tiny dangling dog free. 'In about half an hour. Sorry, remind me again — what is a house group?'

'It's a group of people from our church who meet every other week to study the Bible and pray together. We usually meet at Simon and Hannah's because they have little children, but today they are all coming to us. Right, I must dash. See you on the twenty-seventh?'

Nodding, Lily took her pen, and slipped it back into its slim leather case. Then she put pen and notebook into her handbag which was sitting in a corner of her desk. That was how she liked things to be: a place for everything, and everything in its place. 'Yes. I'm very much looking forward to that. Anything else you want me to bring?'

'Nope. You go and have fun feeding carrots to the ponies!' grinned Beth. 'And tell me all about it when you get back — bye then, Lily, have a blessed Christmas!'

When Beth was gone, Lily looked about the empty library and sighed. Suddenly she just wanted to get home. Even if she did not have a husband waiting for her, at least she could curl up on the sofa with a book or watch a bit of TV.

She took out her phone to check her messages, but there were none. Of course not, she thought, and slipped the phone back into her handbag. *I have just seen Beth, I will see Spencer tomorrow, and I am going to see my family at Christmas.*

Who else would text her? She was lucky enough if she got as many as twenty Christmas cards.

With another sigh, she got up and started to tidy her desk. What did it matter, anyway? She loved Christmas, and she was looking forward to spending it in Yorkshire with her family this year. A few days away would do her good and stop her mind from brooding. At least she hoped that it would.

***

Spencer surprised her by not only bringing her an ostentatious bouquet of dark red roses but by presenting her with a small black velvet box as well. He took her hands, made her sit next to him on her little sofa and placed the box in her lap, smiling.

'For me?'

'Do you see anyone else in the room who might want to claim it?'

She laughed a little nervously. 'No! No, of course not. Oh, Spencer, that is so kind of you. Thank you!'

'Well then — open it.'

Her heart was beating fast as she loosened the silk tie around the box, hoping it was not a ring. Just a few months ago, she would have given anything for a ring, but now she was not sure — actually, she was, but …

She let out a tiny sigh of secret relief when she saw the silver heart pendant nestling on a red velvet cushion. With trembling fingers, she lifted the delicate piece of jewellery out of its box, holding the sparkling diamond-cut silver chain against the candlelight.

'Oh, Spencer, this is beautiful! I don't deserve it!'

And she meant it, too — but Spencer just laughed, taking the pendant from her to put it around her neck. 'Of course you deserve it. It's Christmas, isn't it? And you,' he said, lowering his voice as he began to plant soft kisses along her neckline, 'are a very special woman, Lily. A very special woman …'

Turning around to respond to his caresses, as he was expecting her to do, she knew it would not be long before she would be wearing only the necklace and they would tumble into bed. But hard as she tried, she just could not feel any desire, not even for this one night. She would much rather sit next to him all evening, snuggled up on the sofa with a glass of wine, and let things develop slowly and more naturally — and if she had the courage to tell him …

She shook her head. Not tonight. Not before Christmas. She had waited three months, perhaps even longer, surely this could wait another few days now. And anyway, she knew he would not listen. He would not see her for a week, he would want to make love to her and go home, so that he could go on his early morning run before work tomorrow. Lily did not do any sports, except riding her bike to work and walking Silky, her parents' ancient Irish Setter, when she visited them in Burford. She wondered if they would bring Silky with them at Christmas. They would have to, with no one else to look after the old girl.

'Hey … what's wrong with you, honey?' Spencer had pulled back and was looking at her with a mixture of concern and hurt. Hurt pride, probably. 'Anything troubling you?'

Lily hurried to shake her head. 'No. I'm sorry. It's just — I'm still trying to unwind, you know. Work and stuff. My head needs a little time to adjust to holidays. I'm sorry. Would you mind if I just poured us a glass of wine and then — um ... we could sit on the sofa for a bit and — talk?'

'Talk?'

'Yes.'

'What do you want to talk about? Do you want to tell me the names of all of your crazy aunt's animals again? The dog is called Theo. And she has got ... five horses? Six?'

Lily did not know why but something in the way he said this made her angry, the way he referred to her as the *crazy aunt*. She loved Abigail, and she loved the farm. But she bit her anger down, as she always did with Spencer, though why she did not know. There seemed to be a lot of things she did not know, and not only about Spencer ...

'No. Of course not.' *And I won't talk about anything else tonight, either. There will be a better moment. After Christmas. Or whenever.*

Leaning in to kiss him, she ignored the churning in her stomach and whispered, 'Glass of wine?'

***

IT WAS STILL dark when Lily was woken by the sound of a teacup being placed on her bedside table.

'Morning, gorgeous!'

She opened her eyes to see Spencer towering over the bed, fully dressed and ready to go at — she peered at the red digits on her radio alarm — half past seven.

Groaning, she sat up and rubbed her eyes. 'It's only half past seven! Why can't we stay in bed for a bit longer? Have breakfast together?' She knew the answer of course. He never stayed for breakfast. Sometimes he came back for it, yes, but only after a five-mile-run, or however long it took to have him fit and ready for the day.

Remembering what Beth had said about her friend's husband, she said, 'Oh, by the way, we have been invited for an after-Christmas brunch at Beth's. It's on the twenty-seventh. Will you come with me? Please?'

Here she was again, begging. Why did she so often resort to begging? *He* never did. His yes was a yes, and his no was a no. Mostly she got nos these days. Like now, two in one crushing sentence. No breakfast in bed, and no brunch at Beth's.

'You know I can't stay, Lily. I have to practise for the big New Year's Race in Blenheim. I'm sorry,' he said, forcing a smile. 'I know you would like me to meet your friends more often. Tell you what, why don't we go to Paris in January? Just the two of us. Let's have a look at hotels when you get back from Yorkshire. Okay?'

She bit her lip and nodded. 'Okay. Yes, that would be lovely.'

Would it though?

She drank her tea slowly, as she knew he would not leave until she had finished it, and tried not to cry. She almost wished he would go now and just leave her to it. Or better still, not come back at all. *Maybe I should tell him now. Get it over with.*

'Goodbye then, gorgeous, and let me know how things are going on the farm. Okay?' He leaned over to kiss her. 'See you soon!'

Too late, she thought. *As always, I leave things too late.* Biting her lip, she looked down at her necklace and then up at him, putting on a smile, even if it did not reach her eyes. He wouldn't notice the difference. 'Yes, see you soon. And thank you for the beautiful necklace. I will — I will treasure it forever.' Goodness, what a bad liar she was. Just as well he was not listening, anyway. 'Oh, and Spencer?'

Already on his way, out, he turned in the door. 'Yes?'

'Merry Christmas.'

He smiled. 'Merry Christmas, Lily. I'm glad you like the necklace.'

A minute later she heard the front door being shut, and he was gone.

CHAPTER TWO

Lily. Spencer had a heart attack while running. They have taken him to hospital, but it does not look good. Please come ASAP. Amelia

'Oh no!'

Putting a hand to her mouth, Lily sat down on her bed quickly before her knees gave way. She had been about to go downstairs for Boxing Day lunch when her phone had bleeped. Thinking it would be a message from Spencer, she had picked it up. But although it had been sent from Spencer's phone, it was his mum who had written the message.

Cold sweat began to form on her forehead as she stared at the screen, reading the message over and over again. A heart attack! But Spencer was only thirty-five! And very fit. These things did not happen to fit young men, did they?

There was a knock on her door. 'Are you coming, Lily? Lunch is ready.'

Her mother's voice seemed to come from much further away than just the other side of the door. It sounded like it came through a very thick wall of fog. For some strange kind of reason, images of the 1952 smog that had paralyzed and crippled London for five days and killed thousands came to Lily's mind. The trouble with too much imagination, she thought and tried to get up, but her legs would not obey her brain's order. She could not shake the images off now — she had read about it only recently that it wasn't until undertakers had begun to run out of coffins that the lethal impact of the smog had been realized by the authorities.

This is how this feels now, she thought, *like a smog. It's seeping inside me and there is nothing I can do about it.*

I can't hear. I can't speak. I can't breathe.

What if the next time she saw Spencer he was lying in a coffin, pale faced and hands folded across his broad chest …

'No!'

At that moment the door opened, and her mother stuck her head in. 'No? But Lily, it's — oh dear!' Rushing towards her daughter, Mrs Henderson sat down next to her on the bed and gently took her hands in hers. 'Whatever is the matter, Lily? What's happened?'

For a paralyzing minute, Lily said nothing and just stared at the door. But suddenly she jumped up, tearing her hands free as she did, and reached for her handbag. 'Spencer! I must go to Spencer! At once! — Oh, where are my keys? Have you got them? No, you were driving. Oh God, how will I get there? Is there a train? Where is the nearest station? Why don't I even know these things? And why do I have to be stuck here in the middle of nowhere — I have to go home! Now!'

'Lily! For heavens' sake, calm down! — Bob! Bob!' her mother shouted. 'Come quick!'

***

AN HOUR LATER (an hour!) Lily was bundled into her dad's

Volvo and Abigail pressed a basket into her hands, no doubt filled with leftover Christmas goodies. *If anything happens to Spencer before we get there, I won't eat a thing*, thought Lily as she slumped even further down in her seat. *If he dies, I will never eat again.*

She closed her eyes and tried to zone out while her mum said goodbye to Lily's brother and sister-in-law and coaxed a reluctant Silky, their thirteen-year-old Irish Setter, into the boot. Silky did not like riding in the car. Lily hoped she would not get sick.

'Ready to go?'

Her dad fastened his seatbelt and looked across his shoulder to Lily. She nodded. *As ready as I will ever be. If only we can get there in time. If only I can tell him how much I love him before it's too late.*

She frowned. *But do I love him?*

She felt for the silver pendant underneath her sweater. Was it really only twenty-four hours ago that everybody had admired the sparkling little heart? Even Stephen had been impressed. Lily knew her family did not care much for Spencer. Her brother especially did not think him good enough for her. He did not trust him to look after his precious sister. Sometimes she thought he still saw her as the silly eleven-year-old who had sat on the bathroom floor crying because she had tried to dye her dark brown hair blonde, but it had turned an ugly shade of green instead. He had helped her to wash it half a dozen times before he finally took to the scissors, cutting off her lovely hair, all the while she cried like a baby.

To be fair, he had been the best brother she could have wished for when they grew up, and she did not want to be ungrateful. He just wanted to look out for her. They all did.

But sometimes her family's over-protectiveness just got a little too much, no matter how kindly meant. After all, her illness was ten years ago, she had got over it – or most of it, anyway. She ate enough now, she ate everything, what more did they want? She was still slim but not underweight and the anxiety had got a lot better, too. There were no more panic attacks. Sometimes she almost felt normal.

When her mum had finally settled in the passenger's seat, her dad started the car and steered it through the farm gate and onto the lane that led to the village of Bishops Bridge. Lily did not wave; she did not even look back. Her eyes were firmly fixed on the little silver heart with the sparkling diamond. She bit her lip.

I do love him. I don't want to leave him. I don't want to lose him. Please, God, let him live, so I can tell him.

I love him.

***

IT WAS SIX-FIFTEEN when they got to the hospital. Her dad rushed to open the door for her and gave her a quick bear hug before kissing her forehead and gently pushing her towards the automatic doors behind which the neon light seemed too bright for her tired eyes. She already had a headache. There had not been another message from Amelia even though she had checked ever so often.

'We'll walk Silky for a bit and wait for you in the car,' her mother called through the open car window, but Lily had already slipped through the doors. Self-consciously crossing her chest — she did not know why she did that, she was not even Catholic — she disinfected her hands and walked up to reception.

'Hello,' she said in a small voice and felt like twelve again, 'I have come for a patient who was admitted with a heart attack this morning — Spencer Seymour?'

'Are you related to him?'

'No, I'm — I'm his girlfriend,' she said, feeling for her necklace as if this would get her in.

'Sorry, only family. He's in ICU.'

'I know but —'

'There you are, Lily! God, whatever took you so long?'

Amelia Seymour, wrapped in festive Dior from head to foot and smelling like it, too, came rushing towards her, grabbing her hands. 'We thought you would never come! — She's with us. Our son's girlfriend.' She spoke with confidence bordering on authority. Did that come with the money? Or the status?

The woman at the reception nodded. 'Five minutes. He's unconscious from what I have been told.'

Lily's heart sank. He would not even know she was there. He would not even see her or hear her voice. And they would not be alone. She could not tell him how much she loved him, not in front of his mother.

But she had to let him know! Before it was too late …

***

TRUE TO THEIR word, her parents took her home later. They asked if she wanted to spend the night at their house, but Lily wanted to be alone, claiming she had to sort this out for herself. This mess. The tubes, the wires, the plastic bits and pieces that were stuck to his chest, the monitor above his bed with the dreaded green zigzag line. She hoped to God it would stay green and not turn straight and red overnight.

It might though. The doctor had said as much when he had come to speak to them.

'Better say goodbye,' he had said and gently squeezed her hand. Around sixty and decidedly overweight, he had reminded her of her dad, especially with those warm brown eyes that were looking down at her from his six foot five. There had been a nurse, too, a young brunette called Patsy. Why she should remember her name, Lily did not know. It did not matter.

Nothing mattered.

Not even that the heating had been turned off for three days and the flat was freezing as well as dark and empty. It did not matter. Nothing mattered.

She *had* said goodbye. Quietly. Her lips had moved but the words had not come. She had held his hand — it had felt warm, and she had been glad for that, it made him feel alive – and closed her eyes as she said the words she so wanted him to hear even if she was not sure she meant them. Yesterday she had not been sure. Today was different. Today could be the last day, the last moment, the last chance.

I love you, Spencer. I know I did not say it as often as I should have — you never did — but I know you loved me. Your heart showed me. And I loved you. I wanted you to marry me. I wanted you to build a house with me, in the country, and have four children. Well, maybe two would have done. And a dog. A setter like Silky. You could have gone running with her. Setters like running. I'm sorry I don't. If you get well, I promise I'll start. Couch to 5K and all that. I'll do it for you. I promise. If only you will live.

A tiny movement had made her heart stop beating for a second. Was he waking up? Had that been a flicker of his eyelid? She had held her breath, waited. No. No flickering. No movement. Nothing.

If this is goodbye — please know that I loved you. Please know that — I loved you …

***

Tea, she thought, *I'm going to make myself a cup of tea.* She walked into the kitchen, switched on the light, and picked up the kettle. She opened the Bettys tea caddy Abigail had given her last Christmas and popped a teabag into a mug. She checked the fridge for milk, glad to find there was enough to last her through the night, and opened a packet of chocolate digestives.

Not eating won't help. You must eat. You must be strong.

When she saw the Morris cushions on the sofa, she cried, remembering her birthday, only three months ago. Picking them up, she sat on the sofa with the cushions on her knees and her mug of tea, trying to get warm as well as trying to stay awake. She did not want to sleep. She did not want to let him down; she had to stay awake in case they rang to tell her he had woken up, that he was going to be alright.

But she must have fallen asleep at some point because the shrill ringing of her telephone made her jump, and it was broad daylight when she opened her eyes. Without thinking, she reached for the phone.

'Hello?'

'Lily? It's me, Amelia. I'm so sorry, Lily. He's — he's gone.'

CHAPTER THREE

LILY DIDN'T KNOW how she ever got through that day. She drank lots of tea, ate nothing at all, didn't answer the phone, didn't go out. And all the time she kept thinking *It isn't true. It cannot be true.*

Well, it couldn't be, could it? Spencer had been young and fit and healthy. People like him did not have heart attacks, did they? She shook her head. To her, it didn't make sense at all. Nothing made sense, and nothing mattered anymore. For all she cared the sun could stop shining. Not that it usually shone much in winter, of course, except today of all days it had to make a rare appearance, as if to mock her.

The more she thought about it, the more her head hurt, and still she could not figure it out – it had to be a terrible mistake. She kept feeling for her heart pendant, as if to make sure it was still there – his last present to her. His parting gift, so to speak. It was the only truly romantic present he had ever given to her, which was why it had meant so much to her. *Still* meant so much to her, or maybe even more now that he was gone …

Hadn't she said she would treasure it for ever? And even felt bad about it at that point because she was not sure how long they were going to be together after Christmas? How could she have known that this *for ever* was to last for only six days — and not because she had left him, but because he had died? Died!

Lily wiped her eyes with the back of her hand and gulped. Had it really been less than a week? She glanced at the calendar on the wall. 27th December. *Brunch at Beth and Matthew's. Cheese scones.* She had completely forgotten about that. It didn't matter, anyway. Nothing did. She would stay right here, drink tea, cry her heart out and hope to be able to go back to work after the New Year. At least she had another week.

***

THE NEXT DAY, her brother was standing outside the door of her apartment, a shopping bag under his arm. As soon as he saw the forlorn look on her tear-stained face, Stephen dropped the bag, opened his arms wide and enveloped her in a tight hug. They stood there for a long time, until finally Lily's flood of tears seemed to have run dry for the time being, and Stephen ushered her inside. He made her sit on the sofa and went back into the kitchen where he began to put the shopping away, and make tea as he tried to think of anything he could say to her to make her feel better — but there wasn't.

'So who found him then?' Stephen asked later over yet another cup of tea. 'It was quite early in the morning, wasn't it — and Boxing Day, too, which means most people would still have been asleep or nursing their Christmas hangovers.'

Lily put her mug down and looked at her hands in her lap. 'It wasn't that early, it was around half past ten, I think.

There were dog walkers coming along the path, and they called the ambulance right away. I wish they had practised their resuscitation skills on him, that might have been useful! Lifesaving, in fact. But they didn't, it seemed. Or maybe they did but it didn't help? Oh, Stephen, I don't know! I wasn't there, was I? I think his mum told me but … it all came through a sort of thick mist, or fog, you know? I did not hear half of what she said. I think she talked for ten minutes non-stop. How could she talk so much? Her only son had just … oh God, I can't say it!'

Stephen put an arm around her shoulder. 'I think she just needed to get it off her chest. Say it out loud, to help her grasp what had happened. Like you said, he was their only son. — Do you want to go and see her? Shall I take you over later?'

Lily shook her head no.

'As you wish. But I think you should get in touch with them later this week. They will want to see you, I'm sure. Amelia is quite fond of you, isn't she? Even though you are not posh enough,' he added at an attempt to make her smile. It didn't work.

***

'I FEEL SO bad leaving you like this, sis … Are you sure you don't want me to call Beth?'

Stephen was standing in the tiny hallway, his coat over his arm.

'No,' she whispered hoarsely, shaking her head, 'please don't — don't bother her now. She has her family staying, and she deserves a break. I will call her tomorrow. Maybe.'

'Okay. But I still think you should go and see her. Or

at least call her. She would understand. I'm not sure she would understand you *not* calling her — she is your friend, isn't she? And that's what friends are for — to offer a shoulder to lean on, to be there for you. This is by far the worst thing that could happen to anyone, and I'm so sorry it happened to you, Lily!'

Lily shrugged. 'It didn't only happen to me, did it? It happened to Amelia and Henry Seymour, too. I dare say they can do without me sobbing my way through their stock of starched linen hankies.'

'I'm sure that is not true, but okay, I won't press you any further. You will know when the time is right. Talking of time, I'm afraid I really have to go. But I can come back tomorrow if you like? Make sure you're ...' The word stuck in his mouth when he saw her flinch. *Eating.* That had been the cause for countless arguments between them when they were flat sharing in their uni days. Lily had resented the idea of him looking out for her, or *controlling her* as she had called it when she had finally drawn the line and moved in with two other girls instead.

When she had first started uni, she had been all too happy to move in with Stephen. Their parents had not lived in Burford back then but in Norfolk, so it had seemed like the perfect arrangement at the time, what with Lily having just overcome her illness. To this day she was glad she had moved out when she had, thus protecting the bond between them. She knew that neither of them would have forgiven themselves had this been the cause of a lasting rift between them. Today they were the best of friends again — only sometimes Lily felt Stephen was slipping back into overprotective mode, and then she told him.

Usually. Not today.

'Anyway, if you're sure there isn't anything else I can do for you now ... I'll call you later to say goodnight, okay? Make sure you're alright.'

As soon as the words were out, he shut his eyes wishing he'd never said them. Why wasn't he *thinking*, for goodness' sake? She'd just lost the only man she had ever allowed herself to love, of course she wasn't alright – and wouldn't be for a while yet.

***

AS A COLLEGE counsellor, Beth had seen her fair share of grieving students and professors, and when Lily finally turned up on her doorstep three days later, she gathered her up in her arms immediately, knowing from the distraught look on her friend's face that something terrible must have happened.

Lily and Beth had met five years ago when they had both been new to the college. Lily was still suffering from her anxiety — thank God not from anorexia which had, in comparison, been the 'easier' part of her healing, even though it had been hard and there had been relapses along the way — and had found that talking to Beth helped more than all the years spent in therapy. Maybe that was why she liked Beth so much. She never asked the obvious questions like 'Has anything bad or even traumatic happened to you when you were at school?' (*No, I just did not fit in*) or 'Did you want to be as slim as a model or a Hollywood star?' (*No, I just wanted to be invisible so people wouldn't notice me being different*).

Beth's questions went along the lines of 'How did you feel in that particular situation?' or 'How did you see yourself — and how did you see others? How do you think they saw you?'.

Lily's favourite part was the 'intention bit': 'What did you do that for? What were you hoping to achieve — or avoid?' According to Beth, there was always a reason for our behaviour (the *Why* question), as well as an intention (the *What for* question) — what did you hope to achieve? What did you hope to avoid? Lily thought that was extremely interesting, and when she had said as much to Beth some time ago — they had been friends for a while then, rather than counsellor and client —— her friend had suggested she go into counselling herself one day.

'You'd be really good at this, Lily. You *listen*. You look at people and actually *see* things. Not everyone has this gift. Why don't you use it?'

But while it was true that students tended to unload quite a bit more than a stack of books to be returned onto her desk at the library, she just couldn't picture herself as a counsellor. For one thing, she didn't have the patience, and for another, she felt she was still too anxious about life herself. Even with her master's degree in English and her dream job at the distinguished college library, her self-esteem was still pretty low. And now, without strong, confident Spencer by her side to guide and protect her, it was lower than ever, even if she had sometimes wished she had stood up to him more often. Made him see her for what she really was – a woman with dreams, hopes, and ambitions, and a will of her own. Only now it did not seem to matter what she wanted. The only thing she wanted now was Spencer.

Remembering how over the last three months she had tried to summon up the courage to end the relationship, she cringed. Why on earth had she thought she'd be better off without Spencer? It was blatantly obvious that she wasn't.

'You know what — when Amelia called …' Lily bit her lip, realizing she was slipping back into *client* mode and hoping Beth wouldn't mind. 'When she told me he was … It felt like — like somebody had drawn a rug from underneath my feet. I lost my balance and fell.'

Beth nodded. They were sitting in the conservatory with a pot of coffee between them and a large plate of homemade cinnamon chocolate fudge cake. Normally Lily, who was passionate about baking, would have admired the little gingerbread trees that were stuck into the ganache, and the effect the edible gold glitter had, making the cake look like a fairy tale forest.

'It was good of Amelia to call me,' Lily said — but she wasn't talking to Beth. She was talking to herself. 'I was actually surprised that she should remember me at all …' Tears made her vision blur and she had to put her mug down. Her hands were shaking.

Beth was by her side in an instant, wrapping her in her arms. 'Oh, Lily! Of course she would remember to call you, sweetheart — you were the person who mattered the most to her son. He loved you, and she knew that. Because you are wonderful!'

'Am I?' Lily sniffed and reached for a fresh tissue from the box on the table.

'Of course you are. You are absolutely most wonderful — and now I am going to cut you a slice of this winter-wonderland-cake, okay?'

Lily nodded but did not look convinced. 'Okay.'

The cake was just what Lily needed, and when she had finished the enormous slice Beth had cut her and pushed her plate aside, she said, 'I'm so glad I came, Beth. Do you think — would Matthew mind very much if I stayed the night?'

'Of course not! Why should he? I think he would rather have scolded me for not asking you to stay if I let you go now. I'll make up the bed in the spare room.'

'Thank you.'

'No problem at all. More coffee? Or straight to bed?'

***

THE CARD ARRIVED before Lily had had a chance to go and see the Seymours. She wished she had because now she felt even less worthy to pay a visit to their grand house.

Spencer David Henry Seymour ...

She traced the name with her finger. Spencer David Henry — oh yes. He had told her about his middle names on their first date. He had taken her to a posh restaurant, where they had eaten caviar and lobster and she had felt thoroughly sophisticated and grown up. She had not liked the caviar much, but the lobster had been something else. The next summer he had taken her on a surprise trip to New York and Long Island where they had eaten more lobster, as well as bagels stuffed with cream cheese and salmon for breakfast, and frozen yogurt, her favourite dessert ever since. It had been the most indulgent holiday Lily had ever had, and the only thing she had regretted was that they had not been to any museums, because he thought them boring. They usually did what Spencer liked, and mostly that had been fine with Lily. Now she wished she could do even more of the things that only he enjoyed — even going to the racecourse with him suddenly seemed appealing enough. Anything was better than this dull ache in her heart, the numbness she felt both physically and emotionally now that most of her tears had been cried. She felt empty, drained, and tired. She could not remember the last time she had felt so tired.

It took her a couple of times before she could bring herself to read the rest of the card and pick up the information she needed if she wanted to attend the funeral. Of course she didn't *want* to — but, as Spencer's girlfriend, she would have to, wouldn't she? Even if she wished she didn't because that would only make it final.

'All a funeral can ever do is to make the things that one has desperately tried to deny until then dramatically clear,' she had once heard somebody say at somebody else's funeral — it might have been her grandfather's, but she wasn't sure, and it wasn't really important. Whoever had said this was right.

***

LILY WAS STANDING in front of her open wardrobe, trying to pick a suitable outfit for her boyfriend's funeral. *A suitable outfit*, she thought and grimaced. *What was that when it was at home?* But try and deny it as much as she liked she knew that come next Friday she would finally have to face the truth — that Spencer was gone. Dead.

Feeling fresh tears welling up in her eyes, Lily quickly placed a pair of black trousers and a simple black crewneck sweater on a shelf in her wardrobe and shut the door with a bang. She could wear her charcoal winter coat and her dark blue beret he had loved so much. Of course she wouldn't wear the red cashmere scarf he had given her last Christmas …

Another thoughtful gift, actually — why had she never acknowledged that before? He *had* cared after all, perhaps more than she had given him credit for — more than they had all given him credit for, come to that.

Suddenly feeling overwhelmed by a sense of guilt, she shook her head and quickly left the bedroom and the memories it held of him. Some mornings she found herself making two cups of tea, which was funny, because Spencer had rarely stayed the night. He had stayed the last night though. The night after he had given her the beautiful heart pendant and made love to her so gently — had she known it was to be the last time …

She took her journal from the table where she always kept it, along with her special black pen, and opened it, carefully avoiding giving in to the temptation to turn back to the week before Christmas, when Spencer had still been there, and her life had seemed so perfect. It did not matter that she had not thought it to be perfect at that point. Looking back now, she knew it was as close to perfect as she could have wished and hoped for.

Taking up the pen, she smoothed down the fresh page with her hand and began to write.

My darling Spencer!

I cannot believe you are gone. The card arrived today. The funeral is on Friday. Your funeral. Oh, Spencer! How can I survive this? I am not strong enough! I need you, my darling. Why have you left me like this? Why did you have to go?

I can still feel your arms around me when you said goodbye – how could I have known it would be the last time? Did you know? Did you have a feeling or something? Is that why you held me so very, very tight? I don't know. But I do know that I loved you and that

there will never be another you. Never.
 How I miss you, my darling!
 It hurts so much. It just hurts. So. Much.

   She dropped her pen and cried, not even noticing the hot tears blotting the fresh ink.

CHAPTER FOUR

LILY CLOSED THE door behind her and leaned against the wall, still clutching her keys. The flat was in darkness, but she didn't switch on the lights. She didn't take off her coat and she didn't put down her handbag either. She just stood there, trying to breathe, trying not to cry.

You have survived the funeral; you can take one step at a time now. No need to rush. Just don't cry.

Swallowing hard, she closed her eyes and tried to concentrate on her breathing. In, out. In, out. *There, that was better.* In, out. *You can do this. Take off your coat, put the kettle on …*

The first tear spilled down her cheek, followed by another.

Oh God, I can't. I just can't handle this.

She put her hands over her eyes, shaking her head. *I can't.*

Her shoulders began to heave, and she felt herself sliding down the wall, her sobbing becoming ever more desperate. She didn't care if anyone could hear her through the thin walls of her flat. She was past caring. And what did they know, anyway? Nothing. Nobody knew anything about her. Sometimes she thought she did not know herself, did not know who she was, really – a daughter, and a sister, yes. And a librarian. But she wasn't Spencer's girlfriend anymore because he was gone. And what else was she? Who was she?

The funeral had truly been the worst, and certainly the most heart-wrenching thing Lily had ever had to go through in her whole life. If Stephen had not been there to hold her, she thought she might have fallen headlong into the open grave. She had cried all the way through the service, and through the few words of comfort the vicar had said at the grave before they had all joined in the Lord's Prayer. At least, she thought they had all joined in. Maybe she hadn't — she couldn't remember now. But then, she couldn't care either. They had all gone back to the Seymours' house where they had drunk endless cups of tea while sharing their grief and their memories of Spencer. His parents had put up a large photograph of their son and set it on a chair in the centre of their huge living room, so everyone who came in had to pass it.

Lily had found it unbearable. She had been more than happy to go home early when Stephen, sensing she was fast reaching her meltdown point, had asked her if she wanted to leave. He had offered to take her back to his place, or their parents' house, but she had said no. Assuring him she would be fine, Stephen had finally given in and taken her home.

So here she was now, at a loose end with herself because really, what did you do when you had just buried your boyfriend??

***

IT WAS HALF past ten when Lily was woken by the sound of the doorbell.

'Parcel for you, Miss — have a good day.'

Before she could shout *Thanks, but I don't think* so after the annoyingly cheerful postman, he had already disappeared in the elevator, humming to himself as if he did not have a care in the world. Well, maybe he didn't, but she did. More than she could cope with.

Taking the parcel to the sofa where she sat down with a mug of coffee, she looked at the sender — it was from Francesca. Francesca had read English Literature in Oxford with her and was the only one she had kept in touch with. Sadly, she had never been to see her in Venice, as she had so often promised she would. Maybe she would go this year, to have a change of scenery, and take her mind off things. If Venice could not do the trick, she did not know what could.

Inside she found a whole selection of Italian treats, like pesto, oil and vinegar, and a few jars containing sundried herbs she knew Francesca would have picked in her Nonna's garden last summer. Lily picked up the letter, knowing it would be long, uplifting and beautifully written. It even smelled faintly of lemon verbena. No one could write letters like Francesca — but then no one did write letters these days, did they?

Dearest Lily, I am sorry I did not get this parcel to the post office in time for Christmas, but I do hope you had a lovely Christmas and a brilliant start to the New Year!

Brilliant, yes. Lily shook her head.

How are you, my dear? Are you still happy with that wonderful man you sent me the pictures of? He is very handsome! Any wedding bells to ring soon?

Lily inhaled sharply. Wedding bells! Hardly. Gripping her mug of coffee with both hands, she stared at Francesca's elegant handwriting on the thin sheet of pale blue writing paper before her, wondering how she was ever going to tell her. *By the way, thanks for asking after my handsome boyfriend, he just died?* She couldn't do that, could she? She could not even imagine herself writing it down, or even saying it out loud. He died.

No, Francesca, she thought sadly as she sipped her coffee. *There will be no wedding bells.* The bells that had tolled for him yesterday had been low and solemn, and were still echoing in her heart. Twenty-four times they had tolled, though why she had bothered to count she did not know. She did not know why she had done any of the things she had done yesterday, like knelt in prayer when everybody else had. She never prayed. There was nothing she had to say to the God who had taken Spencer away from her so soon and so cruelly.

Taking a deep breath, she read on.

Guess what, I have been offered a job in Florida! I am quite excited to go. I know, leaving my beloved Italy behind will be a wrench but the offer is too good to turn down. Besides, I would be back every holiday. And I need a break after my Nonna has died – did I tell you she died in October? I am not sure that I did. What is worse, my fiancé has left me to live with a girl from Switzerland — they are actually moving to Switzerland. I suspect she is pregnant, too. So you see, I need a fresh start!

That makes two of us then, Lily thought and put the letter aside. Tears were rolling down her cheeks. *I need a fresh start, too — or I will before long.*

Maybe she could go and visit Francesca in Italy in the spring, while she was still there? She had always wanted to go but never got round to it. With Francesca going to the USA soon, it seemed to be a question of now or never.

Yes, she thought as she looked at the grey skies, *that is a very good idea. I'm sure Francesca will be delighted, and the change of scenery will do me good — never mind the sunshine.*

How she was to get through the rest of this winter was quite a different matter.

***

LILY HAD CONSIDERED taking a couple of days off but then decided not to. Work would do her good, would get her out of the house, give her some sort of purpose. Something to do. She was relieved to find that it actually helped her get through the long winter days. When she got home in the evenings, all she could do was collapse on the sofa with a mug of hot chocolate and a book, trying to escape from reality for a blissful couple of hours. Most days she did not cook — she just could not be bothered. If it weren't for Stephen who would sometimes pop round with a takeaway or insist she come and join him and Emily for Sunday lunch, she would happily have lived on toasted cheese sandwiches, apples and chocolate. And as much as she loved her family for showing so much kindness and concern, by the end of the winter she felt almost suffocated by their constant checking and asking. Her patience was wearing thin, and she got irritated and snappish even with her mum. She was always sorry afterwards and told her so, too, and her mum invariably said, 'It's alright, darling, we know you're grieving' — but Lily knew something would have to change.

She would have to change.

But how, she wondered, when everything here reminded her of Spencer? Every time she walked passed the *Horsebox Café* where they had so often met for breakfast, or passed the gates to the University Park where he used to run, she had to keep her eyes firmly fixed on the ground, or she would cry.

She still had not asked Francesca if she could come and visit her, and she had not looked at flights either. She had not even asked her boss for a week off work, even though she had not taken a holiday since September, and even that had only been for a week. The week around her birthday …

Something was holding her back, and she did not know what — guilt? Fear? Or was it just her not being able to make up her mind as usual?

***

'BUT WHY SHOULD you feel guilty about going to Venice? Only last week you said you wanted to go. Don't you think you deserve a break after the ordeal of this winter?'

Lily and Beth were sitting in the café of the Ashmolean Museum. It was pouring with rain, so they had abandoned their idea of a walk in the Christ Church College Gardens. They always opted for the Ashmolean on rainy days; it had become a running joke between the two friends — if it rains, we can always spend a happy hour looking at paintings at the Ashmolean and have a coffee afterwards. Also, it was one of the few places in the city that did not remind Lily of Spencer.

Stirring her cappuccino, Lily shook her head. 'No, it's not that. I just don't feel like going to such a romantic destination without Spencer. He wanted to take me to Paris in January — and to think I was not even sure I wanted to go!' *Worse still, I was not even sure I wanted to stay with him.* But Lily felt too ashamed of herself to tell Beth. In fact, she felt more ashamed, and guilty, than anything else these days. *I didn't deserve Spencer. I didn't deserve going to Paris, or ....*

'Okay ... Let me see: the romantic destination bit I can understand. Fully and completely. I don't think *I* would want to go to Venice without Matthew, although to be fair, he did go to Rome without me only last year, but that was a church thing, and I had to work. Anyway. This friend of yours — Francesca, right? — is going to America in the summer, so if you want to go and see her before she leaves, it'll have to be now. Correct?'

'Yes.'

'Do you want to see *her*, or do you want to visit Venice? Because if it's about seeing her, you can always go to Florida at some later point. There is plenty of sunshine there, too.'

'And alligators.'

'Sorry?'

'There are alligators in Florida. Sometimes people find them taking a dip in their swimming pools in the back yard.' Lily shuddered. 'I hate alligators! I wish they hadn't survived Noah's Flood. I'm sure there must have been some mistake.'

Beth stared at her for a few seconds, then laughed. 'Oh! Right. Well, I'm glad you haven't quite lost your sense of humour. That's a good sign, Lily! I miss your dry humour — and your laughter. And of course you don't have to go to Florida if you don't want to — but you could still go to Venice in the spring and see her there. Unless you think it's too romantic, and too soon after Spencer.'

'It is, yes. Both.'

'I see. So … where else could you go? Because honestly, Lily, I do think you need to get away for a bit, it will do you good. What about Yorkshire? Fresh country air, horses, and your great-aunt's cakes — that should do the trick, shouldn't it?'

Lily shook her head wearily. 'I don't know …'

'Oh, come on! Didn't you say Auntie Abigail was getting on a bit and that you worried about her working too hard? You could help her muck out the stables or whatever it is you do on a stud farm. Can you ride?'

'A bit, yes. I used to ride Ronnie, that's her oldest and gentlest horse. He's a Welsh Cob — and then there is Willoughby, he is lovely, too. Or I could just walk Theo … yes, perhaps I should do that.'

'There you go — go to the farm, ride a horse, help your aunt — and forget about your worries for a bit. Talking of worries, I'm afraid I have to go — I have a counselling session in an hour. Will you get home alright?'

Lily nodded but her eyes were full of tears, and Beth got up to hug her. 'Oh, sweetheart! I'm so sorry! I wish I could stay —' Glancing at her watch, she shook her head and sighed. 'I can't though. But Lily, please promise me you will at least think about going to Yorkshire in the spring. Okay?'

Spring. That seemed a lifetime away. At the moment, it was about seven degrees, and it was raining. The sun had not been out for three days, and Lily felt drained of all energy. She was even too tired to cry.

'Okay?'

Lily looked up at her friend who was still standing beside her, reluctant to go. 'Oh, Lily. You poor, poor thing. — Oh! Have I ever told you the story of the rainbow?'

A faint smile appeared on Lily's pale face. 'Yes. Hundreds

of times. It's the symbol that God sent after the rain, as a reminder that He would always be with us. Or never be so angry with us again. Or something like that.'

Beth smiled. 'Yes, something like that. Because however sad, miserable, lonely, and crushed you are feeling now, having just about survived your own personal flood, God *knows* — and He will lead you back to dry land, and into the light. He will not leave you in this dark place forever. I promise, you *will* smile again, and be happy.'

Is that so, Lily wondered, when they had hugged each other goodbye, and she had watched Beth walk towards the door. Sometimes she envied Beth, and not only for the happiness she had found with Matthew, but for her unfailing optimism and cheerfulness. *Was life easier when you had faith? Or was it just easier to bear?*

CHAPTER FIVE

WINTER WAS SLOWLY turning into spring, as the snowdrops were reluctantly making way for the crocuses and the first of the daffodils were pushing their tender green heads up, eager to see if the March sun was warm enough for them to bud yet. Soon every bit of green in the city — from the sweeping parklands of the immaculate college gardens to the tiniest front yard in the neighbourhood — would turn into a sea of golden yellow, and for the first time in months, Lily felt a little bounce in her step as she walked home from work one evening and found that it was still light at half past five.

She was still thinking about what Beth had said last week when she let herself into her flat and hung up her coat. *You need to get away for a bit ...*

Filling the kettle with water, she looked about her tiny kitchen and wondered whether Beth was right, and a few weeks in Yorkshire would do her good. Her boss, Hugh, had said as much to her the other day.

'Morning, Lily,' he had said when he had approached her desk, and sat down opposite her, ready for a chat. 'Had a good weekend?'

'Um … yes. Thanks. I didn't do anything much, but — yes, it was good.'

Well. But what could she say? That she had left her parents' house in a rage on Sunday because her family had been getting on her nerves with their constant fussing? Hardly. Not even Beth was helpful these days. In fact, she was just as bad with her kind but persistent reminder of her 'needing to make up her mind'. *What if I don't want to go away? What if I just want to stay here and grieve?*

She knew it was probably unfair, but she couldn't help feeling that people were cushioning her too much on the one hand while pushing her to do things she was not ready to do on the other. It was a paradox, she knew. Everything seemed to be a paradox these days, and decisions impossible to make. Her headaches had become worse, too.

But then it wasn't only about grief, was it? There was this growing sense of guilt and shame, too. Nobody knew about *that*, not even Beth. Lily would rather die than tell anyone how close she had been to ending things with Spencer. She knew it should not matter now, but the thought kept her awake at night, haunted her in her dreams, and made her head ache all day. Sometimes she wondered if she, or her whole life for that matter, would ever be *alright* again.

'Lily,' Hugh had said, steepling his fingers while looking at her with great concern. 'I know you are not well. I can see you are trying your best to put on a brave face, but I'm afraid bottling it all up will not help ease the pain. My brother lost his wife six years ago, and he is still seeing a counsellor. I know that some things take a long time to heal — and nobody should be the judge of just how long. We are all different.'

She had nodded, not sure where this was leading.

'I know you are still grieving that young man, and I'm sorry. You must have loved him very much. But, Lily, you must not forget to look after yourself. I'm sure that that is what he would have wanted, too. Wouldn't you agree?'

Again, Lily gave a slight nod, and he went on, 'I think you should give yourself a break, Lily. Why don't you take three or four weeks of leave, and have a proper holiday for once? Go somewhere nice and sunny. What do you think?'

Oh great, Lily had thought. *Here we go again* ... Why did they all seem to want to get rid of her? But knowing it was kindly meant, she had said, 'I don't know. When would I take this leave? Now?'

'Why not? You could take time off until Easter if you like. As a matter of fact, I have just appointed a part time assistant who is very eager to start, and I'm sure the young man wouldn't mind putting in an extra couple of hours. Debbie can show him the ropes. I've already asked her. She thinks it's a good idea that you take a break, too.'

Does she, thought Lily. *Interesting. Well, you seem to have it all worked out between you. Good for you guys.*

'Okay ... can I think about this for a day or two?' She would have to, because the last thing she wanted was to be stuck in her apartment for a month, for that would completely defeat the purpose, even she could see that.

'Think about it by all means,' he had said, getting to his feet. 'Just let me know what you have decided to do by — say Friday? That okay?'

'Yes. Thank you, Hugh. I appreciate that.'

And she did. She just hoped things would sort themselves out by Friday, or else she would have to take this holiday at some later point, and she actually wasn't sure she could go on like this for much longer, so — something had better come up.

***

Later that evening, Lily was sorting through her wardrobe, replacing winter with spring wear — even if her heart did not feel like spring, there was no point in wearing cashmere jumpers at sixteen degrees, was there? — when her mother rang.

'Mum! Goodness, what's up? You don't usually call this late — something happened?'

'No, nothing's happened. Well, not *to us* anyway — and just for the record, it's only quarter past nine, isn't it? We don't go to bed before ten, not in the summer we don't.'

'It's only March.'

'Yes, well — but days are getting longer, aren't they? Anyway, how are you, sweetheart?'

Lily sat down on her bed. 'I'm fine, Mum.' She wasn't of course and her mum knew that, but there was no point in dwelling on that now, was there? She was getting so tired of this question. *How are you?* Well. *Coping.*

Trying to change the subject, she asked, 'But what happened? *To whom* if not to you?'

'Sorry?'

'You said *not to us*, so something must have happened *to somebody else*. What? And *to whom?*'

'Oh!' Her mum laughed. 'Sorry. It's Abigail's neighbour, that nasty Mr Nettleton. He had a stroke, and will be in hospital for a while yet, hopefully recovering, but you know how it is at that age — they don't usually, you know?'

'They don't usually what?' She knew she sounded impatient, but she couldn't help it — and anyway, what was Abigail's neighbour to her?

'Recover. People at his age don't usually make a full recovery. Either they cannot speak or walk or …'

'Yes, Mum. I know. Now please tell me — how is this Mr Nettleton's business any of your, or even my, concern? Why are you telling me all about it, if it isn't?'

Her eyes fell on a card that was stuck to her fridge. Beth had given it to her some time ago. It said, *When given the choice between being right and being kind — choose kind.*

She sighed. 'I'm sorry, mum. I didn't mean to be rude. So, what will happen to Mr Nettleton now? Has he any relatives who will come to look after him?'

'He has a daughter, but she lives in Cornwall, so it's quite a leg of a journey for her and of course she won't be able to stay for long. Then there's a stepson, I can't remember his name, but they haven't spoken in years, apparently, I doubt very much that *he* would come. Anyway, Abi promised his daughter that she would look after his farm while he is in hospital, but I think she really has enough on her plate as it is with her ponies, seeing as she is getting on a bit herself, so — I thought I'd ask you.'

'Ask me what exactly?'

Choose kind indeed. Her mother didn't expect her to travel to one of the remotest parts of the North York Moors and look after an old man's *pets* now, did she? Seriously! She was not sure why she should remember this, but she could have sworn there was a bunch of very naughty goats involved. Abigail must have mentioned them on one of her visits.

'Well … I thought maybe you could go up and stay with Abigail for a bit and help her. You know, shopping, cooking, cleaning —' Suddenly she stopped and burst out laughing. 'Not looking after old Mr Nettleton's *farm* of course — oh, Lily, I hope you didn't think …'

Yes, that was exactly what I thought, but just as well you were not actually going to ask me. I would have refused flat out, even at the risk of not being 'kind'.

'Oh, all right then, I'll ask my boss,' Lily said, trying not to sound too pleased. Actually, this was the answer she had been waiting for — but her mum did not have to know that, did she? 'I'll let you know on Friday, okay?'

As soon as she had rung off, she texted Beth.

I'm going to Yorkshire after all. Good idea of yours. Sorry I've been such a stranger all week — will you come and have tea with me on Friday? Lily X

The answer flashed up almost instantly.

If cake is involved — always. Beth xx

CHAPTER SIX

It was a bright, sunny day, and Lily felt almost happy as she sped along the A1 early on Monday morning, singing along to the Beatles. She had spent most of the weekend reading — like she usually did, especially when it rained — and then suddenly realized she had not packed yet, which sent her into a flurry of activity on Sunday evening. And now she was on her way to have her very own Yorkshire Adventure, and with every mile made, she felt a bit lighter and happier.

'Spending some time on the farm will do you good,' her brother had said, 'And Auntie Abigail, too, even though she wouldn't admit it.'

'Well, she won't try to mollycoddle me, that's for sure, which is just as well. You don't know how sick I am of being fussed over.'

Her brother had stopped drying the dishes and looked at her. 'We aren't that bad, are we?'

'You are. But it's okay,' she had said, putting a hand on his arm, 'I know you mean well. I'd probably be the same if it was you.'

Relief had shown in his eyes, and they had talked about something else. Lily, though, had thought that this was exactly why she was looking forward to going to Yorkshire. Abi would be far too busy bossing her around to even dream of pampering her.

***

WHEN SHE ARRIVED shortly after lunch, she found Abigail in the kitchen, putting the kettle on.

'I heard your car,' she said by way of explaining, 'so I thought I'd make us a nice pot of tea. Did you have a good journey?'

'Yes,' Lily said, 'very good, thank you. Oh! You've made cake, too — lovely!'

She put down her bags and went to hug Abi but nearly tripped over the dog who was lying in the middle of the kitchen. 'Oops! Sorry, Theo! I didn't see you there, boy.' As she bent down to pet him, he rolled onto his back, exposing his belly which seemed to Lily quite a bit rounder than the last time she'd seen him. 'You're too small.'

'He's not *that* small, and you know he always drops down in the most inconvenient place when he comes in. Better get used to it now that you're going to be here for a bit. — Hello, lass, nice to see you.' She kissed Lily affectionately. 'It was good of you to come. Now go and wash your hands and then we can have a nice brew. Is that all the luggage you've got?' she added with a nod towards her two navy canvas bags.

'Oh, no — the suitcase is in the car, as is all the other stuff I've brought. I'm afraid I don't do light travelling.' She thought it best not to mention the eiderdown duvet and pillow she had brought along with her patchwork quilt and matching cushions.

'Well, you will be here for a while, won't you, so of course you want to be comfortable. And I want you to feel quite at home. Right! Tea and cake whenever you are ready.'

Having deposited her bags at the bottom of the stairs – and taken extra good care not to fall over the dog again who was still lying in the same spot (Theo probably wouldn't move an inch for the Queen herself, even if she brought all of her corgis along!) – Lily sat down at the kitchen table just two minutes later.

'So,' Abi said when she had tried and failed to make Lily eat a third piece of her homemade (and alcohol-infused!) fruit cake, 'what do you want to do first? Go upstairs and settle in? Have a bit of a lie-down perhaps after the long journey? Or would you rather go and have a look around Mr Nettleton's place? It's in a terrible state, I can tell you, just like himself, stuck in hospital as he is, and neither able to speak nor move. Your mum did tell you the poor old bugger had a stroke, didn't she?'

'She did, yes. But — but I won't have anything to do with your neighbour's farm, will I? Or his … pets and — any other animals?'

'Lord, no, of course not!'

Relief flooded through Lily when she heard that. As much as she wanted to go out and stretch her legs, having a *look around* that Mr Nettleton's place was not exactly on her list of favourite things to do right now.

'I just thought you wanted to see what I have got myself into with that rather hasty promise I made to *Madam*. I'll have to check on his goats, anyway. They're nothing but trouble. Give good milk though. Oh well, I suppose Mistress Mary will have to sell the lot, goats and all, if he doesn't recover. And it doesn't look like he will, or not too soon, anyway.'

So there *were* goats. Well, well. Deciding she had better make herself useful, Lily got up, took the plates and mugs over to the sink and rinsed them before putting them in the —

'You haven't got a dishwasher by any chance, have you?'

Abigail snorted. 'What would I want a dishwasher for? Just leave the stuff in the sink and let's go outside. I can help you bring your luggage in and then we'll take Theo for a quick walk before it's time to feed the horses. You would like that, old fellow, wouldn't you?'

No sooner had they dumped the rest of her luggage in the hall ('you're not planning on staying for ever, are you?'), than a tractor came rumbling up the lane. A young woman was waving from the driver's seat.

'Hello, Lucy,' Abigail shouted, 'how's your dad? Leg still in plaster, is it?'

Lucy stopped the tractor and popped her head out of the cabin. 'Yes, I'm afraid it is. He makes a terrible patient, too! Bosses us around the place all day, especially mum and Sam. I can't wait to get to the shop in the mornings!'

Then she spotted Lily. 'Hiya. I'm Lucy Bell, I live next door — well, about a mile up that track, on Upper Rye Farm. Are you visiting?'

'Yes. I've come to stay with my great-aunt for a bit while she's looking after Mr Nettleton's … um — animals.'

'Oh dear! How is he then? Any chance of a quick recovery? I mean, the goats alone would drive me nuts, you are a proper heroine, Abigail, I'm nothing compared to you! — Oh, do be quiet, Hamish!'

She had now stopped the motor of the tractor and Lily noticed the beautiful rough collie who was standing (presumably so that he could get a better view of his surroundings) behind Lucy. *A proper Lassie dog*, she thought dreamily. She had wanted a dog like that for as long as she could remember. *Some girls*, she thought with a glance at Lucy Bell's glossy chestnut curls that were trying their best to escape from underneath a red-and-white polka dot handkerchief that was tied under her chin, *have all the luck*. Lucy reminded her of the young Queen — she could have auditioned for the part in *The Crown*, if it hadn't been for her tell-tale Yorkshire accent.

'I haven't heard any news, no. I might drop in at the hospital sometime next week though, or even tomorrow if Lily doesn't mind going to Scarborough. We can have fish and chips and take a walk along the beach, and then do the shopping on the way home. You don't mind going into town tomorrow, do you, Lily? The nearest supermarket is in Kirkbymoorside but it's not very big so I'd rather we went into Pickering. They've got a Tesco *and* a Sainsburys.'

'I don't mind at all. That's why I came, remember? To help you.' *Well. And to forget about my own problems for a while.* But the less said on that matter, the better.

'Oh, that's so lovely of you — I'm sure Abigail appreciates the company as well, not just the service!' Lucy was about to start the engine when she looked at Lily and asked, 'Would you like to join us for a pint or a glass of wine up at the *Red Grouse*? We usually meet up on Tuesday nights, to catch up with each other and — yeah, have some fun. — Sorry, Abi, it's not that you are not fun to be with — but …'

She grinned, and Abi pretended to shake a stick at her. 'Aw, get away with you, lass! I'm sure Lily here would appreciate a night out with you young folks, wouldn't you, Lily?'

Lily wasn't sure at all that that was what she would appreciate — she had come here to hide from the world for a bit and try to find some rest after the winter's ordeal, not to spend her evenings at the pub with people she had never met before — but as it would have been rude to say no, she smiled and said, 'That would be nice, yes. Thank you. Um … shall I give you my phone number?'

'No need,' shouted Lucy who had already got the engine running again. 'I never look at my phone. Too busy! I'll pick you up at half eight.'

In spite of herself, Lily gave her the thumbs up. *And why not*, she thought, as they made their way along the track with Theo bouncing ahead of them. What did she have to lose after all? She didn't have to make friends if she didn't want to. She would go back to Oxford at the end of the month, and that would be that.

***

THE NEXT MORNING, Lily woke to the sound of a donkey braying his head off in the yard. It was so loud she almost fell out of bed.

'What in the name of …' she mumbled when the animal had decided to catch his breath, but having done so for a very short time, continued as before, or perhaps even louder if that was possible. It took her a while to realize that it actually *was* a donkey, for she had neither seen one in the yard the day before — they had gone to feed the ponies before tea — nor had her great-aunt mentioned any Eeyore living on her premises. *Mind you, the donkey might well belong to that wicked Mr Nettleton*, Lily thought, as she tried to pull the sheets over her head so as to muffle the deafening noise that seemed to penetrate the walls of the farmhouse and fill her entire room, but as that was to no avail, she decided to get up and make herself a cup of tea. *Country life*, she thought, as she made her way down the creaking old stairs, *how perfectly charming.*

It was only half past five and dawn was beginning to creep in when she came into the kitchen to find Theo rolled up in his basket by the Aga. He looked up at her from beneath his bushy eyebrows as if to say, 'What on earth are you doing here at this unearthly hour?'

'Good morning, Theo. I know it's early, but I had a bit of a rough awakening. Do you know if there's any donkey about in Abi's yard? You don't? Mmm,' she said, 'pity. Oh well, we can always go and have a look around the stables later, can't we? A nice little early morning walk. What do you think?'

Theo wagged his tail slowly, clearly not enthusiastic at the prospect of going out.

'Okay,' she said, making for the stairs. 'I'll just finish my tea and put on some jeans and a sweater. Back in five.'

She wasn't though — the minute she had sat down on her bed to finish her tea, she felt an irresistible urge to lie down, and promptly fell asleep.

***

WHEN SHE WOKE up again, it was nearly nine and the delicious smell of bacon and coffee was wafting up from downstairs.

'Why, of course there is a donkey! Faithful old William — didn't you see him last night? He's Delilah's best mate, you know, the little dapple white mare in the last but one box on the right. I heard him too, mind you, but I couldn't be bothered to get up. There's no stopping him once he gets going, anyway.'

Now why doesn't that surprise me? thought Lily, and spread her fried bread generously with butter. 'Mmm,' she sighed with half-closed eyes, 'this is heaven, Abi. Heaven on a plate.'

Abigail handed her the breadbasket. 'Have some more then. You'll be on your feet all day, and I don't want you to collapse carrying the shopping bags back to the car. Talking of which — you don't mind if we take the Range Rover instead of your smart little racer, do you, the boot being slightly bigger?'

Lily grinned. 'As long as you drive that temperamental old beast, I don't, no.'

'Well, I think the sooner you get used to driving it the better since yours will be of precious little use here, especially in the winter, but I'll spare you today because you have only just arrived. Eat up now, lass, and let's get going.'

Especially in the winter?

'But I won't be here in the winter, will I?' At least she hoped very much that she wouldn't. Where else she hoped she would be instead she did not know, but here? Winters on the Moors would be cold, dark, and very lonely, and she was not sure how much loneliness she could take. Although Oxford would be lonely, too, without Spencer ...

But Abi wasn't listening, anyway. She was concentrating on her shopping list, mumbling to herself as the pen moved swiftly across the paper. *Oh well*, thought Lily and picked up her knife and fork to tackle the scrambled eggs, *she must have been having me on. She knows I'm not cut out for country life — not as long as that crazy donkey is around, anyway!*

***

They were driving through Kirkbymoorside on their way home when Abigail pointed to a sign that said *Talbot's Hardware and Farm Machinery* on the right.

'See that shop over there? That's where our Lucy works. Nothing you can't get there and nothing they can't fix for you either. It's her uncle's shop — has been in the family for generations, but he is getting on a bit now, and as they haven't any children of their own, it looks like Lucy is going to take over.'

Lily was astonished. Beautiful young Lucy, working in a hardware store? Now that was something altogether different to do with your life. Well, she could drive a tractor obviously but then she had grown up on a farm, so that was hardly surprising. But tools and machinery, too?

'Wow,' she said because she couldn't think of anything better to say. 'That's cool.'

Her aunt nodded, indicating right. 'It is rather, isn't it? Bit unusual of course, but that lass has lain underneath tractors and leaking taps alike before she even went to school. Will make that Greg of hers a very useful, hands-on sort of wife. Well, mind you, he's a mechanic himself — works in his dad's garage right here in Kirkbymoorside, so it's very convenient. I dare say they are well-suited — childhood sweethearts, those two, you know. Have known each other all of their lives.'

Lily nodded thoughtfully while trying hard not to picture herself and Spencer walking along the Thames River Path, holding hands … or through Christ Church College Gardens … or down Oxford's High Street, looking at shop windows at Christmas time …

Stop it. You and Spencer were over before he died. You knew it. Perhaps he did, too.

A stubborn little voice inside her piped up, *He can't have. He would not have given me a silver heart pendant if he had, would he?*

Well, maybe not but ... it was only a necklace, not an engagement ring. He would not have married you. You knew that!

'Lily?'

With a jolt, Lily came back to reality. Her great aunt was giving her a concerned look. 'You were miles away! Poor lass. Now, I suggest you look out of the window because I am taking you along the scenic route today, through Hutton-le-Hole and up Bank Top. If we are lucky the rain will hold back until we get there, then we can stop and enjoy the view over the Dale.'

They stopped in Hutton-le-Hole, a village Lily quickly decided had to be one of the prettiest she had ever seen. It was nestled into a natural hollow or hole — 'Hence the name,' Abi explained as she parked the car outside the village pub. 'Let's get out and walk around for a bit. It will do you good — and if we are lucky, the village store will be open, and we can treat ourselves to some ice-cream. It's locally made and absolutely delicious.'

Lily was not sure it was warm enough for ice-cream, but determined to get the upsetting thoughts out of her head, she followed her resolute aunt down the road and past the Ryedale Folk Museum which was just closing.

'Oh dear, we might be too late for that ice-cream — no, look, there are people queuing, she's got to be open yet.'

While Lily tried to keep up with Abi, she wondered why on earth people would be queuing for ice-cream in this remote little village, and on a rainy Tuesday, too, but she soon knew why: it was the best ice-cream she had ever had!

They were standing on the bridge that went over Hutton Beck, a clear moorland stream which wound its way through the soft, pillowy mounds that formed the village green. There were sheep grazing peacefully, and Lily could feel herself relax amid the serenity of the place.

'See those limestone headlands over there? Those are the Tabular Hills, and if you look north, you will see the land rising steadily all the way up to Spaunton Moor. We will drive up that hill in a moment,' Abi explained, 'it's a steep climb, but I dare say the view is worth it!'

***

ONCE THEY HAD reached Bank Top, which was — in contrast to the sunny valley — covered in a dense mist, Abi stopped the car on the gravel by the roadside. Theirs was the only car, and when Lily opened the passenger door, she was at once engulfed in an eerie, misty silence. Looming above the quiet dale, the clouds were dark and heavy with rain, and Lily could feel the hair on her arms standing up.

'There is an information board over there by the old iron kilns,' Abi explained, 'you can go and have a look if you like. I'm staying in the car.'

Lily walked along the crunching gravel path for a couple of yards before stopping to look back over her shoulder — the car had disappeared completely in the mist, and she felt a chill down her spine. *This is spooky*, she thought, wrapping her arms around her shivering body. *I would not be at all surprised if there were some brilliantly scary ghost stories about this place, too.* Thinking that she would rather hear those in the comfort of the farm house — in front of a blazing fire with a mug of hot chocolate —, she decided to go back and leave the information boards for her next visit. She took out her phone with numb hands and took some pictures before she hurried back to the car, slamming the door shut behind her.

'That was quick. Did you take any pictures?' Abi started the engine.

'Some, yes. But it was very misty, and cold, too. I did not get as far as the kilns — I could hardly see my own feet in that fog! The atmosphere up here is quite gloomy, isn't it? Almost spooky. Are there any ghost stories about Rosedale?'

'Oh! Plenty!' Abi laughed, as she steered the car back onto the road. 'Why, didn't you know that people believe that the devil himself lives up there, guarding a treasure he has buried in the hillside? And during thunderstorms, when lightning hits the rocks behind the old iron kilns that you can see from the farm, people believe that it is him getting angry! At what or who, I do not know, but they say that he is sending the sparks flying off those rocks to warn people off. And of course it's him growling at us and not boring old thunder that we hear on such nights. It's nonsense, of course, but you'll find that there is a lot of good old superstition around here.' She chuckled. 'And of course we love telling a good old yarn to unsuspecting newcomers! Mind you, some of the thunderstorms we get in the summer months are quite severe, so you can guess what that does to spark people's imagination!'

Well, it has certainly sparked mine, thought Lily, already trying to put some verses together in her head. Or perhaps it would even set the scene for a short story or novel?

And who would doubt the sweet old lady in the lone stone cottage at the end of the lane who swore she had seen a giant black shadow moving about on the cliff the night before?

Lily could feel an unexpected rush of excitement creeping over her, and she could not wait to get home and write down some of the ideas that were coming to her fast now.

***

WHEN THEY CAME home, Lily ran upstairs to her room to scribble down 'just a few ideas' for the ghost story. She wrote a lot, and fast, almost without thinking, and when she had filled two pages, she leaned back in her chair, looking out of the window to where the stables were.

This is it, she thought. *A writer's paradise. I could spend my days roaming the moors and come back and write in the evenings … Yes*, she thought, chewing her pen. *I would love this. Unless of course …*

At that moment, William the donkey started to bray. Loudly. And relentlessly.

'Oh dear — perhaps I'd better go and meet him. If I ever decide to come and live here as a writer, I will have to teach him some manners.' She closed her journal and got up. 'Or perhaps I'd better stay where I am. I can always visit.'

The truth was, she would never have the courage to leave Oxford behind, and she knew it. She would never have the courage to quit her job and be a writer either. She just wasn't a courageous woman — she just had a little too much imagination. And imagination did not get you anywhere in life, did it?

***

WILLIAM WAS SURPRISINGLY small, white, and utterly adorable.

Lily's heart melted when she approached his stall and saw just how cute he was. He was busy eating hay from a net that hung from one of the side walls. How could a creature so small and so sweet make such a racket?

'Hello, William,' she called softly, 'nice to meet you at last. I'm Lily.'

William turned his head and looked at her for a long time, munching slowly, without coming forward to meet her. Little Delilah on the other hand was more than happy to let Lily stroke the warm, velvety skin on her gracefully arched neck. As soon as William saw that his friend was getting all the attention, he too came to be cuddled. Delilah was one of the ponies who had been born on the farm, when Abigail was still in the breeding business. She had been sold to a neighbouring farmer, but when his daughter had outgrown the little mare, Delilah had duly been returned to the farm.

Abigail had been a well-established breeder of Welsh Mountain Ponies and travelled across the country to show her horses, winning many prizes, too, which were displayed in the hall and in the living room. Few of her ponies were ever sold, and most of them, like Delilah, eventually came back. This was mainly because the children they had been purchased for had outgrown them or moved away, which was what most of the younger generation of Bishops Bridge did these days, as very few wanted to become farmers — and who could blame them?

Abigail had been quite happy to let her brother Thomas do the farming (he had kept sheep) while she built her own business with the horses, a concept that had worked well for almost four decades. After Thomas's death, Abi was forced to sell most of the land — and sadly most of her horses, too. She said it didn't matter because she had felt she was getting too old to be travelling the country in a horse truck, but Lily knew it had broken her heart. Now there were only five ponies left — and the donkey.

William rubbed his broad forehead against her shoulder, leaving a layer of dust and hair on Lily's fleece jumper. 'Why, thank you, William, that is most kind of you,' she laughed and patted his shoulder — just to shower herself with more dust and hair. 'Tell you what, if you promise not to wake me quite so early in future, I reckon you and I are going to be good friends. Perhaps I could walk you up the hill one of these days, seeing as I am too big to ride you. What do you think?'

William obviously thought he had had enough and, after another friendly nudge, retreated to the back of the stall and resumed his hay-eating.

She laughed. 'Oh well — each to their own, eh? I'll see you tomorrow then. And remember, no braying before seven!'

At the door she turned around and called back, 'Better make that eight!'

CHAPTER SEVEN

It was raining heavily when Lucy came to pick up Lily at eight. The sky was almost black, and the wind was howling so loudly that Lily could not understand a word Lucy was saying as she climbed into the passenger seat of the little Citroën. A bucket was tossed across the yard and Lily was about to open the door and get out again, but Lucy quickly put a hand on her arm, shaking her head.

'Just leave it!' she shouted. 'You'll get soaked if you get out now!' — or at least Lily thought that was what she said.

They did not speak for the ten minutes it took them to reach the pub up on the ridge. It would have been useless, too, what with the rain drumming against the windscreen and the wipers moving frantically back and forth, making a terrible squeaking sound as they went.

Lily was surprised to find the car park full — they even had to turn and park in a layby opposite.

'I'm so sorry! I should have dropped you at the entrance!' Lucy was holding the hood of her anorak with both hands as she sprinted across the dark road. Lily followed her blindly, jumping from puddle to puddle and feeling the cold water soaking her Converse sneakers. *Stupid idea to wear these in the rain,* she thought. The others would think her an ignorant townie, and it would only serve her right.

Lucy's friends were waving to them from a large table in the far corner. There were three of them, and Lily was just stepping forward to introduce herself, when one of the men took hold of her sleeve and cried, 'Watch out!'

It turned out to be just in time, or Lily would have tripped over the enormous basset hound that was lying half-hidden between the table and a chair which was occupied by a young man with glasses and a mop of dark brown hair. Lily could not tell if the basset was his or not, because he didn't say anything (so probably *no* to that question), but just gave her a lopsided smile and went on to study the menu.

'Never mind Churchill,' the first man said and let go of Lily's sleeve, holding out a hand instead to help her step across the dog (who did not so much as lift his head, never mind move). 'He's the pub dog here. Lazy and stubborn as a mule — and always lying around somewhere about the place, usually in the most inconvenient of spots where people are bound to trip over him.' He bent down to stroke the dog's silky, long ears that were spread across the floor like a pair of giant brown mittens. 'Aw, but we love you anyway, old boy, eh?'

Lily's heart melted as Churchill deigned to lift his head at last, looking up at the man with his big, sad, caramel-coloured eyes. He thumped his tail on the floor a couple of times before he dropped his head again with a heavy sigh, and closed his eyes.

Turning to Lily, the man said, 'I'm Ben, by the way. Welcome to Rosedale, Lily. You're staying with Abigail at Fern Hill Farm, right?'

'That's right,' said Lily. 'I've come to help her a bit while her neighbour is in hospital. She looks after his farm, and I help her with the horses. Well, a bit, anyway.'

Ben nodded. 'Great. Well, let me introduce the lot here — this is Sam, he's Lucy's brother. And this is Jessie, she has got the café in the village and makes the most amazing cakes, never mind her cinnamon swirls. — Oh, and here's Greg now, Lucy's boyfriend.'

'Fiancé, actually,' Lucy said and sat down next to her brother. 'Hey, Sam, I didn't know you were coming, or I'd have picked you up. I've come straight from Kirkbymoorside — well, I stopped at Fern Hill Farm, obviously. Haven't you brought Hamish? He would have liked a night out.'

'Nah, he was sick after eating my bacon butties at lunchtime. Thought we'd better leave him at home.'

Lucy frowned. 'Eating your bacon butties? Why on earth would he even get a chance at snaffling those?'

'Because I had left them on a chair, that's why. The phone was ringing and — oh, gee, thanks, Greg.' He turned to take a pint of Guinness from the tray a tall, muscular man with cropped brown hair was offering, and downed half of it in one thirsty go. 'Aah, that's more like it! — Hi, Lily, I'm Sam. Good to meet you.'

'Nice to meet you, too. — Oh, and who's that?' An elderly chocolate Labrador with rheumy eyes sat down in front of her, looking up at her in silent expectation. Lily bent down to hug her.

Greg set the heavy tray down on the table. 'Hi, Lily, I'm Greg,' he said, extending a strong hand, 'and this is Hazel. She wants a treat — Hazel, lie down, there's a good girl. Sorry you missed the first order, Lily — can I get you anything? A glass of wine perhaps?'

'White wine with a splash of lemonade would be nice,

thank you.'

Everyone helped themselves to their drinks, and Lily sat down next to Jessie, a pretty but very shy looking petite blonde who was just finishing a phone call. Whispering 'love you', she put the phone away and turned to Lily with an apologetic smile. 'Sorry, that was a bit rude of me. But I've left my daughter at home, and I just wanted to make sure she's alright. I don't usually leave her on her own, but …'

'But Louisa is *twelve*, Jess, and quite capable of looking after herself, as well you know, so please stop fretting now and enjoy your night out,' Ben said and put an arm around Jessie's shoulder, pulling her towards him. 'She'll be fine. Don't worry. Okay?'

Jessie nodded and smiled at him but at the same time withdrew gently from his arms.

Thinking that this might turn out to be an interesting sort of evening, Lily absent-mindedly patted a cool, wet Labrador nose that had somehow found its way to her knees along with a big, heavy head which was promptly rested on her thighs now. Either Ben was just looking out for Jessie, or he was keen on her, which was more likely.

'I'm a single mum,' Jessie explained, 'always have been, since the day my daughter was born — I was only nineteen then.' Her small, heart-shaped face clouded over for the briefest of moments, then she shook her head slightly as if to dismiss any painful memories and went on to say what seemed to be a well-rehearsed sentence. 'But we're fine now, Louisa May and me, and, as Ben pointed out, she is old enough to look after herself. She has a friend staying over as well, so she isn't alone, really. They are probably watching movies and turning my kitchen into a mess, but that's alright.'

When their food arrived — Lily had ordered stir-fried rice with crispy duck — she and Jessie got quite animated chatting about baking, finding they had a lot in common, even down to their favourite cakes.

'Oh, you must come to my café while you are here,' Jessie said, putting her knife and fork down and looking at Lily. 'I want to show you everything — and treat you to a cappuccino.'

Lily smiled. 'I would love that, yes. Where is your café then, on the High Street?'

'Yes. The Bridge Café. You can't miss it, really, since there isn't much else on Bishops Bridge High Street except Miss Lavender's village store, the pub, and the church. We're right opposite the school. I'm open from Wednesdays to Sundays, so you can come any time you like. How long are you staying then?'

'Until Easter. I had some holiday left from last year and … um … I — just needed a break. I'm also here to help my great-aunt on her farm while she is looking after her neighbour's place while he is in hospital. Rosedale is so beautiful — I'm already falling in love with this place!' And she was, too. She had not felt so calm and relaxed in months, that was for sure, so it seemed like the mission of 'taking her mind off things' was already accomplished. How long it would last once she was back in Oxford was a different matter.

Jessie laughed. 'It's easy, isn't it? I love it here, too, and I have never regretted coming here when Louisa May was little. I needed a new start at that time, you see, and I must say it was the best idea I ever had. Although Oxford … that sounds pretty lovely, too. All those cafés and bars and theatres and museums … not to mention the colleges and parks. Or the shops! I bet that after four weeks of working on a farm and hanging out at the pub with the locals you can't wait to get back there! What did your friends say when you said you were going up here for a whole month?'

What friends, Lily thought but did not say. But she felt her throat go dry, as always, when people assumed that she had dozens of friends and a fun-filled life back in Oxford, when really it was only Beth these days. They did not know she spent most of her evenings alone in her flat, reading. They did not know anything, did they?

And I don't mind if they don't. They can all leave me alone, for all I care. I deserve to be alone. I did not deserve Spencer. I don't deserve anyone.

'Lily?'

Startled, she looked up find Jessie scrutinizing her. 'Sorry, what did you say?'

'Would you like another drink? The waitress is just here, waiting to take our orders. And you have not answered my question — about missing Oxford?'

'Missing Oxford ... um, no, not very much.' *I don't miss it at all. I certainly don't miss the loneliness.* But she would not tell them that, would she? There was no need for them to know. 'I — um, I need the bathroom,' she said, getting to her feet. 'And I think I would like another glass of wine. A small one though. With a splash of lemonade.'

When she came back from the toilets, she was relieved to find Jessie in lively conversation with Lucy. She sat down with her glass of wine, listening to the music, and fiddling with her pendant, hoping the others would leave her alone. Thankfully, they did.

***

'BUT YOU MUST promise to come and have a coffee at the Bridge Café while you are here. That is, if you are not too busy helping your aunt?'

They were all standing in the car park, and although it had stopped raining, Lily was shivering in her wet shoes and could not wait to get back to the farm. 'I don't think I will be too busy, no. I might have to help her feed Mr Nettleton's goats perhaps but —'

'His *goats*? Oh dear, you'd better watch that lot. Although they are nothing compared to his *geese*!' Ben grinned at Lily. 'You do realize he has geese as well, don't you? They are a nasty bunch! Make sure you don't get near them.'

'I have no intention whatsoever,' Lily deadpanned.

Ben raised an eyebrow. 'I'm glad to hear that. Right, I'll be off. See you round, Lily.' And kissing Jessie on the cheek, he said, 'Night, pretty one,' and strode over to his car, whistling as he went.

'He's such a terrible flirt,' Jessie sighed, but Lily noticed her face had turned pink and she was unconsciously holding a hand against her cheek. 'And such a charmer!' *Well, I hope there is more to him than that and a posh car*, Lily thought to herself as she watched him getting into a gleaming white Tesla. She had a strong feeling that Jessie was already in love with him, and as a young single mother she deserved more than a bit of flirting. She deserved to be happy.

'I'll come and see you at your café as soon as I can. Good night, Jessie!' And she surprised herself by giving Jessie a quick hug before following Lucy across the road. 'Good night, all!'

***

As it was still raining, they went over to Mr Nettleton's farm the next morning, airing the house, and checking the fridge and larder for food that wanted throwing away, since the bins would be collected the next day. Lily was surprised to find the house reasonably tidy and clean for an old bachelor. When she mentioned as much to her great-aunt, Abigail laughed out loud.

'Brian Nettleton, an old bachelor? Never! He was married three times, and even then he always had affairs right, left and centre. Couldn't leave the girls alone, that one. Anyway, I promised his daughter I would help, and as long as it does not involve washing his underwear or changing his bed pan,' she winked mischievously, 'I don't mind. His daughter does not come up here often – she lives in Cornwall now, Mary does, and I bet she's glad about the distance, too. I know I would be. Although she really is just as bad as he is.'

'Oh?' Intrigued, Lily put her cloth down and turned around to her aunt with questioning eyes. She always loved a good story, and she had a feeling she would get to hear one. She was right.

'Well,' Abi began, 'his first wife died when Mary was only five, so he hired a woman who came in to do the washing, cooking, and cleaning for him. She was a young widow herself and had a wee lad, David. When Brian Nettleton discovered what a marvellous cook Sarah Stanton was, he began to see her in a different light, if you know what I mean. She was a pretty little thing and had already turned quite a few heads in the village. He didn't marry her right away though because his daughter was against it — in fact, she was so against it she would have refused to attend the wedding, had the old man let her get away with it. People said she sat in the church pew looking like thunder all through the ceremony. My parents didn't go, they said they did not want to witness that lovely lass making the biggest mistake of her life. Sarah was such a quiet, gentle little soul. I think she just wanted a safe place for herself and the boy. A home.'

Lily imagined Sarah Stanton to be a small, slender woman with dreamy blue eyes and blonde hair tied in a neat bun, an apron around her slim waist. 'What happened next?' she asked as she picked up her cloth again, swiping it idly along the windowsill.

'What happened next? Mary, that spoilt brat, made her stepmother's life a nightmare for as long as she lived, and even more so for little David. The poor lad! He had never known his father — he died in an accident when his wife was pregnant, can you imagine the tragedy? — and now he wasn't to have a new one either because Mistress Mary wouldn't have it. Mistress Mary,' she chuckled, 'yes, that's what we called her — and quite contrary, she was, just like that nasty little thing in *The Secret Garden* — before she turns nice. Which is something Mary Nettleton never did. Or whatever she is called now that she is married.'

Abigail began to shut the windows. It was windy outside, although the rain had ceased a little. 'Before the wedding, she made her father promise never to adopt David,' she went on, 'and she did not want him to take her father's name either — so his mum, bless her, refused to take it too! She should have refused him in the first place, of course, and left while there was still time. Poor lass.' Abi sighed. 'Anyway, they were married for ten years or so when she died of pneumonia. David was eighteen, and had just been offered a place at Durham University. He was such a bright lad! The death of his mother broke his heart though — he left Rosedale and never came back.'

'Oh. That's sad.'

'Yes, it was. Very sad. But Nettleton, sure enough, found himself another wife soon. She was so young, she could have been his daughter! She did not stay for long. Wouldn't tolerate his infidelities — and, needless to say, she did not get on with his daughter, either. No one did. She's a nasty piece of work, just like him.'

Lily shook her head. She was less keen than ever to meet Abi's neighbour now, or at any point in the future, if she could help it!

Closing a cupboard door, Abi said, 'Right, I think that will do for today. Shall we go back to the farm for some tea and cake?'

Lily stared at her aunt. 'Tea and cake? I could do with a bloody whisky!'

CHAPTER EIGHT

The weather remained depressingly wet, cold and windy throughout the week, turning the fields into proper swamps, and making the daily job of leading the ponies from field to barn and back a tiresome, and very muddy business. And while the horses did not seem to mind the rain, even Lily had to admit they looked downright disgraceful in their mud-caked, shaggy winter coats.

But when Lily walked into the village on Friday morning, the sun was finally breaking through the clouds, turning the scenery around her into something so stunningly beautiful that Lily had to stop and catch her breath. The High Street of Bishops Bridge was divided by a stream, and while there was a long row of charming little cottages lining the right side of the street, there were fewer but larger houses on the lane to the left of the stream, each hidden away behind neatly trimmed laurel or yew hedging. Opposite a wooden footbridge, Lily could see the *Dog and Partridge*, the village pub they were going to next week (she could not remember how she had been pressganged into agreeing to another night out, but apparently, she had) when it was quiz night.

Some people were walking their dogs along the bank

of the stream, letting them splash about for the sheer fun of it. Lily stood and watched an especially cute springer spaniel dashing repeatedly into the water to fetch the red ball his owner was throwing for him. He was incredibly fast, dipping in and out of the water in a flurry of black and white. *If they go on like that, his master will not be able to lift his arm tomorrow*, she thought wryly. Although he did look very fit even from a distance. Probably one of those outdoor types who would walk the three peaks over in the Dales in a single day, or a farmer. But he wouldn't be playing fetch with his dog by the village stream on a Friday morning if he was a farmer, he'd be far too busy.

Suddenly Lily felt something wet and hard hitting her forehead. 'Ouch!'

'Sorry!' came a man's voice from the other side of the stream. Then she heard a couple of splashes, and the next moment the voice was much nearer. 'Sorry, sorry, sorry — you're not hurt, are you?'

When Lily looked up, she found herself face to face with a very tall man — well, not really face to face, since he was at least six foot four, but he was looking down at her with genuine concern. His eyes were of the most amazing blue Lily had ever seen, and his brown, curly hair looked like he had forgotten to brush it this morning. Lily thought she could see bits of straw stuck in it, too.

'I'm fine,' she mumbled and bent down to stroke the dog who was now sitting obediently at his owner's side, his tongue lolling and — hold on, was he *grinning* at her? She could swear he was. Laughing, she ruffled his ears. 'Just got caught a bit off guard, that's all. — Hello, sweetie, you are quite the charmer, aren't you?' Turning to his owner, she said, 'I guess I just wasn't expecting a wet ball being flung at me the very first time I entered this village. It looked so peaceful.'

He groaned. 'God, I'm so sorry! It slipped out of my hand and … well. Can I treat you to a coffee by means of compensation? Or were you in a hurry to go somewhere?'

'As a matter of fact, I was just on my way to The Bridge Café. So yes, a coffee would be nice — you don't have to treat me though. It's okay.'

'Oh, but I want to. I'll buy you a cinnamon swirl, too — Jessie's speciality. She has Swedish ancestors, Jessie has. That's why her cinnamon swirls are so delicious. Old family recipe. Have you been there before?' He fastened a red lead to the dog's collar and held out his hand to Lily. 'I'm Joseph Hancock, by the way.'

'I'm Lily. Lily Henderson. And no, I haven't been to the café before, I'm only visiting. I met Jessie at the pub the other night, when I was out with — with …' She hesitated. She could not call them friends, could she? 'With a few people from the village.'

'Ah!' He nodded. 'I think I can guess — that would probably be Lucy, Sam, Greg and Ben. The Rosedale Young Farmers' Gang. I know them alright. Nice bunch. Where are you from then, Lily?'

Relieved to find that she did not have to explain herself, she said, 'I'm from Oxford. I'm staying with my great-aunt for a couple of weeks. Abigail Lewis from Fern Hill Farm?'

'Oh! Yes. Good for you. She is one formidable old lady, Miss Abigail is. And in case you were wondering, I know everybody around here, at least every farmer — and probably every single sheep. I'm the local vet.' Glancing at his watch, he sucked his breath. 'Actually, I'm already running a bit late on my rounds so I might not join you for breakfast if that's okay with you. I'll just get myself a coffee and a bacon butty — Jessie's bacon butties are to die for.'

Lily laughed, trying to keep up with his long strides. 'Very well, coffee and bacon butty it is. And a cinnamon swirl for me. So, do you treat horses as well then? Or donkeys, for that matter?'

'I do occasionally, yes, but there is another chap from Farndale who specialises in horses. For me, it's mostly sheep and cows around here. And the odd goat.'

Lily grinned. 'Would that be Mr Nettleton's goats?'

'Yes. They are very naughty. And the geese!' He shuddered, making Lily laugh. 'But you mentioned a donkey — do you mean old William? Have you met him yet?'

'I have indeed. I *heard* him before I saw him, mind you — woke me up on my first morning at six o'clock. What a voice! Not the three, but only *the one tenor* — do you remember which one was the smallest one? Pavarotti?'

Joseph chuckled. 'I don't know. Wasn't he the fattest one though? William isn't fat. Unless you've been feeding him treats since the day you arrived.'

'Which was only on Monday afternoon.'

'Hm. Not likely he'd have got fat since then.'

'No.'

She looked at him, deadpan, and they both burst out laughing. The dog joined in, barking, and jumping about happily as they approached the café on the other side of the stone bridge.

The Bridge Café was small but very cosy, and the smell of coffee, cinnamon and bacon was definitely inviting, as was the menu, which was stuck to the glass front of the door. For a place like Bishops Bridge, it read surprisingly eclectic — Americano, café latte, a wide range of fruit and herbal teas, quiches and paninis, cakes, and of course the full English as well as the Scandinavian breakfast with rye bread, scrambled eggs with dill, and organic smoked salmon.

'Morning, Jess!' Joseph called, sticking his head in. 'I'm wearing my muddy boots and I've got Inigo with me, so could you kindly bring me a coffee and a bacon butty to take away, as usual? Oh, and I've brought you a visitor, too. Met your new friend Lily down by the stream. As a matter of fact, I'm buying her a coffee and a cinnamon swirl by way of compensation — she had Inigo's wet ball flung in her face.'

Jessie laughed. 'Oh dear! You'll never find a girlfriend if you go on flinging grubby old dog balls at them. — Do come in, Lily!'

'It was a brand new ball, but you are right of course, it's not exactly the way to win a girl's heart,' he said, winking at Lily. 'Or even introduce oneself to a pretty young lady. Sorry, Lily.'

'That's alright,' Lily laughed and went inside to say hello to Jessie. 'It was nice to meet you — and Inigo. He's really cute.'

'Oh, aye, he knows that alright,' Joseph laughed and sat down on the step outside the shop, stretching out his long legs. 'But he still has to learn some manners, I'm afraid.' Inigo flopped down beside him, and closed his eyes with a contented sigh.

'I'll bring your coffee out in a moment, Joseph, but I'm afraid I've just sold the last bacon butty,' Jessie called as she emerged from behind the counter to give Lily a hug. 'Can I tempt you with a cinnamon swirl instead? Fresh from the oven?'

Joseph's face lit up. 'Oh, yes, please! I'll sit right here and wait if that's okay. Be sure to put an extra cinnamon swirl and a coffee on my bill. — Bye, Lily! Very nice meeting you. And sorry about that ball again.'

'No harm done. Bye then!'

While Jessie was busy getting Joseph's coffee ready and slipping two delicious smelling pastries into a brown paper bag, Lily took her time choosing a table. They were all different, she noticed, as were the chairs that looked like they had been purchased at some auction or other, which they probably had. On the left, there were some shelves along the whitewashed wall, boasting an impressive collection of Toby jugs, pots, and bowls. There was an enormous Victorian Welsh dresser on the right, and two windows overlooking the cobbled yard. Lily took a curious step towards the dresser and gasped when she saw the collectors' plates on the shelves behind the glass: there were six of them, each one bearing a hand painted scene from the old nursery rhyme *This is the house that Jack built*.

'Wow!' she said, turning to Jessie. 'Wow! I can't believe you've got those! Do you know, I saw three of these in an antiques shop in Burford some years ago, and I was so sad I neither had the money to buy them — nor the right sort of cabinet to put them in — oh, and never mind the right sort of *house* to put the right sort of cabinet in — well, you know what I mean. And you have got all six of them!'

'I know. Aren't they gorgeous? My grandma gave them to me when I had Louisa May. My sister and I used to argue about — oh, well, never mind. So, what can I get you? A cappuccino or a latte — or just a cup of tea with your cinnamon swirl?'

Again, there was a fleeting look of sorrow on her face, as if she carried the burden of some tragic secret with her. 'Cappuccino sounds lovely, thank you,' Lily smiled. If Joseph insisted on paying, she did not want to take advantage, and anyway, she had never seen the point of those flavoured lattes when regular tea or coffee would do just as well. It was just a lot of hot, frothy milk, wasn't it?

'Bye, Lily!'

Lily looked up to see Joseph waving at her, and lifted her cup, mouthing a *thank you*. When he had gone, she turned her attention to the deliciously sticky pastry on her plate, even licking her fingers when she had finished. Spencer would have died of shame seeing her do this in public …

At once Lily froze. He *had* died. If there was one person who should die of shame, it should be her. She had no right sitting here enjoying her cappuccino and sticky bun — bought by another man, at that! — just three months after his death. Whatever was she thinking?

Lily was just about to burst into tears when her phone rang.

'Hello?'

It was Abi. 'Oh, Lily, thank God! Listen, I must take Theo to the vet for his vaccination and tapeworm treatment, I had clear forgotten about the appointment, else I would have told you. Anyway, I wasn't sure you had taken a key. I can always leave the door unlocked of course, I usually do, anyway, but I wanted to make sure you got back alright. There's more rain coming in just now. Do you want me to pick you up?'

When she looked out of the window, she saw that the sky was quickly turning from blue to dark purple. 'Yes, please! I'm at the Bridge Café on the High Street. Thank you!'

***

While they were feeding the ponies that evening, Lily asked Abi if she sometimes missed the breeding and the horse shows.

'I do, yes. Quite a bit, to be honest. I miss the travelling, too, the excitement and buzz at the horse shows. The Great Yorkshire was always my favourite. And Ronnie won HOYS twice. That's the Horse of the Year Show,' she explained. 'Very grand. It takes place in Birmingham every year in October. I haven't been back since — could not bear to just stand there and watch and not be a part of it anymore …' She closed her eyes briefly, then shook her head.

'Anyway, as I wasn't getting any younger myself, selling up seemed the right thing to do when Thomas died. The sensible decision — sometimes one has to be sensible, eh? Even if you don't want to. What about you, Lily — are you always sensible?'

'Me? No. Never. Would I have come here if I had been sensible?'

Abi roared with laughter, making Dancer shy away. But she managed to soothe him quickly by speaking to him in a low voice and gently rubbing his neck. Wiping the tears from her eyes with the back of her hand, she turned to Lily and said, 'No, indeed, you wouldn't! But I'm glad you did, lass. I'm glad you did.'

And so am I, thought Lily, at the same time surprised at her own cheekiness. *She was sensible, wasn't she? Normally. But perhaps*, she thought, briefly burying her face in Clover's mane, *it's time I tried something different. I can always go back to being sensible if it doesn't work.*

Whatever it might turn out to be.

CHAPTER NINE

It was Saturday night, and Lily was about to change into something comfortable after the much needed and well-deserved hot bath she had just enjoyed. She had volunteered to help Abi looking after Mr Nettleton's animals today and was covered in sweat and stinking mud by the time they had come home. Even though she had been warned, she had not expected a few old goats to be quite so cheeky and temperamental — and they were nothing in comparison to those geese! They were really, really horrible, just like Ben had said.

When she had tried to get past them in the yard, two of them had actually attacked her, while the other two had watched with what Lily could only describe as 'goosy glee'. She had come away with a nasty red mark on her left thigh which hurt a lot more than she had let on when Abigail had asked her if she was alright. Grimacing in pain, she carefully applied some soothing cream to her now very colourful thigh — it had changed from boring red to a vivid greenish-purple and hurt like hell at the slightest touch — and vowed never to go near those geese again unless they were safely locked up in their pen. Which they were now, thanks to her brave and resolute aunt.

'We're not going to let this lot get out again, unless he wants us to roast them on the spit!' Abigail had muttered while she had shut the gate and put the lock on. 'And if you want to get fed by us, you'd better stay on that side of the fence, do you hear me? — And don't give me that look, Master Gander! You can call yourself lucky if any of us will throw you some grain after this!'

'Well, it certainly won't be me,' Lily had said, rubbing her thigh. 'I'm not going to get near this lot again.'

'You won't have to, I promise. And I'm sorry I put you in this dangerous situation in the first place, I should have known they were loose. Well, half-loose, they cannot get out of the farmyard as such, but — you know. Will you be alright walking home, or should I go get the car?'

Stupidly Lily had insisted she could walk, but it was a very long and painful walk indeed, even if it was little more than a few hundred yards. Now all she wanted was a quiet evening in front of the telly with a glass of red and Theo snuggled up in the crook of her legs, as had become the little dog's habit. Well, maybe not too close to her legs tonight.

She fell asleep during the ten o'clock news and dragged herself to bed, leaving Abigail to it. Theo followed her upstairs, and she was too tired to stop him, even when he jumped onto her bed and settled himself comfortably on her duvet where he would probably snore away all night. She knew because he had done so before, even if she hadn't told Abigail. She wasn't sure what the rules were in this house when it came to dogs on the beds, but she was the guest after all, and if she didn't mind, why should her aunt?

***

When she woke up the next morning, the first thing she heard was the rain hammering on the roof, and the next thing was William.

'Ooooh,' she moaned and hid her head under the pillow, 'no! For heavens' sake, not again,' meaning both, the rain, and the donkey.

She was just trying to decide whether she should attempt to get up and have a shower when there was a knock on the door.

'Thought I'd better come up and check on you in case your leg had taken a turn for the worse,' Abi explained when she came in with a mug of steaming hot tea — she wasn't normally the fussing, tea-bringing kind. 'And have you seen Theo anywhere about? Only he wasn't in his bed when I came down, and I know he has a habit of sneaking upstairs when he thinks nobody's looking. Especially when there's a fair chance of slipping into somebody's bedroom – and, *if he is very lucky*, even into somebody's bed.'

Lily reached for the mug. 'Oooh, lovely, thank you!'

She knew she was deliberately ignoring Abi's question, but as Theo didn't stir, she thought they could both get away with it. It was hard not to burst out laughing though because the moment Abi left the room, Theo came out of hiding, looking up at her with his soulful brown eyes.

'*You* are such a joker! Come on then, out you go.' Putting down her mug, she limped to the door, and watched the little dog as he slipped out and went pitter-patter down the stairs. Then she finished her tea and made for the bathroom at the other end of the landing, taking it very slowly and very, very carefully. The last thing she needed was a fall down the stairs.

***

'Lucy called to ask if you would like to come to the pub with them on Tuesday. I said you'd ring her.'

'Great,' said Lily and took her time sitting down. The leg hurt terribly. If her aunt offered her whisky instead of coffee now, she was not sure she'd say no. Anything to numb that pain.

As if reading her mind, Abi said, 'I have made us a nice pot of coffee. And after breakfast, I suggest you take some painkillers. Are you sure you shouldn't go and see a doctor?'

'Absolutely. Painkillers will do fine, and a bit of distraction.'

'As you wish.' When she had poured the coffee, Abi went to retrieve two plates of scrambled eggs and bacon from the oven and set one before her niece. 'Eat, lass. This will do you good. And then we will have a nice day out. Have you ever been to Ampleforth Abbey? They have a lovely tearoom there. Would you like to go?'

'Sounds good. As long as it doesn't involve too much walking.'

'Oh no, I'll make sure of that. But we can go and see the White Horse of Kilburn on the way, enjoy the view from Sutton Bank, and visit the showrooms at the *Mouseman*. Then we can have lunch or tea at Ampleforth Abbey.'

Lily did not know who or what the *Mouseman* was, and she had never heard of Ampleforth either, but she nodded. 'Lovely. I'm afraid I won't be much use to you for a couple of days though, what with this leg. I'm really sorry about that.'

Her aunt tutted. 'Nothing to be sorry about. It wasn't your fault that gander attacked you, was it? If it was anyone's fault at all, it was mine. Just take it gently now, Lily. There's no rush — I can manage. Okay?'

Lily smiled. 'Okay. I'm sorry though — I came here to help, didn't I?'

'Oh, you will help me again before long, don't you worry. And come Christmas, you can eat that gander, with all the trimmings, I promise!'

Lily laughed. 'But it isn't your goose to kill, is it?'

'I'll ask for his neck in return for my kindness to look after the farm. What do you think? Is that a deal?'

'Oh, that is really wicked! I love it. Even I could not have come up with such a cunning plan.'

'You couldn't, no. But I'm made of sterner stuff, I'll have you know, and I'll make him pay. I'll make him pay alright.'

And by the look on her aunt's face, Lily wasn't sure she was talking about the gander.

***

THEY HAD A fabulous day out visiting not only the famous White Horse of Kilburn and the *Mouseman*, but enjoying the view from Sutton Bank, too, which James Herriot had described as 'one of the finest views in England'. Lily could not agree more. By the time they were sitting in the tea room at Ampleforth Abbey, it was already half past two, and Lily was tired but happy. They ordered cheese scones and coffee and sat at a table in a quiet corner near the patio doors overlooking the garden. Lily loved the café and was surprised to see it was full of the beautifully crafted oak furniture with the little signature mouse of the *Mouseman*. It really was the cutest thing Lily had ever seen. The furniture was exquisite, and each piece unique in itself, but the mouse just added that little extra touch. From what Lily had seen at the workshop they had visited in nearby Kilburn, the furniture in the café must be worth a fortune. Of course all the bespoke items on display at the *Mouseman* were well out of Lily's financial reach.

As she took a bite of her cheese scone, she sighed with sheer pleasure. 'Mmm, this is good. Not as good as yours but nice and fluffy. — So, butter, clotted cream, and cheese to take back to Oxford then. I will have my little freezer stuffed with Yorkshire goodies.'

Abi looked up. 'But you will be back, won't you?'

'Of course I'll be back. I absolutely love it here — I almost wish I could stay forever!' Even as she was saying it, she knew she meant it, too. Where had the first week gone? She did not miss Oxford one bit. Definitely not her lonely little flat or the lonely nights spent on the sofa reading. *Perhaps I'll get a cat*, she thought, *to keep me company*. Spencer had not liked cats. *But then*, she thought, frowning, *neither do I, really. Not enough to get myself one, anyway.*

She was fiddling with her pendant when Abi took her by surprise by saying, 'Do then — stay, I mean. What's keeping you?'

'Um … lots of things? A job? A flat? Um …' She faltered. Two things were not really a lot, were they?

'Well,' Abi said, picking up her scone, 'if you ever change your mind, you know where I am.' And she left it at that.

When they got back to the car, Lily was surprised to find a *Mouseman* bag on the passenger seat. Inside was the cheeseboard she had admired in the shop earlier, oval shaped and of course with a mouse 'sitting' on the handle.

'For you — I know how much you love cheese, so I expect you to use it, too.'

Lily hugged her. 'Of course I will use it. Thank you, Abi!'

'You are very welcome, lass. Very welcome.'

And Lily knew she was not only referring to the cheese board.

***

THE NEXT DAY, it was raining again, and Abi had gone to visit Mr Nettleton, leaving Lily to rest her leg. Settling into the sweet-smelling straw in the barn, Lily picked up her book, and soon enough she was captured by J. M. Faulkner's *Moonfleet*, a fascinating tale of smugglers, diamonds, true love, and betrayal. It was while she was reading that a tiny spark of an idea began to form in her mind ...

An idea that, when the rain finally ceased to fall in the course of the afternoon, led her to investigate the derelict barn at the top end of the farm. It was nestled against the heather-covered hill and half hidden between two enormous oak trees that looked as though they had been there for centuries.

The path leading up to the barn was overgrown and quite steep. Nobody ever went up there these days, but when you turned around once you had made it to the top, the views were stunning. You could see the old iron kilns on the other side of the valley and, if you had very good eyes, you could even make out the fine line that ran below the kilns. That would be the railway line, which had been built to transport the ironstone out of the valley and was now a public footpath frequented by ramblers with a taste for history and fine views.

Touching the old stone walls of the barn, Lily bit her lip and nodded thoughtfully. They were solid enough, but the windows were all long since gone but for a few rusty frames still stuck in the holes where the glass panes used to be, and the roof had collapsed almost completely over the years. Lily could see birds roosting in the blackened beams — those that were not broken, that was — and in the empty frame where the door had once been brambles had begun to grow and overtake most of the front wall.

'It's such a shame,' she mused, her hand still on the wall. 'Such a terrible shame …'

Just then she heard Abi calling, and a minute later Theo came hurtling up the path, and the moment was over. With a sigh, she turned and made her way back to the farmhouse. It was probably a silly idea, anyway.

CHAPTER TEN

TWO DAYS LATER Lily went to the paddock and put a bright red headcollar over William's head. It was now or never — her leg felt strong enough and the sun had decided to give Rosedale another go today. As if sensing her nervousness, the friendly little donkey stood still all the time and waited patiently until she was ready to go. Abi handed her a lead rope, which she fastened onto the headcollar, and watched the pair of them as they made their way down the track.

William was surprisingly easy to lead and also quite sensitive in adjusting to her slow step; it almost seemed as if it was *him* who was leading *her*, the way he kept turning his head and looking at her with as if to say, 'you alright there, lass?' Lily was touched. Soon she found herself talking to the donkey as if he were a human, and the way his lovely long ears twitched she was almost sure he could actually understand what she was saying.

'So now you know why I'm here, and I'm glad I've come. Want to be let in on a secret? I'm not even sure I want to go back. Yes, I know, I've got a job and an apartment waiting for me —and yes, Oxford is the most beautiful city in the world — but I just find that that is not all there is to life.

Beauty, I mean. It doesn't make me happy. And with Spencer gone … I don't know. It just seems there is nothing left for me there. There is Beth of course, but she doesn't even live in Oxford, and she is always busy with her church. So here I am now, talking to a donkey. Takes all sorts, eh?' Stroking him affectionately, she said, 'But I'm very glad I found you, William! You really are the sweetest donkey I have ever met.'

Just then the sweetest donkey stopped as they passed a house near the end of the lane, twitching his ears as if to decide what to do next. A woman was working in her front garden, totally oblivious of the donkey that was looking at her questioningly with his gentle brown eyes.

'Come on, William, let's move on. We want to go up that field, see? Maybe even go up to the Bells' farm and get some … oh, hello! Sorry, I was …'

Looking up from her weeding, the woman did not seem the least bit surprised to see a donkey passing by, and grinned. 'Talking to your donkey, are you? Nice to find that I'm not the only crazy one around here. My name's Susanna Harper. I'm an artist,' she added, as if that would explain. 'I do animal portraits — well, mostly. Some landscapes if I get the chance. That's a lovely donkey you have there. Looks kind of familiar, actually …'

'I know. He belongs to my great-aunt, Miss Abigail Lewis on Fern Hill Farm. I'm Lily, by the way. Lily Henderson.'

Susanna Harper pushed back a stray curl of her incredibly long, red hair which went all the way down her back. Lily put her in her mid thirties, and she looked like an advertisement for *Country Living*, complete with blue dungarees and a checked shirt with the sleeves rolled up to her elbows. But even with her tangled hair and a smudge of earth on her freckled nose, she looked strikingly beautiful.

'Ah, that's why. I suppose you must be William then, hey? Hello, old fellow. Abi's rescue donkey. Did she tell you how she got by this one?'

'She didn't, no. I have been wanting to ask her because I cannot remember a donkey living on Fern Hill Farm. We don't visit often, and mostly in the winter when they are all tucked up in the stables but I'm sure I would remember his braying. He wakes me up every morning at eight. Well, he does now — on my first morning on the farm he started his concerto at half past five! I told him very firmly that that wouldn't do if we were to be friends, so eight it is now,' she said, deadpan.

Susanna shook her head laughing. 'You clearly *are* Abigail's niece — great-niece, was it? So, about this donkey — I can't remember what year it was exactly, it was shortly after her brother had died, I think, so probably three or four years ago. He was found grazing among the ruins of the old fort up on the hill — you know, where the abandoned village is, Broughton Hill? He was in a bad state, poor fellow, and lucky it was Joseph, the local vet, who found him. Joseph took the little donkey straight to Fern Hill Farm, knowing Abigail would not have the heart to turn him away. Besides, she had horses to keep him company, and donkeys need a companion to be happy. They never found out who left him there in the first place, or how he had got there at all. Anyway! He's happy now, isn't he? Would you like to join me for a cup of tea? I could do with one.'

'I'd love to, but I think I'd better get on, seeing as I told Abi I'd be back for lunch, and it's already past twelve. Thank you for telling me about William though, I think I love him even more now that I know he had a hard life before he came to live on the farm. I can almost forgive him his early-morning-braying! Almost.'

Susanna laughed. 'Alright then, I'd better let you go. Do pop in for a cuppa though while you're here. How long are you staying?'

'I'm here for another two weeks, so plenty of time for tea and chats. I'd better leave the donkey at home then though.'

'That might be better, yes,' Susanna said, picking up her hoe. 'Well, enjoy your walk then. It's been lovely to meet you, Lily.'

'And you. Bye!'

Tugging gently at William's lead rope, Lily walked on, pleased to find that Abigail had some nice neighbours as well, who didn't come with an assortment of ill-tempered livestock!

***

WHEN LILY RETURNED to the farm an hour later, she was surprised to see Joseph Hancock leaning across the gate, a tail-wagging Inigo sitting by his side.

'Hi!' he called as she got nearer. 'I've been waiting for you.'

She nodded, trying to ignore the flutter in her heart. *I shouldn't even notice how handsome he looks*, she thought. *I'm still grieving Spencer, am I not?*

Concentrating on William as she led him towards the gate, she nodded. 'So it seems. Not for too long, I hope?'

He opened the gate for her, watching her as she passed through. 'Not at all. I was just passing by and thought I'd ask for a cup of tea, knowing of course that Abi always has something fresh out of the oven if you happen to drop in at the right time …' He grinned sheepishly. 'Anyway, she told me you'd gone out with our long-eared friend here. Was he good then?'

'He was, mostly. I met Susanna Harper, the artist who lives down the lane. She's very nice. We didn't stay for tea though.'

'Susanna? Aye, she is nice. Good thing you didn't have tea though — she brews up the most dreadful stuff! Always leaves her teabags in the pot, milk and all, and just pops another one in when she feels like it. I *think* she empties and rinses that pot from time to time — once a week or so. At least I hope she does.'

Lily laughed. 'I'm sure she does. Right, I'm just going to put William in the paddock there with Delilah, will you open that gate for me, too, please?'

Once Lily had taken the head collar off, William cantered off to meet the little mare who had been waiting for him to come back. She was the only one who hadn't gone with the others to the larger field behind the farmhouse. They sniffed each other briefly, tails swishing happily, and then Delilah whinnied and beckoned William to follow her. He trotted after her like a pet dog, which made Joseph and Lily laugh and Inigo bark.

'They are an odd couple, aren't they?' Joseph remarked.

'They are indeed — and it's very clear which of them is wearing the trousers!'

'Three cheers for Miss Delilah, yes. She is quite attached to her William though. You won't be able to take him for long walks, or you'll have to ask his lady along, too.'

Lily rolled her eyes. 'I know! Abi told me. Now then, shall we have that cup of tea? Walking a donkey is thirsty work, I can tell you.'

Abigail was just retrieving a tray with scones from the

oven when they entered the kitchen through the back door. 'How was William then? — Come in, Joseph. And very welcome you are, too. — Oi, you, get down there!' She shooed Inigo away who was trying to jump up at the worktop, probably because he, too, had smelled the scones. 'My Theo won't like that, and you don't want to get on the wrong side of a dachshund!'

'Oh, no, you don't,' Joseph said, giving Inigo a stern look. 'I used to get my heels bitten by that nasty dachshund from our neighbours next door when I was a young lad delivering the newspapers.'

'Well, some have dogs, and some have — geese.' Shrugging, Lily began to butter her scone.

Abi sniggered, and Joseph gave her a quizzical look, so she told him the story of Lily and the Nasty Gander, making it sound almost funny — well, almost.

'But talking of ganders, I'd better go and check on them beasts. You don't fancy coming along, do you, Joseph? Meet the gander that attacked poor Lily here?'

Joseph stroked his chin, pretending to think hard. 'Um — actually, I don't think I have the time — in fact, I really must go I'm afraid. Duncan is waiting for me to take over at the surgery. He's taking his wife out — anniversary, I think.' He rose to his feet. 'Another time perhaps?'

Abi gave him a playful slap. 'Get away with you, Joseph Hancock.' Already making for the door, she called back, 'I'll see you later, Lily. Better check there's enough whisky in the jar when I come back — or in the cabinet, for what it's worth.'

'Would I serve that before or after seeing to your wounds?' Lily retorted, but Abi was already gone.

Joseph laughed and whistled to Inigo as he got up. 'I can

see you are a tonic to your aunt, Lily. She is sharper than ever. Go easy on that whisky though, will you? We need you to have your wits about you when you join us for the pub quiz tonight.'

Lily frowned. 'Oh. I'd quite forgotten about that. Are you coming, too?'

'I hope so, if I can finish surgery in time for once. Mind you, I'm no good at those quizzes. They ask the most ridiculous questions, like *what was the name of Shakespeare's mother?*'

'Oh, but that's easy! Mary Arden of course. Don't tell me you didn't know!'

'I thought it was Anne Hathaway. That was his wife then, right? Oh well. I'm just an ordinary country vet, what do I know, eh? Come on, Inigo!'

Halfway through the door, he turned and asked, 'Shall I pick you up? Seeing as you are not fit to drive, let alone walk one and a half miles into the village. Please say yes — it will give me the perfect excuse to finish early!'

Lily laughed. 'Okay then, if it makes you happy.'

'It does. I'll pick you up just before eight then. Bye!'

It was only when he had gone that she remembered Lucy had said she would collect her tonight. With a sigh, she reached for her phone. What on earth had she got herself into by coming here?

***

'HERE'S AN EASY one to start with - how many of Henry VIII's wives were called Catherine?'

Ben scoffed. 'Very easy! Two?'

Lily shook her head at Jessie who was about to write

down Ben's answer. 'There were two Annes, but *three* Catherines. Sorry.'

'Oh, that's alright. I shouldn't have guessed. General knowledge is not exactly my forte — wait till we get to the music questions.' Ben emptied his pint glass and made a start on his second one that was already standing in front of him. Lily had noticed Ben could put away quite a bit, but then he was a big man, at least six foot three and quite strong, and he did not strike her as the kind that drank regularly. She only hoped he would not drive tonight. Hadn't he mentioned he lived in Farndale though?

'Who has a Heinz ketchup tattoo on their arm and always carries a bottle or two of it on tour?'

'There you go — music question for you, Ben!'

Joseph slapped his friend's shoulder, and Lily almost choked on her drink with laughter. *Heinz ketchup tattoo, my foot,* she thought — *who is supposed to know that?*

But Ben took the pen and wrote *Ed Sheeran*, then put the pen down and grabbed a handful of crisps as if it was the most natural thing in the world to know the tattoos on Ed Sheeran's arm.

'What is the name of the first Beatles album?'

'*Please Please Me,*' said Ben without thinking, making Lily look up. She loved the Beatles, but even she was not sure she would have got this one right. Maybe she was not the great asset everyone had assumed she would be. It didn't bother her though. For the first time in months, she was having fun.

'Babies of which animals are known as Joeys?'

Joseph took the pen and wrote *koalas* into their booklet, then added *kangaroos*.

'Really?' she said in a low voice. 'That's cute!'

'Give me animal questions over general knowledge, or, heaven forbid, music all the time!'

She was sure he knew a lot more than he let on, but Joseph was not the kind of man who would show off his knowledge in front of others. He was much quieter than the other men, boisterous Ben in particular. Taking a sneak look at Joseph, Lily noticed he had put on a clean blue shirt which enhanced the colour of his eyes, and was wearing a pair of glasses. He was drinking Appletizer. *Sensible man*, she thought. Not only would he have to drive himself home as far as Pickering — had he mentioned he actually lived in Pickering or was that where the animal practice was? — but perhaps get up in the middle of the night to help a cow in distress.

'Who plays the Prime Minister in the film *Love Actually*?'

'Hugh Grant,' Lily, Lucy and Jessie chorused, causing the men to look at them very sternly because they were not keeping their voices down.

'Well, everyone knows that, so it's not really hard, is it? But we'll be more careful with the next answer. Oi, listen — general knowledge! Lily, that's for you.'

'In which Jane Austen novel do we learn that 'Netherfield Park is let at last'?'

Lily wrote *Pride and Prejudice* before any of the others could ask what Netherfield Park was. *It does pay to be a bookworm*, she thought and grinned.

Greg came back with more drinks, kissing Lucy on the cheek before he sat down next to her. 'What have I missed?'

'Oh, nothing much. Ben knows the tattoos on Ed Sheeran's arm, we wonder why,' Lucy said jestingly.

'The tattoos on — come on, you're having me on!'

'No. But then he does have a lot of them, and he doesn't

mind displaying them either. I suppose if you like him you'll notice at some point.'

'I like Ed Sheeran. *One life* is brilliant, I can listen to this all day long,' Jessie said and took a sip of her wine. 'But I also like the Beatles,' she added with a grin, 'and ABBA.'

Right on cue, the next question was 'From which country do ABBA originate?', causing everybody to laugh.

Lily could not remember having had such fun in a long time — well, not since Spencer died, to be precise. They had never been to a pub on Quiz Nights. They had hardly ever been to pubs at all, come to think of it. He had preferred restaurants, or the really posh country pubs where fish and chips came at twenty quid.

'What is the name of the coffee shop in the US sitcom, *Friends*?'

Lily wrote *Central Perk*, pushing the booklet back towards Jessie as the host announced a food question next.

'Right, here's a food question that every British person in the room should find easy to answer — what confectionary product is traditionally bought as a gift from a seaside holiday?'

'Well, sticks of rock of course,' said Greg at the same time as Jessie wrote it down.

Nobody knew what food you had a phobia of if you were diagnosed with *Lachanophobia*, but they all had a good laugh at that one, together with the other contestants.

Jessie knew the answers to most other food questions though and Lily thought they had done pretty well when the final question was asked at half past nine.

'In which Italian city is Shakespeare's *Romeo and Juliet* set?'

'Oh, how romantic! Verona, of course, isn't it? Or was it Venice? I keep mixing those up,' said Lucy, and wrote

Verona because everybody was giving her a stern look. 'Okay, okay, okay! I get it. Right, I'm going to have another glass of wine. Lily?'

***

THE NEXT MORNING was sunny and bright, and Lily tucked into her porridge with gusto. Abi had made rhubarb compote, which took the simple breakfast to the next level, especially with some cinnamon sprinkled on top.

'Do you mind if I take Theo out for a walk today? It's supposed to be nice all day, and I would welcome the exercise after all this leg-resting.'

'I don't mind at all. I'll be making jam next, and perhaps a nice pie for us to enjoy when you get back — first of the rhubarb.'

'Ooh, lovely. I'm looking forward to that.'

'How was the pub quiz then? Did you win?'

'No, but we came second. And do you know what the most expensive spice is in weight?'

'Saffron, I should think. Why, didn't any of you know?'

'We did — but what on earth is Lachanophobia? It's a fear of one particular food. But which one you'll never guess!'

'I didn't even know there was such a thing as a fear of food, but — hm. Milk? Dairy?'

'Vegetables,' said Lily and hid her grin behind her coffee mug.

'Veg — oh, come on, you're trying to pull my leg! One can't be afraid of vegetables! Oh, Mum, I don't think I can eat this carrot, it might bite my nose off … no way!'

Lily shrugged. 'Well, I know at least one around here who

would never say that, and that is William. And me, of course. I love vegetables, especially carrots! Why don't we make a carrot tarte tonight? With your homemade puff pastry it would be even better. Do you have any in the freezer?'

'I think so. And I have plenty of carrots, too. Yes, let's make that tonight. A nice crisp salad, a glass of white wine — you would not want Joseph to come and join us, would you?'

Lily almost dropped her spoon. 'Joseph? Why?'

But Abi just shrugged. 'Why not? The poor lad probably does not get a lot of decent meals, what with living on his own and working all hours.'

'I see. Well, I haven't got his phone number so I can't call him. Another time perhaps.'

Abi shrugged. 'You could always ask Jessie, I suppose. Anyway — more coffee?'

***

Lily enjoyed her solitary ramble. When she reached the kilns and the lone chimney Abi had told her about, she was delighted to find there were information boards put up by the North York Moors National Park. She learned about how people had first found ironstone up here and began mining the hills in 1855, soon transforming the quiet valley into a busy centre of Victorian industry. Not only were the first mines opened but the giant roasting kilns were built where the miners roasted (or calcined) the iron ore to reduce its weight for transportation and cleanse it from any impurities. Reading on in fascination, Lily could just picture how the vast quantities of ore would have been tipped into the kilns from the railway line above, and then — mixed with coal — set alight.

Lily thought she could almost hear the noise, smell the smoke, and see the blazing firelight. What a busy place this must have been in those days! 'Nothing like the quiet little dale it is today, eh, Theo?'

But Theo wasn't listening. He was busy sniffing the ground and marking his territory, so that by the end of the day every single sheep would know he had been there.

The text said that a huge workforce had been needed here, so they had had to build cottages for the miners as well as the railway men. The railway line was built in the 1860s, winding fourteen miles over the moors, across difficult terrain, all the way from Bank Top to Battersby Junction near Great Ayton. Here in Rosedale — as Lily could see when she craned her neck to look up the hill — the railway branches were split into two levels: While the upper line would have led to the iron mines above the kilns, the lower one (the one she was now standing on) would have served the kilns. The information board said that the remains of the railwaymen's cottages could be seen if you walked on towards Rosedale Abbey, but as her leg was already playing up, Lily decided to leave it for another day.

'Hm,' she muttered, her eyes still glued to the ruined kilns. 'I suppose the tiny houses on Bishops Bridge High Street must be old miners' cottages, too — I'll ask Abi when we get back. She will know.'

As she made her way back to the farm, she thought about what Abi had suggested the other day — about her staying here in Rosedale. It was a tempting idea. Because after all, what was left in Oxford — beautiful as it was — that really kept her? There was her job, which she loved, and all the places one could go to, the things one could do … But somehow, without Spencer her sense of belonging had diminished over the last three months, had crumbled and gone like the railwaymen's cottages on the other side of the dale.

Or maybe she had never really belonged in the city? She had always wanted to live in the country at some point, hadn't she, and had worried that Spencer, who had not cared much for the country at all, would not want to go with her. A cottage, a dog and three or four children ... had this only ever been wishful thinking on her part? She would never find out now, would she?

CHAPTER ELEVEN

LILY WAS SITTING in the hospital café, trying to make up her mind about the cappuccino she had bought — she really ought to return it, it was almost cold, but she did not like to make a fuss — when she heard the sound of a woman's raised voice complaining to whoever was listening that 'this was simply out of the question' and 'who did they think she was, her old man's *nurse*?'

Curiosity getting the better of her, she looked up to see a tall, slim woman with a neat bob of jet-black hair holding a red iPhone to her ear. She was dressed in tight-fitting black jeans, a ridiculously short red top that revealed her bellybutton, and a Hilfiger denim jacket. She was also boasting the most impossibly high heeled red suede boots Lily had ever seen. They looked as expensive as they looked uncomfortable.

'I know, Charles. And no, I can't do that! I'll have to ask that stuck-up neighbour of his if she would mind looking after the farm for a bit longer — yes, I know. Only until we have found a place. — Okay, now don't shout at me. I'll call you back in half an hour, or better still, when I'm at the hotel. More privacy. — Yes, me too. Bye.'

Ha, thought Lily. *Privacy! You would not shout down the phone like that if you wanted your conversation to be private, would you? And certainly not in a hospital café of all places.*

The woman let out an exaggerated sigh and stuffed her iPhone into the pocket of her jeans. Lily rolled her eyes.

'An americano, please. Black, two sugars. — Oh, I see. Yes, I'll help myself. Have you got any decent sandwiches? Only these? Hm. — No, just the coffee then. — How much?'

Lily forced herself to take a sip of her lukewarm cappuccino, feeling even less inclined to complain now. That woman was so embarrassing!

Hold on, Lily thought, putting her cup down again. What had Hilfiger Lady said on the phone about having to ask *that stuck-up neighbour of his if she would mind looking after the farm for a bit longer*? What farm? And what stuck-up neighbour? Had she referred to Abigail? But that would make her —

Just then Abi walked in, swinging an empty basket. She had brought Mr Nettleton some cake and homemade shortbread, bless her, though Lily could not for the life of her work out why she would do that if she did not even like the man. She probably just wanted to be a good neighbour, just like everybody else in the dale — well, everybody except Mr Nettleton, obviously. And if that was his daughter ...

'Hello! Are you ready to go, or should we have a coffee first? I must say I could do with one.'

Abi was about to sit in the chair opposite Lily when the dreadful lady approached her, all smiles and charm. Her long fingernails were of the same colour as the top and the phone.

'Mrs Lewis! What a lovely surprise to see you here! You may not remember me, I'm afraid, I am Mary Bradshaw, that is, or *was* rather, Nettleton — Brian Nettleton's daughter. I live in Cornwall now, so I don't get up here very often these days. Dreadful business with Dad's stroke. I'm so glad I caught you, Mrs Lewis. Now I can finally thank you for looking after his animals so well. — Have you just been to see him?'

Abi glared at her. 'It's *Miss* Lewis, and yes, I have been to see him. I have brought him fresh clothes, too, as well as a slice of cake and a tin of shortbread to last him through the next week. And I don't mind looking after his farm. I don't live in Cornwall, do I? But then, I am not his daughter either. Good day, Mrs Bradshaw.'

Lily took this as a cue to get up and leave, and she could not say she was sorry — neither about the cappuccino nor about Mrs Mary Bradshaw née Nettleton. Her aunt had certainly not exaggerated. Mistress Mary indeed!

'Wait! Mrs — Miss Lewis, please — wait!'

Before they had reached the door, Nettleton's daughter had caught up with them, flashing her white teeth at Abi as she plunged into her desperate plea. 'I know it's a lot to ask, but do you think you could hold the fort for another couple of weeks? Just until I have found a place for him in Cornwall of course. I will ask him to sell the farm as soon as I can discuss things like that with him — which is, as I am sure you will have seen for yourself, a bit tricky at the moment. So would you do me the favour, please — or him, rather? As a good neighbour? I'm sure you would not want me to sell the lot to the butcher's right away, would you, without my poor father even knowing.'

Abi huffed. 'Don't worry. I'll see to that gander and all of his subjects, two— and four legged alike. I would never let an animal suffer.' *Not even if they belong to Brian Nettleton,* was clearly written all over her face. Although Lily had to give it to her, she kept a poker face all the way out until they reached the car park.

'Insufferable woman! Just as bad as her father. Come on, lass, let's get home. There's a nice drop of whisky waiting for us.'

Lily found herself being catapulted against the back of her seat as Abi put her foot hard on the accelerator and they sped out of the car park at a speed that was most certainly illegal.

***

'I THINK WE deserve a special treat tonight — what do you think? The *Red Grouse* or the *Dog and Partridge*? Or should I get into the car and get us some pies in Helmsley?'

Abi glanced at her watch. 'They close in fifteen minutes, so unless your Mini can fly — But I don't feel like going out either, to be honest. Why don't we just order something by telephone, and you go and pick it up?'

'Good idea. The *Dog and Partridge* then? Do they have a homepage, so we can have a look at the menu online?'

Abi frowned. 'How would *I* know if they have a *page at home*, or whatever you call it? I'm going for a steak and ale pie, so I don't even need to bother with a menu. You can try and find one on the line then if you like.'

'Okay, I will then,' Lily laughed. 'Just let me have a shower first, and then I'll check out the menu. Have you got any cider, or do you want me to get some from the pub?'

'Try the larder, there should be a few bottles left. Unless you want any of that fancy stuff, blackberry flavoured or whatever it is they do to cider these days.'

Having found four bottles of orchard apple cider, Lily put them in the fridge, and headed upstairs for her shower, humming cheerfully.

With her hair wrapped in a soft towel that smelled of sunshine and clean, fresh air, she sat down on her bed with her phone and was about to study the menu when she saw that two messages had come in while she was in the bathroom, one from her brother, the other one from Beth.

Good news, sis! You're going to be an auntie by the end of November! Stephen X

Lily was surprised because she had always put Emily down as the 'career first, then house, then perhaps when I am forty and we have seen the world and enough money on the side' … She stopped herself even before she had finished thinking the word — type. *You should not think in types, Lily*, she scolded herself as she tapped in a quick reply. *It's petty, and petty doesn't suit you. Be kind.*

Congratulations! I'm so pleased for you both X — which she was, despite the fact that she was not particularly fond of perfect Emily with her perfect teeth and perfect nails and perfect everything — and pressed *send*.

Then she read Beth's text, hoping for something to cheer her up.

Do call me, please, Lily, I have some news I would rather not share via WhatsApp. Beth X

Oh dear, she thought. *That sounds ominous.* With a sigh, she dialled Beth's number.

Beth answered right away, as if she had been waiting with

the phone in her hands, which she probably had. 'Oh, Lily, I'm so excited!' she cried, unable to contain herself. 'We are just back from Israel and guess what, it was not indigestion that made me so sick over there … I thought I must have eaten something wrong for honestly, Lily, I was sick *all the time*! But now I know why, and I'm sure you can guess, too — I'm pregnant! With twins! Would you believe it? And that is not all! Oh sweetie, I don't know how to tell you …'

Lily shut her eyes. *Another one.* And she could guess the next bit, too. They were probably emigrating to Canada or something. She swallowed. 'Go on then, spill.'

'Matthew has been offered the position of vicar at St John's in … oh, sorry, I forgot the name of the town, but it's in Devon. We're going to live by the sea! Isn't that wonderful? I know it's a long way from Oxford, but — it's such a great opportunity, Lily. A really large congregation, and evangelical, too. The vicarage is huge! And the gardens are overlooking the sea! I cannot believe how privileged we are to go there. How blessed! Oh, Lily, I'm just so sorry it's going to take us away from Oxford, and from you.'

Too stunned to speak, Lily sat down on the bed. She probably ought to say something like 'congratulations' or 'I'm really pleased for you', but somehow the words got stuck in her throat.

'Oh, I know — it's Kimpton. The place where we're going. Kimpton-by-the-Sea, actually. Just found it on the map. It's not far from Dartmouth, in case you want to look it up. We are going to move down in September when the vicar retires and … oh, Lily, but you're not saying anything! You are not angry, are you?'

'Angry? Why ever should I be angry? I'm just …' *Stunned. Shocked.* 'Um – surprised.' *That's it, settle for surprised.* Anyone would be surprised at how fast things were falling into place for Matthew and Beth. She knew he had been hoping to become vicar in one of the pretty Cotswolds towns so they would not have had to move away from their family and friends but of course they would have to accept what was on offer, even if it meant going as far as Devon. And a vicarage with a view of the sea was not exactly bad, was it?

Beth laughed. 'Yes, so are we! You can't imagine what that felt like — first the letter from Devon, offering Matthew the position, and then the revelation we had when we went to my first scan. Twins! There are no twins in either of our respective families. Well, I suppose there is always a first time for everything. They are not due before November, so at least we will have moved into the vicarage by then and hopefully settled in a bit.'

'I'm sure you will settle in fine. And I *am* pleased for you. Really. I'm just — well. Surprised. It's quite sudden, isn't it? And twins — wow. Do you know what sex they are?'

'We don't, no, and even if we did, we wouldn't tell. We're thinking about names of course, but they will also be kept secret. When are you due back home then? We can meet for a pizza in town. Jamie's Italian? You like Jamie's, don't you?'

Lily shut her eyes for a moment, trying not to picture herself and Spencer sitting at one of their rustic tables, sharing a platter of antipasti and a bottle of Chianti. 'I do, yes. To be honest though, it would remind me of Spencer, and … perhaps we can go somewhere else?'

'Of course. Sorry, I wasn't thinking. And don't worry about Devon — we'll keep in touch. We can write to each other, like they did in the old days, and you must visit us of course, just as soon as we are settled.'

'That will be lovely, yes.' She knew it probably sounded

lame, but she could not help it. Why was everybody leaving her? It was not fair. But then life hardly ever was, was it? Not even for the Mr Nettletons in this world who had no choice but to leave their lifelong home behind and spend the rest of their days in a nursing home in Cornwall.

'Great. So when are you back then? Easter?'

'Yes. I'm planning to come home on Good Friday as there will be less traffic.'

'Good thinking. So, how do you like being on the farm with only your great-aunt and the ponies for company? Is it as peaceful as you hoped it would be — or is it perhaps rather too quiet?'

'Quiet? Are you joking? There's a donkey, too, I'll have you know, and he's got a mind of his own. And a voice to match! Then there is Theo, Abi's notorious dachshund, and a whole lot of new people I have met here. I have been to the pub more often these past two weeks than in the whole of last winter, and …'

'Oh, but that's lovely, Lily! Good to hear you're getting out a bit more often. And making new friends, too. I'm really pleased for you, sweetheart.'

Lily was just going to explain that Lucy, Jessie, and the others were not really *friends* when out of the blue, Beth asked, 'So maybe you won't want to come back at all?'

Lily shut her eyes. How did Beth always seem to know what she was thinking? Did she have something like a sixth sense, and if so, did that come with being a counsellor? Or a Christian, even? Had God *told* her about Lily's secret hopes and dreams?

'Lily?'

'Um … I don't know. I might, or I might not. I — I'll tell you all about it when I get back.' Suddenly feeling very tired, she was eager to end the conversation. 'Right, I've got to go — I was supposed to order food from the pub and then go and collect it. Give my love to Matthew, will you? And congratulations. I'm really happy for you.'

Thankfully, just then Abi called and asked, 'Are you going to take long on that line, Lily? I'm just nipping out to Wood End Farm, make sure the geese aren't loose.'

Lily rolled her eyes and laughed. 'You heard her! Bye then, see you soon!'

Well, she thought, as she made her way down the stairs, *perhaps I am glad to go back to Oxford after all. At least there are no geese!*

CHAPTER TWELVE

Lily was walking back from the village where she had spent a blissful hour sitting in Jessie's café, drinking coffee and dreaming about her barn idea. If she really wanted to do something about that barn, she would have to talk to Abi soon. She only had another week now. How could three weeks have gone by so quickly? And yet, it almost felt like longer ... like she had always been here. Or rather — she stopped to wave to an old gentleman and his Golden Retriever who she had frequently met in the village — *like I belong here*.

Because one thing had become clear now: she did not belong in Oxford — perhaps she never had belonged there in the first place. She had been busy with her job, and there had been the odd night out with some colleagues, and with Spencer of course, but now that he was gone ... and with Beth leaving soon ... what would be left then?

Nothing, she thought bitterly, kicking a stone. *An empty flat, an empty life.*

Here, she had Abi, Theo, and William, and — much as it surprised her — friends. And fun. In other words, she had a life. It felt good. Here, she was happy — or at least, a lot happier than when she had first arrived on the farm, when she had thought she would *never* be alright again. So why couldn't she come back here? Make it work …

But how?

She walked past the Marstons' field and smiled when she saw the spring lambs frolicking about in the early April sunshine. By now she knew which farmer owned which fields around here — on this side of the dale there were only three farms: Brook Farm, Wood End Farm, and Fern Hill Farm. There was a row of cottages tucked away in a quiet lane opposite the Marston's place, too — Jessie lived in one of them, renting from Ben's parents, apparently — and then there was the village of course, with its picturesque High Street, church, village hall, and vicarage. There was a tiny cottage for sale, called the Old Post Office, which made Lily's heart ache with longing just by looking at the estate agent's sign. She had looked it up online but of course it was way beyond what she could ever afford, even if she sold her flat in Oxford. Small as it was, Bishops Bridge was a popular village, and — in the summer months at least — teeming with tourists. These cottages, if they ever came on the market, were advertised as 'the perfect second home' or to be let as holiday cottages. *Well*, thought Lily, kicking another stone, *good for those who can afford that sort of thing*. But then, who had ever said life was fair?

'Hello, sweetie,' she said to a lamb that had come to explore the drystone wall with its little brother or sister. Smiling to herself as she walked on, she tried to think of what to wear to the pub tonight. She had brought one skirt, but it was — *had been* — a favourite of Spencer's, and she was not sure she was ready to wear it again yet. She was not even sure why she had brought it in the first place.

She swallowed, trying to keep the emotions under control. That was how the trouble with her anxiety and eating disorder had started all those years ago. She had always felt inferior, and undeserving. And she had always compared herself to others, especially the girls in her class. They all seemed to be so much prettier, cooler, self-confident, and more popular. She did not fit in, no matter how hard she tried. What with her self-esteem already being low when she was in Year 9, all it took was a couple of thoughtless comments from one of those girls at a party she had miraculously been invited to. She still remembered to this day how excited she had been to go, especially when she learned that the boy she had a crush on would also be there …

But for one thing, he just drank and smoked a lot while ignoring her all night, and then, when she had just been about to call her parents to come and pick her up, she had seen him kissing another girl — and not just any girl but Sandra, the only girl in her class she had considered a friend. And what was worse, Sandra knew Lily was in love with Derek.

Frozen to the spot, Lily had stood there, waiting for them to move somewhere else, and then … then she had heard Sandra telling him about her *crush*, and they had laughed at her. The last thing she remembered about this dreadful night was Derek taking Sandra's hand and leading her upstairs, and her rushing to the bathroom and being sick.

Lily stopped, put a hand to her chest where her heartbeat was gathering speed at an alarming rate, hammering against her ribcage as she remembered some of the things they had said.

Too fat. Too geeky. Too clumsy.
Who does she think she is? She will never have a boyfriend!

Quickly, she felt for the pendant. *You are not fat. You may be a bit of a geek, but that's okay. You love history. You love classics. And now you love donkeys, too. So what? Lucy, Jessie, and the others don't seem to mind. And in Spencer's eyes, you were special. Special enough to be given this pendant. Loved.*

She swallowed back her tears. *Don't cry now. It's a beautiful day. It's going to be a beautiful evening. You'll be with friends. You'll be alright.*

But would she? Would she be alright? Or was she just building sandcastles with her ideas for the barn, knowing she would not have the courage to really do it? Was this just a very special time, and once she got back to Oxford, life here would go on without her, as it had before?

Of course it would. Just like hers would go on — without Spencer, and without Beth. Without anyone to call a friend.

***

As soon as she had closed the farm gate behind her, Lily ran up to the paddock where Delilah and William were grazing. As soon as he saw his new friend, the donkey came over to the fence, as if to see what the trouble was. 'Oh, William! What shall I do?' Lily cried, flinging her arms around the donkey's neck. 'Whatever shall I do?'

She had been standing there for a while, crying her heart out to the little donkey, when she heard someone calling her name.

'Lily?'

She didn't look up but she recognized Joseph's voice at once. Not trusting herself to turn around with her swollen eyes and red nose, she just whispered, 'yes?' and held her breath when he gently touched her shoulder.

'Hey there ... have you been crying?'

She swallowed, her head still buried in the donkey's shaggy coat. 'No, I ... it's just ... well —' But it was no use, she had to be honest with him. 'Yes, I suppose I have.'

'Oh, Lily, I'm so sorry.' Turning her gently around, he cupped her face in his hands and she could see the genuine concern in his eyes. 'Is there anything I can do for you? Do you need a tissue? A cup of tea? Shall I ask Abi to put the kettle on?'

Lily shook her head, but leaned into him now, resting her head against his chest and inhaling the clean, fresh scent of him. It felt good. Safe.

'Are you sure? About the tea?'

'Tea would be lovely.'

'That's my girl,' he smiled, wiping a tear from her face. Then he put an arm around her shoulder and walked to the farmhouse with her. 'You're not crying because you don't want to go back to Oxford, are you?'

She hesitated. 'I suppose I am, actually. I would just love to stay ... but I don't know how. I am not exactly the adventurous kind of person. That's not me. I like to play it safe, even if that makes me sound like a terrible bore.'

He stopped and looked at her, almost hurt. 'You are not boring! You are Abigail Lewis's great-niece, and you walk her donkey. You are funny, helpful, and kind, and — Lily, what is it? Whatever have I said to make you cry again?'

But she shook her head, determined not to let her emotions get the better of her again. 'It's nothing, really. I'm fine. Or I will be after a cup of tea.'

'I somehow doubt that ... but if you don't want to tell me, that's entirely up to you of course. By the way, I'm afraid I won't make it to the pub tonight. I would have texted you, but it seems I haven't got your number — perhaps it would be a good idea if I let you have mine before you swan off to Oxford again, so we can stay in touch. Only if you like, of course. You might be quite eager to get back and enjoy the fun of city life again after a month in the company of — well, country bumpkins like us.'

She stiffened. 'What makes you think that?'

'Well,' he said, suddenly embarrassed. 'I don't know … I just thought four weeks of being stuck in the middle of nowhere would be enough for you. For anyone, really, who isn't … sorry. That was stupid of me. You are not *anyone*. You are — special. Very special. And I know you love it here — I just wish …' He shook his head and looked away. 'It doesn't matter.'

'It does though, doesn't it?' she whispered, and this time it was her hand that reached up to his face. She swallowed. 'It does matter. But Joseph, no matter how much I love this place here, how much I would like to stay — seeing how very little I have to go back to now that my best friend is moving to Devon and …' She closed her eyes briefly, forcing herself to go on. To say it. 'My boyfriend …'

His arm slipped off her shoulder as if she were a hot potato. 'God, I'm sorry. I didn't know — of course I should have thought … you being so pretty and charming and … sorry!'

'It's okay,' she heard herself say. They had reached the farmhouse, and she pushed open the door to let him in. 'I don't have a boyfriend now. He is dead.'

***

WHILE JOSEPH BUSIED himself with making tea and cutting cake, Lily told him about Spencer, and the real reason she came to Rosedale. She did not tell him about the doubts she had had before Spencer died, nor the overwhelming sense of guilt and shame that had been with her ever since … just about her grief. For now, that seemed quite enough. And she *was* grieving him — missing him, too. More than anything, she wished he was still alive, so she could set things right between them. Set him free to love someone else. *Someone worthy of his love …*

When she had finished, Joseph got up, took her in his arms, and held her tight. He did not say anything. There was no need. For the first time since Spencer had died, Lily felt someone understood exactly what she needed — and what she didn't.

'I'm afraid I really ought to be going now,' he said when they had finished their tea and polished off the last of Abi's fruit cake. 'I wish I didn't have to but …'

'Don't worry. I'll be fine. Abi will be back any moment, and,' she added with a smile, 'there is always William.'

'Of course. Donkey therapy at its best. How about we meet at the weekend? Go for a walk perhaps — would you like that? I have the Sunday off, so we could make a day of it, if you like?'

Her tear-stained face broke into a smile. 'I would like that very much. Shall I bring a picnic?'

'Oh, yes, please! Absolutely. No walk without a picnic. If it rains, we'll take shelter under a tree — if we are lucky enough to find one. Better bring your rain jacket. You can bring Theo, too. But don't bother about William, please, not this time — I know you love him, but we're going to be at least four or five hours, and that might just prove to be a bit too much for your long-eared friend, especially if he can't bring Delilah.'

Lily blushed. How did he know she had been thinking about it? 'Of course not.'

'Good. So that's settled then — walk and picnic on Sunday. Now I've got your number, we'll be in touch.' He bent to kiss her lightly on the cheek. 'Bye, Lily. Take care.'

When he was gone, Lily put a hand to her cheek and closed her eyes, smiling softly to herself. *Good,* she thought. *This feels good.*

CHAPTER THIRTEEN

'WELL, IF SELLING is what you want, I cannot stop you. I was just saying that it does not seem fair on your father when he is still recovering in hospital — you don't know what he might have to say about this, do you? Or how he might *feel* about it, come to that?'

Lily, who was just on her way downstairs, stopped dead when she recognised Nettleton's daughter. What was *she* doing here at eight o'clock in the morning? Carefully retracing her steps, Lily sat down at the bottom of the stairs and strained her ears to listen.

'Well, he would not want to sell of course — and I would not dream of forcing him away from his beloved farm and lifelong home if I had an alternative, but sadly, I haven't. So all I'm asking you to do is look after the livestock until I have sold the lot off, and perhaps show the odd prospective buyer around. If that's alright with you, I would like to give your phone number to the estate agent so when there's somebody interested, you could show them around and answer some questions. You know the place nearly as well as I do after all.'

Lily sat up. *You know the place nearly as well as I do.* Had she been missing something here?

Abi turned around sharply, and Lily ducked, hoping she would not see her. 'Oh, now why does that not surprise me? You always know when it is a good time to drag up an old story, don't you, especially if it's to your advantage. You don't even know what happened — at least not from me, you don't. And of course you would believe everything your father told you. You're as bad as he is. But alright then, give that estate agent my number if you think that will help. I don't expect anyone to show the remotest interest in buying that rundown old place.'

'Well, that remains to be seen, doesn't it?'

Mary Nettleton left shortly after that, and Lily sat in stunned silence until Abi came into the hall, a tea towel in her hand.

'Lily? What's the matter? — Goodness, you look pale! Have you been sitting there long?'

'Um … just a few minutes. Long enough to hear though, I'm afraid. I'm sorry.'

Abi flapped her hand dismissively. 'Aw, don't worry! She's just as bad as her father. The sooner the place is sold, and he's bundled off to Cornwall, the better. Good riddance and all that. Breakfast?'

It was clear that Abi had no intention of talking about her neighbour, so Lily thought it best to let sleeping dogs lie for the time being, but she had to admit she was curious now. Had Abi had an affair with Nettleton at some point? Had they not always been sworn enemies? Maybe they had just had different expectations, or maybe …

'Coffee or tea? Oh, and your mum called. You might want to ring her back later. Have you got any plans for today?'

Lily shook her head. 'Not really, no.'

'Why don't you try riding Willoughby then? You have

not ridden at all since you came. You used to when you were a teenager, as did your mum. It might help you, you know. Come to terms with things, I mean. Or you could just walk William. He has become a good friend, hasn't he?'

Suddenly, Lily's throat was tight with emotion. 'He has, yes.' A single tear spilled down her cheek. 'A really good friend.'

'Oh, lassie. Come on now, eat your breakfast, or you will have to go on an empty stomach and that won't do. Tea or coffee?'

'Coffee, please.' Lily followed her into the kitchen and sank onto a chair while Abi put a large plate of bacon and eggs before her. Knowing that resistance would be futile, she began to eat, but put her knife and fork down after a couple of bites, realizing that Abi had never made her talk about Spencer's death. Or referred to her grief in any way. Instead, she had done what she was so good at and why she loved her so much: She had just let Lily *be*.

'Abi? You never really needed me here, did you? To help you on the farm? Be honest with me, please — was it mum who set this up? Did she tell you I needed a break or something?'

Abi sat down with her own breakfast and placed a hand over Lily's. 'Don't be angry with her, please, for worrying so. You are right — she thought it would do you good to come here and enjoy a bit of fresh air. So when Brian Nettleton had his stroke, I thought now was as good a time as any … But as the old saying goes, *in war and in love*, … or in times of grief, for that matter …'

Lily smiled. 'I thought as much. Well, well.'

'It worked though, didn't it? You do seem a lot happier now than when you first came.'

'I am. Very much so. And I will miss being here — you know I have always wanted to live in the country myself. A cottage, four children, two dogs ...' Her voice trailed away, as did her thoughts. 'Spencer did not want any of that. I think. Or maybe I was wrong about that. Like I seem to have been wrong about so many things ... but I'll never know now, will I? What he really wanted — and what might have been.'

Abi gave her hand a squeeze. 'No. But there is no point in dwelling on the *might-have-beens* in life, is there? As you said, you will never know. I'm glad you had a good time here and are feeling better. And if you find that Oxford does not suit you any more, you can always come back here. Any time, lass.'

'I know. And I love you for that. You are one in a million, Abi.'

'Well now, I don't know about that.' She picked up the cafetiere. 'More coffee?'

***

'IF JOSEPH SAYS you can't come with us on Sunday, then I'll have to take you today, or we won't get to spend much time together at all,' Lily said, leading William along the path. 'And I know I will miss you terribly when I'm back in Oxford. You know ... I do wonder what that Nettleton woman meant when she said *You know this house as well as I do*. Shall I ask Abi? No? Hm. You're probably right, better leave it be. Although I have a feeling this will not be the last we have seen of that horrid woman — or her father, for that matter. I have never taken such a strong dislike to a person I have never even met before!'

She walked up to Upper Rye Farm, where she bought clotted cream, cheese, and butter, and then stopped at Susanna's cottage for a chat before returning home.

Home, she thought, as she closed the gate behind her, and led William back to his paddock. It came so naturally to call it home. Why couldn't she make this work?

Well, a voice inside her head said, *why don't you try it? After all, what have you got to lose?*

She sighed and looked up at the barn. 'Nothing much, I suppose. Nothing much. Just like this barn — if I don't help it come to life again, nobody else will. It will just stand there for another fifty years and rot …'

Suddenly a thought struck her. What would become of the farm if Abi got frail and sick like Mr Nettleton? Who would look after the ponies, and William? Abi would probably leave the farm to her niece, since there was not anyone else but …

Lily frowned. But her parents would not want to move up here, they were happy as they were in Burford. *I am not happy where I am though. I could do with a fresh start. And if I were to come up here …*

Looking up, she saw the crumbling old barn standing against the backdrop of the fields that stretched almost to the ridge where the road ran. Sometimes Abi would put the horses to graze there but today the field lay empty with just the breeze moving through the high grass. Lily bit her lip. *It's perfect,* she thought. *Just perfect.* And then she broke into a run, up the steep and winding path, muttering 'that will have to be paved of course', until she reached the barn. Leaning against the wall, she ran a hand up and down the rough surface of the stone.

'Yes,' she whispered, 'that's it. If I come here … and help

Abi turn the farm into a working business again – not as a stud farm, of course, because I know next to nothing about horses — but surely I — we — can think of something else … anything to save the farm — *her home* — from being lost.'

Because that much Lily knew, losing Fern Hill Farm would break Abi's heart beyond repair, and the more she thought about it, the more determined she became not to let that happen.

CHAPTER FOURTEEN

JOSEPH WAVED WHEN Lily came to open the gate for him. 'Lovely day for it, isn't it?' he called as he jumped out of the car and slammed the door shut, leaving an indignant Inigo behind.

'Yes! Perfect. Why aren't you letting him out then — we aren't going anywhere by car, are we?' She pointed at Inigo who was jumping up and down behind the passenger window, barking like mad.

'We are — I thought I would take you to the Hole of Horcum, seeing as it's such a fine day. It's about half an hour's drive, forty minutes at the most.'

'The Hole of Horcum? I'm not sure I have ever heard of it.' Tossing her rucksack into the boot of Joseph's Land Rover, she whistled to Theo. 'Come on, Theo, we're taking a ride with Inigo!' The moment she opened the passenger door though, she found herself being almost knocked over by an excited Inigo who came bouncing down the same moment she was going to step inside.

'Inigo!' Joseph grabbed him by the collar just in time. 'Come here!' Picking him up, he walked round to the back of the car and opened the boot. 'I'd better put you in here.

Much safer for a bouncer like you, anyway. Lily and Theo can sit in the front, they know how to behave. Or Lily does, anyway,' he added with a wink.

'The Hole of Horcum is one of the most spectacular features in the National Park — it's a huge natural amphitheatre 400 feet deep and more than half a mile across,' Joseph explained as they drove along the A169 towards Pickering. 'Legend has it that it was formed when Wade the Giant scooped up a handful of earth to throw at his wife during an argument.' He turned to Lily and grinned. 'Nice man, eh? Although to be fair, she must have done something to rile him like that.'

'Probably. Like reminding him to wipe his feet before he got in?'

They both laughed, and not for the first time Lily thought how easy it was to be with Joseph. He managed to make her laugh, and she felt comfortable even when they were not speaking. With Spencer, she had never felt so relaxed. Often enough she had thought that make-up was not the only thing she put on when she went out with him, even though she never usually wore any during the day. But for Spencer, everything had to be perfect, including her. For Joseph she seemed to be enough as she was.

Having left the car in Levisham, a quiet little village just off the A169, they walked past the *Horseshoe Inn*, where Joseph promised they would stop for a drink when they got back. Following a lane, they soon came to a signpost marked 'Hole of Horcum'. Here they turned left, crossed two streams, and stopped to let the dogs drink.

'I never got around to asking, but did you actually name him Inigo after that Inigo Montoya character in *The Princess Bride*?'

'Of course. It is one of my favourite films, and I used to joke that if one day I owned a spaniel with black ears, I would name him Inigo Montoya, even if it wasn't an I-litter. Which it was, believe it or not, so the name even made it into his official papers!'

Lily shook her head laughing, then followed Joseph along the path that had a wall to its right. 'Golly. So if I had an Irish Wolfhound, would I call him Fezzik?'

'You might. But you've got a donkey named William, haven't you? Don't you think that will do?'

'Well, for one thing he is not *my* donkey, and for another, I don't live here, remember? I'm only visiting. And I'm leaving on Friday.'

I really must talk to Abi before I leave, she thought, biting her lip. *If I don't do it now, there won't be time until ... well, later. Very much later.* It was not the sort of thing you discussed on the phone, was it?

'But you'll be back, surely? Now that you have made friends here? And I don't only mean the donkey.'

She knew he meant to make her laugh but when she turned to him, she was unable to hide the sadness in her eyes. 'I know. But it isn't quite the same, is it?'

He reached out to touch her cheek. 'No. No, it isn't. I'm sorry. I wish you could stay though.'

Lily felt a lump forming in her throat and shook her head. 'S'okay. I'll be fine.'

She could see his brow furrowing as he scrutinised her, but he did not say anything, and she was glad. She was not sure what it was she wanted to hear, and from the look on his face he was not sure what she expected him to say either, so it was with a certain relief that she felt him taking her hand and leading her on. A few minutes later, he stopped her and covered her eyes with his hand.

'Miss Henderson, may I proudly present to you — the Hole of Horcum!'

She opened her eyes and gasped as she took in the stunning scenery — the Hole of Horcum lay stretched out before her like a giant green punchbowl, drenched in April sunshine and dotted with thousands of daffodils which were gently swaying in the warm breeze, like miniature dancing girls in their dainty little yellow frocks.

'Oh, Joseph,' she whispered, gripping his arm, 'this is so beautiful!'

He nodded and put his arm around her waist. 'It is quite something, isn't it?'

'Indeed … Oh, I'm so glad you took me here today. Thank you, Joseph!' Without thinking, she leaned into him and sighed, wishing she could freeze this moment. *This is right*, she thought dreamily as she gazed into the valley. *This is where I belong.*

'I'm glad you like it. Shall we sit down and have our picnic now? Then we can enjoy the view for a bit longer.'

'Yes. That would be lovely.' Her voice sounded as if it came from somewhere else. She was mesmerized. She felt Joseph gently pulling her closer to him, and together they stood there in silence, cherishing the moment.

Only when Joseph let go of her to take the picnic rug out of his rucksack and spread it on the grass, did she find her way back to the present.

'You were miles away,' he said, when they sat down to eat. 'I can't tell you how glad I am that you like this place — it's magical, isn't it? This is definitely one of my favourite walks.'

'I can clearly see why. It must be stunning in the autumn, too, when the leaves turn all orange and red …'

'It is. You must come back then, Lily — promise that you will?'

She nodded but still her heart was heavy. What if her plan did not work out? What if she was only dreaming — being so hopelessly romantic, as everyone said. Well, she would have to show them that you could be romantic and realistic at the same time. All she needed was to come up with a really good plan ... And talk to Abi. If Abi did not want her on the farm, then that would be the end of that. But somehow she had a feeling that Abi was just waiting for her to say something ...

Perhaps, she thought as she watched the dogs scamper off and then turned to look at Joseph who had stretched out beside her as if it was the most natural thing in the world, *she is lonelier than she lets on.* Because, as she had just found out for herself, there was a fine line between being alone — and being lonely. A very fine line.

She let out a soft sigh.

'Hey,' Joseph said, slipping an arm around her shoulder. 'Thinking about going back to Oxford?'

'M-hm ... yes, I suppose.'

'So why don't you stay?'

She shook her head. 'It's not as simple as that.' She could not tell him about the barn. He would think her completely crazy.

'Isn't it?'

'No. I'd need to find a job, and somewhere to live —'

He frowned. 'Don't you think Abi would let you stay on the farm with her? I'm sure she would love to have you.'

'Yes, well, maybe she would but there is still the small matter of finding a job. I can't open a riding school.' *I can open a book shop maybe. But for that I'd have to talk to Abi first ...*

'Lily.' Cupping her face in both hands and, gazing deep into her eyes, he said, 'You are the loveliest girl I have ever met, and I know you are hurting, but please don't let what happened in the past determine your future. You've got to let go. And if I can help you in any way ... I will. Perhaps this,' he kissed her very softly on the lips, 'might be a good start?'

She tried to close her eyes and enjoy the moment, but she couldn't. Her heart was racing. Was it excitement, or was she panicking? Sometimes she could not tell the difference. She felt dizzy.

No, she thought. *This is not a good idea. It's too soon. I'm still raw with grief. And we have not known each other long. We should take things more slowly. Much more slowly.*

'Please, Joseph,' she began but did not get any further because just then Inigo came hurtling across the grass, carrying a large, mud-caked stick, and came to a skittering halt on the rug, sending the leftover sausage rolls flying as he did. Theo, who had been dozing nearby, got up, yawned, stretched lazily, and ate them one by one.

'Ugh! Inigo!' Grabbing him by the collar, Joseph jerked him away while Lily sat there, laughing helplessly as she watched the pair of them. 'Naughty dog! Aren't you ashamed of yourself? Now look what you've done! And what's that you're carrying?'

The spaniel did not look the slightest bit ashamed, and Lily laughed even harder. 'You don't even know what shame is, do you, Inigo? Come on, I'll throw the stick for you.'

But Joseph took her by the elbow, holding her back. 'Erm, Lily — no, that's not a good idea. I'm afraid that isn't a stick.'

'Oh? What is it then?' Lily looked closer at the long,

brown object that was stuck between the spaniel's teeth. Suddenly she paled. 'Oh … please don't tell me it's …'

'Yes. A hare's front leg — and a rotting one, too, by the smell of it. Inigo! Drop it! Now!'

They were still laughing as they packed up the picnic, and Lily was glad for the distraction. Now she would not have to think about whether she wanted Joseph to kiss her, or not. She could leave it for another day.

'Sorry,' he said, lightly touching her shoulder. 'That was not quite what I had in mind when I kissed you. But perhaps it was a bit too soon, anyway. You are still grieving that Spencer guy, I don't want to rush you. I'm sorry.' He raked a hand through his hair. 'So, shall we start again and take things slowly? Just get to know each other first?'

'Okay.' Lily nodded, remembering how Spencer had rushed her from the very beginning, making love to her too soon, when she was not nearly ready. She knew Joseph would not rush her like that, and yet she did not trust herself to meet his gaze, knowing that if she looked into those blue eyes now, she would be lost. And then? She would go back to Oxford, and he would stay here. How would they make that work? Wasn't her life complicated enough?

'Okay? As in — okay, let's get to know each other and see what happens? Or okay, if that's what you want?'

When she looked up and saw the confused look on his face, she detected a vulnerability in him that she had not seen before. Maybe he was not the confident, laid-back, easy-going guy — maybe he had his own demons to fight? For all she knew he might have been in an unhappy relationship, or maybe he had even been married, like Spencer? In any case, getting to know each other seemed a good idea. *A safe idea.*

'No, let's start again and get to know each other. Let's start by — being friends. If that's okay with you?' Holding out her hand, she said, 'I'm Lily Henderson, I'm twenty-seven, I work as a college librarian in Oxford where I also have a lonely little flat that does not feel like home anymore since Spencer died ... I drive a red Mini, I love the Beatles, and donkeys. And,' she drew her breath, 'I suffer from anxiety. Quite badly, actually. But these days, I can handle it. Well, most of the time.'

'Wow,' he said, shaking his head. 'That is a lot of information, Lily Henderson. My life is not nearly as interesting, I'm afraid. Come on, let's walk, and I'll tell you more about it.'

They followed the footpath through a field gate and climbed up a steep path that led them to a broad track over the moor. With spectacular views of the Hole of Horcum now to their left, Lily felt herself relax once more as she listened to his account of his life as a Yorkshire vet. He had always wanted to be a vet, and he had always wanted to stay right here, in Yorkshire.

'I grew up in Bransdale, so not very far from here. My parents were farmers but had to give up the farm after a case of foot and mouth disease. They were going to retire anyway, and they were tenants, they did not own the farm, but still, it wasn't easy for them.' He offered his hand to help Lily over a stile and lifted the dog flap for Inigo, while Theo simply crawled underneath the bottom rail.

'I can imagine that. Where do they live now? And do you have any brothers or sisters?'

'Nope. There's only me. My parents moved to Hutton-le-Hole, and I live in Pickering, alone with my dog. I must say, though, that I am really committed to my job. I don't even have time for hobbies, except walking, and I often get to do that in between visits to farms. It's why I always take Inigo along. The other reason being that I never trained him to be on his own.'

Lily shook her head laughing. 'A vet and his dog, eh? I love it. Well, I hope you know how lucky you are, Joseph Hancock. You know — living in this beautiful place, loving what you do, and having such a naughty but incredibly sweet dog for company … seems pretty perfect to me.'

'I know I am lucky. The only thing that's missing in my life is —' He stopped himself, as if sensing that would be a step too far, too soon. 'Never mind. I am lucky, and I am happy to share this with you today.'

She smiled, and they walked in silence for a while, until they reached a signpost at a corner of a stone wall, where they turned right, following a track across the moor. Lily could have walked on for hours, even though the skies had clouded over, and the air smelled of rain. It was just so good to be with Joseph, and out walking on the Moors. He had not told her much about his private life, other than that he had been in a long-term relationship that had not ended well. In the end, she had run off to New Zealand with a colleague of his.

'I want to show you something,' Joseph said and took her hand, 'it won't take long. Come on, this way.'

Curious, Lily followed him until they reached the edge of an escarpment, where they had to put the dogs on their leads because there were so many rabbits about. Then they walked down a path through a hollow way, until the ruins of a tower came into view.

'This is Skelton Tower — I don't know anything about it, other than it might have been one of those hunting towers. But what I really wanted to show you is this,' Joseph said, leading her across the grassy headland until they were standing at the edge.

Lily gasped. 'Oh!'

'I thought you'd like this — that's Newton Dale down there, and if we are lucky, we will be able to see the steam train. It runs between Pickering and Whitby, stopping at Goathland, Levisham, and Thornton-le-Dale. We could do that some other day, if you like … oi, listen! I think I can hear a whistle.'

Lily put a hand above her eyes and looked to the right, and there it was — a nostalgic black steam engine pulling six carriages came huffing and puffing around the corner, making her feel like she was one of the Railway Children. If she waved, would an old gentleman in a top hat wave back at her, she wondered and unconsciously raised her hand.

'They wouldn't see you from down there, they …' But he didn't finish his sentence, because in that moment they both saw a hand reaching out of a window of one of the carriages — and it was waving a large, white handkerchief at them.

'See?' Lily turned to him, her cheeks glowing with excitement. She had no idea how lovely she looked in that moment. 'They did — or one of them did, anyway. Oh, Joseph, this is the most romantic of all places! Look, there is an information board next to the tower. Let's see what it says.'

'Built around 1830 by Robert Skelton, rector of Levisham, the tower was used as overnight lodgings after a day's shooting on the moors. The grassy headland is a wonderful spot for a picnic, and you'll hear the whistle of the steam trains below in plenty of time for a photograph,' she read. 'Hm. Not very exciting. But it really is a great spot for a picnic — let's have one here next time we come back.'

'Deal,' he said, taking her hands and looking down into her eyes (he really was incredibly tall! If she ever wanted to kiss him, she would have to stand on her toes. And she would still suffer a stiff neck afterwards.). 'And in the meantime, Lily, remember you have friends here, a great-aunt, a donkey, and — if you want to, I'm sure you've got a home on Fern Hill Farm. Sometimes, you know, we don't know where we belong until we get there. My grandma used to say that, and I think it's true.'

Lily did not answer. The great, big lump was back in her throat, and she knew she was going to cry any minute now.

'Come on,' he said softly, taking her hand. 'Let's get back to the car before it starts to rain. I don't want you to catch a cold.'

***

SOMETIMES WE DON'T *know where we belong until we get there.*

Lily was lying in her bed, listening to the rain beating against the window, and repeated the wise words of Joseph's grandma. *Yes,* she thought, and closed her eyes, *that is definitely true. I never knew I belonged here, but I do now. I just know it. The only thing left for me to do is to find a way to make this work.*

CHAPTER FIFTEEN

'So ... would you mind?'

It was the evening before Lily was to leave for Oxford, and Lily and Abi were sitting in front of the fire sharing a last bottle of wine. The weather had turned cold, and the rain hadn't stopped for three full days, turning the fields into positive swamps. Lily had just told her great-aunt about her ideas for the old barn.

'Mind? Of course I wouldn't mind — I'd be delighted! That's a very lovely idea, Lily, and kind, too. To be honest, I have been pushing the question of what is to become of the farm to the back of my mind for years. It's not wise, I know. One has to make plans, take precautions. To be honest — and as much as I love the idea of a wee bookshop on the farm — but it may perhaps not be the most ...'

'... viable business scheme?'

Abi pursed her lips. 'I don't want to say that but — well, I suppose you can always give it a try. I'm just warning you, there won't be a great many customers in the first place, and in the winter, when it gets really lonely up here ... there may not be any for weeks.'

When she saw the crestfallen look on Lily's face, Abi

put a hand on her knee. 'Now the best thing for you to do,' she said, 'would be to find a job outside the farm, outside Bishops Bridge even. You could try the bookshop in Helmsley? They are quite good, and they might want some help, even if it's only part-time. You are a fully qualified Oxford librarian; I dare say you'd stand a good chance. I know you're a romantic, Lily, but you need to be practical, too — not always, but when it comes to the really big decisions in life, I'm afraid you do. I should know.'

'But — but what about the farm?'

'Don't worry about the farm for now. I'll be fine for another couple of years, especially if you come to help me. Why don't you talk this barn idea over with your dad? He's a builder, and he's got his own business, he will know what's best to do — hm? What do you think?'

Lily tried to keep her sigh in. 'Yes, well, that is if he doesn't think me completely crazy. You know he always tells people exactly what he thinks, even if he does it in an annoyingly nice and gentlemanly way.'

'True. But you can only find out if you ask him. And just for the record, you, my girl, are no crazier than your eccentric great-auntie Abigail, take hope and warning from that!'

'Oh dear,' Lily said into her wine glass, and when she looked up and met Abi's eye, they both burst out laughing.

'Here's to us Yorkshire lasses then, one born and bred, and the other one adopted!' Abi raised her glass. 'I dare say that two of us will be just about enough to keep off any evil neighbours, may they be men or geese!'

Lily nodded solemnly, but her eyes were twinkling when they chinked glasses. 'May they be men or geese!'

Theo — probably thinking they had both gone completely round the bend — got up, yawned, stretched, shook himself, and walked away with that dignified expression on his whiskery face that only a wire-haired dachshund could carry off.

***

THE NEXT MORNING, Lily stopped at the Bridge Café to say goodbye to Jessie and to pick up some cinnamon swirls to put in the freezer. 'If you don't give me the recipe, I'll have to buy the lot and freeze them all,' she said, getting out her purse and putting it on the counter. 'Your choice.'

'I only have four left, so you might as well have them. But I recommend my simnel cake, too, as well as my twist on Yorkshire gingerbread — you can tell me about the hidden ingredient when you find it. And I can't let you go without a piece of quiche for lunch, can I? How long have you got to drive?'

'Depends on the traffic. Anything between three and a half and five hours.'

Jessie gave a low whistle. 'Oh, that far. You won't be coming back for weekends then, will you?'

'It depends. But I will definitely be back in the summer!' Pocketing her goodies, she paid with a twenty-pound note and insisted Jessie keep the change. 'Thank you, Jessie. We'll keep in touch, won't we?'

'Course we will! You're one of us now.' Emerging from behind the counter, Jessie hugged Lily. 'Goodbye then, have a safe trip.'

You are one of us now. Lily dropped the brown paper bag into the woven basket she kept on the passenger seat and got behind the wheel of her Mini. She looked at her face in the rear mirror and sighed. *If only that were true.*

Then she started the engine and drove away, leaving the quiet village of Bishops Bridge, and a piece of her heart behind.

***

THE FIRST THING that caught Lily's eye when she came into her living room were the Morris cushions on the sofa. She stopped in the doorway, clutching her handbag. The cushions he had given her on her last birthday. In September. That was not long ago, was it? Seven months. He had been gone three months. No – three months and six days today. She knew because she still counted the weeks, and the days, whenever she opened her journal. She knew because it still hurt. Because she still missed him, and loved him, so much.

'Beth? I know it's practically Easter and you are probably out at some church thing or other, but … can you call me as soon as you can? Please? I need you …' Ending her voice message, she tossed her phone onto the kitchen counter and threw herself on the sofa, sobbing into the pretty cushions.

***

BETH CALLED HER back an hour later. 'Okay, so there is no way I can see you before Monday, but if you think you can wait that long, we could go for a walk and have coffee? And of course you can tell me what's troubling you right now — is it about Spencer?'

Lily closed her eyes. 'Yes. That and — some other things. I'm already a little better so I think I can wait until Monday. I'm going to stay at my parents' tonight, seeing as my fridge is empty and we are all going to be there for Easter brunch tomorrow, anyway. And a walk sounds lovely. We can walk to Minster Lovell and come back to that cosy pub for a glass of — no, of course not. You don't drink. Well, a cup of coffee then. Decaf.'

Beth laughed. 'Alright, I'll see you on Monday then — but only if you promise you'll call if you feel a meltdown coming, or worse. Preferably *before* it gets worse. Do you hear me?'

'Yes, ma'am. Thank you, ma'am.'

***

'So, YOU CAME in and saw the cushions — how did that make you feel?'

They were sitting on the bench on Crawley's village green, nursing coffee from the thermos flask Beth had brought because it was so cold. Lily pulled her old university sweater around her shoulders and blew at her coffee. 'I don't know … just an overwhelming sense of loss and sadness.'

Beth nodded. 'Of course. And … how did you see yourself in that moment?' She was slipping into counselling mode, but Lily didn't mind. On the contrary, it was just what she needed: sound counselling and warm friendship in one neat package.

'Lost. Completely lost.'

'What did you do?'

Lily frowned. 'Well, I — I called you, didn't I? You know that. And then I threw myself onto the sofa and cried. I held the cushions to my chest, and cried until I felt I could not cry anymore. Then I made myself a cup of tea, and then, thank God, you called back.'

Beth smiled. 'Well done, you. Always call the ambulance first.'

'I know. And being with my family actually took my mind off things. I walked Silky — well, she doesn't walk far now, just a quick sniff around the village, but at least I got out for a bit of fresh air — and I helped mum prepare the Easter feast. Oh, and we went to church, too.'

'Did you?'

'Yes. Emily insisted — must be her hormones or something. But it was a really good service, not boring at all. In fact, the vicar was brilliant — I actually listened all the way through. You would have loved it. Have you ever been to Burford? To the church, I mean?'

'Oh, yes. Quite often, actually. I'm glad you liked it. So, what else has been on your mind? You said there was more than grief. Are you ready to tell me?'

Fiddling with her pendant, Lily tried to find the words to explain how she had come to feel about Rosedale. 'Well. Um … it's like this — I think I'm about to make a really big decision and I'm not sure I can — or even should — do it.' She faltered. 'Because I'm not sure I am brave enough … never mind strong enough … it would take a lot of courage, I suppose. Not to mention money. And …'

'Hold on! One thing after the other, please. I'm a pregnant woman, I can't think so fast these days.' Beth moved a few inches away, holding up her hands. 'So, a big decision — let me guess, you are thinking about leaving Oxford and moving up to Yorkshire to live on the farm with your great-aunt and the donkey?'

Lily stared at her friend. 'How do you know?'

'Because,' Beth said, putting an arm around her shoulder, 'I am your friend and I know you. Besides, it is written all over your face. *I love Yorkshire*, it says. If you cared to look in a mirror, you would see the writing quite clearly.'

Instinctively, Lily put a hand up to her forehead, then dropped it again. 'Oh.'

'Well — not literally, of course. But yes, there is something in your eyes. A spark that wasn't there before.'

'That's probably because I'm dreaming. You know what I'm like, always dreaming away ...' Her gaze dropped to her shoes, her hands gripping her mug of coffee. 'It can't work. I know it can't. It's crazy. Giving up my job, my flat, my life ...'

'But you aren't happy with your life, are you? You haven't been happy for a long time, Lily, not even when Spencer was still alive. You were always dreaming of a life in the country, of having children, and a dog ... He didn't want any of that, did he?'

'No. He didn't even want to marry me. But Beth, I *loved* him! I really did! If I do this now ... won't that be like a betrayal? As if I was ... I don't know — leaving *him* behind?'

Beth shook her head. 'No, Lily. It's not a betrayal. And you are not leaving him behind — he is gone, sweetheart. He won't be back.'

She could see Lily swallowing hard. Then the first tear fell. Then another. And another.

'Oh, sweetie. Come here!' Pulling her friend close, Beth stroked her back in long, slow movements, until the sobs began to cease. Finally she offered her a tissue, saying, 'I know you loved him, Lily. And I'm so sorry for your pain. Which is exactly why I think you *should* leave all this behind and start afresh on the North York Moors. You deserve to be happy. Give yourself a chance!'

Lily blew her nose and turned away, gazing across the green. 'I'm not sure ... It's such a crazy plan ... you would laugh if you knew! And my parents, and Stephen — they will all think I have gone mad. They will talk me out of it, just you wait. I needn't even bother telling them.' She finished her coffee without looking at her friend. 'It's hopeless, Beth — *I* am hopeless.'

Beth frowned. 'No, you're not. So, what is your plan then? Something to do with books?'

Lily spluttered. How come Beth *always* knew what was going on in her mind?

'Well — yes. I was thinking of converting an old barn on Abi's farm into a ... a bookshop. But as I said, it's totally crazy — it would cost a fortune, I have never worked in a shop before, and of course I have no idea where the customers would come from, especially in the winter. So I need to come up with a Plan B. Probably a Plan C and D as well, just to be on the safe side.'

'But it's a *lovely* idea, Lily! You know a lot about books, and if there is a charming old barn ... why not? You might want to find something else first, not only to give you something to do while the barn is being converted, but also to bring some money in. Have you talked to your aunt yet?'

'I have, yes. She would love to have me. To be honest, that is part of the idea ...' She told Beth about old Mr Nettleton next door and how he was going to lose his home. 'He is a horrid old man, but I still think it's sad. I don't want the same thing to happen to Abi, you see. So I thought if I moved up there, I could help her, and — yes. That was the idea.'

'And it's a great idea, too. I'm sure she appreciates that, even if she does not sound like she needs looking after just yet.'

Lily laughed. 'No, she doesn't. She is very fit considering her age, and her mind is razor sharp, as is her tongue! But I have a feeling she is lonelier now than she used to be, when she still had her business, and her brother was alive. Of course she would never admit that much. But the building project will keep her busy, and make her feel useful, even if I have to go and work in the nearest town. Which I just might have to do …'

'Yes, but even if you do, you can go and live in Rosedale. You have found your home, Lily! Isn't that exciting? I'm so pleased for you. I will feel so much better about us leaving now that I know you, too, have a plan.' Beth finished her drink and shook the last drops out of her mug. 'And you can ask your dad, you know, about the barn conversion. I'm sure he would be happy to help even if he can't actually take on the project as such, being too far away. But he might know somebody in the area.'

Lily was not convinced. 'He might. I'm not sure that asking dad at this point is a good idea though. I know just what he will say. *You are a sensible person, Lily. You always play it safe. Why give up all your safety on a whim like this?*'

'Because it isn't a whim,' Beth said with empathy. 'It's an adventure, and it's good for you. And as for the *why* question — well, because you need to get out of here. This place is suffocating you, smothering all your hopes and dreams like — I don't know, like bindweed. You need to be free, Lily. Free to follow your dreams!'

'But … what if it all goes wrong? If I can't do it after all?'

'Lily,' Beth said, sounding just the right side of stern as she took her friend's hands. 'You will never know if you do not try. Just look at your assets — you have family up there, a home … you are sensible, kind, compassionate, and willing to work hard. Plus, you know more than I ever will about books. That is more than most people have when they start an enterprise like this. And once you have sold your flat, you will have money, too. It won't last you forever, but it will probably pay for the barn conversion. House prices have gone through the ceiling over the past two years! You'll make a fortune.'

'Well, I still have a mortgage — which means I only own about a third of that flat,' Lily said, taking the tissue. 'As I'm sure my brother will be kind enough to point out. He will say …'

'Oh, forget about Stephen and what *he* might have to say on the matter! It's *your* life, Lily, not his. You are a grown-up woman, free to make your own choices, even your own mistakes. But this is not a mistake. It's a chance! Take it, Lily, do!'

'But …'

'Ah!' Beth held up her index finger. 'No more buts. Go to Rosedale, shake them all up with your book barn ideas, and whatever else has been hiding inside that pretty head of yours for too long.' She pulled Lily closer, giving her shoulders an encouraging squeeze. 'You'll be fine.'

Lily looked at her, tears shimmering in her eyes. 'Will I?'

'Of course you will. God loves you and He …'

'… has a plan for me, I know. You told me so a hundred times.' But she smiled, anyway, because even if she was not sure about *God* loving her, she knew that Beth did.

'And I'm telling you again because it is true. Come on,' Beth said, getting to her feet. 'Let's go back to my place. Matthew is cooking steak and chips for tea. He's worried about my iron intake. You are staying for tea, aren't you?'

'I'll definitely stay for steak and chips, yes.'

CHAPTER SIXTEEN

Susanna was closing the gate behind her when she heard a car coming up the lane. She turned to see if it was going to stop — people popped in at the strangest of times to ask her to paint a portrait of their pet, obviously thinking that artists never slept — but it didn't, and she walked up the path to her house. It was so dark inside, she had to switch on the light. Shaking her head in dismay, she went into the kitchen, put her shopping bags down and flicked the kettle on.

When she had put the groceries away, she stood at the window waiting for the tea to brew, wishing once again her mum was here. It was on days like these that she missed her the most. She missed her dad, too, but he had been gone fifteen years now, while her mother had died only eight months ago — a sudden heart attack — leaving Susanna heartbroken and all alone.

It was then that David Stanton had begun to creep into her thoughts again, softly like a cat on its paws, and even as she painted, she sometimes thought she saw his face reflected in the windowpane of her studio. What she saw was the face of the 18-year-old boy of course but still, there it was, as clear — and as dear — as it had been then.

They had been together for the best part of their teenage lives, and somehow, she had always assumed they would get married and settle here in her beloved Rosedale. Her parents had liked David a lot and would probably have been more than glad to see him marry their only daughter. Susanna's mum had been one of the first to welcome Mrs Stanton into the neighbourhood, and they had soon become close friends, although Elaine Harper could never understand why quiet, gentle Sarah would marry a heartbreaker like Brian Nettleton. When she died, David had been only eighteen and just finished school. He had left Rosedale shortly after the funeral, leaving Susanna and all her hopes of a life together behind.

She had never seen him again.

Ever since Brian Nettleton had suffered a stroke some weeks ago though, Susanna's thoughts had wandered to David more frequently. She wondered where he was, what he did … and whether he had a wife, and a family. Probably. Because even if deep in her heart she knew she had never stopped loving him, she could not expect him to spend his life alone. She had not always been alone either. As a student, she had moved in with Adam Bates, a fellow art student, during her first term at Leeds University, and if he had not turned out to be what her friend Annabel had called a Cheating Pig, her life might have taken a different turn. As it was, she had found him making love to her best friend on the kitchen table one afternoon when she had come home from a lecture. She had moved out the next day.

A few years later, when her dad died, she had gone home to support her mum, and never left again. She had her art, her cottage, her beloved hills, and her cat, and found that most of the time she was quite happy with her solitary life.

If nothing else, it was peaceful. She taught Art to Years Five and Six at the village school one day a week, and otherwise she was happy enough to stay at Rose Cottage and paint.

With a sigh, Susanna turned back to her tea, only to find that almost twenty minutes had passed, and the tea was not only far too strong but also stone cold.

'Now what, Marmalade?' she said, turning to her ginger cat who was looking up at her, meowing softly but persistently, as if she knew Susanna had forgotten to buy her food. 'Shall I put the kettle on again, or shall I get you some food first? Food?' She sighed and grabbed her purse. 'Thought so. You really are a selfish creature. I hope Miss Lavender stocks some decent cat food because I am not going into Pickering again, not in this weather!'

***

THE WINDSCREEN WIPERS were on full speed, and Susanna was trying her best to see through the rain and the impenetrable mist as she made her way down the potholed lane. A sudden thud followed by a bleating sound made her break hard.

Shaking, she switched off the motor and climbed out of her car. At first she could not see anything, but then she spotted the shape of an animal lying on the grassy verge of the lane.

It was a goat.

'Oh, you poor thing!' she cried, bending down to the animal. 'I'm ever so sorry! I just didn't see you ... yes, I know, it is quite dark, isn't it? And you probably didn't see my car either — I'll just go get my phone and call the vet, okay?'

With a heartbreakingly pitiful bleat, the goat gave up a

feeble attempt at lifting her head and went to lie quite still while Susanna went in search of her phone. This took a while, due to the terrible mess the car was in, and because the phone must have slipped under the passenger seat when she braked. Luckily Joseph Hancock was in her contact list because he was Marmalade's vet, so she ran back to the goat with the phone pressed to her ear, willing him to pick up. As soon as he did, she explained the situation.

'You're lucky,' he said, 'I'm just on my way to Upper Rye Farm, as it happens, so I'll be there in five minutes. Stay right there, and keep her warm. See you!'

Slipping the phone back into her pocket, Susanna bent down to hug the goat. 'Everything's going to be alright, sweetie; doctor is on his way and will be here in no time!'

It wasn't long before she could hear a four-wheel drive approaching, and saw Joseph jumping out of the car just as soon as he had pulled the handbrake.

'Hello there,' he cooed, squatting down beside the goat, 'what are you doing out here, eh? You should be snuggling up to your pals in the stable in such nasty weather. Let me have a look at you …'

He examined the animal carefully and then turned to Susanna, who had been watching anxiously. 'Don't worry, she's going to be alright. It's just the shock and that hind leg looks as if it might be broken. I'll do an x-ray as soon as we get her to the practice. It wasn't your fault,' he added reassuringly when he saw the troubled expression on Susanna's face. 'She should not have been out in the first place, but as she really is quite old and probably almost blind, I'm afraid she must have panicked when she heard the engine of your car. As she didn't know where the sound was coming from, she just bolted.'

Susanna nodded, still cradling the goat. 'Can I come with you? I could hold her while you are driving — would that help, do you think? She does seem a little frightened.'

'Sure, if you like. Can you leave your car here, or do you want to take it back to the cottage? I'll make a quick phone call and explain things to Mr Bell. His cow will have to wait for another hour or two, I'm afraid, while we take this little one to the surgery.'

'I'll take the car back if you don't mind. I don't want to risk anyone crashing into it when I leave it here. See you in five?'

'Sure. Come on now, old girl, let's get you a bit more comfortable.' Joseph carried the goat to his car, and together they placed her gently on the back seat, pulling a rough blanket over her body. Inigo, who was sitting in the footwell of the passenger seat, was given stern orders to stay just where he was.

'If we can't find out where she escaped from, the pair of you will have to get along for a while, anyway. Unless we find someone to take care of you — and I think I know just the person for the job …'

***

SURPRISED TO FIND not only her neighbour but also Joseph Hancock on her doorstep, Abi said, 'What brings you two here on this rainy day? I'm sure I would have remembered calling the vet — oh! Hello,' she said when she saw the goat in Joseph's arms. 'Who's that then? Don't tell me it's one of Mr Nettleton's wicked lot. Is she hurt?'

Joseph laid the goat carefully down by the Aga and covered her with the blanket he had brought from the car.

Turning back to Abi, he smiled apologetically. 'She is, I'm afraid. Hello, Abi. Sorry to barge in like this. We were hoping she might find shelter with you for a while — you may well be right in thinking she escaped from Wood End Farm, in which case there wouldn't be anyone to take care of her, anyway. I did try to call you and give you fair warning, but you were out.'

'I was in the barn. Oh, you poor thing!' Abi knelt down beside the goat, looking her over. 'Of course she belongs to Mr Nettleton! I think it may well be old Myrtle ... are you Myrtle? Hey? Aw, don't worry now, you'll be alright here, and quite safe.' Giving the goat a reassuring pat, Abi got up and stretched her back. 'Right, let me just put the kettle on, and then you can tell me what happened.'

After Susanna had filled her in, apologizing over and over again for her carelessness, Abi put a hand on her arm. 'Don't blame yourself, lass. You could not have reckoned with *a goat* coming up the lane in this weather, could you? And you couldn't have seen her either. Isn't it dreadful? I'm sure we haven't had such a wet and windy April in years!'

She got out a biscuit tin and put it on the table. 'Coconut oat biscuits. Careful, they're quite solid — you might want to dunk them. By the way, I got a phone call from Nettleton's daughter the other day. Seems he is doing really well in rehab and can even move about a bit, pushing a Zimmer frame. So guess what? He's coming back to the farm! She would rather sell the place of course, lock, stock, and barrel, but he wouldn't hear of it.' She sighed as she poured the tea. 'Silly old fool. Although I must say I can't really blame him ... It's his home after all. Although who is to look after him, I don't know. Mary was a bit lofty about that. But then, he's not my responsibility, is he?'

'I never thought I would live to see the day, but I almost pity the old man,' said Joseph, grabbing a couple of biscuits as he got to his feet. 'I'm afraid I must love you and leave you. Mr Bell has been expecting me, I'd better not let him wait any longer. Thanks for the tea, Abi, and for looking after Myrtle. You're a star!'

'Pity Mr Nettleton?' Susanna scoffed when he had gone. 'That'll be the day!' Dunking her oat cake into her tea, she frowned and said, 'But he won't be able to do the chores on the farm for a while, will he, when he can't even walk properly? I dare say you might end up looking after his beasts for a while longer, Abi.'

Abi shrugged. 'That's okay. As long as I don't have to wash his unmentionables.'

They both laughed, but when Susanna left half an hour later, Abi turned to Myrtle and said, 'I'd much rather look after you for the rest of my life than after him for 'just a few weeks', as that wretched woman put it — but we won't tell anyone I let myself be talked into that, will we? He could always suffer another stroke, or decide that the sun does shine brighter in Cornwall after all — which I'm sure it does.'

CHAPTER SEVENTEEN

Lily knew that eating cherry jam wasn't the cleverest idea when you were wearing white jeans and reading a newspaper at the same time, but by the time a blob of the dark red preserve dropped from her bread and onto her thighs it was too late.

'Bother!' She reached for a napkin, casting the newspaper aside. It wasn't as if there was anything remotely interesting in the papers these days; it was only out of habit that she picked up *The Guardian* on Saturday mornings, along with a freshly baked farmhouse loaf from the artisan bakery around the corner. But now she could hear the post coming through the letter box and went to collect it. She was waiting for an e-mail from the builder Abi had recommended. She had not met Pete Burns yet, but they had spoken on the phone last week, and he had promised to do a rough calculation for her and send it before she was going to drive up to meet him next Friday, just so she knew what she was getting herself into, should she decide to go ahead with the project.

'While I agree it would be a shame to let the barn fall to ruins, I do not think that turning it into a bookshop will get you any of the money back that you must be willing to part with in the first place — and I'm talking *a lot* of money. Barn conversions don't come cheap, even if the building is not listed. You might want to think about a more ... say, *viable* alternative. A holiday cottage for example, providing the barn is big enough,' he had explained. 'But we can discuss that when you come up next weekend. I might bring a friend who could do the woodwork for you, see what he thinks.'

Well, that it's a rubbish idea, of course, Lily thought as she finished her coffee, *what else? I'm just a dreamer after all, or so everyone tells me. Everyone except Beth, that is. And Abi.* But where the money for the project was going to come from, neither of them had been able to say. She would have to think about that though, and preferably before she quit her job. But she had been back in Oxford for a month now and found it increasingly unbearable, especially with Beth talking of nothing but babies and the forthcoming move to Devon. Lily knew she probably did that on purpose to help her make up her mind, but she couldn't. She needed more time.

Or do I, she thought, glancing at the calendar on the wall. Next week she and Spencer would have been together for three years. Three years ... and he still would not have asked her to move in with him, or even proposed. She would just have been wasting her life waiting for something that was never going to happen.

Well, I'm not waiting now, she thought, tossing the paper aside. *On Monday I will tell Hugh I am leaving. No more hesitating. I have made my choice, I've got to do this now, or I'll never do it at all.* And as soon as she had talked to Hugh, she would pop into the next best estate agent's and ask them to come and value her flat. Set things in motion. *Before* she told her family.

***

It was with a churning stomach that she sat down opposite Hugh's desk on Monday morning. He was busy shifting some papers but looked up and smiled encouragingly every now and then, which somehow made Lily even more nervous. He did not know she was about to drop a bomb, and she was beginning to feel she did not want to drop it after all. Was there time to leave yet?

But just then Hugh cleared his throat. 'Sorry to keep you waiting. Now then, what can I do for you, Lily?'

She was fidgeting with the heart pendant, nearly ripping it off its delicate chain as it got stuck in the lace trim of her cotton top. It was uncharacteristically hot for early May, and the air conditioning in the old building was not working properly, if at all. Lily felt beads of sweat forming on her forehead and gratefully accepted the glass of water Hugh was offering.

'I … um … I would like to — I think I would like to … resign?' There, she had said it. Her heart was hammering inside her chest, her throat was dry, and her hands were clammy against the glass, but she had said it. *Step one, taken.*

Hugh's eyebrows shot up. 'Resign? Oh. That's a bit of a surprise. I know you haven't been happy for a while, but I always assumed that was for private reasons — you mourning your boyfriend, mainly — and nothing to do with your job. May I ask what's brought this on?'

Lily took a deep breath and then spoke quickly before her courage failed her. 'Of course. And it has nothing to do with the job, really — I still love it. I would like to stay but — I want to move to Yorkshire, you see. I'm thinking of opening a bookshop on my great-aunt's farm. We are going to convert an old barn and …' She faltered, suddenly feeling stupid for thinking she could do this. How did she expect Hugh to understand when he hardly knew her at all? How could she explain?

'Oh,' Hugh said, refilling their glasses, 'I see. That's a lovely idea, Lily. Very romantic — but isn't it very remote up there in the Dales? Or was it the Moors?'

'It's the North York Moors. And it is remote, yes, but it's a very popular place, there are lots of tourists — holiday makers, walkers, … even in the winter. I think. It's a beautiful place, and full of history. There are ghost stories and abandoned villages and haunted kilns … I'm sure I can make something out of that.' *Perhaps I will even write my book. But I don't have to tell him that, do I?*

'Well', said Hugh, taking off his glasses and cleaning them with the back of his tie, making Lily cringe. 'I'm sure that is all very nice, Lily, and I quite understand your need to get away, especially after what you have been through. Can I suggest something a little less *finite*?'

'Um — yes?' She was not sure she wanted to hear his suggestion, sensing that he might want to talk her out of it yet. Because no matter how fast her heart was beating, she was determined to stick to her decision. She was leaving by the end of this term. She was not going to come back. She was not going to stay.

'Why don't you take a sabbatical? You can take six months, or a whole year, and see how it goes. If it works out the way you hope it will, you can resign, and if it doesn't, you would still have your job when you come back. *If* you come back. *If* it doesn't work out. Which I hope it will, seeing as you have set your heart on this idea.'

'I have, yes. And that's why I've got to go — and I'm not coming back. Not next year, not ever. Oxford … is not my home anymore. Thank you for your kind offer,

Hugh, I appreciate that it's very generous of you, but I'm afraid I have to decline. A sabbatical would not make me feel free — and I need to be free.' Relieved to have got this over with, Lily sank back in her chair, took her water glass with shaking hands, and drained it. She did not dare look at Hugh — if she had, she would have seen him smiling.

'Well,' he said with a sigh, 'there is nothing more to say then, is there? Except good luck, of course, and all the best. We will miss you, Lily.'

She looked up and met his eyes, which were twinkling in a friendly, almost grandfatherly way. But there was a sadness in them, too, that touched her heart. 'I'll miss you, too', she smiled. 'This place, this city … But I hope you understand that I have to go. You can't start anything new if you stay where you are. You've got to move on. In my case, to Yorkshire. I'll take some good memories of Oxford. The sad ones … well.'

He nodded. 'It's good to take the happy memories along as you go. Leave the unhappy ones behind if you can. And Lily?'

'Yes?'

'I'm proud of you. It's a very brave thing to do.'

'Or a very foolish one,' she muttered, suddenly doubtful again. Had she really just quit her job? Her parents would think her mad! It *was* mad. Reckless. Irresponsible. Whatever was she thinking?

'No,' Hugh said with a shake of his head, 'not foolish — just brave. And now if you'll excuse me, I have a job to advertise.'

***

When she got home, she found her dad waiting for her outside the apartment block. He was holding a dripping umbrella — there had been an enormous thunderstorm in the afternoon, just as Lily had got back from her lunch break, and it had not stopped raining since then — and looked like he had been standing there for a while. 'Evening, Lily. How's things?'

'Um ... good, thank you. What are you doing here, dad? Why didn't you call?'

'I did but you did not answer. I have some news I'd rather you heard in person — it's about Silky ...'

Lily's hands flew to her mouth. Silky! She knew she was old and had not been well lately, and she remembered her mum had said something at Easter ... about having to take her to the clinic for some tests ... But surely that did not mean ...

'Is she — oh, dad, please tell me she isn't ...'

Her dad nodded slowly. 'I'm afraid she is, love. Come here.' He held out his arms, and she fell against his broad chest and cried.

***

Later, over a cup of tea, he told her that the results of the tests had shown what their vet had already suspected: that the cancer had spread from the kidneys to the liver and would ultimately have led to heart failure, so they had decided to have her put to sleep immediately. Lily's mum had cried all the way home, insisting she could not possibly be the one to tell Lily. So her dad had dropped her off at home and driven straight to Oxford.

'Of course there was no space to park the car, so I had

to walk the best part of a mile and got soaked ... not that it matters, of course. And perhaps it was only half a mile. Oh, Lily, I'm so sorry. That is a lot for you to take in. First Spencer, and now your dog ... Mind you, she had a good life, eh? And what fun times we had with her. Do you remember the time she ate the brandy-filled chocolates Auntie Abigail had brought? My, but she was drunk! Silky, not Abi of course. But the poor dog couldn't walk straight the next day, and drank from every puddle along the way.'

They both laughed and cried at the same time. Looking up at her father through her tears, Lily asked anxiously, 'Where is she now?'

'We left her at the clinic, love. She'll be cremated and then we can ...' Her dad swallowed. 'Then we can bury her ashes. Or scatter them somewhere she liked to run, like perhaps on the Broads — oh, I don't know. She was your dog, love. You decide.'

'I can't!' she wailed. 'And anyway, Silky was a family dog. We should all get together and decide what to do. Does Stephen know?'

'They're still in Cornwall. They are not due back before Sunday, and I don't have the heart to call them. Knowing your brother, he would drive straight back home, and that isn't fair on Emily. It's their last holiday together as a couple — before they have a baby, I mean.'

She nodded. 'Of course. I had forgotten about that.' It made sense now that Stephen had not answered her messages. He must have turned off his mobile while on holiday — *good for him*, she thought. *At least he knows how to spend quality time with his wife.* She had never seen Spencer without his iPhone in his hand ...

She shook herself. *Don't. Don't go down that road again.*

They sat in silence for a while, drinking their tea, until her father got up and put a hand on her shoulder. 'I hate to leave you like this, love, but your mum's waiting for me … I don't suppose you want to come? Spend the night perhaps?'

Secretly, Lily had been toying with the same idea, thinking that perhaps this might be a chance to let her parents in on her secret, but then she thought better of it and shook her head, no. This was a not the right time, not when their beloved family dog had just died. She could always postpone her meeting with Pete the builder and stay here …

No, she thought, as she took the tea things into the kitchen. *I'll go. I have been miserable here ever since I came back, I need something to look forward to. And even if the book barn is not meant to be, I can still think of something else. Anything is better than being stuck here for the rest of my life.*

CHAPTER EIGHTEEN

It was Pete who called to say he couldn't make it the next Saturday, and could they postpone, so Lily went to see her parents after all. Somehow, she found herself helping her mum in the garden, and while she did not normally enjoy gardening, handling the soft, fresh soil was surprisingly soothing. They planted pink and white baby's breath to compliment her mother's roses, and Lily was pleased with herself when she finally got up and stretched her aching back. Her hands were dirty, but she didn't mind — she wouldn't worry about things like manicure when she lived on the farm, would she?

'You know, mum,' Lily said, washing her hands under the tap, 'I've been thinking — I really would like to go and live in Yorkshire. I could stay with Abi on the farm. What do you think?' She closed her eyes. *Wrong question again. It doesn't matter what she thinks, does it? It's* your *life.*

'Oh?' Her mum looked up from the flower bed she was kneeling in. 'What's brought that about then?'

'Well — for one thing I found that those four weeks on the farm really did me some good. Working outside, handling the ponies, mucking out stables, walking the donkey …' She noticed her mum's eyebrows shooting up and hurried on, 'all of that has done wonders to restore my health, both mentally and physically. Not to mention emotionally. Also, I believe I need a fresh start after … after everything. I cannot bear to think of having to spend another winter in the city, missing Spencer. And Beth. She and Matthew are going to Devon in September, and they are going to have a baby, too — twins, actually.'

'Oh. That's nice. And twins!'

'Yes, mum, it is nice for them. But it also leaves me … pretty lonely here. So what it comes down to, um … I asked Abi if I could move in with her, and she says she is happy to have me.'

Her mum dropped her secateurs and stared at her daughter. 'Abi *knows*? And — and we don't?'

Lily could see the disappointment in her mum's face — she had always confided in her parents first, and now her mum was hurt. But while she was grateful that her parents, and her brother, had always looked out for her, she knew she would have to stay firm now if she ever wanted to be independent, and free. After all, it was for Abi to decide whether she wanted her to come and live on the farm or not, or what was to happen to the barn. It was her home, and her life — and Lily's.

'I'm sorry, mum. I know you just want to look out for me. But surely you can see I had to ask Abi first? If she had said no, I needn't have bothered to tell you at all, simply because there wouldn't have been anything to tell.' Taking the secateurs from her mum, she put them down and put her hands on her mum's shoulders. 'Aren't you pleased for me, mum? I'm moving on! Isn't that what you have been waiting for? Ever since … ever since Spencer died?'

'Yes, of course but ...' Her mum looked confused. 'But Lily, are you sure? Do you really want to leave Oxford — your good job, your nice flat, your friends ...'

'I don't *have* any friends, Mum. There is only Beth, and, as I said, she is leaving for Devon by the end of the summer. There will be no one left, mum — no one, not even Silky!'

Tears were spilling down her face now, and her mum sighed. 'I'm sorry. I'm sorry, Lily ... I thought you were ... oh, never mind. Come on, sit down, I'm going to make us a nice cup of tea. And tonight, we can talk it over with your dad. He will know what's best to do.'

I'm sure he does, thought Lily, sniffing. *He will talk me out of it, that's what. Especially when he hears about the barn idea.*

***

To her surprise, he didn't, or not at once, anyway. He just sat there and listened, and when she had finished, he put his glass down and said, 'Well, well. I must say you seem to have it all worked out between you. And Abi has even found a builder for the project! That was quick then. Well, she is not one to put things off once she has made up her stubborn old mind, is she?'

'Bob!' Maureen shot her husband a reproachful look. 'You are talking about my favourite auntie and surrogate mother!'

'Sorry. It just seems ... rather sudden. Who did you say he was? The builder?'

'Pete Burns. He's from Rosedale Abbey, so he knows the area, and the people ... we thought it would be best to keep things in the hands of local businesses. The barn conversion, I mean.'

He nodded. 'That makes sense. But — Lily, what about your job, and your flat? You can't travel between here and ...'

'I can't, no.' Lily took another deep breath — she seemed to be taking a lot of those today — and went on to explain, 'And I won't either because I have already quit my job, and I'm going to put the flat on the market, too. If I don't earn, I can't pay the mortgage, simple as that. But don't worry, I'm going to find myself a job in Rosedale. Abi says ...'

'You have done what?'

Her dad had knocked his wine glass over and her mum jumped up, her face pale with shock, to get a cloth.

'I quit my job. And I am going to sell my flat. It was a ridiculously expensive flat in the first place, I don't know why I ever thought I needed that kind of luxury. All I want is a home,' she went on, her voice softer now, 'and I have found it in Rosedale. I just know that that is where I want to be. You should understand, Mum — you grew up on the farm!'

Lily's grandmother — Maureen's mum and Abigail's oldest sister — had died of leukaemia at the age of thirty-five, leaving her ten-year-old daughter and her husband shellshocked. Amos Woodcourt, a quiet, kind, and generous man who had first met his wife when she had come to buy pasties in his parents' little grocery shop in Thirsk, found the prospect of running the shop and bringing up his daughter on his own overwhelming and was only too happy to let Abi and Thomas take charge. So Maureen was duly sent to school in Kirkbymoorside and spent most of her teenage years on Fern Hill Farm, doing her homework in the farmhouse kitchen, and helping Abi in the stables.

Lily's mum had always said that despite it all, she had had a wonderful childhood, with the kindest and most caring of fathers, and an extra set of parents in Abi and Thomas — not to mention the ponies who had helped her a great deal to overcome her grief.

Just like William has helped me overcome mine, thought Lily, still waiting for her parents to say something. *Not that losing a boyfriend compared to losing your mother of course, but ...*

'Also,' she said, trying to fill the uncomfortable silence, 'I want to make sure Abi can stay on the farm as she gets older — it would break her heart if she had to give it up, don't you see that? Mum?'

Her mother sighed. 'Of course I can understand *that*. It's very sweet of you, Lily, to want to help her, even look after her as she gets older — in fact, it's a relief of sorts but ... but, Lily, Rosedale is such a remote place! Won't you be very lonely up there?'

I am lonely here, mum. You have no idea just how much!

'I won't. There are actually quite a few people my age in and around Bishops Bridge. There is Lucy who lives on Upper Rye Farm, then there is Jessie who runs the village café, and Joseph, he's the local vet ...' She felt her face flush and hurried to add, 'and there is Susanna Harper, she is an artist and lives next door at Rose Cottage. So no, I don't think I will be lonely — or any lonelier than I am here, anyway.'

Her dad sighed. 'Don't get me wrong, I don't think it's a bad idea, all things considered. But Lily, why can't you take this *more slowly*? You are such a sensible girl. You have never done anything so ... *rash* in your life. What will you do if your plan does not work out? You will have no job and no home to come back to once you have sold the flat. And whatever will you do once you are there? For a living, I mean? You've got to think about that, sweetheart.'

'Oh, I'll find *something*. I can always become a shepherdess. There are plenty of sheep in Rosedale.' Lily did not know what had got into her but somehow her dad's words provoked her.

'Lily!' Her mother looked shocked, and hurt. 'How can you talk to dad like this? You know he means well. A bookshop is a lovely idea, but your dad is right, you can't make a living from it — not in Rosedale!'

Digging her nails into the palms of her hands, Lily clenched her teeth. This was not going well. She should have known of course but still, she had not reckoned with quite so much opposition. Not that she needed her parents' *permission* to go to Rosedale, but she had hoped for a little more understanding — or perhaps even some support.

'Dad,' she said in a desperate attempt to make him see how much this meant to her. 'I know I have never done anything like this in my life. I know I am always sensible. But I have never had an adventure, either, I have never really stretched my wings! I want to *fly*, dad. I want to be free!' She knew she was back to pleading but she did not care. She was tired, she just wanted to get this over and go to bed.

Her dad put a hand on hers. 'Of course, love. I understand — really, I do. I suppose we just can't stand here and watch you throwing your life away …'

'What *life*?'

Now both of her parents were staring at her.

'What do you mean, *what life*?' Picking up his wine glass, her dad found it was empty and got up to fetch the bottle from the fridge.

'Exactly that — what life? If you mean getting up every morning to go to work and coming home to my empty flat and spend the evenings reading on the sofa …'

Her dad turned in the doorway. 'Oh, Lily, it can't be that bad, surely? You must have some friends you can meet at the weekends and …'

'No, dad. I *have* no friends. Spencer is dead, and Beth is moving away in the summer. There is no one. No one to miss me and no one for me to miss either. Except you, of course. But you must see that that is not the same. You don't live in Oxford and …' She shook her head wearily. 'Anyway, it's not the same.'

There were tears in her mother's eyes, and when her father returned from the kitchen to top up their glasses, he put a hand on Lily's shoulder and said, very gently, 'Of course it isn't, love. I'm sorry to hear that you have been feeling so lonely in Oxford. I never knew … we always assumed … well.' He shrugged helplessly. 'Seems we were wrong.'

'Yes,' Lily whispered, her eyes fixed on the tablecloth, 'you were.' Her hands were trembling, and she nearly spilled her wine as she reached for her glass.

Suddenly she felt her dad's hand covering hers. He cleared his throat and said, 'So, let's start again, shall we? What about a project manager, have you got one? For the barn project, I mean?' His voice was soothing, reassuring, and calm.

'A project manager?' Lily looked up. 'Um … no but — won't that be terribly expensive? And what do they do, anyway?'

'Basically — everything. Planning, getting the necessary paperwork done, sorting out any problems that might arise during the project — and there will be problems, there always are — that sort of thing. Most of them charge a lot of money, but if they are good, it's worth thinking about. I'm sure your builder can recommend someone.'

Lily nodded. Suddenly feeling overwhelmed, she turned to her dad and said, 'Will you come up to Yorkshire with me and have a look at the barn? I would like to know what you think. We could make a weekend of it — you could come, too, Mum. You haven't been since … you know. I'm sure Abi would love to see you both.'

Bob's face broke into a smile then, making the corners of his eyes crinkle. 'That's a lovely idea, Lily. I'm sure we can fit that in, Maureen, can't we? How about next weekend? And if your builder has time, you could ask him to come, too. I promise I'll keep my big mouth shut as well.'

***

As soon as she got back on Sunday, Lily phoned Abi, to tell her they would all come up next weekend, and then Joseph, to tell him she was coming. He was out though — probably on duty — so she texted him and spent the rest of the afternoon sorting out her things in the spare room.

By eight o'clock, she had three boxes full of stuff ready to go to the charity shop, and was so tired and hungry she decided to order a pizza and watch TV. Joseph still had not answered her message, and she was just beginning to feel anxious — perhaps she was wrong about him having feelings for her? — when her phone beeped.

Great news about you coming! So sorry to hear about your dog. Feel tightly hugged. Good night. J. xx

This night, she fell asleep with a smile on her face.

***

THERE WAS NO smile on her face when Lily had her brother on the phone on Thursday. He was not his usual calm and composed self but uncharacteristically short-tempered — in fact, he was shouting so loudly that she thought it best to hold the phone well away from her ear. She would have hung up on him but made herself shut her eyes and count to twenty after his last verbal assault had gone down the line and straight through her heart. Finding it difficult to keep her breathing under control as she felt a panic attack coming on, she blinked hard to hold back the tears.

When she had first told him about her plans, he had not said anything for a full minute and then barked, 'Are you mad? Whatever possessed you to quit your job — and on a whim, too! Have you completely lost your mind now? And anyway, Dad promised to fix our conservatory next weekend, he can't go to Yorkshire to look at your stupid old barn!'

'For one thing, it is not my barn, but Abi's, and it's not stupid either because we are planning to turn the farm into a viable business again, which should make sense even to you. And no, I haven't lost my mind and I am really hurt that you should think so. You are my brother, you of all people should know how much it means to me to have a new start!'

He sighed. 'I'm sorry. But you know what I mean. This grief business is wearing you out. It seems to bring back the anxiety, too. I'm really worried about you, sis — you haven't been yourself since Spencer died, and that's five months ago!'

Four months, two weeks, and five days.

Lily did not say anything.

'You know I love Auntie Abigail but even you must admit she's as mad as a hatter!'

'Well, that makes two of us then.'

'Sorry?'

'You said I was mad to quit my job, and now you said Abi was mad. In my book, that makes two madwomen. We should get on very well together, don't you think?'

'Stop it, Lily, it's not funny! Abi may well be family, but she is not your *responsibility*. It was Mum who was brought up by Thomas and Abigail, not you. For goodness' sake, Lily, you have been struggling to look after yourself for months! How do you think you are going to cope with that loneliness up there — with only Auntie Abigail and her ponies for company? You'll get depressed!'

The blood was rushing inside her ears like a torrent now, and she had to sit down. Her knees were shaking, and her throat felt like sandpaper.

Don't cry. If you do, he will only think he is right in believing you are not fit to look after yourself.

She gulped. Once, twice. Then she took a deep breath, and another one — a technique she had learned in therapy, and which normally helped. She closed her eyes and counted to twenty, then shook her head in frustration. It didn't work. The blood was still rushing, her throat was still dry, and her heart was still beating much too fast. Her hands were clammy as they tried to press her knees down to stop them from shaking.

Finally she found her voice — or some voice, for it did not sound like hers at all. It sounded strong, confident, and quite angry. It was like she was sitting next to another person, another Lily. A Lily that asked her brother, 'Not been able to look after myself for months? You'll get depressed? Care to explain that? Take it back, even? Because I'll have you know that, apart from being discouraging, this was really a very rude thing to say — and about your own sister, too! Who you always claim you love so much.' She knew this was his sore point — it would hurt him more than anything if she doubted his love for her. *Well, it hurts me too*, she thought and bit her lip, waiting for him to defend himself. Good thing he did not see her shaking knees.

'You know I love you, Lily. And I'm not saying this because I want to hurt you — in fact, I'm saying this because I want to *protect you* from getting hurt again. Because if that barn idea comes to nothing — and I hate to say it, but it *is* a stupid idea! I can't believe Dad even agreed to look at that wretched barn, he should never have encouraged you ... Anyway, if it doesn't work out, you will feel lonelier and more lost than ever up there. Lily, don't you see, I just want to ...'

'Yes, well, I have heard quite enough about what *you* think and what *you* want. This isn't really about me, is it, Stephen? It's not about my hopes and dreams, it's not even about my pain and how I can best cope with it. It's about you being in control. Because if I move up north, you will not be able to check up on me any longer, and you can't bear that, can you? You may think I am not fit to look after myself, but you are wrong! All I need is a new start, a new chance in life, and I'm going to take this chance. I don't need your approval. I have made up my mind, and I will go. Oh, and one more thing — if you think I was not lonely and lost *even before Spencer died*, then you really don't know me at all!'

She banged the phone down hard and hurled it into the far corner of her living room. The moment it hit the sideboard, the other Lily (the bold and brave one who told people exactly what she thought) got up and left, and she was her old, anxious self again. Shaking, sweating, and now sobbing desperately.

CHAPTER NINETEEN

Having left Oxford at lunchtime the next day, Lily made straight for the motorway, knowing it would take her at least four hours to get to Rosedale. Traffic on the M40 north was an absolute nightmare, and by the time she finally hit the M1 at Northampton, it was already gone three o'clock. She would be lucky if she got to the farm in time for dinner.

The row with her brother had left her shaken and unable to make any sort of decision until late in the evening when she had sent an email to Pete Burns asking him if he could come to the farm on Saturday morning. His reply had been immediate, and positive. Childishly satisfied, Lily had called her father to let him know she was going alone, but would be happy to go again just as soon as he could spare the time.

'I would still like your opinion, Dad, but I appreciate you promised Stephen to fix their conservatory first. I'm just really eager to set things in motion, so if you don't mind too much, I'll go alone.'

'Well, it's your project, so you can go anytime you like. You don't need my approval. Just send me some pictures, or better still, give me a video tour via WhatsApp. Will you do that?'

She had promised, and felt much better afterwards. She knew her dad would have loved to come but of course he could not let Stephen down, and she did not want him to either. Not when it was *her project*, as he had pointed out. He had no idea how much that meant to her, but she loved him for saying it.

My project.

I will show them what I am made of, she thought and gripped the steering wheel. *I will show them all.*

***

'OF COURSE IT is *possible* — everything is possible if you have the money for it. The question is, Miss, how will you get your money back? Because frankly I don't see how that could work. A bookshop in the middle of nowhere — where do you expect the customers to come from? Or do you want to teach the sheep some reading? That might be interesting — a book club for sheep!'

Pete laughed but stopped as soon as he saw the crestfallen look on Lily's face. He seemed like a kind man — *a bit like dad, actually*, Lily thought. But of course he knew his business, too, and he knew what worked — and what did not.

'So, what you're saying is — I should abandon the whole idea?' It was one thing to hear her dad express his doubts, or even her brother, but to hear it from the local builder was a different matter. Lily held her breath as she waited for his verdict.

Pete scratched his head and looked around the farmyard. 'No, I'm not saying that, lass. This is a great place, and we could certainly convert this barn here into something worthwhile — what about holiday cottages? They would earn you some money. There is a shortage of holiday accommodation in this lovely area, and I should know. We have a cottage in Rosedale Abbey and another one near Bank Top that we rent out. They are fully booked year-round. Well, almost. January and February are not terribly busy, and neither is November. But the rest of the year — now don't look so down in the mouth, lass. I'm sure we can do something with this barn, even if it's not a bookshop. Why don't you let me introduce you to an architect, and then you can have a look at some plans before you decide what to do. Does that sound good?'

No, a stubborn voice inside Lily's head piped up, *it doesn't! This is my dream! My book barn dream. If I can't make this come true here, I won't make it come true anywhere. I can't give it up yet. I haven't even started!*

But she nodded, biting her lip. 'Okay. If you give them my details, he — or she — can get in touch. I'll talk it over with my great-aunt. It's her farm, and her barn.'

She knew of course what Abi would say — that it was her project, and her decision. But if it hadn't been for Abi, who knew Pete's wife, they wouldn't even have a builder now — and consequently no project whatsoever — so the least she could do was ask her opinion.

'You do that, lass. Your aunt is one formidable old lady, and certainly not afraid of people, I'm sure she'll agree that this is the sensible thing to do. And in the meantime, you could always work in our little bookshop in Thirsk, or in Helmsley — they have a nice one, right opposite *Hunters* Delicatessen. Have you tried those pies?'

Are we talking about pies now, thought Lily. She could have cried. *The sensible thing to do.* Now where had she heard that before?

***

'Well,' Abi said and put a plate of freshly baked cheese scones on the table, already split and thickly buttered, just like Lily loved them. 'Firstly, he is not the one to decide what you — or I, for that matter — want to do with that barn. Pete Burns doesn't get paid for giving his opinion. Secondly, I think holiday cottages *are* a good idea — you have an eye for interior, Lily, and all those little details that make a room cosy and cheerful. I can see how you turned that dingy old bedroom into something really lovely back in April. And you were only visiting then! If I give you a pot of paint or two, I dare say you'll make it look like three-star accommodation! Also, you are a stickler when it comes to cleanliness, so we'll always get the highest marks for that, too. And I know I said you should ask in the bookshops nearby but honestly, I don't think you have to travel that far. In fact, I believe you can even make that dream of yours come true after all …'

Lily stared at her, butter dripping from her scone. 'Can I?'

'Well, yes — you might have to compromise a little but —'

Just then there was a loud knock on the door and a man's booming voice called — or rather shouted — Abi's name.

'Abigail Lewis! Oh, where is that infuriating old bat now?'

Lily was not in the least bit surprised when an old man wearing a stained checked flannel shirt and baggy brown corduroy trousers that were held together by a piece of rope in place of a belt, marched into the kitchen, his unshaven face like thunder.

'Abigail Lewis, what have you done with my goat?!'

Lily could not resist the temptation to get up and hold out her hand, even if she hoped he would not take it. His hands looked decidedly unwashed, and he stank. 'And you must be Mr Nettleton — how very lovely to make your acquaintance at last. My name is Lily Henderson. I am Miss Lewis's great-niece.'

***

'Right,' said Ben, putting down his empty pint glass. 'So nasty Nettleton turned up in your auntie's kitchen and seriously demanded *his goat back*? How did he get there in the first place? I thought he was still in hospital, or rehab, or something.'

They were all sitting in the *Red Grouse*, where Jessie had arranged an impromptu meeting (and presumably pulled some strings as the pub was usually fully booked on a Saturday night), and Lily was just telling them about Nettleton's memorable appearance in Abi's kitchen.

'Well, yes, he had been to rehab in some place on the coast, but his daughter had just picked him up from there and taken him home. When he found he was short of a goat — honestly! And an old one at that! — he made his daughter drive him over to Fern Hill Farm where he promptly burst into Abi's kitchen. He just walked in, muddy boots and all, swearing at poor Abi and demanding he was given his goat back. I saw his Zimmer Frame standing in the yard, so walking in without any aid must have meant a lot to him. Not that it helped, mind you.'

Greg shook his head. 'So what did you do?'

'Nothing much. I said 'oh, you must be Mr Nettleton, how very lovely to meet you at last', and then I held out my hand and introduced myself.'

Everybody laughed, and Ben shook himself. 'How very lovely to meet you at last,' he mimicked, slapping his knees.

'Oh, God, I wish I had seen that! What did he do then? He didn't stay for dinner, did he?'

'No, but I offered him a cup of tea.'

The girls were in hysterics, nearly doubling over in laughter, and Greg shook his head in amusement. But Ben stared at Lily, clearly impressed. 'You did, eh? Don't tell me, he demanded a double scotch!'

'He didn't, no. But he didn't want tea either, thank God. And then his daughter came barging in, stopped dead for a moment, gave me one look — and ignored me. Ignored both of us, in fact. She grabbed her father by his shirtsleeves and dragged him out, hissing, 'Don't bother with these people, dad, they don't know how poorly you are, or they might have come over to welcome you. No manners, some of them.' Or something of that sort. Abi and I just looked at each other and shook our heads. We were just about to burst out laughing, thinking they had gone, when Nettleton turned in the doorway and barked, 'I want that goat back by tomorrow or fifty quid, Abigail Lewis! Your choice. But I won't wait!' And do you know what Abi did?'

'Well, she didn't give him the goat,' Greg remarked drily. 'Or she wouldn't be Abigail Lewis.'

Lily shook her head. 'No. She got up, walked over to the kitchen drawer, got out her purse, and counted three twenty-pound notes into his hand. 'You can keep the rest for damages to your pride,' she said and turned his back on him. He roared like a wounded lion when his daughter more or less pushed him through the door. We both had a hard time keeping our faces straight until they were gone. Though why we even bothered, I don't know. They might as well know how ridiculous they are. All that fuss about an old goat, honestly!'

She joined in with the others as they laughed, and when she felt Joseph slipping his arm around her waist, Lily thought that she could almost see her life back in Oxford fading away, like the colours of an old photograph that had been exposed to the light for too long. Like the colours of that photograph, her memories, and her sense of belonging — if she had ever had one to begin with — were slowly beginning to dissolve and fade into nothingness.

***

'So, what's the plan?'

Lily looked up from her sticky toffee pudding to meet Lucy's scrutinising gaze. 'Sorry?'

'I'm sure you did not come here for a weekend just because you could not wait to meet the infamous Mr Nettleton, so there must be some ulterior motive. I hope Abi is not unwell? But you would have said, wouldn't you, if anything was wrong? My parents are good neighbours, they would help.'

Joseph was in serious conversation with Greg just now, talking about his dog — poor Hazel was not in the best of health, but she was almost sixteen, so Greg might have to be prepared to say goodbye to his beloved Labrador, and let her go. Lily shook her head, tears in her eyes as she thought of Silky. It's just a dog, some people would say. But that was just it, wasn't it? To most of us, they weren't 'just dogs'.

'I know,' she said, and gave Lucy a smile. 'And it's not about Abi. At least, it's not only about her, it's —' She hesitated. She hadn't even told Joseph about the barn, she couldn't tell Lucy now, could she? But what else could she say?

'I'm thinking about moving up here so I would be able to help Abi with the farm and … look after her when she gets to the stage that she needs looking after. Not that she does now, or would even let anyone hint that she might one day! You know what she's like. Stubborn independence and all that. But,' she added quickly before Lucy could switch into overexcitement, 'I'll have to come up with a plan. For a start, I'll need a job, won't I? I can't spend my days feeding ponies, or walking William.'

'Oh, Lily, that's fantastic! You could work in my shop — I need help! But that might not be the kind of thing you would like to do, would it? No books, no good. Oh, you'll think of something. A bookshop perhaps? There is one in Helmlsey, right opposite …'

'Yes,' Lily cut in, 'opposite the delicatessen, I know. But please, Lucy, it's early days. We are just … brainstorming some ideas at the moment.'

Well, it was a little more than that, but Lucy did not have to know — at least, she did not have to know before Joseph did. *I will tell him later, when he takes me home*, she thought, and scraped the last bits of pudding from her dish.

'Who's having ideas? — Oi! You said you were going to share that with me! There's nothing left!'

Joseph looked from the empty plate to Lily and back until she laughed. 'Sorry, it was too good to resist. Shall I order another one?'

'It's okay. I'm pretty full after that pie. But you can buy me an ice-cream next time we go to Helmsley. They have very good ice-cream there.'

'That is not a problem. I love ice-cream.'

His face lit up. 'Me too! So, Helmsley tomorrow?'

'Maybe. But first, I want to show you something. Will

you take me home later?'

***

'So we had a builder come to look at it today. To see what we can do with it. Sadly, it does not look like my original plan is going to work.' Lily shrugged. 'But then I suppose one has to be realistic.'

They were standing in the moonlit farmyard, and Lily had just told Joseph about her barn project. It felt good to talk so confidently about her plans, even if she did not *feel* very confident about them. But that was the thing about Joseph: He always took her seriously, no matter how romantic her ideas were, or how high her head in the clouds. Unlike Spencer, he would never laugh at her dreams.

'Well, yes, but I don't think you have to give up on your dream yet, Lily. It would be a shame, especially if it's something that you have always wanted. And getting Pete on board is a very good idea. Apart from the fact that he is brilliant at his job, he will always be impeccably honest with you. He would never do anything just for money — unless the client has more money than brain of course, but even then …' He looked over to the barn and nodded. 'No, it's good, really. Well done, Lily. I'm glad you have decided to come and make a home here — when will you come then? Soon, I hope?'

She felt warm inside from all the praise and encouragement. It almost made her believe she could do it now. 'Um … I don't know — in the summer? August perhaps? I have to sell my flat first, or I'll have no money at all to start with, whatever we decide to do about the barn.'

'That sounds very sensible.' And pulling her close, he

whispered, 'Tell me, Lily Henderson, are you always this sensible? Or would you perhaps consider being just a little bit reckless tonight and kiss a country vet who has been wanting to kiss you ever since he first set eyes on you at the village stream?'

'Set *eyes* on me? You were flinging a wet ball at me!'

He laughed. 'I know! And I'll never hear the last of it, will I?'

Pulling back, she shook her head laughing, and her eyes were dancing with excitement. She knew she was flirting now, but she did not care. It felt good. And right.

Joseph caught her by the waist and pulled her close again, closer than before. 'Oh Lily,' he whispered, his lips brushing her neck, 'did anyone ever tell you how beautiful you are?'

And then his lips found hers, and he kissed her with an unexpected passion that took her breath away. Closing her eyes, she kissed him back just as passionately, until they were both gasping for air.

'I'm sorry,' he said, raking a hand through his hair, and trying his best to look embarrassed. 'I don't know what came over me.'

'I think you did — and I didn't mind, did I?' She smiled. 'And I don't mind if you do it again either.'

'Don't you?'

She shook her head slowly, her eyes never leaving his. He kissed her again, slowly, and so intensely that she thought she was going to faint with happiness, glad that his arms around her felt so strong that even if she fell, he would catch her, keep her safe.

***

It took her a long time to fall asleep that night but when she finally did, she dreamed that she and Joseph were running down a hill, picking daffodils as they went, and laughing. She was wearing a pale blue dress and a large, wide-brimmed straw hat, and he caught her by the waist, making her squeal with laughter. Turning her around, he kissed her and …

'Lily?'

She turned her head on the pillow, struggling to open her eyes. Even speaking was hard, and her *yes* was not more than a hoarse whisper.

'Lily.'

She sat up, rubbing her eyes. 'Yes? Who is it? What …'

There was no one in the room. It was dark, and she could not hear a sound but for the ticking of her watch on the bedside table. But as soon as she had laid down again and closed her eyes, she could hear the voice again, and this time she was sure it was Spencer's. She could not see him, but the hill, the flowers, and Joseph, even the image of herself had disappeared, swallowed up by a cold, impenetrable mist that was making her shiver. Spencer's disembodied voice was thick with emotion as he spoke.

'Lily, what are you doing? Have you already forgotten me?'

She woke with a start, her heart beating wildly, and when she sat up with a jolt and switched on the light, she realized she was covered in sweat.

'I haven't. I haven't forgotten you, Spencer! Please, believe me, I haven't …' she sobbed, clutching her sheet, 'I haven't …'

Four months, three weeks. No. She had not forgotten.

CHAPTER TWENTY

'I THINK CONVERTING the barn into holiday cottages would probably be a good investment. If you want to do it, you have my blessing. And you might still be able to have your bookshop if you asked Miss Lavender about that empty shop on her premises — seeing as it has been empty for a while now, I don't see why she would object. There used to be a flower shop, but it didn't last long ... Pity, really, the young woman was so enthusiastic about it. But then there aren't many who would buy flowers in Bishops Bridge, with most of us having flowers in the garden, and little occasion for grand bouquets, except for the odd wedding. So,' Abi said, buttering her crumpet, 'what do you think?'

'I think,' Lily said, slipping Theo the crust of her bread, 'I'd better get going soon if I want to be home before five. Lord knows I have slept long enough!'

She had sat in bed crying for a long time and by the time sleep had finally overcome her, the first faint pink of dawn had appeared in the east, slowly lifting the darkness into light. By the time she had woken up, it was past ten and she had found a mug of cold tea on her bedside table, and a note saying, 'I'm outside. Back for elevenses, or breakfast, whichever it will be for you then. A.'

Setting down the cafetière now, Lily reached for Abi's hand. 'I'm sorry. I know you want to help, and it's very kind of you but ... can we perhaps look at that shop next time I'm here? I really haven't got the time today, and ...' She put her head in her hands. It was all getting too much. The barn, the bookshop, the kiss last night, and then the dream ... She needed to clear her head first. *Go home, sit down, write a list. Call Beth. Talk it over with her. She will know what to do. She always does. And if she doesn't, she will pray for you.*

'Of course. There's no rush. You have a lot on your plate, lass, and I'm sorry I just piled even more onto it. Silly me. But I could speak to Miss Lavender if you like, ask her if she would let the shop to you, and then you can come and see her next time you're here. Does that sound alright?'

Lily nodded, slowly lifting her head. 'Yes, that ... oh, but, Abi, we haven't even talked about where the money would come from! For the barn conversion, I mean. I know I should have thought about that before and of course I'm going to sell the flat but that might not be enough, and — well, you know what I'm like. Heads in the clouds and all that. Whatever people call me.'

'But you aren't *whatever people call you*, Lily. You are *you* — wonderful, kind and caring *you* — and sometimes,' Abi added, wagging her finger, 'just the right side of naughty, too! Remember how you put old Nettleton in his place. I dare say, you will be a real asset, should I ever have to fight him off my land again.'

'Yes, well, that's as may be, but we still need to think about money. I don't know how much I will get for the flat — I'm going to put it on the market just as soon as I have sorted things out with my brother. He might even help me, seeing as he is an estate agent. But still, it might not be that much …'

'Oh, don't worry about that, lass — I may not be rich, but I do have a few savings from when I sold all of my horses and expensive equipment like horse trucks and the large Mercedes four-wheel-drive. And there's always the paintings in the attic.'

Lily almost choked on her coffee. 'Paintings in the attic?? You are not telling me you have some Da Vincis stowed away there, are you?'

'No,' Abi said calmly, 'but genuine Dawsons — some are Margaret's, some Donald's. Margaret left me some of their paintings when she died,' she explained. 'Their son has most of the others, and of course he got the house and what money there was left after death duties, but she insisted I get most of hers, and some of her husband's, too, should I ever need to sell them in order to save the family farm. Well, the farm doesn't exactly need *saving* now, but investing — and what is the point of hiding those pictures in the attic until I'm gone, eh?'

Lily was still staring at her, trying to take this in. She knew her Uncle Donald had been a famous artist, some of his paintings having sold for thousands of dollars to rich Americans, according to her mum. Her parents had a seaside scene hanging in their sitting room, which she and Stephen used to joke about sharing — it could hang in Lily's house for one year, and in Stephen's for the next. 'Because it would not be fair if only one of us got to have a real Dawson', they said, possibly only half joking.

Perhaps they could turn the barn into an art gallery and display her aunt and uncle's work as well as Susanna's and other local artists? In books, people did that sort of thing all the time. But somehow Lily sensed that this idea would not go down well with Pete the Builder either. After all, what did she know about art in the first place? Nothing.

'Can I see them?'

'Of course. We can go up now, if you like? Unless you are in a hurry to get back to Oxford?'

Lily scoffed. 'Not now, I'm not!'

Just then the room turned dark and cold, and the next minute heavy rain was being whipped across the yard and against the window, making it impossible to continue the conversation. Abi put her mug down and tutted. 'Well, whatever reason you might have for wanting to move to Rosedale, it can not be for the weather!' she shouted and indicated for Lily to follow her.

***

MOST OF THE paintings were landscapes — the moors, the coast, Whitby Abbey, and a well-captured scene depicting Goathland's historic train station where people were saying goodbye on the platform while the shining black steam train was about to roll out of the station. It looked so real Lily could almost hear the hissing of the engine and smell the thick smoke that filled the air. The initials *DD* were painted in the bottom right corner of the picture, just visible above the wooden frame. The paint on the frame was peeling, but that made it look even more special. Lily knew she would never have the heart to sell this picture — or any of the others, for that matter — and hoped that they wouldn't have to.

There were some still lives, too, depicting pottery and wildflowers, as well as a picture of a little boy and girl sitting on the beach in Robin Hood's Bay, with their backs turned to the artist. The boy was busy building a sandcastle and the girl was washing shells in the shallow water, possibly to add to her brother's sand castle later.

'These are so beautiful,' Lily whispered. 'How will you ever part with them? I know I couldn't — well, with the still lives perhaps, but then I am not particularly keen on vases and fruit bowls. Though they are well-depicted, I must say.'

'Well, they have been in the attic for fifteen years now, haven't they? It's fifteen years since that dreadful accident ...'

Abi's sister and brother-in-law had died in a boating accident in the South of France, where they had lived in one of the picturesque fishing villages on the coast. They had not been happy for a long time, and the accident happened because they had both been drinking, and arguing all evening. Raging with fury, Margaret had got on the boat, and Donald had followed her. And then the storm had hit the little sailing boat ...

Abi's finger was tracing the surface of the oil painting depicting the children on the beach. 'Fifteen years ...' Still mesmerized, Abi shook her head and said, 'But you are right, they are too good to be rotting away in the attic. Why not give other people a chance to admire them in their living rooms? We should get a professional to come and value them. — Oh! What is that?' She picked up a small envelope that had been tucked inside the back of the frame and turned it over in her hand, eyes widening in recognition. It had to be of some significance, or else she would not seem so flustered now, but much to Lily's disappointment Abi just said, 'oh' and quickly tucked it inside her jacket.

Suddenly a cold wind blew through the cracks in the wood, making Lily shiver. They had been sitting on the dusty floorboards for almost an hour now, and she got up, straightening her back. 'I think we'd better get downstairs. It's too cold up here, and I must get going, anyway.'

Abi nodded, but Lily could tell she was still thinking about Margaret. Lily knew the sisters had been estranged from one another, though why nobody knew, not even her mother. On the rare occasions Lily had seen their Auntie Margaret, it had never been without some glass or other in one hand, and a cigarette in the other. *Poor Margaret*, she thought. And poor Abi for losing her sister like that. *I must make sure I make up with Stephen when I get back*, she thought and offered Abi a hand.

'Well,' Abi said, dusting down her jacket when she had got up. 'I suppose you must then — but you have time for a quick cup of tea, haven't you? And I must give you some sandwiches to eat on the way, in case you get stuck on the A1 again. I have cake, too.'

There is always cake in this house, Lily thought, smiling as she followed Abi down the stairs. And love, and warmth, and laughter, and friendship. The perfect place to call home.

***

THE FIRST THING Lily did when she got back to Oxford was to call her brother.

'Hey,' she said when he picked up, 'how was your weekend? Conservatory sorted?'

'No, I'm afraid we'll have to get a specialist in. But never mind that blasted conservatory — how was Yorkshire? Have you only just got back?'

'Yes. I haven't even hung up my coat yet. I … I wanted to …'

'Yes, me too.' She could hear Stephen settling into his favourite armchair. The one she had helped pick for his first apartment, just before he met Emily and Emily declared the armchair to be 'the most hideous thing she had ever seen'. As soon as they had moved into their house, the armchair had been banished to Stephen's study or his 'man cave', as Emily called it. There was a desk, a chair, a bookshelf, and most importantly, his model railway. Most of the tracks and engines went back to Grandpa Henderson, which was why Lily knew Stephen was already dreading the day when everything would have to be packed up and stored away in the attic because his study would be needed as a nursery. Poor Stephen. Hopefully they would be able to move into a bigger house soon, where he could have his model railway back and running. But with Emily proudly declaring she would be a stay-at-home-mum, Lily did not know where the money should come from, so the poor engines would probably be in for one long period of hibernation.

'Are you sitting in your armchair?'

'Yes. The best armchair we ever bought.' She could see him smiling, and smiled right back at him, knowing he would see her even if he didn't.

'It's the *only* armchair we ever bought together. Anyway, about last week — I'm sorry …'

'Me, too. Do you want me to come over for a hug?'

'No, you're alright. I just wanted to let you know I was sorry. Not about going to Yorkshire but … you know.'

'I know, yes. And it's okay. I mean, I still think it's crazy, obviously, but … it's alright. *You*'ll be alright. Listen, I've got to go, Emily's parents are coming for dinner. See you soon?'

After they had said goodbye, Lily stood in the middle of the room, trying to figure out what to do next. Suddenly she felt an overwhelming sense of loneliness. Whyever had she thought buying a two-bedroom flat in Oxford would be a good idea? She had been nothing but lonely here, even when Spencer was alive. Most of the time she had been on her own here, with only her books for company. Remembering her dream, she went to the antique linen cupboard she had inherited from her grandmother and flung the doors open. The cushions were right where she had stuffed them only weeks ago. She took them out, sat down on the sofa, and hugged them tight.

'I haven't forgotten you, Spencer. I haven't. And I never will either. I won't kiss him again, I promise — or … or not for a long while yet. If he really loves me, he'll have to wait.' The tears were falling now, hard and fast. 'I loved you, Spencer. I did. And I miss you. I still do …' But even as she was saying it, she knew it was not quite true — what she *was* missing was her old life. Her routine, her sense of safety and belonging. All of which had gone. This place felt cold and empty now, and not like home at all.

It was time to go.

CHAPTER TWENTY-ONE

DAVID STANTON PUT the phone down and raked his hands through his dark brown hair that had grown far too long over the last couple of weeks. He had inherited both the colour and the curls from his mother — well, to be fair, he could not remember his father much because he had been only four when he died, but he had seen photographs, and Mike Stanton had been blonde and blue-eyed, so no match there. He had been a carpenter though, so the love for wood and anything to do with woodwork clearly came from that side of the family.

David had planned to do business studies at Durham University but when his mother had died, he had given up his place, knowing he would not be able to afford university. So instead he went to work for a carpenter who specialized in bespoke garden furniture and tree houses. Seeing that his new employee was not only willing to work hard and eager to learn the trade, but also extraordinarily skilled, his boss took him on as an apprentice. Some years later David was offered a job with the *Mouseman* in Kilburn, where he would happily have stayed for ever had it not been for the global financial crisis in 2008/9 which cost him, being the most recent one to have joined the team, his job. Determined to make a living from his skills yet, he decided to take the risk and set up his own woodcarving business in Lofthouse, Nidderdale.

He made everything from rustic garden furniture to delicate small items such as wooden dishes, and had chosen the squirrel to be his trademark, which he now carved onto every piece he made. At the beginning it had not been easy, but over the years David had not only made friends in the village he now called home, but earned himself a reputation which had begun to spread even beyond Yorkshire. And now, twenty years after he had left Rosedale as a young lad, he got a phone call from his mate Pete the builder who wanted him to look at some old barn on — of all places! — the farm next to the one on which he had grown up.

As a rule, David did not do restoration work, and if he did, it was perhaps the odd stable door or some ancient shutters which needed a bit of TLC, so he was intrigued to hear why Pete had recommended him of all people. Pete knew that David had an issue with Rosedale, and Bishops Bridge in particular, and, being a good friend, he also knew why.

'Aw, just come and have a look. I'm not even sure she will go through with that book barn idea, it is rather crazy, and I told her as much. But if she does, I thought it would be fun to work on a project together. What do you say?'

David had not said anything much — he was not remotely interested in barn conversions, and the only reason he could think of that would make him go and have a look at the crumbling old building was his curiosity to see the place again after such a long time. But was he ready to go back? What would he find — and who? Would

Susanna still be there? He had a feeling she might. She had always been a homebird, never happier than when sitting in her mum's kitchen, sketching while Elaine made jam or preserves. She loved the moors and the ragged hills, and the atmosphere the unpredictable weather created in the dale, skies turning from brilliant blue to purple or black in a matter of minutes.

Pete went on to explain that perhaps the young lady — Miss Abigail's great-niece apparently — could still be persuaded to convert the barn into a holiday cottage instead, which would be a lot more profitable, especially in the winter. David heartily agreed with his friend on that point. A book barn in the middle of nowhere! Utter nonsense.

***

THE *GREEDY GOOSE* in Risplith was packed that evening. It was a very popular pub — they served the best Thai food in the area — and David was looking forward to his first proper meal this week. He knew he should make more of an effort to eat well — and regularly — but he simply did not enjoy eating alone, never mind cooking. So when Pete, even though he was coming all the way from Thirsk, had suggested they meet at the *Greedy Goose*, David had agreed most happily, even if it involved discussing that stupid barn proposal.

'So, what exactly does the young lady have in mind with Miss Lewis's barn? And where do I come in? I'm not a regular carpenter, or a joiner, I'm a woodcarver.'

'I know! And that is exactly what you could do — *the interior*. Bookshelves, a counter, and all that. I just thought that you might want to come and have a look, you know, and tell them what you think. I know you would be impeccably honest when it comes to telling them whether it is worth the money and the trouble, or not.'

Well, of course it isn't, thought David, but Pete was like a runaway train now. 'You could make the door, perhaps, you know, with a wee squirrel on it. You know, squirrels, trees, wood, books …' David was staring blankly at him. Pete shrugged. 'Anyway, I thought it would be nice, and brilliant advertising for you, too. Everyone who comes to that book barn —'

'Oh, yes, do remind me of all those people who will come flocking to the book barn on a cold and snowy winter's day *in blooming Rosedale*!'

The waitress brought their food and David took a long, thirsty swig of his beer, still shaking his head. Sometimes Pete could really be infuriating!

'I honestly don't know what's got into you, David,' Pete said once they had agreed who got which plate. 'You said your business wasn't exactly prospering at the moment and you could do with a larger commission for a change. Something other than the usual garden bench.'

'I like to think that my work is not quite *your usual*, thank you very much. In fact, I think it is rather unique, as do all of my customers.'

Pete sighed. 'Come on, David, you know I didn't mean it like that. I know you're passionate about your work, and that's great but — well, passion doesn't exactly pay the bills, does it? This project could earn you *a lot*.'

'*If* she wants me to do it. And *if* she really wants to go ahead with her book barn. That is two big Ifs, Pete. I can't make a living from Ifs. And besides, I swore I would never go back.'

Putting his fork down, Pete gave his friend a stern look. 'David. I know you don't want to go back. You have told me often enough, and I understand, but I also think it's time you buried those ghosts from the past. Come to Rosedale. Get it over with. If it still feels weird to be there — or even wrong —, then at least you know. You don't ever have to come back again then. I promise I will come to Nidderdale for the rest of my life to have curry with you. Come on, lad,' he said, picking up his knife and fork, 'give yourself a chance.'

David sighed. 'I'll think about it. Okay?'

'Good.' Nodding, Pete took another mouthful of curry. 'And there's no way this curry here is three chillies — have you got mine?'

***

IT WAS LATE when David got back to the cottage. He went through to the living room without bothering to switch on a light, poured himself a whisky and opened the French doors to the small back garden. Leaning against the doorframe, he gazed out into the descending darkness. There was a red brick wall on the far end that would soon be covered in fragrant yellow honeysuckle, and borders on either side of the patio. The borders were strictly low-maintenance: just a couple of low-growing shrubs, some sturdy perennials, an ornamental stone urn that some well-meaning person had given to him with lavender in it (sadly, the lavender had not survived its first summer), and a birdbath. Pale pink clematis were covering the wooden fencing to both sides, and there were some persistent sweet peas that David had tried to get rid of several times — to no avail. He had finally given up, seeing as they were obviously made of sterner stuff than him. Thinking of his conversation with Pete tonight, David wondered if those sweet peas were somehow symbolic of his enduring love for Susanna — suppressed over the years, ignored, even yanked at, and yet impossible to destroy.

He shook his head, but the image of Susanna was still there, even when he shut his eyes and opened them again. Ever since Pete had come up with that crazy book barn idea, she had been on his mind, her face was in everything he saw. If she was still there though, or had come back, surely she would be married by now, wouldn't she? With children, too. They had always wanted a big family, Susanna and him. Even at seventeen, they had talked about it, made plans for their future … only that future was never to be. Or not for the two of them together, anyway.

Did he want to see her there, happily married with adorable children?

Some other man's wife. Another man's children.

He knew he could not bear it.

And then there was the risk of bumping into Brian Nettleton … David wondered if *he* was still around. Probably. Life was unfair, wasn't it? His mother had not been forty when she died of pneumonia, and that ghastly old man would likely live forever, or at least until he was a hundred and shaking his stick at any intruders to his precious farm. David knew that Wood End Farm was the last place he ever wanted to set foot on again, never mind seeing Brian Nettleton.

He stood there for a long time, watching the bats silently circling the night sky, thinking about what to do. His eyes never leaving the sky, he lifted his glass to his lips, finished his drink and nodded. Pete was right.

It was time.

He went back into the house, picked up his phone and messaged Pete, saying he would go and have a look at the barn after all, and would he arrange for him to meet that young lady from Oxford whenever it was convenient, thank you.

CHAPTER TWENTY-TWO

SINKING DOWN ON her sofa with a sigh, Lily left the phone to ring in the kitchen, determined to ignore the flood of messages that had come in while she was at work. It could all wait now. She would sit here and watch an episode of *Downton Abbey* or two, and perhaps order a pizza. There was a bottle of Chardonnay cooling in the fridge, too. *Even if I don't have anyone to share my pizza and wine with here*, she thought, *there is no reason why I should not enjoy my Friday night in.* Next week she would drive up to Yorkshire again, to meet Pete, as well as the architect, and some woodcarver Pete thought she might like to 'have a chat with'.

'He could do the shelves for you — he's very good! It is worth having a look at his workshop in Nidderdale. Nice place for walking, too. You can check out his website first, see if you like what he does.' She had, and she did, but of course *The Squirrel of Lofthouse* was well out of her price range. If she had money to spare, she would fill the shop with *Mouseman* furniture — but as it was, she had none.

The last couple of weeks she had been busy trying to work out how to change that. For one thing, she had finally plucked up the courage and called Miss Lavender — she was due to meet her on the premises on Friday afternoon — and she had put her flat on the market, too. The estate agent had already called her to say he had a few clients who were very keen, offering more than the asking price without even having seen the flat, so the first viewing would be on Monday evening — a prospect that made her feel just a little bit sick. What on earth was she doing?

She had just slipped the DVD into the player when the doorbell rang.

'Oh, for goodness' sake!'

She scrambled to her feet, nearly fell over the rug, and opened the door just as the bell rang again. 'Yes! What is – oh! Hello, stranger,' she said when she saw her brother standing on the doorstep. 'This is a nice surprise. What are you doing here on a Friday night?'

'Just passing by on my way home,' he said, kissing her cheek. 'And hoping for a cup of coffee as well as an explanation perhaps.'

'Oh?'

'Yes. I passed Barnet & Farrell's on the way. Offers in excess of £300,000? Have you gone completely mad? It's an outrageous sum, even for Oxford! You'll be lucky to get £270,000! And why didn't you ask me? I could have pulled some strings for you.'

Lily forced herself to take not one, but two deep breaths before she spoke. 'Because that would not have been ethical, would it, with you being my brother? Anyway, since you made it blatantly clear what you thought of the whole scheme last time we spoke, I didn't think you would even care to help me. And just so you know, I have already had four offers — two of them at £310,000 — and the first viewing will be on Monday evening. With any luck, I'll sell the flat by the end of next month.'

She could not help feeling very smug with herself as she saw her brother pale. '£310,000? That's insane!'

'I know. And just as well, because that means Abi doesn't have to sell Auntie Margaret's paintings, and we can go ahead with the barn conversion just as soon as we have decided what to do with it.'

Stephen put his briefcase down and hung up his jacket. 'I thought you were going to turn it into a bookshop?'

'I was, but as everybody keeps saying it is a crazy idea, I might not after all. Anyway, it's Abi's barn, so it really isn't for me to decide. Even if she insists I can do what I like. The point is, I can't though, can I? Not as long as I don't win the lottery. So, selling the flat for a good price is a good start.'

Stephen shook his head, probably wondering where the sister he had known had gone to — this clearly wasn't Lily. It was not like her to be so flippant. It wasn't like her to be so determined and strong-willed, either.

'Have you got any decent coffee in the house, or shall I get us some from the deli?'

Without so much as a word, Lily walked into the kitchen and banged her *Colombia Coffee Roasters* tin on the counter. 'That good enough for you?'

Stephen frowned. 'Hey! What's the matter? Did you have a bad day at work?'

'No. I'm just tired. And you know that I always buy my coffee at *Colombia*, so there is no need for such a stupid remark. Decent coffee, my foot.'

'Do you want me to go? I'm sorry, I just thought we could talk about it. Get the elephant out of the room, you know. And I'm sorry about the coffee bashing. I guess I'm just teasing you because you are going to live in the country soon — no more fancy coffee bars. Colombia is excellent. The best, actually.'

Lily started to spoon coffee powder into her cafetiere. 'It's okay. So what was it exactly you were going to talk to me about? Except coffee?'

'Well — the flat sale, obviously. I would still like to help you — as I suppose none of us can stop you, anyway, I thought I might as well. Or rather, I kind of expected you to ask me. That was stupid of me, of course, since you seem to be determined to do it all by yourself. Even Emily says she hardly knows you since you are back from Yorkshire! She admires you, by the way. She must be about the only one who thinks it's a great idea — moving to Rosedale, and opening a bookshop. Or whatever it is you will do.'

Lily held the kettle in mid-air. Emily admired her? Intelligent, ambitious and sophisticated Emily in whose company she always felt so inferior she avoided talking about anything more serious than the weather?

'Does she?'

'Yes. She says it will do you good. She also says we should all have a little more faith in you and … and let you go.'

'Oh?' Lily was so stunned, she could not think of anything else to say. Maybe she had been wrong about her sister-in-law who had always seemed such a cold fish to her. *Maybe*, she thought, *I should be having coffee with Emily instead. I might get more fun out of it. And encouragement.*

'That's what she said, yes. I was beginning to think she was right, but then I saw the advertisement and … sorry.' He held up his hands when he saw her thunderous face. 'So, um, what time are you leaving tomorrow?'

***

LATER, LILY WAS lying in bed with her phone in her hand, exchanging messages with Joseph at lightning speed.

> So, when are you going to be back in Yorkshire? The weather has been really nice lately, with temperatures almost reaching twenty degrees. We could have that ice-cream ;-)
>
> Next weekend actually. Another meeting with Pete the Builder — this time he's bringing the architect, too. Maybe I'll need something stronger than ice-cream after that.
>
> That can be arranged ;-) How did Abi find an architect at such short notice? Does she know *everyone* in Rosedale?

Lily smiled.

> She knows a lot of people. But actually, Pete is enough — he knows the rest. He is even talking about bringing a woodcarver, though whatever for I don't know. I won't be able to afford hand carved furniture, will I?
>
> Perhaps not now. But you never know ;-)
>
> Never know what?
>
> What lies around the corner.
>
> Good things, I hope.
>
> With us? Definitely. Just keep on walking, Lily.

Yes, she thought when they had finally said goodnight, *I will. I will walk on until I'm home. And I won't look back either.*

CHAPTER TWENTY-THREE

Miss Lavender was one formidable old lady — nobody knew how old she really was, but she had to be well past retiring age, probably nearer seventy than sixty-five. She was tall and angular, and with her silver hair tucked into a neat bun at the back of her head as well as the horn-rimmed glasses on her long, hawk-like nose, she looked very much like a fearsome nineteenth-century schoolmistress. Her eyes had the colour of a pale blue winter sky, and although she rarely smiled she did not look unfriendly. Rumour had it that she was of an aristocratic background, but as she was an intensely private person who kept herself to herself, nobody knew for sure where she had come from, and why she should have settled in Bishops Bridge of all places. As it was, she had become what people called 'the salt of the earth' and was held in high esteem for her kindness and generosity, as well as for her shrewd sense of business.

She lived in a flat above the shop and was just returning from a walk when she saw Lily standing outside her shop, stepping nervously from one foot to the other. As soon as she felt the old lady's piercing eyes on her, Lily stood still, suddenly feeling very much like a little girl who had been caught chewing gum in the lesson. She just managed not to curtsey.

'Good afternoon. You must be Lily Henderson. Do come in, dear, don't be shy. Would you like a cup of tea? It's warm enough to sit outside — if you would like to follow me?'

When they were seated at a white cast-iron table in the tiny back garden and Miss Lavender had put down a tray with tea things, Lily felt herself begin to relax.

'So, you want to come to Rosedale and live with your great-aunt on the farm? That is a brave decision for a young woman like you, to leave city life behind and come to live on the North York Moors. Winters can get very lonely up here, you know?'

'I know. But I really love it here, and I don't mind the loneliness. And as for that city life ... I'm not really leaving much behind either.' She hesitated, not sure how much to tell the old lady. 'My — my boyfriend died some months ago. And my best friend is moving to Devon soon, so there will be nothing left for me.' Except sadness, and loneliness.

The old lady looked up. 'Oh dear. I'm sorry you had such a hard time. Of course, you need a fresh start after all that. — Do you take sugar in your tea?'

Lily looked at the gold-rimmed sugar bowl with a pale pink rose pattern and shook her head. 'No, thank you, I don't. Although the dish is very pretty. About the shop — um ... I was telling you on the phone that I would like to rent it and open a bookshop. You see,' she went on before her courage left her, 'I have always wanted to have my own bookshop, ever since I can remember. As a proper book worm, I cannot not imagine anything better than being surrounded by books — which is why I chose to become a librarian. I like my job, don't get me wrong — but, as I said, I don't want to stay in the city. I must confess I am also a hopeless romantic, so maybe you will think this idea is crazy, just like everybody else … especially my family …' She sat up straight, as if that would increase her chances with the stern old lady. 'But I am ready to work hard, and unless you have other plans for the shop, I would very much like to give it a try.'

'I have no other plans, no. And I think a bookshop is a wonderful idea. Especially as the shop is right next to the Bridge Café. A very neat combination, wouldn't you agree?'

Lily smiled. 'I would, yes. So — you would let me have the shop?'

'Absolutely.' Taking a sip of her tea, Miss Lavender said, 'I think it could be just what Bishops Bridge needs. As I said, winters can be long and hard here, and there is nothing like snuggling up in front of the fire with a good read.'

Lily nodded enthusiastically. 'I agree. And people would not have to go as far as Helmsley to buy a book, or order online. Online shopping is convenient of course — especially if you live in a remote area like this one — but it just isn't the same as browsing through a lovely little bookshop and finding your perfect read. Um … what about the rent?' she asked, feeling a little embarrassed. 'How much would it be?'

She had no idea how she was going to pay the rent as well as for the furniture and the stock she would have to order. If she did not buy the books, she could not sell them, it was as simple as that. She could not put them in cardboard boxes on the floor either. In her dream, there were lovely honey-coloured pine shelves lining the pale green walls of her shop, and a counter with stands and neat little boxes on it, displaying postcards and small gifts people might be tempted to buy. But that was in her dreams — this here was reality.

'I have just resigned from my job in Oxford, you see, so money is a bit … um …' *Tight. Just say it. Money is tight.*

'Oh, don't worry about the rent,' Miss Lavender said, brushing away a tiny crumb — or maybe it was a mere gesture, for as far as Lily could see, the table top was spotless. 'In fact, I have a proposition to make, if you don't mind. Seeing as you want to save as much money as you can but get the shop up and running as soon as possible — would you consider working for me? If it were my shop?'

Lily frowned. 'I — I'm not sure I know what you mean, Miss Lavender.'

'Just that. If I turn the empty premises next door into a bookshop, you could work for me. You don't have to pay rent. You don't have to worry about furniture and stock orders. You get paid for selling books. And while I know it is not the same — I can see the disappointment in your eyes now, lass — I'm just saying it would save you a lot of money, and a lot of trouble, too, never mind the risk. What do you think? Or would that be defeating the object? I understand if you say it would. I know something about dreams, even if I am old.'

'Oh. Um … I don't know what to say, to be honest.' While she knew she would be a fool to say no, she also knew that that meant giving up her independence before it had even begun. It would not be her bookshop.

'Oh, dear, I'm sorry — I have put you on the spot now.' Miss Lavender reached out to put a gnarled, speckled hand on Lily's. 'You can always say no. Just think about it for as long as you like. I will not give the shop to anyone else.'

Lily was lost for words. Why was this old lady so kind to her when she did not even know her? Why would Miss Lavender trust her, a newcomer and complete stranger? And why would she be willing to take the risk with a new shop when she did not have to? She had to be at least sixty-five, she ought to be thinking about retiring, not opening yet another shop!

'That is very kind of you, Miss Lavender. And I promise I will think about it. You see,' Lily said, taking a deep breath, 'the original plan was for me to have my own bookshop on my great-aunt's farm. We are planning to convert an old barn, but sadly, the builder does not think a book barn would be a viable project. Nobody thinks it would be.' She shook her head and reached for her teacup, but her hands were trembling, and she had to put it back. The last thing she needed was an accident with Miss Lavender's precious tea set. 'I may be a hopeless romantic, but even I have to accept reality sometimes. Even if it hurts.'

'A book barn? Oh, but that is a lovely idea! Very romantic. I like it! And Lily, I don't know why you should keep calling yourself *a hopeless this* and *a hopeless that*. You are doing a very brave thing in leaving the life you have known behind, and coming here to live on a farm. That is quite a big step! And even if you'd officially be working for me, you could still think of it as your bookshop. I don't mind. *Lily's bookshop* sounds very nice, doesn't it? Much nicer than *Miss Lavender's bookshop*.' Her spectacles wobbled as she wrinkled her nose, almost making Lily laugh. 'You can call it whatever you like of course. And you can choose the furniture, the colours, everything — and the books. Especially those! — Shall we go and have a look at the shop? Would you like that?'

Lily nodded faintly. She could not believe this was really

happening to her. Looking down at her heart pendant and then at Miss Lavender, she said, 'Yes, please. But, Miss Lavender, what if …'

'Courage, dear heart — it will all work out. The key is in the waiting. And now come and have a look. Remember never to buy a cat in a bag!' Her pale blue eyes were twinkling, and Lily wondered if she might have found a kindred spirit in Miss Lavender.

The shop was perfect. It was surprisingly light and not as small as it looked from the outside though smaller than the café and Miss Lavender's shop. There was a large window to the front, and a tiny back room which could serve as an office-cum-kitchen. The floorboards were dusty but looked alright; they could probably just be sanded down and resealed, and the walls needed painting, of course. Sage green or duck egg blue to go with the honey-coloured pine shelves?

'It's lovely,' Lily said, turning around to Miss Lavender. 'I don't think I will have to think about it!'

Miss Lavender smiled. 'Good. Then I suggest I'll get in touch with the builder, see when he can fit us in, and you will choose the furniture and the colours. If all goes to plan, you can place your first stock order in early September. Does that sound agreeable?'

'Very agreeable, thank you.'

***

'I THINK IT is a very sensible choice — taking over Miss Lavender's new shop, I mean. And you know, it might actually work in your favour — you'd be right on the High Street, which means more people would drop in, and you would be neighbours in business with both Jessie and Miss

Lavender. Don't underestimate the importance of getting the locals on your side! Yorkshire folks are friendly, but they can be terribly stubborn, too. You don't want to get on the wrong side of them.'

'I'd definitely not want to get on the wrong side of you.' Lily helped herself to another slice of quiche. She hadn't eaten all day and was ravenous. 'Oh, I can't wait to tell Jessie tomorrow! It's her birthday, and we're all going to the *Red Grouse* — I hope that's okay with you?'

'Of course. Is Joseph coming, too?'

'Abi!'

Just then her phone rang, and when Lily saw who it was, her cheeks flushed a deep red, and she turned away quickly before Abi could see — and worse still, comment.

'Lily! I never knew you were coming! I have just heard from Greg. Do you mind if I come over? We could go for a walk.'

'What, now?'

'Yes, why not? It will be light for at least another three hours. Please, Lily, I can't wait until tomorrow. Inigo is wagging his tail. He says he can't wait either.'

Lily laughed. 'Oh, alright then, come over. Where are you now?'

'Um … in Bishops Bridge?'

'In Bishops Bridge? But not outside the farm gates?'

'No, not quite that close. I have just had a look at Mr Barnsley's Honey, she has an upset stomach. She is a terrible hoover, that one, and he never sees her picking up all that rubbish of course, him being nearly blind. Anyway. See you in five minutes?'

When Lily had put the phone away, she turned to Abi and said, 'And before you jump to any conclusions, it's only a *walk* we're going on, not a trip to the registrar's office, so no need to get your hat out.'

Feigning innocence, Abi tutted and said, 'I don't know what you are talking about. A walk with who? William?'

'He hasn't got a phone, has he? Not that he needs one,' she added, rolling her eyes at Abi when the donkey started to bray.

'You've got that one well trained, I must say!' Abi cried, wiping tears of laughter from her cheeks. 'He has been ever so good even while you were in Oxford. Don't allow him to sleep in your room as well when you move here though. I'm not sure the old floorboards will hold *his* weight.'

Now it was Lily's turn to feign innocence, and she tried very hard not to look at Theo. 'What do you mean, him *as well*? Who else do you think sleeps in my bedroom?'

'Oh, what do I know. Theo? Myrtle? Both?'

Shaking her head, Lily rose to her feet. 'I'll put my boots on.'

CHAPTER TWENTY-FOUR

THE SMELL OF cake fresh from the oven wafted up from the farmhouse kitchen, and Lily opened a reluctant eye to glance at her watch on the bedside table. It was quarter to eleven.

'Bother! Bother, bother, bother!'

Had she really slept so long? Why hadn't her aunt woken her? Pete and his team would be due any minute, and she was not nearly ready to meet them!

Pushing back the duvet, she cursed herself for not having set an alarm. It had been nearly three o'clock in the morning when she had crept up the stairs and into bed. They had walked up to the kilns and sat there, talking for hours, and she would have happily spent the entire night up there, had it not turned so cold.

On the way home, she had told him about her meeting with Miss Lavender, and how she was trying to figure out what to do, even though she had already said yes.

'I would have been a fool not to accept her proposition — but I keep asking myself, why? Why on earth would she do this? Do you know anything about her? Why would she trust a total stranger to run a bookshop for her — in Bishops Bridge! And I thought Abi was crazy. And me, obviously.'

'Whoa there!' Spinning her around to face him, he had placed his hands on her shoulders and said, 'First, you are not crazy. You may be a dreamer, you may be a romantic, but you are also sensible and clever, and you would never do anything that you hadn't thought through. And you are compassionate and kind — and so is Miss Lavender. She has a kind heart, for all that she appears to be such a fire spitting dragon. *Don't touch this*!' he mimicked, making Lily laugh. 'Anyway, I think there are two reasons why she would offer you the job — the first being her sense of business: the premises have been sitting empty for a while, so they don't earn any money. And what with all those greeting cards, calendars, comics, magazines and paperbacks in her little convenience store I'm sure she thinks she could just as well sell them next door, if she had an assistant. Also, this would bring new customers to Bishops Bridge, and to her shop, even Jessie's café. Everybody would profit, should you be able to turn this bookshop into a success. With your qualifications and your passion, she obviously believes that you will — and so do I, by the way.'

Although she had nodded, she had not quite been convinced. 'And the second reason?'

'The second reason is that I believe that beneath her prickly exterior and all that fuss about not touching things and drinking your loose leaf tea from fine bone china cups, Miss Lavender is an incurable romantic at heart. She knows you have a dream, and she wants you to follow it — and so do I. I hope you are going to accept?'

'I already have, haven't I? I just can't stop wondering if this is really the right thing to do.'

'You will find out,' he had said, squeezing her hand. They had walked back in silence, and when she had asked him in for a cup of coffee, he had said, 'I know I shouldn't because I'm working tomorrow, and you need your sleep as well, but yes, I'll stay for a cuppa. Just the one.'

In the end, he had stayed until the sky was beginning to turn a pale pink in the east and they could hear the first birds singing outside. 'I think it's time I went home — I should have left long ago,' he had said, gently helping Lily to her feet. They were sitting on the sofa by the Aga, and Lily had nearly fallen asleep. Or had she actually? She couldn't remember.

'What time is it? Oh dear! Nearly four. Where did the time go?' Sitting up with a jerk, she had knocked down the empty mug that she must have put at her feet. 'I'm so sorry I kept you all night. Will you be alright? You said you have to work today.'

He had kissed her hair and smiled. 'I'll manage. I'm glad you told me a bit more about yourself. Your illness and all that ... I'm sorry you had to go through so much. Poor you.'

'Oh.' Frowning as she tried to remember what exactly she had told him, she had got up and walked to the kettle, then stopped. How much did Joseph know about Derek and the disastrous results of that party now? About her teenage angst getting to the point where she could not sleep without the lights full on because of the nightmares, and her slipping into anorexia in an attempt to make herself as little of a nuisance as possible?

Remembering Joseph had to go, she had put the kettle down again and shrugged. 'It's a long time ago. I'm fine now.'

They both knew she wasn't, but Joseph had been wise enough not to say anything. Instead, he had kissed her good night, and left her to get some sleep. 'And don't worry about me, I'll have a really strong coffee when I get home, and not bother about going to bed. It's okay, I have done it before. And it's only a half day. Duncan will take over at four. That's my boss, by the way.'

She had been too tired to protest that working from six to four was not what she would call a half day.

Deciding she would not bother getting dressed for now but just make herself a cup of tea and ask Abi to hold the fort until she had had a shower, she dashed down the stairs and burst into the kitchen.

'Morning! So sorry I'm late! Why didn't you … oh!'

She stopped dead when she saw a tall, dark haired, and strikingly handsome man standing by the Aga, a mug of coffee in his hand.

Trying her best to shrink back into the hall, she found it was too late, as he had already seen her. What was more, he was making his way towards her now, holding out a strong, tanned hand. 'Morning, Miss Henderson — or is it alright for me to call you Lily? I'm David Stanton. David, if you like.'

Although he smiled warmly at her, Lily could not have felt more embarrassed, and she felt the blood drain from her face. David Stanton! What on earth was *he* doing here?

'Hello,' she mumbled, and let him take her hand. 'I'm Lily.' For some reason her knees felt like butter, and she knew she was staring but she could not seem to take her eyes off him. It felt like a dream, meeting the man she had heard so much about. The man no one had ever expected to come back. And here he was, standing in Abi's kitchen, with a mug of coffee in his hands, and introducing himself to her as if he was a neighbour who had just dropped in.

His eyes were the colour of the ocean after a storm, and they crinkled in a friendly smile as he shook her hand warmly. 'Pleased to meet you, Lily Henderson. I have come about the barn, only to learn that the meeting is to take place tomorrow and not today — I suppose I'll have to throttle Pete for not bothering to tell me. Could have spared me an eighty-minute drive.'

Abi, who was busy preparing bacon sarnies, looked up from buttering thick slices of fresh white bread. 'Well, yes, but Pete only called me half an hour ago to say that the architect could not make it today and could we meet tomorrow instead,' she said, pouring Lily tea from the pot on the stove. '*You* were still fast asleep then, Cinderella, and after Pete's phone call I didn't want to wake you either. What time *did* you get back last night? I never even heard you.'

'Um … Could you just give me five minutes to get dressed? I'll be right back. Unless you will be gone then?' Trying to avoid David's gaze, which she somehow found unnerving, she took the mug of tea Abi was offering and stepped back into the safety of the hall.

'No, no, I'll be right here. I thought we might as well take a look at your barn, seeing what potential is there — even if it is not going to be a book barn after all. Your aunt has already told me that Pete has shattered that dream of yours to pieces. I'm sorry about that. He is right, of course, you would never attract enough customers. Much better idea to build holiday cottages instead — I know!' He held up his hands. 'It's not the same. We'll take a look, okay? And don't rush, please, not for my sake. I'll be ready when you are.'

***

AFTER THE QUICKEST (and coldest) shower ever, Lily put on a pair of cropped denim shorts and her favourite T-shirt with *Here comes the Sun* written on it, and rushed downstairs again, giving her hair a quick brush on the way.

There was a plate with bacon sarnies on the table, but no sign of David when Lily entered the kitchen, and she wondered if she had only imagined him being there.

'David's gone to look at the barn,' Abi explained, handing her another mug of tea. 'Do you want to take your sarnie along, and just have your tea now?'

'I'll have one now, thank you, and come right out. You go ahead.' Lily took one of the juicy sandwiches and put it on a plate. Determined not to embarrass herself in front of David Stanton again by dribbling brown sauce down her T-shirt, she sat down on a chair.

'I'll take the rest along if you don't mind then; poor David has not had any breakfast either,' he said. He lives by himself,' Abi added with a wink, 'poor lad. I bet he has carried a torch for that Susanna lass ever since.'

Lily stopped chewing. This was getting better and better. 'Susanna? As in, Susanna Harper?'

'There is no other Susanna around here. They were childhood sweethearts back then, her and David. We all thought they would stay together, you know, get married, settle here … Mind you, I have never noticed a man living in Rose Cottage either, apart from her dad, bless his soul, so she might well have been waiting for *him* to come back.' She sighed wistfully. 'We never thought he would though. Not after all these years.'

'But he has.'

Abi nodded. 'Yes. He has indeed. Well,' she said, gripping the tray, 'I suppose I'd better bring him some breakfast then, hadn't I, so at least he doesn't have to face the ghosts of his past on an empty stomach. If there are any, that is.

He may well be over it for all we know and just never cared to come back.'

Funnily, Lily could not imagine that that was the case, as she watched her aunt carrying the tray across the yard. There had to be something that had enticed him to come back after all these years ... Or was her imagination running away with her again? But surely, he must have better things to do than to come here and look at a crumbling old barn, only to tell them there was nothing he could do to save it ...

Like fixing his love life?

Stop it, Lily. Shaking her head, she got up and took her mug and plate to the sink, where she stood for a minute, looking out at the hills beyond the farm gates. *You are being too romantic. These things happen in books, remember, or in films, not in real life.*

***

'Wow — how long has the barn been like this, Abi?'

David was looking up at the remains of the wooden beams that had once formed the roof, letting out a low whistle.

Putting a hand to the small of her back, Abi followed his gaze and shook her head. 'I don't know really. It used to be the dairy, back when my parents had cows. But it hasn't been in use since then, and don't ask me when it was built in the first place. About a hundred years ago perhaps?'

David walked around the building and looked back at them through a gaping hole where there had once been a window. 'Yes, that is a good guess. I would have dated it back to the turn of the century. So, with any luck it is not listed — that's important, Lily, if you want to take on this project. Have you got a project manager yet? I could recommend someone. Becky Jessop in Ripon. She's very good, but also very busy. She owes me a favour though, so maybe I could put in a good word for you. Only if you like of course,' he added, looking from Abi to Lily.

'That would be lovely, thank you. My dad said we might need a project manager. He's a builder, too. Down in the Cotswolds,' Lily explained. 'So — what do you think then? Would holiday cottages be a good idea? I mean, instead of the …' She still found it difficult to let go of her original idea but made herself think of Miss Lavender's shop and said, 'book barn?'

Of course it did not matter what David Stanton thought, but somehow Lily needed to hear another opinion, if only to reassure her they were doing the right thing. She could not afford to fail — and Abi couldn't either, seeing as the future of Fern Hill Farm was at stake.

'Oh yes,' he said, nodding enthusiastically, 'absolutely. You could even have two cottages — the barn is big enough, and you could always have an extension built on each side to accommodate the kitchen, or even create an extra room?'

And create an extra source of income, you mean, Lily thought. *But why not? If I can't have the book barn, I might as well make the most of the alternative. The sensible alternative*, she reminded herself. 'Yes, that would be good. We could create an enclosed courtyard with those extensions … yes, I like that.'

And she did — in her mind, she was already picturing the cottages now, with pretty ceramic name plates on the whitewashed walls — the *Curlew* and the *Lapwing*, named after her favourite moorland birds. She especially loved the soft call of the curlew which she could often hear when they circled above the fields behind the farm.

'So, do you want me to contact Becky? About the barn?'

Snapping out of her reverie about cottages and curlews, Lily realized David was smiling at her. 'Oh! Yes, please do. We'd appreciate that very much, thank you.' She exchanged a glance with Abi, who nodded and said, 'Yes, indeed we would. Thank you, David. More coffee?'

David nodded, already searching the contacts on his iPhone. 'Yes please. Tell you what, I'll give her a quick ring now. No time like the present. If she is too expensive, you can always say no. You are aware this barn conversion won't come cheap though, aren't you?'

'We are, yes. I'm sure we can always put the farm down as security when it comes to the mortgage, can't we?'

Lily felt something pulling her stomach together as she heard her great-aunt talking about the farm. *I must not let her down*, she thought. *Whatever I do, I must not let her down.*

'Oh, there are specialist lenders who deal with that sort of thing. Becky will link you up with one of those, don't worry. They have specific criteria that need to be met, and the type of holiday let mortgage will also depend on the type of building, in this case, a barn you already own but which needs to be converted first. Excuse me a minute —' He stepped aside, leaving Lily and Abi to wait.

'I say, he is not a man prone to dawdling, is he? Gets right to the point. I like him.'

Lily rolled her eyes. 'Of course you like him. He is nasty old Nettleton's long-lost step-son — or not stepson, rather.' She frowned. 'What is he to Nettleton?'

Abi shrugged. 'Nothing, I suppose. Same as Brian Nettleton is nothing to him. And why should he be, the way he treated him and his poor mother?'

Lily nodded absent-mindedly. But then suddenly a thought

struck her. 'Are you sure you didn't know it was David Stanton? The woodcarver Pete Burns was talking about?'

Abi bristled. 'Of course I didn't! I had no idea! If I had, I would have told you, wouldn't I?'

'I suppose you would, yes,' Lily grinned, 'and all of Bishops Bridge, for that matter!'

Abi huffed. 'You make me sound like an old gossip!'

'Aren't you?'

Watching David as he talked into his phone while walking up and down the track, raking a hand through his hair, Lily couldn't help but wonder — had Pete set the whole thing up to get his friend to come back to Bishops Bridge, mixed up dates and all? Because he wanted him to see Susanna again? She shook her head. No. Matchmaking was a woman's business, wasn't it? Most men weren't even romantic enough to think of such things. Maybe Pete didn't even know about Susanna. And even if he did —

'Right,' David said, slipping his phone back into the pocket of his jeans and picking up his mug. 'That's settled. Becky says she can come tomorrow, when Pete and the architect are here. I thought that would save you another trip up here. She also says I am to give you her number so you can be in touch should anything come up.' He winked. 'In the meantime, I'll text Pete and let him know Becky is coming. He has worked with her before, he won't mind, especially as I take it you won't be here all the time. If you go back to Oxford, I mean?'

Feeling a bit overwhelmed, Lily — who had not expected things to develop quite so quickly in only one weekend — hurried to say, 'Oh. Yes, of course — good thinking. Thank you, David. And I'm sorry you came here for … well, nothing much really. To look at a crumbling old barn.'

David grinned. 'Aw, don't worry, that's alright. I got a good breakfast, didn't I? And I think the holiday cottages are a great idea. This is a lovely place — you'll be booked out all year. And if you do have any money to spare,' he winked, 'you can always commission a nice bench in front of the cottages. I'll leave my business card with you, just in case.'

'Sure — just in case,' Lily said, taking the card and wondering if she should drop it outside Rose Cottage when she was next walking Theo — quite accidentally, of course. And with no romantic intention at all. 'But thanks for coming, David, and for organizing a project manager for us. That was really kind of you.'

'Not at all. Right,' he said, draining his coffee and putting down his mug. 'I'll be off then. Thanks for the sandwiches, Abi. And good luck with your barn, Lily!' He gave her the thumbs up and took the last bacon sandwich before he walked back to his car, waving cheerfully. 'Bye!'

They were just getting back to the house when there was an almighty crash coming from the lane, followed by door slamming and a woman shouting furiously.

'What *on earth* did you think you were doing, reversing out of a farm entry without looking? Honestly, you'd think that …'

But they did not get to hear what Susanna Harper thought because she had either broken off or dropped her voice to a whisper. Lily had a hard time stopping Abi who would have run to the gate to see what was happening.

'I'm sure they can sort it out between them, Abi, they are grown-ups,' Lily said, fighting her own urge to look across to where Susanna and David were now standing in the middle of the lane, staring at each other in disbelief.

Twenty years, she thought, shaking her head as she took up the coffee tray. *So it does happen in real life. And right here in Bishops Bridge, too.*

CHAPTER TWENTY-FIVE

'So, what's it to be — tea, gin and tonic, or a walk?'

David stared at Susanna as if she were a ghost. She had to be — this couldn't really be happening to him. He could not speak. He could not move. Had he known whose car he had hit, he would not even have got out of his in the first place. Of course she was absolutely right, he should have looked more carefully. But then this lane was so quiet, if you happened to meet more than two tractors and a car in one day, you'd call that heavy traffic. How could he have been so stupid?

'Hello? Did you hear what I said? Tea, gin and tonic, or a walk? Up to you, really, but I'm not going to stand in the middle of the road until the cows come home.'

David shook himself, blinked, swallowed, and — no. Try as he might, the words would not come. There was absolutely nothing he could think of to say to her.

You are as beautiful as ever. He cringed. Ugh! Too cheesy. True, but still — no.

You haven't changed at all. Nice, but not really true. She *had* grown older, same as him. And yet ... her emerald eyes were the same, and her sensual lips, the colour of cherries and so deliciously full, he could have kissed her right here in the street. And that gorgeous red hair — had it always been this long? It almost went down to the back of her knees. She was *so* beautiful.

And then she did something that brought him right back to reality: Closing the space between them, she stood in front of him and kissed him full on the mouth.

Startled, he took an involuntary step back. 'Susanna!'

She shook her head, smiling mildly. 'Yes. It's me. Glad you still recognize me after all these years — twenty next week, isn't it? On the nineteenth.'

'But — how do you …?'

'It was two days after my birthday. I could hardly forget that, could I?'

He shook his head. 'No. Of course not. I'm sorry, Susanna — for the pain I caused you, and the mess I left behind when I walked out of your life.'

'Don't be. We were both very young, we made mistakes and … anyway,' she said, exhaling visibly, 'shall we go for a walk? We can have a look at the damage first, and leave the cars in my yard. Unless you have other plans?'

'No. I came here because … oh, never mind. I can tell you all about that while we walk. I was just wondering — can I perhaps do that again?' He was thinking of the kiss, of course, but either Susanna didn't get the hint, or she misunderstood him deliberately. Knowing her, he supposed it had to be the latter.

'What, reverse into my car? I don't think so. It was my dad's car, by the way. He died fifteen years ago. Cancer,' she explained. 'So I'm rather fond of the car, old as it is.'

'Gosh, I'm so sorry.' He raked his hands through his hair. 'Can you forgive me? We'll get it fixed as soon as possible.

Or I will, rather.'

Susanna shrugged. At the sound of an oncoming vehicle, she hopped back into the battered old Jeep and slammed the door shut. 'You'll find the way?'

***

Having left both cars outside Susanna's cottage, they followed the path which led them to Upper Rye Farm where David remembered the Bells breeding their famous Guernsey Cows. There were some grazing in the field, so he guessed they were still breeding. She told him all about her parents and how she had come back to live with her mum after her dad had passed away, and set up her business at Rose Cottage.

'I paint pets and other animals for people, and sell them. Sometimes landscapes, too. I turned Dad's workshop into a studio — you remember he was a luthier, don't you? —, then I asked somebody to design a website for me, and — well, here I am, painting for a living. Oh, and I teach art one day a week, at the local primary school. Bit of extra money …' She looked wistful. 'It worked well — for both of us. Sadly, it didn't last …' She bit her lip. 'Mum died last year. Heart attack. It all happened so quickly … one moment she was pegging the washing on the line in the garden, the next I found her lying on the ground. By the time the ambulance arrived, it was too late. They couldn't bring her back.'

There were tears in her eyes, and his heart went out to her as he stopped to take her in his arms. 'Oh, Susanna! I'm so sorry to hear that. Poor you! That must have been terribly hard … Your parents were very kind. You must miss them dreadfully.'

Susanna let out a long, wistful sigh. 'I do. Especially mum. Dad is … well. That's long ago now. I still have four of his most precious violins. Every time I look at them, I think of him and —' She shrugged. 'Life is not fair. But sometimes we get the most extraordinary surprises —like you coming back to Rosedale after twenty years! I still can't believe you are really here.'

'Me neither,' he said, gently wiping a tear from her cheek. 'I suppose we have to thank Lily for that. If it hadn't been for her and her romantic book barn ideas, I would never have come.'

Susanna nodded, biting her lip. 'I see.'

Placing both hands on her shoulders, he said, 'Susanna. Listen, please. I know I shouldn't have walked out on you like that. I'm so sorry I did. Even today I am full of shame and regret — which is probably why I never came back.' He shook his head and let his gaze wander across the fields, taking in the serene beauty of the dale. 'I was ashamed, Susanna. So I tried to live my life as best as I could, and thought I'd better let you get on with living yours. I thought I would never see you again … And of course I never expected you to still be here after all these years. I would have thought you had married some decent guy and moved away to some — I don't know … happier place. But you always were a homebird, weren't you? You would never leave Rosedale unless you really, really had to.'

Susanna did not say anything. She just stood there, the gentle breeze ruffling her beautiful long, red hair, as she stared into the distance. All was quiet except the distant gurgling of the beck. Finally she said, 'No. I wouldn't. But I refuse to torment myself with questions about what might have been. There is no point. Just like we will never know why we did what we did, or what all this was good for. But in the end, you did come back. And I'm glad.'

He smiled as he lifted her hand, slowly kissing every finger, his eyes never leaving hers. 'Are you?'

'I am,' she nodded, and her lips curved into a soft smile. 'And I will be forever grateful to Lily and her romantic book barn ideas, as you call them. She is so sweet — a bit crazy perhaps, but so am I, so that's alright.' Suddenly she laughed. 'Had I known you were coming, I might have warned you of course. Never trust a girl who talks to her donkey!'

'Her donkey??'

'Yes. Abi has a donkey, William, who is Lily's best friend. She walks him past my cottage whenever she is here, all the way up to the Bells' place and back. And, as I said, she talks to him. But hey, I talk to my cat.'

'Oh dear,' he deadpanned. 'Well, that explains everything of course.'

She nudged him and he nudged her back playfully. They both laughed, and he took her hand as they continued along the way up the hill until they came to the track that would lead them past the kilns and all the way down to Rosedale Abbey. While they walked, he told her about his woodcarving business and the little cottage he had over in Nidderdale.

'And —' she hesitated and kept her gaze firmly on the track ahead, 'is there a Mrs Stanton in Holly Cottage?'

'No. There is no one — no wife, no girlfriend, just me. I've been thinking about getting a dog but haven't got round to it yet. I'm not even sure I have the time … Most days I'm either stuck in the workshop or out and about in my truck, delivering, building …' He shrugged. 'I like to keep myself busy.' *As long as I am busy, I don't have time to dwell on the past. On the things that might have been. If I had never left. If I had come back. If …*

'I'm the same. But at least I've got a cat I can talk to. And some really nice neighbours.'

He nodded thoughtfully. 'So … you live alone, do you? With your cat?'

She gazed up at him with her sparkling emerald eyes. 'Yes.'

Yes. How much meaning, how much promise could there be in one single word? *Yes.*

His chest tightened with emotion, and he stepped towards her at the same moment as she moved, and wrapped her in his arms. 'Oh Susanna,' he said, into her hair, breathing in the sweet scent of her shampoo, like a long-forgotten memory. 'My dearest darling Susanna …'

And as she lifted her mouth to his, he cupped her face in his hands and kissed her.

CHAPTER TWENTY-SIX

When Lily arrived at the *Red Grouse*, the others were waving to her from a table in the garden. Jessie, who looked beautiful in her simple floral dress and her blonde hair swept up in a lose ponytail, was just sitting down with a glass of wine but got up again when she saw Lily.

'Hey! Happy birthday!' Lily kissed her cheeks and placed the wrapped present in front of her. 'I know you don't need anyone to tell you how to make cappuccinos and lattes, but I saw it in a bookshop in Helmsley and had to get it for you, anyway. Hope you like it.'

'I'm sure I will, thank you. It's very thoughtful of you. And there is always something you can learn from a good cookbook. So, it's about coffee, yes?'

Jessie was just beginning to unwrap the present when suddenly a large, black Labrador Lily had not noticed before jumped up, nearly upsetting the table he was tied to in the process.

'Oh, God, no! Bruno, no! Anna!'

At that moment a woman with long hair the colour of milk chocolate came running from the pub and literally dived at the dog's front paws, grabbing him by the collar to pull him down. 'Down! I said, down!' And to Jessie, she said, 'I'm so sorry, Jess. I really thought I could get away with going to the loo and leave him here for five minutes, but no — *you* are a bad dog,' she said to Bruno who was busy searching the ground for food with his huge black muzzle, making indecent slobbering noises whenever he found a crumb. 'I should never have brought you!'

Bruno ignored her. He had found a soggy old chip covered in tomato sauce, and settled down to munch on it.

Jessie shook her head laughing. 'Oh, Anna, you say that *every time* — and you know you could never leave him at home! It's fine, we're outside. Well, for the time being at least.' She looked at the swiftly gathering clouds above. 'It does look like we're in for something, doesn't it? — Come on, Lily, let's get you a drink. Where is Joseph? Isn't he coming?'

Lily flopped onto the bench next to Jessie. 'He is, but he said he'd come straight to the pub, just as soon as he had finished surgery. He should be here any minute. And a drink would be lovely, thank you, although I'm driving, so I'd better stick to elderflower cordial.'

While Ben went to get the drinks, Lucy came over, phone in hand, and kissed Lily's cheeks. 'Hey, Lily, good to see you — look, here's our dream cottage! Isn't it pretty? The Railway Cottage,' she read aloud, 'I love it! It's halfway between Kirkbymoorside and Pickering, so perfectly situated for us. Did I tell you we were getting married in February? I have always wanted a winter wedding — complete with a horse-drawn sleigh! Or a pony-drawn gig, in case it rains rather than snows. Which is,' she cocked her head in the most charming way, '… quite possible.'

Lily laughed. 'Yes, quite. Although from what I hear winters can be quite tough up here. I have seen pictures of this very pub all snowed in.'

Lucy's eyes widened. 'Ooh, yes, I remember. That was a nightmare of a winter. Anyway, I mean to borrow a set of Abi's ponies for the church, Delilah and — what's her name? Clover, isn't it, the other dapple white she bought just before her brother died? He never knew, I think — he said he had stopped counting them ponies! Anyway, so Delilah and Clover are going to pull the sleigh — or gig — and I'm sure they will look perfectly adorable, even if they are only ponies, and only almost white.'

At least it is not the Daisy Cow that is going to draw the sleigh, Lily thought and had a hard time suppressing a snigger — from what she had heard about that wondrous cow it would not have surprised her in the least. But then a plough might have been more appropriate, and you could not very well go to church sitting on a plough, could you?

'I'm sure they will. They are so cute. By the way,' she said, taking a deep breath. 'I've got news, too — I'm going to work in Miss Lavender's new bookshop, and Abi and I are going to convert her old barn into holiday cottages. What do you think?'

'You're going to stay? Yay!' Lucy flung her arms around Lily, almost upsetting her glass in the process. 'That's brilliant news, Lily — does Jessie know? — Jessie!'

But Jessie, who had come back while they were talking about the wedding, was not listening. She had just unwrapped the book Lily had got her, about the *Art of Barista*, and gasped.

'Oh, God! Oh — oh, God!'

'What is it? Jessie, what's wrong?' Ben sat down next to her and put an arm around her shoulder. She was trembling violently.

'Is it about the book? Did I do something wrong? It's only about coffee ...' Lily stammered, but Jessie burst into tears, tore herself free from Ben's embrace, and ran away, sobbing.

'Oh dear,' Ben said, getting to his feet, 'I suppose I'd better go and check on her.'

When he had gone, everyone sat in stunned silence, each of them wondering what on earth could have upset Jessie so much. It couldn't be the book, could it? Surely not.

The first low rumble of thunder brought them back to the present, and they all got up quickly and collected their glasses to go inside, just as the first fat splashes of rain hit the table.

Just then Ben came back — alone.

'Where is she?'

Ben picked up his beer glass, found it empty, and put it down again. 'Inside, talking to Fiona. She's the only one who knows anything about Jessie's past — well, I know *a few* things, obviously, but not enough to explain this — ' he indicated the book that was lying on the table. 'I have no idea why a book about coffeemaking should have brought on this reaction. Is anyone having another beer?' He got up to walk to the bar without waiting for anyone to reply.

'Me, please — hey, what's going on? Where is the birthday girl?'

Without any of them noticing, Joseph had arrived on the scene, bearing a bunch of flowers and looking more than a bit nonplussed.

'With Fiona, crying her heart out over a blooming book your girlfriend here gave her,' Ben retorted and turned his back to them, making Lily's cheeks flush crimson with embarrassment and anger. She had not done it on purpose, had she? For all any of them knew, it might not even be about the book at all.

'A book? How can she be crying about a book? Is it this one?' Joseph asked, picking up the offensive book and turning it around. '*Barista — the art of coffee making.*' He frowned as he looked up, completely clueless. 'Whatever should be wrong with that?'

Greg shrugged. 'I don't know. Maybe it isn't about the book at all. Come on, guys, let's get inside before we get soaked.'

'Good point,' Anna said and picked up Bruno's lead. 'Come on, boy, in you go — oops! Oh no! No!'

At *in you go*, Inigo had plunged forward to say hello in his characteristically enthusiastic fashion, complete with wagging backside, lolling tongue, and happy barking all around. Bruno, always up for a game of chase, thought it was a brilliant idea, and soon they were chasing each other around their respective owners' legs, tying their leads around them in the process.

'Stop! Stop, Stop, STOP!' Anna shouted, her head red as a beetroot. 'Bruno! Sit! Down! Now!' He did, and she quickly freed herself of the lead, and marched him towards the car park. A minute later she was back — alone.

'He is not my favourite dog today.'

'Well,' Lucy said, wiping her eyes, 'at least he has cheered us up — and look who has started it all! Inigo! You really are the worst behaved dog in all of Rosedale.'

'Except he doesn't live in Rosedale but in Ryedale,' remarked Joseph. 'And he will go to bed without his dinner tonight, won't you, Inigo?'

***

They were sitting at a corner table inside the pub when Jessie came to join them five minutes later, eyes and nose red from crying, but with a brave smile on her face. 'Hello there — sorry about that.' She sat down next to Ben and picked up a menu, just as if nothing had happened at all. 'So, what is everyone having? And where is my wine glass? Ben?'

Ben looked up. 'Sorry?'

'My wine? Have you drunk it?'

'Oh!' Lucy cried, looking guiltily at the almost empty wine glass in front of her. 'I'm so sorry, I must have up picked yours out there. I'll get you another one. Are you coming, Lily?' Without even waiting for a response, Lucy dragged Lily with her.

As soon as they were out of earshot, Lucy whispered, 'I think I know what this is all about. Or at least I have a feeling — it may not be the book, but *the author* she got so upset about. Nate Sullivan. I googled him just now, and from what I know about Jessie, I have reason to believe he may be Louisa May's father.'

Lily paled with shock. 'What? Oh no! And I have put my foot in! Oh, why didn't I *think*?'

'Well, you weren't to know, were you? Anyway, *if* Nate Sullivan really is Louisa May's father, Jessie has every reason to be upset of course — especially because I don't think she ever told him. That he has a daughter, I mean. As far as I know, Louisa May has no idea who her father is, which might make things a little more complicated at some stage, if you know what I mean. One day she will want to know. She has a right, after all — but then, so has he ...' Lucy shook her curls. 'Oh dear. What a dilemma.'

'But how did they meet? And why didn't they stay together?'

Lucy shrugged. 'I don't know the details, to be honest — Jessie doesn't really talk about herself … I think he was a boy she went to school with. They were close friends, but nothing more. And then her sister died, and — yeah, I think that was when it happened. Or maybe it was a party, and they all got drunk? I don't know. I don't think she even mentioned his name … only that he went to Africa after school, to volunteer on some coffee plantation.'

'Her sister died? Oh no! Poor Jessie!'

'Yes. It was awful. Michelle died in an accident when she was sixteen. A car hit her while she was roller skating along a winding country lane. They say she was dead the instant the car hit her — as if that would help.' She shook her head. 'Jessie's never got over it, I think. That's why she is so fiercely protective of Louisa May. As for her mother … she has never been the same since. A nightmare!'

A nightmare indeed, Lily thought and nodded. To lose a sister at so young an age — and in such a horrible accident, too! No wonder Jessie was so quiet. It also explained why Lily often thought she saw a shadow crossing her friend's face. 'I didn't know, no. Poor Jessie.'

'Yes. It's a terrible story. She's alright most of the time — I think her coming here with Louisa May was a good decision. And Ben is good for her. Even if he can be an eejit at times.'

'Oh yes,' Lily agreed, rolling her eyes. 'But — if you don't even know the name of Louisa May's father, how can you be sure he is the guy who wrote this book?'

'I'm not. It's just a feeling I have, because she reacted so strongly, and I thought, it can't be the book, so maybe it's the author? I googled him — here, read this.' She held her phone under Lily's nose. 'Nate Sullivan, born 4th August 1982, in Market Deeping, Lincolnshire, is a renowned

Barista, and founder of *The Coffee Experience* in Durham. Nate, who has won several barista competitions in the UK, first fell in love with coffee and coffee production during his time in Kenya where he volunteered on a small, organic coffee plantation run by female farmers after graduating from High School in Market Deeping in 2000 … Okay,' Lily said, handing the phone back, 'I don't have to read more. That's him, no doubt. Now what do we do? Or what do *I* do, rather? I gave her the book.'

'Oh, Lily, come on! It's not your fault. And who knows, maybe this is the kick she needs to put things right … come on, let's grab a couple of drinks and head back, the others are getting suspicious. Look, Joseph's coming to look for you! — How's things between you then?'

Lily blushed. 'Well …'

'Whatever is taking you so long?' Greg called as he came over to find them. 'Jessie has calmed down, and we are all ready to order our food. Come on, girls! Have you got Jessie's wine?'

Lucy rolled her eyes at Lily. 'And don't you think I'll let you off the hook! I'll sit next to you and watch you like a hawk, so I won't miss a thing! By the way, how did that encounter in the lane end, do you know? Between Susanna and David Stanton? Mum says she thought she saw them walking past the farm hand in hand …'

Lily laughed. 'Lucy! For heavens' sake, you are worse than Abi and your mum put together. If they really were holding hands, I'm sure we will find out soon enough. For now, we have a birthday to celebrate, and a friend to cheer up.' Grabbing the two wine glasses from the bar, she walked off, determined to make it up to Jessie. And not to give in to any kind of gossip, no matter how kindly meant.

CHAPTER TWENTY-SEVEN

THE FIRST THING Lily did when she got back to Oxford on Sunday evening was to run herself a bath. She was exhausted from the long drive, not to mention the excitement that the weekend had brought. When she had driven up to Yorkshire on Friday, she couldn't have dreamed of securing a job in a brand new bookshop on the same afternoon, meeting Nettleton's long-lost stepson and inadvertently (but literally!) pushing him into Susanna's way, giving Jessie a book written by her daughter's absent father, and finally, setting things in motion for the barn conversion faster than you could spell 'holiday cottages'! To say nothing of Joseph and how she felt about him — but was it right? Was it real?

She poured bath oil into the hot water and watched it spread slowly, while its fragrance (fittingly called Moorland Heather, bought in a small gift shop in Thirsk on the way home) rose up, filling her nostrils and making her heart ache with longing for that place she had grown to love so much.

But can I do this, she asked herself, her hand making slow circles in the smooth, fragrant water. *Can I really do this?*

You deserve to be happy. Even if that stupid nagging voice in your head keeps whispering you don't, you know you do. Don't listen to the lies inside your head. You did that before, and you know where that got you.

She smiled. *I don't even have to call Beth now to know what she would say*, she thought, and went into the kitchen to see if there was any wine in the fridge. There was, and when she had poured herself a glass, she took it back to the bathroom with her, along with the latest novel by Sarah Maine. Tonight, she would not worry about anything. She would just relax in the bath, enjoy her wine and her book, and then sleep.

But even after two glasses of wine and two hours worth of reading Lily could not sleep. Her thoughts kept drifting back to Jessie and the situation she had involuntarily put her in. She had texted her friend several times, apologizing over and over again, but the reply had always been the same. **Don't worry, it's fine.**

Only it wasn't, was it? But if Jessie refused to talk about it, then there was nothing she could do. Perhaps she could get her to talk when she was back in Rosedale. Because bottling up was never the answer — and being the expert in that department, she should know.

The other thing that was weighing on her mind was the Barn Project. Pete and the architect had arrived shortly after breakfast on Sunday, along with Becky, the project manager. Not much older than Lily, Becky Jessop was the most elegant woman Lily had ever seen, apart from Spencer's mum perhaps. Becky looked like a walking model for Barbour, except for the Mulberry handbag. Lily hoped she would not charge her accordingly.

Tomorrow, there would be two viewings, plus an online tour they would do for an American professor who would start teaching neuroscience at Magdalen College at Michaelmas. He had put down the ludicrous offer of £330,000, no doubt hoping he would snap up the apartment before anyone else had even had a chance to see it.

Putting her book on the bedside table, Lily switched off the light and closed her eyes. *Perhaps I had better try and think of something else*, she thought and yawned. Like of Myrtle, the goat, who was already driving poor Abi round the bend. Only this morning she had interrupted their breakfast by coming into the kitchen with a bunch of carrots in her mouth, dropping clumps of fresh earth to the floor.

'Myrtle! Out!' Grabbing the newspaper from the kitchen table, Abi had chased the goat out of the house and returned a moment later, sinking down on her chair with a sigh. 'That goat will be the death of me, I swear!'

Lily had given her an amused look. 'What did you expect? She's a Nettleton goat after all, she can't help being naughty. Pass me the jam?'

A smile spread over her face. Yes, that was better. Goats and donkeys, jam and cake. Country life at its best. What was not to love?

***

IT WAS TWO weeks later when Lily came back from work in the pouring rain, shedding her wet coat in the hall just as the telephone began to ring. She had stupidly forgotten to take an umbrella in the morning and had got completely soaked. To be fair, she had only bought the flimsy beige trench coat on a whim because it had reminded her of the final scene in *Breakfast at Tiffany's* where Holly and Fred rescue the cat in the rain. She probably didn't look as pretty as Audrey Hepburn in that scene either, but then that was the difference between Hollywood and real life, wasn't it? Obviously, she didn't have a cat either.

If I ever have one though, she thought as she hurried to pick up the phone, *I'll call her Cat.*

'Lily! Oh, I'm glad I caught you at last. I must have mislaid your mobile number ... Listen, lass, I might need you to come back a little sooner than I thought ...'

'What do you mean, *sooner than you thought*? I was going to come up for the village fête — that's in two weeks. Won't that do?'

'Well, I can't drag you up here, obviously, but ... I'm afraid I had an accident this morning. Dancer shied and came down on my left thigh with his front hoof, and now it's all swollen and black and blue and it hurts like hell. Nothing's broken, thank God, but I have had some stitches, so ... I was rather hoping you could come up for a few days. I know you have to work but —'

Lily sat up straight. 'Stitches? Abi, where on earth *are* you?'

'Still in A&E, I'm afraid. We had to wait for three and a half hours but I hope they are going to let me go now I'm all patched up.'

'We? Who is with you then?' Secretly she was relieved to hear that Abi was not alone and had hopefully not sat behind the wheel with her injured leg either.

'Susanna took me, bless her. She said she would help me, too, but I'd rather you did, to be honest. You know how to handle the ponies — and the goat! Not to mention William.'

Lily sighed. 'I can't, Abi. I'd love to, really, and — well, I could come up for weekends, I suppose, but I do have to work throughout the rest of the summer, I'm afraid, having used up all of my leave in the spring. Isn't there anyone else you can ask?' She tried to think of someone and found that she couldn't. She shook her head in despair. That was it, in a nutshell: If anything ever happened to her great-aunt — like this accident now — nobody would be able to do the job for her, and keep the farm going. There was nothing for it, she would have to talk to Hugh.

***

Having agreed to take unpaid leave for two weeks, Lily decided she should let her parents know about Abi's accident as well as her plan to drive up tomorrow. She would call Beth, too, and give her an update — she knew her friend would be thrilled to hear she was really moving on now.

'Hello, sweetheart, that's a nice surprise!' her mum said. 'Dad and I were just talking about you and your project. When were you planning to go up and take a look at the barn?'

'Tomorrow,' Lily blurted out, not even taking the hint about her dad and the barn. 'That's why I'm calling — Abi had an accident, and she needs help.'

'Oh! I see. Poor Abi. But Lily, why didn't you ask me? I could have gone. I have time, you know, and I can handle the ponies, too. I mean, it's very kind of you, sweetheart, but ... wait a minute! How about Dad and I join you at the weekend and perhaps stay for a couple of days? You wanted Dad to see the barn and hear all about your plans, anyway. You have not forgotten, have you?'

Lily closed her eyes. She had, utterly and completely. And of course, she could have asked her mum. Why hadn't she thought of that? Why hadn't *Abi* thought of that? She knew Maureen would do anything for her, and for the horses.

'I'm sorry, Mum. You are right, I forgot completely. Please tell Dad I didn't mean to. And I would love for you to come up to Rosedale at the weekend. Tell Dad I will show him the barn, and make him a nice cheese and onion pie, too,' she added, knowing how her dad loved a good pie.

Her mum laughed. 'Oh, Lily! You don't have to do that. Your dad will forgive you anything — but it's sweet of you to say you'll make a pie. I'll feed him on salad leaves until the weekend then. No puddings!'

When she had rung off, Lily rinsed her mug and put it back into the cupboard, thinking how often she must have done this over the last three years. One of the many little habits and routines she had rigorously kept up in an attempt to make her life feel safe and …

She stopped, her hand on the handle of the cupboard. But it had never been *safe*, had it? It hadn't been a home either. And what was more, it had not even been a life … She had lived, but she had not felt *alive*. Not like she felt when she was with her new friends in Yorkshire. Without realizing it, she had built herself a neatly stacked house of cards — and that house had collapsed the day Spencer had died. With all her certainties in life suddenly stripped away, she had been left with a pile of cards that wouldn't hold together anymore.

It was time she threw them away.

***

THE NEXT MORNING, she was on the road north once more, pushing the poor Mini to its limit on the motorway. She had flung a few clothes into her suitcase last night after she had talked to Beth for nearly two hours and realized it was too late to be fastidious about her packing (which she usually was – but maybe that was the old Lily). *What does it matter if I fold or roll my sweaters*, she had thought, throwing in another couple of T-shirts for good measure, *I'll be living on a farm, not in a castle!*

Predictably, Beth had been excited for her and reassured her that everything would be fine, even if some things did not quite go to plan, like the book barn.

'A bookshop on the High Street sounds lovely! I'm sure you have made the right decision. Miss Lavender sounds an interesting lady. I should like to meet her — and all of your new friends, especially the charming vet!'

Lily shook her head, smiling at Beth's cheeky comment, and the effortless way in which she had then changed the subject. 'I can't wait to come to Yorkshire and buy some books from you. Picture books for the children, a nice, sweet romance or two for myself … oh, you can send me a list with recommendations! And talking of lists, I'm sure you have drawn up a nice long one called *All the things I need to do before I go to Yorkshire*, and pinned it to the kitchen door, haven't you?'

Lily had turned to look at the kitchen door, and taken a sip of her wine. 'I haven't made a list. It's all in my head.'

'*All in your head?*' Beth had said, laughing. 'I see. Well, I won't keep you then, before you forget to pack your underwear. You don't have to take thermals in June, do you?'

CHAPTER TWENTY-EIGHT

'WOULD YOU DO me a really big favour while you are here?'

They were sitting in Abi's kitchen sampling a new recipe Lily had just tried out, sticky toffee flapjacks, but Abi looked pale and tired, which worried Lily. The wound had developed a nasty infection and the GP had put Abi on a course of antibiotics. By rights, she should spend her days on the sofa watching daytime telly, and not hopping around the farm feeding ponies. Lily had had a hard time persuading her to rest these past three days, and was counting the hours until the arrival of her parents tomorrow. She hoped her mum would be able to talk some sense into Abi.

Pouring the tea, she said, 'That depends. Not if it involves Nettleton's livestock — there's no way I'm setting foot on that farm again!'

'And you won't have to, I promise. I haven't been there since the accident — now don't give me that look! I haven't, cross my heart and all that. No, it's about the village fête on Sunday. As member of the WI, I promised to make some cakes and man the WI stall for two hours, too. Seeing as I can hardly *stand* on that leg, never mind walk around, I was wondering if you would go in my place. And help make the cakes perhaps?'

'Of course I will! That's what I'm here for, remember? To help you. And two hours isn't too bad. How many cakes did you promise to make?'

'Oh, just a couple of trays full of scones, a curd tart, and a Victoria Sponge. Do you think you can manage that?'

Lily popped the last piece of flapjack into her mouth and nodded. 'No problem. And mum and dad will be here, too, so you could not have timed this better — sorry,' she grimaced, 'I didn't mean you *planned* to have your thigh kicked black and blue. And believe me, I know what that feels like — I had an encounter with that wicked gander, remember? Although it probably wasn't nearly as bad.'

'Oh, I don't know — I still think we should eat him for Christmas. But now that Nettleton is back, that might prove a little difficult. I just wish he'd stop pestering me about —' She stopped. 'Oh. Never mind.'

But Lily did mind. If there was one thing she was going to find out one of these days it was why on earth Abi had been letting that nasty man bully her into helping him when she did not even like him. What kind of arrangement had they agreed on since his release from the hospital, she wondered. She hoped it did not involve anything beyond throwing the geese some grain. 'Pestering you about what? Don't tell me you have been cooking for him while I was in Oxford! Abi?'

The way Abi winced told her she had hit the spot. 'I know. I should never have offered ... I just felt so sorry for him, you know, when he came back. I don't know what Mary was *thinking* — leaving her father to fend for himself when he can't even walk properly ...'

'Oh, he could walk alright the last time he barged in here! And his precious daughter hopefully has enough brains to think of things like meals on wheels, never mind arranging for a nurse to come in twice a day or something. It's her father, for goodness' sake, so he's *her* responsibility, not yours!'

A message flashed up on her screen, and Lily, hoping it would be from Joseph, hurried to pick up her phone. She had not seen him since she came back because he was at some veterinary conference in Edinburgh and would not return before Saturday. But the message wasn't from him, it was from Jessie.

> Sorry I've been such a stranger, and sorry for getting so upset about your present, too. I know it's not your fault at all. Next time you're in Bishops Bridge, do get in touch. We can share a pizza and a bottle of wine at my place if you like. Jessie x

> Tonight? I'm right here — Abi had an accident with a horse and can't walk. Lily x

Jessie sent her a thumbs up emoji, and Lily put the phone away, returning her attention to Abi. 'That was Jessie, asking if I'd like to come over tonight. You don't mind, do you?'

'Of course not! Why should I mind? You go on and have some fun while you're here.'

'Alright then. But you must promise you won't set foot on Nettleton's farm!'

'I can't, can I?' Abi said pointedly, looking down at her thigh.

'As if that would stop you,' muttered Lily. Turning to Theo, she said, 'I trust you to look after your mistress then. Make sure she does not leave the house. Do you hear that?'

Theo gazed up at her from underneath his bushy eyebrows, as if he would never so much as set a foot outside himself without asking her permission. Then he gave a soft whine and curled himself into a ball at Abi's feet, pushing his nose under his front paws, and closed his eyes.

'Hm. I'm not sure I can trust him, but I'm afraid I have no choice. Right,' she said, getting to her feet, 'I'll get the ponies now and you *rest*. Okay? R.e.s.t. I'll do the shopping tomorrow, so maybe you could write me a list? You can put all the cake ingredients on it, too.' *Maybe add a wee bottle of arsenic for that horrible old man next door, to go with his tea?*

She left the farmhouse shaking her head. *Feeding Mr Nettleton! Of all people.*

***

THEY WERE HALFWAY through the second bottle of wine when Jessie told her about the accident — and how it had led to her falling pregnant. 'My sister Michelle — she was only fifteen months younger than me, so we were very close, almost like twins — was skating along a country road when a car hit her — she was dead the moment he hit her, the police said. There was nothing anyone could have done. One second was all it took …'

'Oh, no!' Lily's hand flew to her mouth. Although she already knew her sister had died in a skating accident, it was awful to hear Jessie talk about it. And to see the sadness in her eyes, too, even after fourteen years.

'It's okay, it's a long time ago now. But I'll never forget that terrible day. I had been out with some friends, and when I came home …' She shook her head. 'The moment I walked into the house, I knew something was wrong. Mum was crying. Dad was crying. Two policemen were there, and the vicar — I remember thinking, *where is Michelle?* When the vicar, who had known us since we were little girls … when he told me there had been an accident …' Jessie bit her lip. 'I remember screaming at the top of my lungs. I remember kicking and biting and pushing my way through all the people who were trying to stop me, up the stairs to my sister's room, calling her name again and again until I lost my voice. I remember sitting in her room all night, willing her to come back.'

Tears were running down her face now, and Lily's heart went out to her. 'I remember how the vicar told me about the accident — he had been cycling along the same lane, and arrived at the scene shortly afterwards. The driver had already tried resuscitation and called the ambulance, but there was nothing anyone could have done. They said she would not have felt any pain. I never believed that though … same as I never believed the driver did not see her, or really tried his best resuscitating her. I didn't want to hear about his shock, either. What did I care about that man? He had killed my beloved sister! And I heard her screaming in my nightmares. Nightmares that would not go away for weeks and months, and sometimes still haunt me.'

Lily went over to her and hugged her tight. 'Oh, Jessie! Poor you! Poor, poor you. I'm so sorry.'

'It's okay now. I have Louisa May, I have my café — lots of things to be grateful for. It's Mum we worry about. She never got over this. No therapy, no counselling in the world could help her. She even went to a clinic in Switzerland. Waste of time.' She sighed. 'She's *always* worried about Louisa May. If it had been down to her, we would never even have bought her a tricycle, never mind a bike! If Mum knew Louisa May had *skates*, she would have a heart attack. It's why I had to move away, you see, when Louisa May was four. We'd been living with my parents, but it didn't work. We needed a new start.'

Jessie got up and poured two large glasses of water. Handing one to Lily, she said, 'So, about Nate — you may have guessed he is Louisa May's father — and how I ended up pregnant ... One night, about three months after the accident, Nate and I were sitting on a bench in the park talking. He was my best friend, so I was crying my heart out to him, like you do with best friends ... about how I was worried my mum would end up in an asylum or something ... or dad would have enough one day and move out ... Nate was a good listener. And then — I don't know ... one thing led to another, and suddenly we were kissing, and ... well. Eight weeks later I found I was pregnant. By then Nate had gone off to Africa, working on some voluntary project, and I was left with — well, not much of a choice really. I never once thought about giving up my baby, even if it meant I couldn't take my place at Cambridge. I had been offered a place, you see. But it wasn't meant to be.' A smile lit up her face as she turned to look at the framed photographs of her daughter on the wall. '*Louisa May* was meant to be. I never once regretted having her. She's my world — and a tonic to my parents.'

'Of course she is.' Lily reached out to touch Jessie's arm. 'And you have done an amazing job in bringing her up on your own. How did you come to choose Bishops Bridge of all places? Had you been here before?'

'Oh yes. We used to spend our summers here on the Moors when I was a kid, so there were lots of happy memories connected with Rosedale. — Do you want a coffee?' Jessie got up.

She is really restless, Lily thought, concerned for her friend. *This must bring back quite a lot of pain — and I thought I was grieving!*

'Coffee would be great, thanks.'

'Anyway, to cut a long story short, we moved to Bishops Bridge the summer Louisa May turned five and started school, and I worked part time in the *Red Grouse* and part time in the village shop. We lodged with Fiona and Dan for a while — they don't have any children, and were quite happy to have Louisa May in the house. They even built a sandpit and hung a swing in the pear tree for her. It's still there, and whenever we go for a meal at the *Red Grouse*, Louisa May insists she is not too old to sit on a swing!' Jessie laughed. 'Anyway. Two years later, having found out that baking was my real passion — I went on a training course for patisserie in York. When the couple who had run the café before me wanted to retire, I was able to take over their lease, and … yeah, everything seemed to fall into place and — here I am.'

'Wow,' Lily said, shaking her head in amazement, 'you are *so* brave!'

Jessie shrugged. 'Oh, I don't know about that — I'm just glad everything worked out the way it did. But then the people of Bishops Bridge are really kind and helpful, as I'm sure you will have noticed. When Ben offered me his cottage, I couldn't believe my luck, but then that's just the way he is — and just the way almost everybody is around here. Except Mr Nettleton, of course.'

Looking at each other, they burst out laughing.

***

Lily did not sleep well that night. She kept waking up from all sorts of different but all very confusing dreams — one of them had skating girls in them, laughing and waving to each other as they approached a bend in the road, another one featured a fell runner who ran straight into a herd of cattle, and the last one, from which she woke with a gasp at around five in the morning, was about her driving a car up a very steep and narrow road which brought her right up into the air — where it suddenly ended.

Throwing off her duvet, she wiped her brow, and crept downstairs to make herself a cup of tea. She sat on the sofa in Jessie's living room and looked at the family photographs on the wall. There were a few of a teenage Jessie and a girl who looked almost exactly like her — *Michelle*, she thought and swallowed hard. The sister Jessie had lost …

When Jessie came downstairs at seven, shouting for Louisa May to 'swing her legs out of bed this minute', she stopped dead when she saw Lily perched on the sofa.

'Hello? How long have you been sitting there? Not all night, I hope?'

Lily shook her head. 'No, don't worry. I just had — some … not so nice dreams. But I'm fine now. And I've got an idea. Are you awake enough to listen?' she asked, picking up her phone.

'Give me five minutes to make coffee, then I'm all yours. But I haven't got much time, really, so you'd better be quick.'

'That's okay, it won't take long.'

Lily watched Jessie as she busied herself with making two mugs of coffee and then sat down next to her on the sofa. 'So, I've been thinking — and what I've been thinking is …' She was almost too excited to speak and inhaled deeply before she plunged into explaining what she thought was the most brilliant idea. 'I think you should go and see Nate. You don't have to tell him about Louisa May. Just — well, go and see him. See what he's like.'

When Jessie did not respond, she went on to explain, ' You could do a training course, you know, at his coffee shop! It's in Durham, so not far at all. Look, I found his website …' Clearing her throat, she read, 'Here at *The Coffee Experience* we offer Barista Training courses as well as fun-and-information-packed behind-the-scenes tours and gourmet coffee tasting, including Nate's Kenyan inspired cakes and biscuits. That sounds great, doesn't it?' Lily turned to Jessie and beamed. 'Isn't that a fantastic opportunity? You can do something you enjoy, improve your skills — I'm not saying your coffee isn't any good or the cappuccinos don't look a picture, but there is always room for improvement, isn't there? — and … yeah, see what he's like. What do you think?'

To her horror, Jessie's face had turned very pale. In a voice that was almost dangerously calm (and did not sound like Jessie at all) she said, '*I think* you should go home now. And mind your own business. Now if you'll excuse me, I have to make breakfast — and no, I'd rather you didn't stay.'

With that, she picked up the mugs and marched through to the kitchen, leaving a confused Lily behind.

For a minute, she sat in stunned silence. When she had got her bag from upstairs, she put her head around the kitchen door, knocking softly on the frame. 'Jessie … I just wanted to say …'

But Jessie spun around, her blue eyes ablaze with fury. 'No, Lily, I don't want to hear your excuses. I don't even want to hear you say you're sorry because you can't be, you don't even understand! You were not listening at all last night. Just leave me, okay? Just leave me!'

***

When Abi found Lily crying in the barn later, she went to hug her and walked her back to the farmhouse, careful not to let Lily see the pain it caused her to walk. 'Let's have a good, strong cup of tea. And then you can tell me all about it — or leave it, just as you choose. Just put the kettle on, lass, and get the flapjack out. Remember you put it on the top shelf so the wretched goat can't get it.'

Over her tea, and in between half a pack of tissues, Lily told Abi all about Nate and the book and the stupid mistake she had made in thinking she could help Jessie find a way to reconnect with the father of her daughter. She knew it was not her secret to tell, but she didn't care. Abi could keep a secret, she knew that, for all that she loved a bit of gossip like most folks round here.

'It was so stupid of me! So very, very stupid!' Lily raged, ignoring the flapjack on her plate. 'Not to mention *thoughtless*! And now I have lost the one friend I thought I had already made — and my future neighbour in business! — before I have even moved here! Stupid, stupid me!'

'Now, you are not stupid — do you hear me? You are a very dear girl, and sometimes you are perhaps just a little … impulsive. You didn't think about the impact your suggestion might have on her, no matter how kindly meant. And that is because you do not know her very well — had you known her better, you would not have suggested she sign up on a course and go to Durham to see him. And certainly not at seven o'clock in the morning, just before her daughter would come downstairs for breakfast!'

Lily winced. 'I know … poor Jessie! But Abi, what do I do now?'

'Oh, don't worry, she'll come round. Just give her a little time.'

'But what if she doesn't? How can we ever be friends again after this? How can I even face her?'

Abi sighed. 'Because in my experience, nothing is ever beyond repair. Look at yourself, how you have recovered from your own heartbreak. Look at how strong you have grown! Jessie will be fine, and you will be friends again, I am sure of that.' Squeezing her arm, she said, 'Go, get your donkey, and take him for a walk. Or take Theo, he hasn't been out much lately. A bit of fresh air and exercise will do you good.'

Lily was not convinced, but seeing as there was little else she could do right now, she went to fetch William. *I can only try*, she thought with a little hiccup, and fastened the lead rope to the donkey's red halter, *to make it right again. We can, and should, always try and do our best. And if we fail, we must try again. Because ultimately* — she had read that somewhere but could not remember where — *we only fail if we refuse to try again.*

'And I can't fail Jessie,' she whispered as she led William across the yard, 'I can't fail Abi. Or any of them. I can't fail this here — it's my one chance at happiness, and at finding a home. I can't, and I won't, fail to make this work.'

CHAPTER TWENTY-NINE

SATURDAY BEGAN SUNNY and bright, with perfect watercolour blue skies and a gentle breeze, bees buzzing, and children squealing with delight as they dipped their toes into the icy cold water of the beck. Miles of colourful bunting was lined along the High Street and Church Lane, and the village green was dotted with white tents and rustic stalls. Lucy's granddad was just setting up the barbecue with his neighbours, Mr Talbot and Mr Wilkinson, while their respective wives were chatting to Abi, revealing the latest gossip — mainly about David Stanton's unexpected return, and him having been asked to design the interior of Miss Lavender's new shop.

'Custom-made shelves! By the Squirrel of Lofthouse – why, he comes almost as expensive as the *Mouseman*! How can she even afford it?'

'Martha Talbot!' Abi looked horrified. 'I hope she did not hear that! And anyway, it's none of our business, is it? If she wants David to make those shelves, that is entirely her decision. Personally, I believe it has more to do with bringing him back to Bishops Bridge than anything else …'

Three pairs of eyes were now looking at her expectantly,

willing her to share more of her private thoughts on the matter of David Stanton, but for once they were in for a disappointment. 'Does anyone else fancy a cuppa? I know I could do with one. Oh, look, there is my niece now, and her husband — they arrived last night, and Maureen is going to stay the week, bless her. — Cooee! Maureen! We're here!'

Martha Talbot and Ruth Wilkinson exchanged meaningful glances with Caroline Bell, who shrugged and poured them all a cup of tea. Meanwhile Abi, clearly not in the mood for gossip, turned to Maureen. 'Have you brought the Victoria Sponge? Did you find it alright?'

'Well — what was left of it. Someone must have left the door open, and I'm afraid someone else — a very naughty someone, possibly with two cute little horns — stole the cake.'

'Oh no!' Lily, who was busy arranging the scones, covered her face with both hands and shook her head in shame. 'It was me — I left the door ajar, thinking you were still in. Sorry! That was really careless of me. Now what?'

Martha Talbot and Caroline Bell sniggered, and Maureen hid her face behind a paper doily, but Abi just sighed. 'Well, there won't be any Victoria Sponge to sell now, that's for sure.' And when she saw the crestfallen look on Lily's face, she put a hand on her shoulder and said, 'Now don't fret, lass, we have more than enough cake, there's another stall run by Miss Lavender and her ladies from the church, and I suppose Jessie will be selling her cinnamon swirls. Look, there she is!'

Lily glanced over to where Jessie was just opening the flap of a cute wooden stall. It even had a sign that said *The Bridge Café*. But then she quickly looked away again, thinking that Jessie might not be too happy to see her.

'You're probably right, but still … I'm sorry. Shall I do the first two hours then, so you can have a little walk around with Mum and Dad?'

'I won't be walking around very much today though, will I? — Oh, look, there's Joseph! Did you know he was coming?' Abi pointed in the direction of the church car park where a small group was just getting out of a mud-splashed Land Rover, their laughter carrying across the bridge.

'No, I didn't …' Lily watched the group somewhat warily. Why was the woman just putting her hands against Joseph's chest, and reaching up to whisper something in his ear? Who was she, anyway?

'Don't you want to go and say hello to your young man?'

Lily turned to her dad who was smiling at her. She could hardly say no now, could she, without making a fool of herself? And what was the worst that could happen?

'Um … yes, I suppose I do. I'll be back soon.'

'Take your time, love, we will manage. Just remember your mum is dying to meet him, so if you have five minutes to come over here and introduce the young man …' He winked at Lily, and she could not help grinning back at him.

'Will do. See you later!'

When she reached Joseph, he was just trying to pull Inigo back from the burger stall. Luckily, there was no sign of the woman now. Maybe he had just given her a lift?

'Hello!' she called. 'I didn't know you were coming! Aren't you working today?'

'Lily!' he laughed, picking her up and whirling her around. 'That's a lovely surprise! I thought you would be busy on the farm. And no, I'm not working — not until Monday, in fact, which is a rare treat. How is your auntie?'

'Oh, she's fine. She's still in pain, obviously, but that

does not stop her from gossiping with her friends at the village fête, as you can see!' She rolled her eyes, indicating the group of grey-haired ladies surrounding Abi who was now sitting in the director's chair her dad had brought, and looking just a little bit like the Queen on holiday. Only the corgis were missing. 'My parents are here, too, and my mum is going to stay for a couple of days. In fact, I promised I would ...' ... *introduce you to them.* But she did not get to finish her sentence.

'*Joseph!*' The high-pitched voice of a woman cut through the air, causing people to turn their heads. 'Why didn't you wait for us? We don't know anyone here, do we? That's not fair!'

And there she was: a strikingly elegant looking woman in her mid-thirties, crossing the bridge, her face a mixture of anger, amusement, and something else Lily could not quite put her finger on. Flirtation? Possessiveness even? But before Lily had a chance to ask who she even was, the woman had reached them and touched Joseph's arm in a disturbingly familiar manner.

'You promised we were just going to have breakfast here, though why we couldn't have gone straight to York I don't know. There are such gorgeously sophisticated cafés there! I don't want to waste any of our precious time together at some stupid village fête, when I'm only here until tomorrow. — What time did you book the table at the *Ivy*, Liam?'

Lily turned to Joseph, unspoken questions burning in her eyes as she frowned at him. *Waste our precious time together? Only here until tomorrow?* What was that supposed to mean? Who is she?

But Joseph did not meet Lily's eye. He seemed strangely

distracted by this woman who was now busy straightening his collar. Why was he wearing a formal shirt when he had the weekend off? What was going on?

'Really, Joey, you can't even dress properly without my help! What are you like?'

Joey? Dressing without my help? This was getting better and better. Or worse and worse.

Lily was just going to say something (although what exactly she did not know, the situation being too bizarre) when a man she had not even noticed until now stepped forward, offering his hand. 'Hi, I'm Liam. I'm a friend of Joseph's, from veterinary college. And this impossible flirt here is my sister, Roisin. We're from Ireland. Well, I live in Ripon now, but … Roisin, take your hands off Joseph, you're embarrassing him!' Shaking Lily's hand cordially, he motioned for his sister to come forward, but Roisin was still busy with Joseph's shirt and took her time turning around. When their eyes met at last, Lily knew that woman was trouble.

With her mass of red curls tumbling down her back, cat-like green eyes set wide apart in a face with skin the colour of buttermilk, Roisin was the epitome of the Irish country lass. She was wearing stylish navy cigarette trousers and an expensive looking white blouse with a silk horseshoe print handkerchief tied around her slender neck. Needless to say, her small burgundy shoulder handbag was Mulberry. *What else*, thought Lily and squinted while trying to decide whether the colour of the handbag clashed with Roisin's hair. It didn't.

Roisin did not offer Lily her hand. She did not say hello either. In fact, she simply ignored her and went on brushing imaginary fluff off Joseph's shirtsleeves while he was busy keeping Inigo away from Roisin's feet. What he found so interesting about these, Lily could not imagine.

'Behave yourself, Inigo! Come on, let's say hello to Abi, shall we? Lily, why don't you —'

But Roisin gave an exaggerated sigh and pulled at Joseph's hand like an impatient child eager to get to the playground. Lily did not even want to imagine what that playground would look like for Roisin, and whether it would include a bed. 'Oh, *come on*, guys, I'm starving! I drove all night to be with you, Joey, and — ugh, Inigo! Stop it! Joseph, you haven't trained him at all!'

Lily smirked, silently applauding Inigo for being his usual naughty self. He had just licked the gold buckle of Roisin's patent leather shoes. With relish. Lily wished he had peed on them.

'Well — I tried my best.' With an apologetic smile, he turned to Lily. 'Do you mind if we just go and find some breakfast first? Roisin came over from Ireland late last night, and drove straight over to Liam's in Ripon. I'm afraid she gets a bit prickly when she's hungry as well as tired.'

I can't imagine her being much fun under any circumstances, Lily thought, *never mind kind. Or polite, come to think of it. How much does it take to say hello when you're being introduced to someone, even if you could not care less about that person?*

She shook her head, half angry, half amused. 'Well, if you must —'

'Aw, don't exaggerate, Joey. It wasn't that bad — what with the roads being empty, it only took me three and a half hours from Holyhead. And I went straight to bed, good girl that I am. Ask Liam. He knows I need my beauty sleep.'

Lily had a hard time not snorting. *Beauty sleep! Good girl.* For crying out loud.

'You are quite beautiful enough, as I am sure your husband tells you every morning.'

Lily, who had just been about to walk away (she was not going to play gooseberry all morning), stopped in her tracks, only to hear Rosin laugh raucously. 'My husband? Fine chance! He rarely even shares my bedroom these days. I do believe he sleeps in the stables. Partners varying in sex and age, too. But then I can't complain, can I? We always said we'd lead an open marriage.'

Lily's jaw was not the only one to drop. It felt like the people around them had frozen, too, in speech as well as in motion. They were staring openly at Roisin, and at Joseph. Lily hoped they did not mistake *him* for her husband. But everybody around here knew Joseph, and they knew he was not married.

Liam had the grace to step in. Pulling his sister away from Joseph, he hissed, 'That is quite enough, Roisin! Come on, I'll take you to York for your breakfast, or we can stop at a café on the way. Preferably somewhere where they don't know me, or Joseph. — Sorry, Lily,' he said with an apologetic smile, 'she doesn't mean half of what she says but she can be a nuisance. And quite an embarrassing one at that! — Come on, sis, let's get out of here.'

But Roisin was not one to be easily stopped, and she certainly was not going to have her brother patronize her. 'I do mean what I say! You know Seamus and I have a contract. Anyway, let's just grab a coffee to go and then drop that annoying dog off at Joey's parents'— you didn't plan to take him to York, Joey, did you? They don't allow dogs at the *Ivy*.'

Lily and Inigo exchanged glances. The poor dog clearly didn't have a clue what was going on either, the way he looked at her with his soulful brown eyes. She was tempted to bend down and pick him up when Liam cut in. 'Yes, well, let's go then. There is a stall over there in the far corner, if we are lucky we can get there before word gets round. Come on! Bye, Lily. Nice meeting you! Take care!' And taking his sister by the arm, he steered her away, leaving a sheepish looking Joseph behind. Inigo dropped to the ground and sighed.

'Oh dear,' Joseph said, scratching his chin. He was clean shaven, and Lily was itching to reach out and touch his face, but she didn't. Something was telling her to be cautious. 'I'm sorry about that. She is only here for Liam's birthday,' he went on to explain. 'And we are going on this trip to America in the summer, so there is a bit of planning to do as well. She will be furious with me when I tell her I have not even applied for bloody ESTA yet.'

'What?' Lily felt hot and cold in rapid alternation.

'We planned a trip to Montana last year, before I even knew you. We are going to stay on a mustang ranch.' He rolled his eyes. 'I can't even ride! Liam and Roisin grew up on a stud farm in Wicklow. Their father breeds racehorses. Liam has been on at me for ages about this trip, so last year we decided we would go and … yeah. I'm sorry, Lily. I should have told you. I also should have told you about Roisin coming this weekend. But there is nothing going on between us, I swear! She is just a friend.'

Lily was stunned. He was going to Montana with this femme fatale? And he had not even bothered to tell her about it? And about *her*?

'But — what about her husband? Isn't he coming, too?' Anxiously waiting for an answer, preferably in the affirmative, she looked up at him, hoping he would detect the hurt in her eyes, if not in her question. She had told him she was an anxious person, hadn't she? He should know this was difficult for her.

'Seamus? Oh no. You heard her, and although it was embarrassing, it is essentially true. He is busy on his farm. He is also a breeder, an even more successful one than her dad. He's quite a bit older than her and … yeah. He is a terrible bore, I don't know why she ever married him. Well — the money, obviously. And his horses. Roisin was born with reins in her hands!'

Was she, thought Lily wryly. *And obviously, she reined you in at some point. Open marriage, my foot. Arrangement.* If she had not felt so sick with anger, she might have laughed. But all she could say was 'oh', and even that came out rather lame. Would he think her a bore, too?

'Yes. But it's all quite harmless, she's really just flirting. I suppose it's just the way she is. And her brother is watching her, as you can clearly see, so no worries.' He leaned in to kiss her, but she turned her face away, irritated by his odd behaviour in Roisin's presence — he had practically ignored her, hadn't he? —, and by his rather lame excuses now. Just flirting. Sure. What about him then? Was he *just flirting*, too? Or did they actually need Liam as a chaperone when they went off to Montana together?

'I think you'd better go, Joseph, and catch up with your friends. I promised Abi I'd sell cakes for her, so if you'll excuse me, I'm busy. You can meet my parents another time.' *Or just don't bother.*

Much to her disappointment, Joseph nodded all too quickly, even ignoring her hint at him meeting her parents. It obviously wasn't important enough. 'Yeah, I suppose I'd better go. Give Abi a hug from me, will you, and tell her to take things easy. Bye, Lily.' And with a quick peck on her cheek (a peck on the cheek, not even a proper kiss!), he turned and walked away, dragging a reluctant Inigo with him.

Or maybe it's just me *who is not important enough. Who did I ever think I was — to him, and to the others? What did I ever think I was doing, selling my flat, quitting my job, and coming here? Did I seriously think I could do this? Stupid me. Stupid, stupid me.*

Lily slowly walked back to the WI stall, forcing herself not to look up when she heard Roisin laugh. She could not bear to see her with Joseph. In fact, she could not bear to be here at all. She just wanted to go home.

CHAPTER THIRTY

'Mum, I want to go home.'

Maureen looked up from rearranging the remaining scones. They had nearly sold out, which was just as well because so had the clotted cream, and scones were not half as nice without. 'To the farm? But you have only just …'

'No,' Lily cut in, folding her arms across her chest, 'I mean, *home*. To Oxford. Now. Or tomorrow, anyway. Do you think dad would take me?'

'Of course he would. But why do you suddenly want to go home? What's happened? Have you had a fallout with that young man of yours?'

'He is not *my young man*! He is …' Lily shook her head. 'I don't know who he is. But he is not — oh, please, mum,' she pleaded, 'can I go back to Oxford with Dad tonight? You can stay the week in my place — you said you would, didn't you?'

Maureen reached across the counter to touch Lily's cheek, concern in her eyes. 'Darling, what's wrong? Tell me, please. What has he done? He must have done something. Are you sure you can't sort it out, whatever it is? He seems such a nice young man, from what Abi told us. Why didn't you introduce us?'

Lily walked around to the other side of the stall and sat down on the director's chair Abi had vacated. She had gone off with her friends to see what the other stalls had to offer. There would be competitions, too, and Lily knew Abi was hoping for her rhubarb and strawberry jam to win a prize as well as her baby carrots which they had miraculously been able to save from being devoured by Myrtle.

'Because he is busy showing his Irish friends around before they swan off to York for the afternoon. Apparently, he has the weekend off — he never has a whole weekend off when I am here!' She knew she sounded like a spoilt child pouting because she didn't get the sweets, but she didn't care. 'Where is Dad?'

'He is chatting to your builder — look, they're over there, drinking cider. Builders always have something to talk about! Now, Lily, why don't you get behind the stall here for a bit, as you promised Abi you would, and help me? I'm sure a bit of distraction will do you good. Look, there is Miss Lavender — she was here before and was hoping to see you. She is the lady you are going to work for, isn't she? The one with the village shop?'

Lily sighed. Her mum was right of course, she had promised to sell cakes. And if Miss Lavender wanted to talk business, even better. *Anything to distract me, and keep me from thinking about that wretched Irish girl and what she is up to when I'm not looking.*

***

BY THE TIME they got back to the farm, she had almost convinced herself she was okay. She went straight to see William though, a clear sign that she was upset.

'Leave her be,' Abi said to Maureen when she wanted to go after her daughter. 'She'll come in when she is ready.'

'Hello, William,' Lily said and climbed onto the top rail of the fence. 'Had a good day? That's nice. I didn't. And shall I tell you what?' And she told the little donkey everything. When she had finished, and he was still standing there, looking for all the world as if he was listening attentively, she laughed and said, 'You truly are the bestest friend I ever had! What are men to donkeys, eh? I don't even need a counsellor these days. I just come to you.'

She patted his neck and turned to walk back to the house, already feeling much better. Maybe she should follow her mum's advice and think about the good things that had happened today rather than the bad things. There was Miss Lavender's astonishing news about having appointed David Stanton to make the shelves for the bookshop — and what was more, he had been more than happy to take on the whole project, counter, floorboards, and all. Privately Lily wondered how much money you could actually make with a village store, but if custom-made furniture was what Miss Lavender wanted, then who was she to argue? The shelves would look great.

'I have a feeling he still has a special connection with this place,' Miss Lavender had said, making Lily wonder if she was referring to David's enduring love for Susanna Harper. Was the old lady telling her that David had fallen in love with Susanna all over again, and was maybe even hoping to return to Rosedale? And to set up his business here, too? In which case of course a commission like this one would be more than welcome, and as fair a start as any.

'Hello, Lily.'

She turned around sharply at the sound of Joseph's

voice behind her, wondering what on earth he was doing here when he was supposed to be in York, dining at the Ivy. With Liam and *Roisin*. Her heart was beating fast, and she could feel cold sweat forming on her brow. How was she supposed to get out of here? Why couldn't he just leave her alone?

'Lily.' He gently took her by the shoulders but let go of her when he felt her stiffen. 'Thank God you're still here. I thought you might have gone home ... back to Oxford, that is.'

'I did think about it. But I am staying until tomorrow. What are you doing here? Shouldn't you be in York with your friends, enjoying a fancy dinner at the Ivy?' She knew she was being unnecessarily flippant, if not unfair, but she couldn't help herself.

'We booked a table for six, and I just dropped the two off at Liam's place and ... Lily, I want to talk to you. There are some things you need to know about — well. Roisin and me.'

Roisin and me. Lily swallowed. She was not sure she wanted to hear this.

'I know what you're thinking,' he said, reaching for her hands. '*I don't want to hear this.* But Lily, you must. Please. I don't want to keep any secrets from you. And I will never forgive myself if you hear it from someone else ... So — can we sit somewhere quiet, and talk?'

If you hear it from somebody else. Hear what, exactly?

For a minute she did not say anything, did not even move. Finally, she nodded. 'Okay,' she said, swinging her legs over the fence and sitting on the top rail, looking Joseph straight in the eye, 'let's talk.' Whatever he had to say, she was not going to do this without William.

***

'I WENT TO see Liam in Ireland over Christmas in our final year at Veterinary College. I did not take much notice of Roisin at first, other than that I thought she was pretty. She was good fun, too, and could drink all the men under the table, even her granddad! On Christmas Day, we went up to a place called the Forty Foot – that's a deep sea water inlet south of Dun Laoghaire, known in former times as a men's bathing place. It's one of those weird Irish traditions — they all jump down from the rocks on Christmas Day, men and women, and think it's great fun.'

He shuddered but Lily did not laugh. 'I didn't mind being a coward. Not until Roisin started teasing me, that was — so of course I jumped in. I was in love, I wanted to impress her … well. We spent a couple of days together, and by the time Liam and I left, I thought I had a girlfriend. Only she wasn't looking for a relationship. She went off to America soon after that, and I didn't see her for a year …'

Lily had a feeling that he was getting to the tricky bit now and slid her hands underneath her thighs. The last thing she wanted was for him to hold her hands now.

'A few months later, she was standing outside the cottage that Liam and I were renting over in Knaresborough, crying, and looking for a place to stay. She had just come out of a bad relationship, and I was fool enough to let her in — into the cottage, and back into my life. Big mistake! I thought we could work it out, even plan a future together, but she went back to Ireland after a couple of weeks and the next thing I knew was that she was getting married to a man old enough to be her father! I was hurt. I would have married her, you know.' Realising that that was probably not what

Lily wanted to hear, he went on, as if to get this part over with as quickly as possible. Meanwhile, Lily was still waiting for him to drop the real bombshell. This could not be the end of the story, could it? Her getting married?

'Roisin was after money, and a grand place with lots of horses. That was the only life she had known, and the only life she wanted to have. I could never have offered her that as a vet. All I ever wanted was a family, a nice, comfortable home, a dog ... I still want that, by the way,' he said, smiling ruefully at Lily. She did not smile back, and he bit his lip. 'Sorry. So, with hindsight, I should have known from the start that we were never meant to be together. But I wasn't so wise then — and no, I'm afraid that's not all. She invited me to her wedding — I didn't want to go, but Liam said I should not miss the chance of an Irish wedding, so ... I think I was kind of hoping that that was the only way to get her out of my head — to watch her walking up the aisle to marry another man. Bad mistake.'

Wishing he would get to the point, Lily made a noncommittal sound before turning her gaze on the hills. She heard Joseph's voice as if it was coming through a mist. 'We were all staying at a small seaside hotel the family were paying for — very chic. Like I said, they didn't do anything by halves. She doesn't, either, as I'm sure you can imagine. And then ...' He put his head in his hands. 'Oh, Lily, you are not going to like this.'

'Go on then. I don't think it can get much worse. Unless — you didn't sleep with after she got married, did you?'

He shook his head. 'No. Not after.'

Not after? Lily's jaw dropped and she felt her fingers digging into the soft wood, but she still did not look at him. 'Please tell me you didn't — not on their wedding day!'

'Not quite. But I'm afraid this isn't much better, and yes, I am ashamed of what I did. Even eight years on, I can't look at her, or her husband, without thinking —' He shook his head.

Lily felt her mouth go dry. Surely this couldn't be true! This couldn't possibly be the same kind, sensible, honest man she thought she had been falling in love with. Or could it?

'I found her crying in the park opposite the hotel the evening before the wedding. She was having doubts, and — yeah, well, I suppose she needed a shoulder to cry on. We had a couple of drinks in the hotel bar, to calm her nerves, and … then it happened.'

Lily turned to look at him at last, her face ashen. 'You — you slept with her the night before her wedding? Oh, Joseph! Don't you know how *bad* this is? Like, really, really bad?!'

'Of course I do! I know now, and I did then. I do know the difference between right and wrong. Normally.' He sounded bitter, and angry with himself. 'I was jealous, Lily, angry, hurt, and confused, and … oh, I don't know. Perhaps I was secretly hoping she would change her mind after … you know.' He bit his lip. 'She didn't of course. I was a fool twice over — three times over, actually. I should never have … anyway. It's in the past now. I swear I haven't touched her since then. Or let her touch me, for that matter.'

'Today, you did.'

'Sorry?'

'Today you did. You did let her touch you. *Oh Joey, you cannot even dress properly without my help*,' she mimicked, feeling hot tears pricking at the back of her eyes. 'I will not let you take me for a fool, Joseph Hancock. If you seriously think I am going to watch you go off to America with that woman, you are badly mistaken. Badly!'

Tears were running down her cheeks now and she wiped them away angrily. But there were too many. A whole torrent of tears. 'Oh, Joseph,' she whispered, shaking her head, 'how could you? How *could* you?'

He reached out to wipe her tears away, but she jumped down the fence abruptly and started to walk towards the house.

'Lily! Wait!'

'No! And you don't have time, anyway. Your presence is required at the Ivy.' *Did you know I always wanted to go there? With you? Because it is such a lovely place, and so romantic?* She could not bear to think that he would be dining there tonight, with Roisin, and not with her. Why was life so unfair?

'I still have a few minutes. I—'

She turned on her heel, fixing him with an icy look. 'A few minutes? How generous. Do you honestly think you can fix this in a few minutes? Go. Just go!'

'Okay,' he said, pushing himself away from the fence. William had retreated to the far end of the paddock the moment Lily had left, and stood there with his back turned to Joseph. 'If that's what you want.'

'I don't know what I want. But I don't want you, or anyone else, to mess with my feelings. Good night, Joseph. Take care.'

She might as well have said goodbye.

***

LILY WAS LYING in bed, the sheets pulled up to her chin, when his message arrived.

I love you * I love you * I love you * I love you * I love you * I love you * I love you *

It had to be at least a hundred *I love yous*. *Sweet*, she thought. But it was not nearly enough to reassure her. He would still go to Montana with the lovely Roisin, riding into the blooming sunsets and sitting around campfires roasting marshmallows. She did not answer his message but cried herself to sleep, wishing she had never come to Rosedale at all.

CHAPTER THIRTY-ONE

Oxford had never seemed so dreary. The rain that had been falling ever since she got back from Yorkshire on Sunday evening — after she had persuaded her father to take her back to Oxford with him, leaving her mother in charge — had not stopped for a full week. She could not even cycle to work, which only added to her frustration, and by the end of the second week her nerves were as frail as a threadbare rug.

She missed Joseph, she missed Jessie, and she was scared she might have lost both of them, but felt there was nothing she could do. Joseph would go on his trip, whether she liked it or not, and if Jessie didn't come round soon, she would have one hell of a wretched start with her bookshop. Lily had received an email from David in which he had declared the Bishops Bridge bookshop his 'priority project', which Lily thought was rather sweet of him. He promised the bookshop would be ready to open its doors by the end of September, a thought that made Lily feel sick with nerves. Was she really doing the right thing? But there was no going back now, was there? Becky had said that the builders would be able to make a start on the barn by the end of August, so that was another project she couldn't get out of now, even if she wanted to (and she had seriously contemplated cancelling the wretched barn!). It wouldn't be fair on Abi, anyway, so they might as well go ahead with it.

And who knows, Lily thought as she stepped out of the college building, looking at the sky and shaking her head in dismay, *what lies around the bend. Perhaps the best does after all*, she thought and opened her umbrella.

Waiting for the bus to take her home, Lily was cradling a cup of takeaway coffee when she heard the soft sound of the curlew — and started. *Joseph*. Although he had sent her a number of messages — most of which, to her shame, she had left unanswered, because she simply did not know what to say after his shocking revelations that night — they had not talked since she left. And that was almost a week ago. She took out her phone, swallowed, then answered.

'Hello?'

'Oh! Hello there. Is this a good moment?'

Lily closed her eyes and took a deep breath. 'Um … yes? I'm sitting in the bus shelter, waiting for the bus to take me home, so …'

'I know. I can see you — and I would just die to have a sip of that coffee because I'm not only knackered but wet and freezing, too.'

'What?' Lily nearly dropped her phone. Catching it at the last moment, she looked over to where Joseph was standing, outside the *Pret a Manger* where she had purchased her coffee five minutes ago. How could she have missed him?

'I'm coming over now, if you don't mind. When is your bus? Would there be time for me to grab a coffee, too?'

Lily shook her head and laughed when she spotted him outside the fast food restaurant on the other side of the road, jumping up and down to keep warm. 'I'm coming over, and we can both have one inside Prets. And then we will take the next bus — or walk.' Slipping her phone into her handbag, she got up and just remembered to look right and left before she darted across the busy High Street, throwing herself into Joseph's open arms.

It was only when he enveloped her in a hug, whispering 'Hello, my darling — God, I have missed you!' into her hair that she remembered she was angry with him. *Too late*, she thought, when his lips found hers and he kissed her, making the butterflies inside her flutter and dance in delight. The butterflies, it seemed, knew better than to say no to this irresistible man who had come all the way to Oxford to see her.

They kissed long and passionately, forgetting the world around them, until they were both so wet the water was dripping down Joseph's neck, and he pulled a face. 'I don't know about you, but I am soaked! Come on, let's go somewhere warm and dry and have a coffee. Or do you want to go straight to a pub? Are there any decent pubs in Oxford?'

'Hundreds! But do let's have a coffee first. You are in no hurry to leave tonight, are you?' She knew she sounded her old anxious self again and nothing like the sassy girl that had told Joseph to bugger off. But if he had taken the trouble to come all the way down to Oxford to see her, surely he would stay for a bit? And fight for her, too?

'Absolutely not. I have been so bold as to take the weekend off, so we have time to talk. I really want to …'

But she held up a hand, not wanting to plunge right into those treacherous waters again. 'Later. Please. No rush.'

***

They went to Lily's favourite riverside pub, *The Head of the River* on Folly Bridge, ordered a bottle of house white and shared a starter platter for two. Joseph then ordered the signature beef burger with all the trimmings, and Lily the wild mushroom risotto, warning him that she would probably pinch some of his triple cooked chips. She had often come here with Spencer — and funnily, for the first time since his death, this had actually prompted her to go here, and not give the place a wide berth as she would have done only weeks ago. She had wanted to come here with Joseph, to show him she could be happy in a place that reminded her of Spencer, even if he did not know it had been one of their favourite places to go. It didn't matter — *she* knew, *she* remembered, and she was going to make new, happy memories tonight.

'I hope you don't mind me staying — you do have a spare room, I hope?'

'That's a lot of hoping, Joseph Hancock,' she teased, cheeks flushed from two glasses of wine. 'And you're right about the first hope, I don't mind you staying, but wrong about the second — there is no spare room. Well, there is, but it's tiny, more of a cupboard really, and it's stacked with boxes, all the way up to the ceiling. So …'

'So what do you suggest? Does this place have rooms?' Joseph looked over his shoulder, pretending to look for a sign advertising rooms.

'It does, but they don't come cheap, and they may well be fully booked at this time of year. You may have to crash out on my sofa. It's not nearly big enough for you I'm afraid, but that's all I can offer at such short notice …' Her amber eyes were twinkling with mischief, and she knew she was flirting. She also knew she was enjoying every moment.

'Right … so upright in your cupboard, rolled up in a tight ball on your sofa, or … any chance I could …?'

'No. Definitely no.'

Yes! Yes! The reckless voice was singing in her head, making her laugh as she shook her head. But the sensible voice kicked in instantly. *No. Absolutely no! He's going to America with a woman he has been in love with before and who is determined to make him fall for her again; you are not going to give in now just because you are drunk! He still has to fight his way back to your heart. You are not going to let him off the hook so easily.*

'Shame.' He shrugged, picked up his wineglass, and put it down again when he saw the confused look on her face, detecting her emotional dilemma. Just as well he did not see her fiddling with her pendant, a habit she had slipped back into since her return from Yorkshire. 'Hey!' He reached out to touch her cheek. 'Don't panic. I'll be perfectly fine wherever you put me, unless it's on the last train back to York.'

She smiled. 'Okay.'

They decided to give the pudding a miss and, because it had stopped raining, walked through Christ Church Meadows before they got a taxi that took them back to Lily's place.

***

True to his word, Joseph slept on her little two-seater and when Lily got up the next morning with a slightly fuzzy head, she could smell coffee. Smiling, she swung her legs out of bed and walked into the living room where Joseph sat reading the newspaper. There were two mugs and two plates on the coffee table, and a bag with fresh croissants from the French patisserie around the corner.

'Morning, sleeping beauty. It's nearly ten o'clock! You promised you would show me the sights today. I took the liberty of starting with the bakery down the street — thus the takeaway coffee. I hope you'll forgive me. I didn't know what you usually had in the mornings. Probably tea, right? But croissants go particularly well with coffee, don't you think?'

'Particularly well, yes. As a matter of fact, I have got fresh coffee, too, but takeaway is okay. Where did you go, Alain's Bakery? Oh, they're good.' She peered into the bag. 'Oooh, lovely, and pasties. You do spoil me!'

'The least I can do in exchange for a night on your comfy sofa. I slept like a …' He caught her mocking eye and gave up, laughing. 'No. I didn't sleep at all. Sorry, not your fault of course. I'm glad to be here, so … breakfast?'

Over breakfast, Lily told him all about her super-fast flat sale (his eyes actually bulged at the mention of the price!) and her plan to move up to Rosedale in late August, hoping he would take this as a clue to tell her he had had second thoughts and was going to cancel his trip to America now. He didn't.

They walked around the city, visiting Christ Church College and hiring a punt afterwards (which was great fun, especially when poor Joseph nearly had to let go of the pole at one point while Lily doubled over with laughter), all the while chatting amiably, but never once referring to his forthcoming trip. By the time evening fell — and with a spectacular sunset, too, bathing the famous Dreaming Spires in golden light — Lily was so nervous she could not contain herself any longer and burst out, 'So, um … are you going to Montana then? With — with Liam and … her?'

Joseph gave her a look that was completely nonplussed, almost innocent. 'Of course. Why wouldn't I?'

'Why — you know. Because of what happened — I mean, back then, and — well. Last Saturday. I thought you might have changed your mind.'

'But Lily, we booked this holiday *a year ago*, we've been looking forward to it! I mean, Liam has, mainly, because he has always wanted to go, and somehow he persuaded me to come, too. He is my oldest friend, so …' He shrugged. 'We're only going for two weeks. You'll be so busy you won't even notice me being gone. There is the barn, and —'

'But — but what about *her*?' she blurted, despising herself for sounding so pathetic. So much for making him fight. And so much for not going down the same road again. The begging road. Maybe she had not come that far after all.

He sighed, then put an arm around her shoulder. 'I told you, there is nothing — absolutely nothing — going on between us. Please, Lily, trust me. Please.'

She hesitated. Why was it always *her* who had to give in? Why did people always ask her, even *expect* her, to trust them? Even if he did not understand her feelings, he might at least try and respect them. She had every right to be jealous, and anxious. He knew about her anxiety. She had told him, hadn't she? And it was not like she was deliberately trying to spoil a holiday for him. She just could not bear to let him go with that woman!

But try as she might, she could not stop herself from crying now. The first tear that had been hanging in her lashes dropped down her cheek, followed by the next, and the next. And then the flood came.

'Oh Lily!' Holding out his arms, he caught her and pulled her close. Her head resting against his chest, she closed her eyes and breathed in the clean, woody scent of his aftershave, trying to commit it to memory. *Scents were keepers of memories*, she had read in a book, and found it was true. Nothing could keep the memory of a person or a special moment alive for longer, and in a more vibrant way, than a scent. Funny then that she did not remember Spencer's scent. She remembered the brand, yes – Dior Suavage – but she could not remember the smell. Like a sample splash on a paper strip in a perfume shop, it had evaporated. Vanished.

But even though she cried so hard, he would not change his mind. Go to America he would, with Liam and his sister, and there was nothing she could do about it. He did promise he would not even look at Roisin if he could help it, and definitely insist he had his own horse to ride — his attempt at a joke —, but he also asked Lily very earnestly to give him some credit and trust him. 'I will think of you night and day, and be back by your side before you know it. Everything will be alright. Just trust me. Okay?'

Just trust me.

'Okay?'

Slowly, and still biting her lip, she nodded. What else could she do?

'And the trip is not until August. You could come up for another weekend? How about the one just before I leave?'

She shrugged, not wanting to sound desperate again, or even clingy. 'I don't know. I'm really busy here, working, and wrapping things up. You'd be amazed to see how much stuff there is in this tiny apartment! Mostly books of course.'

'Of course,' he deadpanned, and she laughed. In fact, they both laughed, and then they kissed, and walked down the street swinging hands. *Today is a beautiful day*, she thought, *and I am not going to let anything, or anyone, spoil it.*

'Of course. But still, it's another month. Tell you what, if you can't make it up to Yorkshire by the end of these four weeks, I will come and get you. Is that a deal?'

She tilted her head. 'Hmmm … yes — perhaps.'

'If I didn't know you better, I'd think you were flirting with me, Lily Henderson,' he laughed, taking her face in his hands. 'Before I kiss you, you must promise you won't let me wait too long. Let's make it the last Saturday in July. Okay?'

'Okay.' She was still upset about the whole business with Roisin, but she had done her best to talk him out of it, and it had not worked, so she might as well let go. And when he kissed her, she did.

***

LILY HAD JUST waved Joseph off the next day when she ran into Spencer's mum outside the station.

'Lily! Oh, it is lovely to see you! How are you? I have been meaning to call you but,' Amelia gave a brittle laugh, 'you know how it is. Always busy, aren't we? I don't know about you, but I have found that as long as I am busy I can bear it. But then of course it is not winter yet …' Her face clouded over, and Lily felt sorry for her. She was just trying to think of something to say when Amelia asked, 'Was that your brother I just saw you walking down the platform with? I have just waved my sister and brother-in-law off, they live in Aberdeen. Shall we go for a coffee?'

Lily wished the ground would open up. *My brother? No, that was my new boyfriend.* She couldn't possibly say that, could she? Not to Spencer's mother.

'Um … I'm afraid I can't, Amelia. My — my parents have invited me for Sunday lunch, and I'm already running a little late. I must go home and get my car and … yes. Perhaps another time soon?'

'Of course. Is your brother not coming then? For Sunday lunch at your parents? Only you just said goodbye to him, didn't you? Funny, I thought he lived in Oxford with his wife. Or perhaps he is going away on business?'

Lily squirmed. *That woman is like a dog with a bone! Why can't she leave me alone?*

'Um … yes, he — no. He is going to see our great-auntie in Yorkshire. She had an accident and needs some help on the farm. He is staying the week.'

'Oh, but that's nice of him. You do have such a lovely family, Lily. I'm sure they do everything to help you. Right, I'll let you get on then. Enjoy your Sunday lunch, and do call me about that coffee. Bye!'

'Will do. Goodbye, Amelia. Give my love to your husband.' *Goodness*, she thought as she watched Amelia walk away, *that was close*. But then she noticed how slowly Amelia was going, pulling out a large white handkerchief as she did and dabbing at her eyes. Was she lonelier than she let on? Would that cup of coffee perhaps have done her good? Suddenly Lily felt ashamed. *I should call after her*, she thought. *We should go for that coffee. It can't hurt, can it?* But she found she could not move. She stood rooted to the spot until Amelia had gone, and her phone rang. Glad for the distraction, she pulled it out of her pocket.

'Hello? — Oh, hi, Stephen! How are you? — You have done what?? Bought a dog? You're joking!'

Good thing Amelia is out of earshot, she thought. *I could not have dug myself out of this one, could I?*

CHAPTER THIRTY-TWO

Lily had never been prone to procrastinating but found that she was still sitting among the boxes in her Oxford flat a week after her last day at work. And what was worse, she was sitting here alone, and with a knot in her stomach that was becoming bigger and tighter as the days slipped by. *I'm leaving*, she thought as she closed another box and marked it *kitchen — Mum & Dad*. She would leave most of her things in the storage room above her parents' garage for the time being. 'No point in bringing my pots and pans to the farm, is there,' she had joked when her mum had stood in the drive shaking her head, as yet another six boxes had gone up the ladder.

Beth and Matthew were already in Devon — they had met up for coffee one last time on Friday, after Lily's final day at work, and said a tearful goodbye, promising to write (!) to each other — and now she was getting hourly updates on the renovation work in the vicarage. But instead of feeling motivated to get moving herself now, she felt strangely detached, almost as if she was living outside of herself. *Am I really ready yet?*

Stephen and Emily were busy decorating the nursery

(and training a very naughty cocker spaniel puppy who would have gone to a rescue centre had Emily not begged Stephen to buy him from the colleague who had not reckoned with his girlfriend's allergy), her parents had taken themselves off to France for a wine tasting holiday, and she should be in Yorkshire by now. Only she wasn't. She was still sitting here, asking herself the same questions over and over again, and being genuinely surprised that she still wasn't getting any answers.

With a sigh, Lily got up from the box she had been sitting on, rereading the message Joseph had sent earlier.

> Good morning, beautiful! I'm sending you a picture of a Montana sunrise, knowing of course what you will say — 'oh, but a Rosedale sunrise is ever so much more spectacular!' You are right, of course. Especially when we get to watch the sunrise together, on Bank Top, with coffee in thermos flasks and Abi's sticky buns. How about we do that again as soon as I get back? Xx

A slow smile spread across Lily's face. She remembered that walk, and she remembered the look of sheer disbelief she had given him when he had suggested he pick her up at four o'clock.

'In the morning??'

'Ever watched a sunrise in the afternoon?' he had retorted, wiggling his eyebrows. And what a lovely walk it had been, more than worth getting up for! They had driven up to Bank Top where they had sat and watched the sun slowly rise from behind the hills on the opposite side of the valley. It had been the most spectacular sight, with the first rays of the sun finding their way tentatively down the hillside, gently pushing back the shadows, and kissing the sleeping valley awake with its soft golden light. Then, as if somebody had switched on the light on a stage, everything had seemed to burst into life at once: Rabbits were coming out of their holes and hopping across the fields, birds were circling in the sky above them, praising the morning with their song, and a group of deer stood quite still in a field, gazing about the valley with their gentle eyes. When a fox with her cubs were making their way from the shelter of the wood to the stream, Lily put a hand to her chest, catching her breath.

'Oh, Joseph,' she whispered, grasping his hand, 'this is so beautiful!'

'It is, isn't it? You wouldn't see *that* on a cruise ship in the middle of the Atlantic,' he'd teased, nudging her. She had shocked him a little the night before when she had told him she wanted to go on a transatlantic cruise, preferably on the Queen Mary 2, one day.

'No, but I'd have nothing but sea around me, which I imagine would also be quite magical.'

Remembering the magic moment of the long and passionate kiss that followed, Lily looked about the mess in her study and sighed. There was nothing magical about a move, unless you could get a Genie to come and sweep all the things you wanted away to Rosedale in one swift ride on his magic carpet. As it was, she only had her parents and her brother to help her, and another month until she would have to vacate her flat.

***

AN HOUR LATER, she had packed up the rest of her books,

which would all travel to Yorkshire with her. Almost ready to make a start on the dreaded chest of drawers in the hall — six drawers full of *stuff!* — she leaned against the wall and briefly closed her eyes. She was so tired. And so worried. Because no matter how many messages and pictures Joseph sent or how often they met for Facetime, she could not shake off the feeling of unease whenever she pictured him together with *her*. And thanks to her vivid imagination and her restless mind, she did a lot of that, mostly at night when she was trying to sleep.

Suspecting her brother would not understand how she could work herself up over something so "trivial", as she was sure he would call it, she had turned to Beth for support. But even she had said not to worry, and everything would be fine. How did they know?

'Trust your heart, Lily, and trust him. You must learn how to trust again after Spencer. Joseph sounds like a good man. And good men don't come along like buses. Don't miss your chance at happiness, Lily. Don't let him pass.'

Good for you, Lily thought as she went to open a kitchen cupboard that had not been emptied yet, *you have been happily married to your childhood sweetheart for three years. I'm sure Matthew has never even so much as looked at another woman!*

A message flashed up just as she was balancing a collection of bowls, and she nearly dropped the lot as she tried to reach for her phone which was lying on the kitchen table behind her.

> Hey, Lily, what are your plans for next Saturday? If you have nothing else to do you might want to do me a favour. Please call me, and I will explain. Jessie x

'I'm so sorry I upset you,' was the first thing she said when Jessie picked up.

'Oh, don't start that again. It's fine, honestly. I completely overreacted, I know that now. It was just a little too much too early in the morning. And you can actually do me a favour to make up for …. Well, for pushing me. I know I need some pushing, so — will you go with me?'

'Go where? When?'

'To Durham. I signed us both up for a Barista Masterclass Course. On Saturday. Louisa May is in Sweden with my parents, and I take it Joseph will still be in America, so … perfect timing, don't you think? Where are you, by the way? Not still in Oxford, I hope??'

'You want me to come to a Barista Masterclass with you? To Nate's coffee shop?'

'Yes. Where are you?'

Lily sighed. There was no getting out of it. 'Still in Oxford. But I'm nearly done with packing …'

'About time, too. Bishops Bridge needs you. I need you.'

'You do?'

'Yes. Because if I don't do this now, I might regret it for the rest of my life, so — will you come with me? Please?'

'Of course I will. It's the least I can do! I'll drive us, too, if you like, so you needn't worry about that.'

'Oh, would you? You're a rock! Thank you. Um — when are you coming?'

Lily looked at the boxes around her and then at the clock. It was half past eleven. If she left here at three … or four, at the latest … 'Tonight. I'm coming tonight.'

***

Lily had not even switched off the engine when she heard raised voices coming from inside the farmhouse. A minute later she burst into the kitchen to find Mr Nettleton, and his daughter, standing opposite Abi who was leaning against the kitchen cupboard, her face drained of all colour.

'How dare you?' the old man was just roaring at Abi, his face crimson with rage.

'No, Mr Nettleton — how dare *you*?'

Lily placed her hands on her hips, jutting out her chin defiantly. 'You can't just come in here and howl at my great-aunt as if she has just set fire to your precious farm when in fact she has been looking after it for you since April! I am not even sure you have said as much as 'thank you', never mind paid her, as would have been appropriate. Leave her alone, Mr Nettleton. Just *leave her alone*. In fact — do you mind if I just throw him out, Abi?'

Nettleton flared his nostrils at her, reminding her of an old dragon who was all smoke but no fire. 'Now wait a minute, young lady — I have not come here to be insulted by an ignorant young woman from bloody Oxford who doesn't know the first thing about …'

'I know more than you think, Mr Nettleton. For a start, I know quite enough of *you*, more than I actually care to know. But as I am going to live on this farm, too, I'm afraid you and I will be neighbours soon, whether you like it or whether you don't.' *And I'm sure you very much* don't, *you cranky old fool, but I'm afraid we neither of us have a choice.* She did not say that though, not sure whether she had already said too much and made matters worse for Abi without intending to. But oh, how this horrid man riled her! *Bloody Oxford*, my foot.

'Are you going to stand there and watch that niece of

yours — or whatever she is — treat my poor father like this? Do you think it was easy for him to come here and beg you to look after his beloved animals, since he obviously can't? Do you want him to have to sell the lot to the butcher's just because you are too high and mighty to throw some grain at his chickens and geese? And you get the eggs, which is more than fair. I did offer you money back in April, as you well know, but you refused. So, I'm afraid you only have yourself to blame. And I would very much appreciate you not telling lies about Dad when he has been …'

'You have said quite enough, Mary. I don't want to hear another word about your lovely Dad — if he is so very lovely, why don't you come home and keep house for him yourself? Or better still, take him to bloody Cornwall with you?'

Abi's eyes were blazing, but Lily could see she was trembling, too, whether with fear or rage she could not tell. *Poor Abi*, Lily thought, wondering for how long these people had already been here, hurling insults at her.

'You know very well that I can't come and live here! And I wouldn't, not with you *and* that nasty little thing from Oxford there! How *dare* you speak to my father like that?' she snarled, turning to Lily. 'You know nothing about him, or if you do, they are just lies! Spread by those mean old farmers and their ever-gossiping wives, no doubt. This is the last place on earth I ever want to come back to!'

'Oh, I'm glad to hear that,' came a deep voice from the door which made everybody turn around. Theo, who had gone into hiding, positively leapt into David's arms. Picking up the little dog, David turned cold, dark eyes to his stepfather and stepsister. 'I don't know what this is all about, but I have dropped in for a cup of tea and I can't imagine the pair of you would be welcome to stay — or would they, Abi?'

'Indeed they wouldn't, no. You heard my niece — and him. Out! Both of you. Now!'

Lily watched in astonishment as Mary took her father by the arm and steered him towards the door. Either she was lost for words, or she was wise enough not to argue with this man, whom she clearly did not recognize as David Stanton.

But David stepped into her way as she tried to get past him. 'You know who I am, don't you, Mary Nettleton? I am probably the last person on earth you ever hoped to see again. But *I* have come back here, Mary. And I will not have you treat my lovely neighbour like this, do you hear me? I will *not* have it, and neither will anyone else in this village. Now good day to you both.'

Lily was so impressed she was tempted to clap and cheer, like they sometimes did in the cinema when the long-awaited hero entered a scene, but she didn't. Instead, she just stood and watched as Mary and her father hurried out as fast as they could — she would have liked to think never to return, but something told her they had not seen the last of the pair.

Turning to David, she smiled brightly. 'Hello, David. Cup of tea?'

***

'I USED TO buy sweets from Miss Lavender when I was a lad, that's how I know her. Spent most of my pocket money in that little shop, I did!'

David grinned as he took another piece of shortbread from the plate Abi had put on the table the moment

Nettleton and his daughter had left. 'Anyway, so I have very fond memories of the shop, and of Miss Lavender. I am absolutely honoured to do the work for her. And when she told me that you would be working in the shop, I thought it best to discuss the interior with you. You got my e-mail, didn't you?'

Lily nodded, not sure she could follow. Why, she had not even recovered from the shock of the Nettleton scene! She would also have expected David to say something about that, but he didn't. Either he just played it cool, or he was more laid-back than she could ever have been, had she been in his place. She thanked God she wasn't, though.

'Good. So when I saw your flashy little Mini turning into the yard, I said to Susanna, I'll go and see her right now. No time like the present and all that, eh?' He popped the last bit of shortbread into his mouth, grinning from ear to ear.

Lily couldn't help staring at him. *What else has been happening since I was here last? Has he moved in with Susanna now, or is he a regular guest?*

'Okay ... so, um — you are going to do everything? Shelves, floors, walls, and all? I could help, you know. I'm quite good at swinging a paintbrush.'

He grinned. 'I was kind of hoping you'd say that. Susanna is going to help, too. We can all work on this together — if you provide the tea, Abi?'

'Of course I'll provide the tea. And the cake. And there is always Jessie of course.'

Lily had not had a chance to tell Abi about their trip to Durham on Saturday and shot her a quick look that said, *I've got something to tell you.* But first, she was dying to know what was really going on between her great-aunt and that wretched Nettleton. *Tonight's the night*, she thought grimly, her fiery eyes nearly burning holes into her aunt's. *Tonight you are finally going to tell me what this is all about!*

'Oh, God, yes. Those cinnamon swirls … mmm!' They all laughed, and David rose to his feet. 'Anyway, Miss Lavender is happy for you to choose whatever you like, shelves, paint, and all. She says you will know best. I could bring a few samples, then you don't have to come all the way to Nidderdale. Unless you would like to, of course. But I expect you will be quite busy — keeping the neighbours off and such like.'

Lily grinned. 'I hope not, now that you've put him in his place good and proper, but you never know. And I think I would appreciate the samples, thank you. I'll be right here, so any time that's convenient for you.'

'Good. Well, I'll be off then, ladies. Thank you for the tea, Abi — and if that man bothers you again, just give me a shout, and I will see him out, daughter and all!'

I don't doubt that, thought Lily, shaking her head in amusement as she watched him leave. *I don't doubt that at all.*

But the moment he had closed the door behind him, she turned to Abi, folded her arms across her chest, and said, 'Right. I think it's time you told me about what it is that makes that ghastly man think he can treat you like a doormat — *and I don't mean David!*'

CHAPTER THIRTY-THREE

'SO LET ME get this straight: You were posing for my great-uncle Donald wearing nothing but *this*,' Lily pointedly lifted a corner of the delicate lace shawl that had been draped over the back of Abi's best armchair for as long as she could remember and had become yellowish with age, 'and then he went to marry your sister — my great-auntie Margaret — which is the reason you fell out and never spoke to each other again? And all these years you never told a single soul about this? Where is that sketch now, if you don't mind me asking? And do tell me, what has all — or any of this — to do with nasty old Nettleton?'

Not that the story about the sketch was not outrageous enough as it was: It seemed that young Abigail, Donald, and Margaret had been in something of a love triangle for some time before Donald and Margaret eventually got married. When he had asked her to sit for a picture, lovestruck young Abi had foolishly believed that he would choose her over her sister, but he didn't. It turned out he had been sleeping with her sister all the time, while Abi — conscious of her age and so afraid of her father's wrath — had only let him kiss her and take her out to the pictures, or for ice-creams.

Abi sighed. 'Oh, Lily — you don't want to know …'

Oh, but I do, Lily thought, leaning forward in her seat. She had not even touched the wine she had poured them both, and neither, she noted, had Abi.

'When Margaret and Donald died in that boat accident in France ten years ago, Margaret left me a letter. She must have written it some years before, but it seemed she never sent it. So after the accident …'

'Wait a minute,' Lily cut in, frowning, 'would that be the letter you found in the attic when we were looking at the paintings?' She remembered how Abi had paled and quickly stuffed the letter inside her pocket.

'Yes, that's the one. I had forgotten it was there — I must have stuck it to the back of one of the pictures when their son brought them up here after the funeral. He's a nice lad, is Jacob. Lives in Canada with his family now. We lost touch soon after that, but then of course we never had much contact in the first place, what with his mum and me having fallen out over his dad … — I doubt that Jacob knows the reason though. And even if he does …' Abi reached for her wine glass but did not drink. 'It doesn't matter now, does it?'

'No. I suppose it doesn't. It's very sad though, for all of you.'

Abi took a sip of her wine. 'It is. Well now, about that sketch and Mr Nettleton …' Suddenly she put her hands over her eyes and shook her head in shame. 'Oh, Lily, I don't know how to tell you — it's really quite embarrassing!'

'That's as may be, but I still think you'll feel better for it once you've got it off your chest.' Lily spoke softly, and reached out to touch Abi lightly on the arm.

Abi nodded. 'Well. I suppose you're right. I was really upset after that accident, you know. Jacob had been to bring the pictures, and while he was there, I realized what I had missed out on all these years. After he had left, I sat here in the conservatory, surrounded by Margaret and Donald's paintings, and cried. For the sister I had lost, the nephew I never knew, and for myself because I had been so foolish ... And then, when I stepped outside for some fresh air, who came along but Mr Nettleton.'

She paused, and Lily held her breath. *Come on, Abi, spill! What happened?*

'Thomas was out walking that weekend with his mates; they were doing the three peaks over in the Dales. He did ask whether I'd rather he stayed, being so upset about Margaret, but I insisted he should go. He so rarely took time off from the farm ... Anyway, there I was, all on my lonesome, when Mr Nettleton came over to bring us some fresh eggs — which was actually rather nice of him. He was in a nice-ish phase at that time, and we got on considerably well. He asked me how I was coping, and I broke down and cried. Cried on his shoulder, I did! I must have been really desperate.' She laughed, but it sounded brittle, and Lily could detect a tremble in Abi's hand as she set down her wineglass. It was clear that she wanted to relieve herself of what had been her secret burden for so long, and Lily's heart went out to her.

'He wasn't married at the time — although to be honest, I don't think that would have stopped that wicked man. Anyway, the next thing I knew he had me sitting in his back garden, drinking homemade eggnog. It was a warm day, and I soon began to feel the effects of afternoon alcohol indulgence. My tongue loosened quickly, and before I could stop myself, I had told him all about that wretched sketch! How beautiful I had been as a young girl, how Donald had admired me … and how it had cost me the precious bond with my once beloved sister. Well.' She pursed her lips. 'Naturally, he then wanted to see it, so — drunk as I was — I went to get it. He liked it very much, and I was so flattered by his compliments — he could be quite a charmer, you know … well, as I said, I was drunk and … yes, well. That was that.'

That was that. Was that Abi's way of telling Lily that she had agreed to sleep with him? Probably. 'You — you are not telling me you gave him the picture after that? Like — I don't know … a love token?'

Abi nodded, shame faced. 'I tried to claim it back the very next day, but he refused to give it to me. He said he would if I agreed to — do certain things for him. Like keeping house, cooking, and — well. I suppose you can guess the rest.' Her cheeks flushed deeply. 'I should never have been so stupid of course. But I thought if I only kept house for him, and pretend to be his friend … you know — that that would be enough. But Brian Nettleton did not want to settle for friendship. So, when I realised he had no intention of giving the picture back, and he started to harass me …'

Lily was shocked. 'He didn't — you know … he wasn't violent, was he?'

'No, no. And it didn't last long either. Thomas began to suspect something, and I was on the verge of telling him when *wife number three* turned up, and that put an end to it, niceties, eggs, and all. We have loathed each other ever since. Or perhaps, on my part, more than ever before.' She looked at Lily and shrugged in a gesture of defeat and shame. 'So now you know the whole sordid truth. I'm sorry, Lily. I hope you don't despise me now. Or not too much, anyway.'

Lily shook her head in disbelief. 'Despise you? Why? If there is anyone I despise, it's Mr Nettleton! But — wait a minute! Is *that* why you have been looking after his farm? Because he still has the wretched picture?'

One look at her aunt's face was all the answer she needed. 'I don't friggin' believe it! Does he blackmail you? If he does, you must tell David, you know. He will not —'

'I don't think he will blackmail me *now*. He used to, in the beginning. It's how he got me to help him in the first place. Well, I would have looked after his animals, of course, he needn't even have asked. Fact is, he hasn't been looking after them properly for some years. When I first went over after he had had his stroke, the stables were dirty and awfully smelly. And the animals were all underfed. Some of them were limping about in their own …' She shuddered. 'Anyway, I got Joseph to check them all and give them their annual jabs while Nettleton was in hospital. I never told him of course. He would have accused me of interfering.'

Lily scoffed. 'So what? You were quite right to interfere — and rather you than the animal welfare, I should have thought!'

'Yes, that's what I thought, too. Anyway, I didn't do much else for him these past few weeks, except bring him some leftovers so he wouldn't starve. That wasn't much trouble.'

'Fair point. But — what was all the commotion about then when I came? Why would Mary accuse you of letting her father down? Did you agree to do anything else, except feed him and his beasts?'

'I most certainly didn't — but it seems he had made Mary believe that I would! She seriously thought I had agreed to be his live-in nurse! Can you imagine that? Me! After all he's done to me over the years! And I don't know what other outrageous lies he told her, but apparently, he made her believe he was paying me, too! Put that together with her somewhat blurred picture of her father and me having been — well, something of an item once, naturally, she believed him, and didn't sign him up for social services, thinking I would do my job. As if! And when she came and found him and the house in a state of utter neglect, she had the nerve to blame *me*!'

Lily was flabbergasted. Now it dawned on her why Mary had said that Abi knew her father's house "inside out". What a bitch! And what a manipulative old man he was, to have his daughter believe that Abi was not only his lover but also his obliging housekeeper and nurse.

'Of course he just told her that lie to stop her from saddling him with a district nurse,' Abi explained. 'Only today Mary found out she had been lied to all along. Naturally, she does not like being lied to any more than you and me. But rather than blaming a father who could do no wrong in her eyes …'

'Except marry Sarah Stanton …'

Abi laughed. 'Except marry Sarah Stanton, yes. Well, now you know what all this was about — I say, let's bring on a toast.' She raised her glass, and Lily was glad to see her aunt's eyes were sparkling again. 'To the future of Fern Hill Farm?'

'Yes! *And* to not worrying about the past, or whether Nettleton still has that picture or not. Although I must say I would love to see it … is it good?'

'Oh, aye, it is very good. A bit like the picture in that *Titanic* movie, only I wasn't wearing a heart-shaped diamond pendant worth millions of dollars. Just — this,' she said, picking up the shawl in exactly the same fashion as Lily had done, and they both laughed.

CHAPTER THIRTY FOUR

The irresistible smell of coffee, cinnamon, and sizzling bacon hit Lily's nose the moment she entered the café, and her tummy gave an embarrassingly loud growl as she weaved her way to the counter where Jessie was just serving a customer. Looking up, she saw Lily and smiled. 'Oh, there you are! Do sit down if you can find a table, I'll be with you in a minute.'

The café was as busy as ever, and it took ten minutes for Jessie to bring Lily a cappuccino. She dropped into the empty chair next to Lily and wiped her brow. 'Phew, this is the first time I'm actually sitting down this morning! It's as if people got up this morning and said, *oh, she's going to be closed on Saturday, let's go now*. I only wish I had more seating outside … but hey, I've got an idea! When you open your shop next door, you won't really need the back yard, will you? Perhaps we can get Miss Lavender to take the trellis down, and expand my tea garden. Actually …' Her face lit up, making her look very young, and very pretty. Poor Nate was in for a surprise when he would meet her on Saturday! Would he have read the names on the list, Lily wondered? And would he recognise Jessie's name? After all, she had never changed her surname, so it was quite possible he would, wasn't it?

'Reading while you have a coffee, and perhaps a slice of cake ... what's not to love, eh?'

'Sorry?'

'Read books, eat cake. Simple business idea. Waterstones does it. In fact, nearly every bookshop offers coffee and cake these days, if they have the space, and the facilities. We have both!' She nodded enthusiastically. 'Just think what we could make of this, Lily. What a chance! What a dream! Oh, I'm ever so glad you came!'

'What, to Bishops Bridge, or to your café today?'

Jessie laughed. 'Both of course! Right, I'll see you tomorrow then. Will you pick me up? At seven-thirty?'

'Seven thirty it is. And now I must go, Abi is coming to pick me up any minute. We have an appointment in Thirsk — with the bank, to talk about the barn conversion, and ask for a loan. I'm terrified!'

'So would I be, if I were you. But don't worry, it will all turn out well. Which is more than I can say for myself ... anyway! See you tomorrow!'

***

WHEN LILY PULLED up outside Corner Cottage the next day, she found Jessie already waiting for her. She was sitting on the step outside her front door, with two coffee-to-go mugs and a small wicker basket next to her. *Probably full of cinnamon swirls*, Lily thought, and wondered who was supposed to eat them all if Jessie's stomach was all tied in knots, as she knew hers would be.

'Morning!' Grabbing her bags and her basket, Jessie came running down the path. 'Gosh, I'm so nervous, I did not sleep a wink! Do tell me all about that bank appointment. Anything to take my mind off things!' She thrust a coffee mug and a cinnamon swirl at Lily.

'Do you seriously expect me to eat while I'm driving?'

Jessie shrugged and sipped her coffee. *Poor Jessie*, Lily thought as she took an appreciative sip of her own coffee before she placed it into the cup holder and started the car. *And I seriously thought a sixty-thousand-pound mortgage was something to lose sleep over!*

'Well — it wasn't so bad, actually. We were able to claim the mortgage, which is good, and it isn't nearly as much money as I had expected it to be, thanks to my mum!'

'Your mum?'

'Yes! She spent her teenage years on Fern Hill Farm because *her* mother — who was Abi's eldest sister — died when she was only eleven. So my grandddad, who had a shop in Thirsk, left her in Auntie Abigail's and Uncle Thomas's care — which is why Fern Hill Farm holds a special place in my mum's heart even today. Naturally, she doesn't want Abi to lose the farm, should anything go wrong with our barn project. What I *didn't* know was that she and dad had transferred a large sum of money to Abi the week Mum was here, and I was in Oxford. I had no idea — and certainly no idea how much! Can you imagine the look on my face when Abi told me on the way to the bank yesterday? Like, oh by the way ... well, you know what she's like.'

'Yes. Oh, but Lily, that is such a lovely thing of your mum to do! She must be a wonderful person!'

'She is — both of my parents are. Mum said — I called her last night, of course, to thank her — she thought it only fair to give back some of what Abi and Thomas had done for her. It was my grandfather's inheritance, actually, so it makes perfect sense. Sadly, he died when I was little, so I never really knew him. And as my dad's parents moved to Spain when they retired, Abi really was the closest to a grandmother my brother and I ever had. — Oh, do pass me a bun, please, I cannot bear to have that smell right up my nostrils all the time and not get to taste them!'

***

The Coffee Experience lay tucked away in a side street in the city centre of Durham, with a few cast iron tables and chairs outside, still wet from last night's rain, and a green and white striped awning above the door and adjoining window. The door was open, and the smell of freshly ground coffee beans hit the girls' nostrils as they stepped inside. Lily was still clutching the paper bag with her half-eaten bun, and Jessie was nudging her, in an attempt to make her put it inside her handbag. But it was too late — already they were approached by a tall, blond woman who was flashing the most dazzling smile at them, exposing her perfect white teeth.

'Good morning! You are early — can I offer you a cup of fresh coffee? My name is Hayley, and I will be your host today, together with my husband of course, who is due to arrive shortly. He is just gone to drop off the kids at their grandparents'.'

It was not only that Hayley looked far too young to even have kids, but the way that she was talking about *her husband* that made both Lily's and Jessie's jaw drop.

'What are your names, please?' Hayley picked up a clipboard from a table and was scanning a list, pen poised. She was still smiling, and Lily hated her for that. And for her perfect teeth. But mostly for being Nate's wife.

'Um … Jessie Nilsson and Lily Henderson, please.' Lily reached for Jessie's hand. It was ice cold.

'Ah yes, you were the last ones to join our group. We only have ten participants today, which should make it nice and personal. Do you both have Scandinavian origins? Only the names indicate that you might.'

'My parents are from Sweden,' Jessie explained, and Lily could hear the tremor in her voice. Poor Jessie! Would she go through with this, she wondered, or make a run for it? She squeezed her hand reassuringly.

'Oh, interesting. They make great coffee in Sweden, don't they?'

'Yes.'

Lily squirmed. How long was Nate going to be? The sooner they could get this over with, the better. Oh, if only I had done my research properly, then I might have known he was married with kids! But Lucy had not found anything about his family status either, not even on Instagram. They had agreed that he must be a very private person.

While Hayley went to fetch the coffee, Lily turned to Jessie and hissed, 'We can leave any time if you want. I don't care about the money. I'll pay you back.'

But Jessie shook her head. 'No. I'm fine. I mean — I'm not, obviously, but …'

'Jessie? Jessie Nilsson?'

Still holding hands like little girls, they both turned around simultaneously to find themselves face to face with Nate Sullivan.

CHAPTER THIRTY-FIVE

'I CAN'T BELIEVE it's you! After all these years! You look great.'

'Thank you.'

Lily watched as their eyes locked and they both stood rooted to the spot, neither of them sure what to do, or even say, next. Nate was very handsome in a geeky sort of way — his dark, wavy hair came down to his collar, and he was wearing a pair of thick, horn-rimmed glasses that almost matched Miss Lavender's. He was casually dressed in a white, open-neck shirt — Lily couldn't help noticing the designer label — and dark navy Marco Polo jeans. He wore a gold watch but no ring, and was holding an iPhone in his right hand, as well as the keys to his Jaguar. *The perfect model of a successful businessman,* Lily thought, *and charming to a degree. Shame he was already married. If he weren't, Ben would stand no chance against this one, even if Nate didn't happen to be Louisa May's father.*

'Are you here for the Barista Masterclass?'

'Yes. We thought …'

'Well, *hello*! I thought you wouldn't come in today at all, what with it being your grandma's ninetieth birthday. Shouldn't you be in Windermere by now?' Hayley was emerging from the kitchen bearing two cappuccinos on a small oval tray. She put it down on a table and kissed Nate's cheeks.

Lily and Jessie exchanged glances. *What was going on here?*

'Yes, well — I'm on my way, actually. I just needed to pick up the present which … God, I can't believe it's you! — Hayley, meet Jessie Nilsson, my long-lost friend from school. I haven't seen her since then, and here she is, all ready to do a Barista Class — and I can't even stay! Bugger!' He raked his hair, took off his glasses, and put them back on again, all the while shaking his head. 'I wish I had more time but … will you at least have a cup of coffee with me? Oh. I see you already have one. Hayley, would you be so kind as to get me one, too?'

Hayley rolled her eyes at Lily. 'You'd better come through and leave them to it. The others should turn up any minute, and my husband, hopefully. Nate, you can make your own coffee!'

Lily nodded, and turned to Jessie as she picked up her cappuccino. 'Is that okay with you?'

But Jessie was not even looking at her, so she followed Hayley to the back room, glancing back over her shoulder just in time to see Nate hugging her friend and kissing her cheeks. She somehow doubted he would still make it in time for his Nana's birthday party.

***

'Well?'

'Well what?' Jessie slid into the vacant seat next to Lily and poured herself a cup of coffee. 'Mmm,' she said after her first sip, smacking her lips, 'good coffee! A nice sticky cinnamon swirl would go very well with this one,' she winked, her cornflower blue eyes shining with excitement.

Without a word, Lily got the crumpled paper bag out of her handbag and held it out to Jessie. A look of mock horror on her face, Jessie pushed it down, hissing 'Stop it!' and slapping her arm playfully before she burst into a fit of giggles.

Just then Gabe, Hayley's husband, walked in, and Hayley got up, visibly relieved that he had made it on time after all. 'Ah, here he is now. I'll leave you all to it then. Have fun!'

'And patience is a virtue, my dear! I'll tell you all about it on the way home,' Jessie whispered and drained her coffee cup. Then she sat in an annoyingly upright position and flashed her best schoolgirl smile at Gabe who, after having introduced himself as the 'Barista Master Number Two here at *The Coffee Experience*, second only to Master Sullivan himself' plunged right into the fascinating history of coffee.

Lily pouted. 'On the way home? I can't wait that long!'

A discreet beep announced the arrival of a message on Jessie's phone. Judging from the way her face flushed as she bent her head to read it, Lily thought she could not be the only one whose strongest virtue was definitely not patience.

***

'So ARE YOU going to meet him then?'

They were sitting in Jessie's kitchen drinking wine and eating crisps from a great value pack they had picked up at the service station, and Lily had given up counting the discreet little *bings* on her friend's phone.

Jessie grinned. 'And wouldn't you like to know?'

'Jessie! That's not fair! You said you would tell me all

about it on the way home, but you were texting all the time, or sitting there with your eyes half closed, dreaming away … come on, you could at least answer my question!'

'Alright, alright. Yes, we are going to meet. Next week. For a meal, in Carlton-in-Cleveland, so not impossibly far from here. Nate says there is a popular pub that offers authentic Thai cuisine, *The Blackwell Ox*. I have never heard of it, but I love Thai food and am quite ready to give it a go.'

Lily sat her glass down with a thud and gaped at her friend. 'I don't think we are talking about *Thai cuisine* here, are we? We are talking about a hot date with the father of your teenage daughter! Who, if I may say so, is quite hot himself. Not my type but —'

'Lily! It's only a meal! We just want to get together and talk — there is so much we do not know about each other, so much to tell …' She blushed. 'And just as much to conceal, I suppose. To quote Jane Austen. Well, I can't very well tell him about Louisa May on our first …'

'Ha!' Lily cried, grinning madly. 'Got you! It *is* a date!'

Blushing even deeper, Jessie tried her best to talk herself out of it. 'No, it's not! It's — we'll just meet up to share a meal, and spend a nice evening together. That's all there is to it, really.' She bit her lip. 'At least I hope it is. What if he asks about my family though? What will I tell him?'

'The truth, I should hope. And you'd better be prepared, because he will ask about your family, your private life … it's what people do when they first meet someone — or meet someone again after a long time. It's what Joseph and I did when we went on our first walks together. We took our time getting to know each other and — well, here we are.'

'Well, if you put it like that I suppose you're right …' Jessie sighed. 'Oh, but Lily, if I tell him I'm a single mum and have a twelve year old daughter, it won't take him long to figure out the rest!'

'I guess not. But why don't you play it by the ear, hm? Let him do the talking first. And then … well, you will know what to say when you get there. He seemed a very decent sort of man. And I'm so glad he is not married to the lovely Hayley!'

Jessie laughed. 'Yes, me, too. She is too good to be true, isn't she? I have never seen fingernails like hers. How does she keep them so long and shiny working in a coffee shop? And being the mum of two little boys, too?'

'I don't know. She was nice enough though, and so was Gabe. And we learnt a lot! In a way, I'm glad Nate was not there to distract you. I can't wait to practise my cappuccino skills on you tomorrow morning. It's alright for me to stay the night, isn't it?'

'I can't let you drive after half a bottle of red, can I? Shall we order a pizza? I'm starving!'

'Good,' said Lily, reaching for her phone to check out the menu of the nearest pizza service, 'so am I. Let's order a large one with all the trimmings, yes?'

While they were waiting for their pizza, Lily showed Jessie the photos Joseph had sent, and asked her if she thought it wise to go down to London and surprise him at the airport when he got back from his trip next Sunday.

'I thought it might be a nice idea, but if that Roisin woman …'

'Oh, bugger *that Roisin woman*! She's married, and he has been texting you about twenty times every day since he left, what does that tell you about his feelings? Eh?'

'Jessie! I never knew you could swear!'

Jessie shrugged. 'There's lots of things you don't know

about me. But seriously, I think you have been mooching about for quite long enough. Go to London, make him smile. He will love you forever — and *she* can bugger off to Ireland just as soon as the plane has landed. Who says she even comes back to Heathrow with the lads?'

Lily pulled a face. 'No one. Just a feeling I have. So, if I go down to Oxford that weekend, I could sort out my flat, move the rest of my furniture to my parents', leave the key with the estate agent, and come back with Joseph on the Sunday.' She scrunched up her nose. 'Gosh, that's a bit too much for one weekend, isn't it? Maybe I should just —'

'Stop it!' Jessie threw the cork of the wine bottle at her. 'For heavens' sake, stop it! It's a brilliant idea, wonderfully romantic, very *Lily*. Just do it.'

CHAPTER THIRTY-SIX

THE FOLLOWING FRIDAY, Lily was heading south for a weekend of packing the last of the boxes, while her brother and father would take apart the furniture that would go into storage. Then she would only have to clean the flat and drop off the keys at the estate agents' on her way to the airport on Sunday. The hardest part, she thought as she stopped at a service station for a coffee, would be to stop herself from boarding the next best flight to Tenerife for a holiday in the sun. After the week she had had, she could certainly do with one.

David had called on Monday to say he would be in Bishops Bridge the next day, and would she like to see the bookshelf he had made (of course!), as well as a few paint samples to help her decide on the colour. So on Tuesday afternoon they had had a very efficient work meeting on the premises — everything was super efficient with David, as Lily had found out (in that respect he was very much like Becky Jessop, who had taken to bombarding her with urgent e-mails regarding the barn conversion) — and decided on the number and size of the shelves, the style of counter Lily wanted, and the colours for the walls (sage green to match the cream pinewood shelves and the rustic white cream brushed oak floorboards). They had just agreed that it would be best for her and Susanna to agree on the day they wanted to make a start on the walls when Miss Lavender had popped her head in, announcing a visitor.

'This is Kelly Graham from the *Rosedale Gazette*. She would like to do a quick interview with you, Lily, about the shop. Do you have fifteen minutes?'

There would have been hundreds of things Lily would have preferred to do instead, as she was shy and hated talking to strangers, but David had encouraged her, reminding her with a friendly wink that publicity was everything. And of course, she had made sure to mention the custom-made shelves David was going to make, and the *Squirrel of Lofthouse* — although for how long it would be called that and not the *Squirrel of Rosedale*, Lily did not know. With David, it was 'Susanna this' and 'Susanna that' in almost every sentence. It was abundantly clear that he was just as much in love with her as ever.

Kelly was young, twenty-five at the most, with blonde hair tied in a prettily plaited ponytail and serious brown eyes behind huge, round glasses. But she was utterly charming, and before Lily knew it she had told her everything — about her coming to Rosedale in the spring and falling in love with the place, her deciding to leave city life behind and open a bookshop on her great-aunt's farm (namely because that gave her the chance to mention the holiday cottages — talking of publicity!), and Miss Lavender's proposition that changed everything.

'And with The Bridge Café on the right, we have great hopes to be able to put lovely little Bishops Bridge on the map good and proper,' she had said, and blushed when

David had raised his eyebrows at her, nodding approvingly as he gave her a big smile.

God, she still could not believe she had said all that! She felt almost like a totally different person — confident, bold, and ambitious, David had called her afterwards. And Miss Lavender had said she was proud of her, and quite looking forward to working with her. She only hoped she would not disappoint the old lady.

Confident, bold, and ambitious. Am I really, she thought, *any, or even all of these things?* Only this morning another message from Amelia had arrived — she still wanted to meet up for that coffee. She knew she would have to tell her the truth, or she would never get out of this. There was no need to mention Joseph perhaps, but she should tell her that she was going to Yorkshire, to start a new life. She felt she owed her that much.

***

SHE HAD JUST poured herself a glass of wine when Beth rang.

'Hey, you! How is Devon?'

'Great,' was the sarcastic reply, making Lily sit bolt upright with surprise and shock. Beth resorting to sarcasm meant that something must be seriously wrong — she just hoped Beth had not fallen out with Matthew, or that something was wrong with the twins. 'Matthew has fallen off a ladder and is awaiting surgery in the hospital. I'm stuck here with all those boxes, paint charts, a half-finished nursery, and back pain that would drive the Holy Mary round the bend. Sorry. I'm not well, really. So, do cheer me up — how's things with your aunt and that nasty neighbour of hers? The last thing I heard was he was blackmailing her into cooking for him. Does he still do that?'

'Well, no, but he is still around and still a pain, so I'd be really grateful if you could pray for something to happen that might take him away for good. He doesn't have to die!' she added hastily, 'just … you know. Go away. And I'm sorry about your back pain and Matthew being in hospital. I hope you'll find some relief soon! I wish I could come and help you but I'm so busy … I have just come back to Oxford to vacate the flat — that's the echo you can hear, it's bouncing off the empty walls …'

'Good. It means you are finally moving out — and *on*! You have come far in six months, Lily. I'm really proud of you. As for that terrible man … I never thought I'd say it and please don't tell Matthew, but I have actually been tempted to pray for him to have another stroke — not a big one, just serious enough to get him out of your hair once and for all. And I didn't actually — pray for *that* to happen, I mean. I was just … tempted.'

Lily laughed. 'Beth! You have changed your tune! Is it the hormones? Or the back pain? Sorry, that wasn't funny. Remind me please, when are the twins due? I'm sure you have told me a hundred times, but I am terribly forgetful these days — too much going on in quiet little Bishops Bridge.'

'The due date is the twenty-first of October. They will probably be delivered by caesarean a couple of days before … scary. Oh well, it's another two months. Now they've got to get my husband up and running first. He managed to twist his knee so badly when he fell that it's most likely torn his meniscus — he's had meniscus surgery before, it seems it's his Achilles' heel.'

When Lily told her about Amelia's persistent invitation

for coffee, Beth surprised her by saying not to bother seeing her in person. 'You can text her. Honestly, it's fine, Lily — she needs to get on with her life, and you have every right to get on with yours. If she hadn't seen you at the station, she might never have got in touch in the first place! Right, I'll let you get on with your packing now; Matthew is just calling on the other line. Take care, God bless, bye!'

Lily stared at the phone in her hand. What on earth had got into Beth? *Don't bother to see Amelia?* Was that kind? She had to be in bad pain — and worried about Matthew of course. No wonder she had seemed so uncharacteristically brusque.

With a sigh and a shake of her head, Lily went on packing until well after midnight, and fell asleep the moment her head hit the mattress on the living room floor.

***

'Lily!'

Joseph only stopped in his tracks for ten seconds, then he rushed forward to sweep Lily off her feet, swing her around and put her down on the floor before him. 'What a lovely surprise! Did you know you were coming when we spoke on Thursday?'

'Of course. I had it all planned — right to the moment when you see me and whirl me around, just like you did!' Determined not even to deign Roisin with a look until she absolutely had to (why was she here at all and not in Dublin where she belonged?), she asked, 'How was your flight?'

He took her face in his hands and kissed her. 'Do you really want to know?' he murmured as he planted tiny and deliciously soft kisses along her neckline, like bubbles rising to the surface of those natural hot springs in Arizona. She was just beginning to feel very hot indeed, when suddenly a hand grabbed Joseph's arm, jerking him away from her as if she was not there at all. Lily was too horrified to speak. This was absolutely inconceivable!

'Hey! You forgot to give me back my pen! It's in your shirt pocket — wait, let me just …' Pushing Lily aside as if she was nothing but an irritating fly, Roisin was just standing on her toes to reach Joseph's pocket when Liam's booming voice sounded from behind.

'Oh *come on*, Roisin, surely you can see the guy is busy!' He grabbed his sister by the sleeve of her jacket and shook his head at her. Turning to Lily, he said, 'Hi, Lily, great to see you. And great to deliver him safely back into your hands — or arms, whatever. I swear he was talking of nothing else for two weeks, it was always Lily, Lily, Lily!'

Was it? thought Lily, still reeling from the shock of being pushed aside by that woman — and with Joseph just letting it happen! It was Liam who had stepped in, not Joseph. She looked at Joseph, stunned — *why isn't he doing anything about it, if he really talked about me every day? Why doesn't he tell her to go away?*

'There you are. Sorry I kept it, I didn't mean to,' Joseph said, getting a silver pen out of his pocket and handing it to Roisin with a smile, all the while holding Lily in his arm. It cost her all of her self-discipline not to tear away.

Holding the pen in her left hand, Roisin reached up to his cheek with the other hand, stroking it slowly and in an annoyingly sensual way that made Lily want to scream. 'Aw, thank you. It means a lot to me, this pen — you gave it to me for my twenty-fifth birthday, remember? So I could write to you. Those were the days, eh?' And then she stood on her toes again and whispered so loudly that everybody could hear, 'You will send me all the pictures, won't you, Joey, and that video you did of me riding last night, when it was so hot I had to take my top off?'

'Roisin!'

Suddenly someone did push Roisin away, and with considerable force, too. Sadly, it was not Joseph but Liam.

'Will you just leave it now?' he hissed at his sister as he pushed her roughly towards a shop window. But even though he dropped his voice to a furious whisper, Lily could not help hearing. 'For goodness' sake, Roisin! Why can't you just leave him alone? God, I am so tired of playing chaperone to the pair of you twenty-four-seven, I can't wait to get home! I will need another three weeks holiday to recover!'

Slap!

Lily's hand left a bright red mark on Joseph's cheek. The moment she saw the look on his face though — a mixture of surprise, hurt, anger, and disappointment — she could have cried.

What have I done, she thought, as her cheeks flushed a hot crimson and tears began to prick at the back of her eyes. *What have I done?*

'I'm sorry,' she whispered, a hand over her mouth, 'I'm so sorry!' And because she did not know what else to do, she turned and ran away.

***

THE THING WITH *dramatic exits*, Lily thought as she sat in one of the airport cafés, an open packet of crisps, a half-eaten panini, and a bottle of Ribena in front of her, *is you never take the time to stop and think about what to do next.*

What on earth has got into me? I don't normally walk around hitting people, do I? And in public, too! Poor Joseph. Whatever must he think of me now?

She shook her head. It didn't matter now, did it? It was too late. She had slapped him, publicly, and walked out on him, that was two big mistakes in just twenty seconds. How could he ever forgive her? She could hardly blame him for not calling after her, or even following her. She certainly would not have run after the man who had just publicly humiliated her. And she had got her fair share of humiliating when she had been with Spencer, even if he had never hurt her physically, and probably never hurt her deliberately either with his snobbish remarks.

Goodness, is that the best dress you have? We are going to the opera, for Christ's sake, not to a pop concert. Oh well, I suppose I'll have to take you shopping. He had, too. He had bought her a beautiful burgundy evening gown, which she had worn once, on another visit to the opera. After his death, she had given it to a charity shop.

But hitting someone! Hitting *Joseph* of all people — kind, gentle, good-natured Joseph ... who probably did not even realize what was happening when that dreadful woman threw herself at him. How could she have been so cruel? He did not deserve that! He did not deserve such a bitch as *her*. He deserved someone who adored him, who ...

She answered the phone the moment it rang. 'Yes?'

'Lily! Thank God. Are you still at the airport?'

'Yes,' she said in a very small voice. She did not know what else to say. She felt like crying.

'Where are you? Can I see you? I'm walking through Terminal 3 right now ... I have been looking for you everywhere. Please, Lily, wherever you are, wait for me!

We need to talk.'

He was too kind! He should not be so kind now! What was wrong with him? Why wasn't he shouting at her? She deserved to be shouted at. And worse.

'I'm ... I'm sitting at Pret's – um ... Terminal 3, actually. Level 1. Will you find that?'

'I'll find you anywhere. Just don't go.'

'I won't,' she choked, 'promise.'

I'll find you anywhere. As soon as he had rung off, she put her face in her hands and began to cry.

'I'm so sorry, Joseph,' she sobbed when he had found her. 'I'm so, so sorry!' She could not bring herself to look at him, even when he crouched beside her and gently took her in his arms. How could he be so kind to her?

'I don't know what came over me! I just — when she ...'

He shushed her. 'Shhh! It's okay. You walking away hurt me more than anything. I suppose I deserved that slap — I should never have let her get near me. *Us.* I'm sorry, Lily. And just for the record, I never took a single picture or video of her, and I certainly never saw her ... you know. Without decent covering. She is such a bitch — and a notorious liar, too. I promise I will never see her again. I won't even invite her to our wedding— oops!' His hand flew to his mouth, but his blue eyes were laughing, and soon enough, Lily, in spite of herself, joined in. But the next moment she was crying again, and he kissed her tears away one by one.

'Do you think you would take me back to Yorkshire after all?' he asked over a cup of coffee and a brownie to share. 'You have brought your car, haven't you? Liam has taken a train, and Roisin is staying in London with her husband for a couple of days. I expect they have got some sorting out to do. But never mind her — this is about us, hey?'

She nodded and reached out to touch his cheek. Thankfully, the red mark had almost gone. 'Yes … I can do that. I will take you home, Joseph — both of us. Home to Yorkshire.'

***

In the end, Joseph did most of the driving, while Lily, exhausted from the emotional toll the last few weeks had taken on her, slept. She hardly even noticed Joseph turning into the drive of Fern Hill Farm and Abi coming to greet them both, Theo following at heel.

'I think I had better borrow Lily's car to get myself home, Abi. Do you think she'll mind?'

Abi shook her head and gently steered Lily towards the stairs. She moved like a sleepwalker. 'As long as *you* are back home safe and sound, lad, I don't think she'll mind anything. But do come in for a cup of tea first. Have you eaten?'

'No, but I'd better get going — I'm expected back at work at seven tomorrow morning. That's the price you pay for a summer holiday! Bye, Abi. Bye, Lily!' He blew Lily a kiss and then he was gone.

CHAPTER THIRTY-SEVEN

ON WEDNESDAY THEY all met for a meal at the *Dog and Partridge*. By then both Joseph and Lily had had enough sleep, and Joseph had found his working routine again while Lily had been busy painting the walls of the shop with Susanna, and ordering the first stock. It was only four weeks until the opening now, and the article in the *Gazette* — as well as her posts on Facebook, Twitter, and Instagram — had drawn a lot of public attention. Suddenly Lily had ninety-six followers — and that was her private account, not the official one she had created for the shop.

They had just finished their starters when Lily's phone rang. 'I thought I had left it at home,' she said, pulling the phone out of her handbag while mouthing *sorry* to the others. 'Hello?'

'Lily, it's me,' said Susanna at the other end, sounding flustered. 'Sorry for interrupting, but can you please come home? Abi is having a major crisis, but she won't tell me what it is about. I have a feeling the Horrid Man has been back, because I heard her muttering his name. I have made her an extra strong cup of tea, David has even offered whisky, but she is still shaking. I can't get a word out of her. Can you come double quick?'

Lily frowned, then turned to Joseph, phone still in her hand. 'How fast can you drive?'

***

'I THOUGHT HE had thrown it away — he *said so* when I asked him some years ago. When he was just getting divorced from number three. But now he claims it to be in his bedside drawer, and threatens to show it to Kelly and make her print it in the *Gazette*, so everybody would see me …' She covered her face with her hands. 'Oh, that dreadful man! Why can't he have another stroke and bugger off to some care home — preferably in the south, so I shall never have to see him again!'

'Good idea,' Lily remarked drily. 'But in the meantime, we will have to come up with a plan to retrieve that blasted picture. — Hold on! How did he get here on his own when he can't even walk? I hope that stuck-up daughter of his is not back for another duty visit to her *dear Daddy*?'

'Lily!'

Eyes blazing with fury, Lily turned around. 'Yes! *Bloody* and *blasted*! I've had enough, Abi — I cannot possibly think of any polite words to describe that horrid man or the impossible situation he is putting you in!'

She was pacing the room, trying to think of even more swear words but found that she was too angry to think of anything much. Joseph, who did not have a clue what all this was about, and thought it best not to ask just now, busied himself with making coffee. Susanna and David had left shortly after Joseph and Lily had come bursting through the door. They had found a distraught Abi sitting at the kitchen table, an untouched glass of whisky and a mug of cold tea in front of her.

Abi sighed. 'He did not actually *come* here. He called me — to tell me he had read Kelly's article about the bookshop in the *Gazette*. Said he did not see why you should come and set up business here and get all the help and support even from the villagers when I, as his neighbour, wouldn't even take pity on him and cook him some decent meals. And as for David's name in the papers ... well, that just about did it, I suppose. He did not comment on that. But Susanna, bless that girl, just happened to knock on my door after he had rung off — she wanted to know if we needed anything from *Sainsburys* as they were going to place an order, and when she saw that I was upset, she first called David and then you.'

'Very sensible. She's a really good neighbour — they both are,' she said, thinking of how effortlessly David had become a part of the Bishops Bridge community again, almost as if he had never left.

Joseph put his arms around Lily's waist and whispered, 'Do you mind if I just leave you to it now? I'll be on early morning duty, so I'd better grab some sleep.'

'Of course. — Abi, do drink that whisky David poured you, it will do you good. I'm seeing Joseph out.'

Outside in the yard, Joseph took her in his arms to claim a proper kiss, and after promising to call her tomorrow, he walked to his car and drove off, leaving Lily to calm Abi. At least she had finished the whisky by the time Lily walked back into the kitchen, and chirped, 'Joseph is a nice lad. So kind and helpful — and discreet, too. He didn't even ask what this was all about. You didn't tell him, did you? About that wretched picture, I mean?'

'Of course not! I haven't told a soul.'

'Of course you haven't. I'm sorry, lass.' Abi got up and

put the tumbler in the sink. 'I've been thinking, Lily — how does that Man always seem to know when I'm on my own? Does he sit there with a pair of binoculars like James Stewart in *Rear Window*?'

Lily sighed. 'I don't know. I'm here now, so we can go to bed. Becky is coming tomorrow, to discuss the time frame with me. She'll be here at eight o'clock sharp, so we'd better …'

But Abi was not listening. 'I really don't know what's eating that man,' she muttered under her breath. 'Perhaps he is jealous? Because I have a lovely great-niece who's come to live with me, and he has a heartless daughter who wants to lock him up in a care home far from —'

'To be honest, Abi, I don't care what's eating him or not,' Lily cut in, tired of discussing that wretched man. 'You reap what you sow, don't you? And some people actually get what they deserve, too. I'll get that picture back for you, if it's the last thing I do!'

'But, Lily, he says he has already sent it to Mary and asked her to make photocopies, and then he'll get Kelly Graham to print it in the *Gazette*. Oh Lily, this is dreadful! What will people think if they see me like that?'

'But they *won't*, Abi! Kelly is a sensible girl, she won't even think about printing that picture. Why would she? And anyway, I think he is just bluffing. Because honestly, what would he gain? Would people really respect you less, or like him more? No! And as I don't even *have* a reputation here yet, and therefore nothing to lose, I am going to stop this nonsense once and for all!'

'How?'

Lily placed her hands on her hips. Shaking her head as she stood at the window, she let out an exasperated sigh. 'I don't know. I'll think of something.'

***

AND BECAUSE THERE was no better place for late night thinking than a cosy stable full of sweet smelling hay and no better listener than a donkey with his long ears, she went to find William after Abi had gone to bed.

'Oh, William,' she whispered, stroking the warm coat on his neck, 'Whatever have I got myself into now, eh? Did I seriously hope to find peace and quiet on Auntie Abigail's farm? I must have been dreaming! Anyway, I think it's time we hatched a plan, don't you think, to retrieve that blasted picture. Move over a little, I want to sit with you. There, that'll do.'

Sitting down in the straw next to the blissfully munching donkey, Lily pulled up her knees to her chest. 'The question is, how can we get that man out of the house without raising suspicion? Now, I was thinking of getting Abi's friends on board, you know, the Bishops Bridge Gossip Crew. Only this time they would have to swear to secrecy — yeah, I know, that's the hardest part. But I'm sure they would do it for Abi. I wouldn't have to tell them exactly what this is about, would I? So, once they have solemnly promised not to breathe a word …'

CHAPTER THIRTY-EIGHT

Lily put down her paintbrush when Jessie stuck her head in. 'I saw you alright — do come in, I could do with a break. Coffee? Although I have only instant on offer, and no milk, so you might want to bring some over — I'll pay, too.'

'No, you're alright, I've got two cappuccinos. Leftover carrot cake, too — um, Lily? Do you mind if we sit outside? The smell of that paint really makes me sick. And before you ask, no, I'm not pregnant!'

Stretching her aching back until it gave a satisfying crack, Lily got up from the corner where she had been crouching for the best part of an hour, painting the 'fiddly bits' as Susanna called them. Susanna had several commissions to see to and had not been able to come in for a painting session today. It was a beautiful sunny day, and Lily did not mind sitting outside in the least. Also, it would take her mind off things — for she had not been able to think of anything much but the retrieval of the wretched picture these days, especially with Joseph working all hours and her great-aunt being constantly on edge since Nettleton had hurled his absurd threats at her on Tuesday.

Although she couldn't for the life of her understand

why Nettleton should still have such power over her otherwise perfectly self-confident great-aunt. Even if he was still in possession of that sketch, surely he wouldn't put photocopies of it in the shop windows, would he, out of spite? And whose shop windows would that be, anyway — Miss Lavender's? Certainly not. Honest, upright Miss Lavender was the last person on earth who would allow a Brian Nettleton to try and get her involved in any silly revenge scheme. He would never hear the last of it.

'So, what's the news?'

Jessie looked at her with round, innocent blue eyes. 'What news?'

'Jessica Nilsson! You went out with him last Thursday and I haven't heard *a thing*! Nothing at all! It's not fair. Come on, what happened? Tell me!'

'Well …' Jessie took her time opening a sachet of sugar and pouring the contents into her milk froth (no fancy hearts today, Lily noted with a wry smile.), then took her teaspoon, stirred, and licked it with annoying devotion until Lily could bear it no longer and snatched the spoon from her.

'Now then. Where did you go, what did you wear, what did you eat, did you share a pudding, did you tell him about Louisa May, will you see him again? You can answer these in any order you like. Just. Don't. Procrastinate.'

Jessie shrugged. 'Okay. Here goes. I wore my usual jeans and my favourite blue silk top, and we met at The Blackwell Ox in Carlton, as I recall telling you we would. The food was lovely, and I had a frightfully spicy vegetable stir-fry, and no, we did not share a pudding. I didn't even have one, I was so full. And yes, I had to tell him about Louisa May. He asked if I had any family, and when I said I had a daughter, he asked to see a picture. He says she looks gorgeous.'

Lily laughed. 'Of course he would say that! She's his daughter — and the spitting image of you! Which means he thinks *you* are gorgeous, too.'

Blushing, Jessie took a sip of her cappuccino. 'Yes, well ... but then he asked how old she was and ... well, you can guess the rest. He was quite cool about it — or at least, he *seemed* cool. I don't know him very well, do I? Not at all, actually. Not now. He says he wants to see me again and — oh, God, Lily! What am I to do? How did I ever get myself into this mess?'

'For one thing, it was me who got you into this mess — and for another, I don't think it is a mess at all. It's a chance! A chance to ... set things right. Sooner or later you would have told Louisa May about her father, anyway, so why not now? And it doesn't have to be tomorrow.'

Jessie nodded. 'True. But what do you think? Should I tell Louisa May first, or —'

'Jessie. One step at a time. Meet him again, get to know each other again, and then — you'll work things out. Louisa May is a smart girl, she will not be fooled. I suspect she will know her father when she sees him.'

'Yes, that's what I thought. Just like he knew she was his daughter the moment he saw the picture. He wasn't even angry, you know — for me not telling him. He completely understood. He remembered the accident, too, and the state I was in that summer ... well. How could anyone ever forget something so awful?'

Lily put an arm around her shoulder. 'No one. Of course not. You are doing the right thing, Jessie. Just take it slowly — there is no rush.' Suddenly she remembered something she had been dying to ask Jessie since Tuesday: Ben had not been at the pub, which she had thought very odd, knowing that he rarely missed an opportunity to see Jessie, or to enjoy a pint or two. 'Um — what about Ben? Does he know? I mean — does he even know anything? About Nate being Louisa May's father and about us going to see him in Durham?'

Jessie bit her lip. 'Yes. I told him. That's why he didn't come to the pub on Tuesday. He says he needs some space — I can't blame him for that, can I? Things are complicated enough as they are between us. For a start, I know he likes me a lot more than I like him. I mean — I like him but … I don't think I'm in love with him. I thought I was, but now I'm not sure I ever was. Not enough, anyway, to want to be in a relationship with him.'

'But you told him that, too? He knows you are not interested?'

'Oh, he knows that alright. He is just the type who doesn't ever give up — I'm not sure he will now!' She sighed. 'It's a bit of a tricky business, really. Not only because we have been friends for so long — I'm also renting his cottage, and his mum looked after Louisa May when she was little, so …'

'So what? You don't owe him anything, except the rent. And if you and Nate should really hit it off and want to give family life a try, why, you can always find another house, can't you? Anyway, as I said, there is no rush at all.'

***

LILY WAS IN no particular rush herself when she walked home later in the fading light of the day, stopping here and there to pick some of the late summer flowers from Farmer Marston's field that she was going to put in a vase on the kitchen table later. The lambs were almost fully grown by now and, at least for Lily, indistinguishable from their mothers. Unlike his next door neighbour, Mr Marston was a kind-hearted man; she had stopped ever so often to chat to him when she saw him in the yard, or when he passed her on his tractor. Abi had told her that the Marstons had had their two children later in life and that both, the boy and the girl, suffered from cerebral palsy. At thirty-two and twenty-eight, Edward and Victoria still lived at home and were lovingly cared for by their parents — for how much longer they would be able to do that was a different matter.

When Lily passed Wood End Farm, her lips formed a thin line of angry determination as she thought of the plan she had hatched to retrieve the sketch. She had instructed Abi's three friends carefully, and all she needed was for Mr Nettleton to rise to the bait they were going to throw him. And of course Abi to be lured away for the day — but thanks to Mrs Talbot, there seemed to be a perfect solution to that problem, too.

'I will ask her to come to York with me next Friday. I need a dress to wear at my grandson's wedding, I could do with some advice — it's not like your great-aunt is an expert when it comes to fashion, but it'll have to do. Two blind chickens finding a grain ... and then we'll go to *Bettys* for afternoon tea, to make sure we won't be back too soon.'

Lily smiled. Mrs Talbot was lovely — actually, all of Abi's neighbours were, except Brian Nettleton! According to Abi, even grumpy old Wilkinson, who reputedly put his precious cows before his own wife, was a sensible man once you got to know him. He had been keen to hear about Lily's plans for the barn and offered to spread the word among their large family circle who frequently came to visit, saying he was sure they would be delighted to stay in one of the cottages.

She pulled out her phone to read the message that had come in.

> How was your day painting? I hope you'll have that green washed out of your hair by the time we meet on Sunday ;-) Can't wait to see you then! Seven o'clock, by the gate! J xx

Laughing at his referral to her traumatic hair-dye-experience which she had told him about, she slipped the phone back into her pocket. They had arranged to meet for an early morning walk and a picnic breakfast, and Lily was looking forward to it immensely, since they had not had the chance to see each other since pub night on Tuesday. If that was what it was like to be married to a country vet, she would have to find something to fill her days — and nights, too! – waiting for him to come home …

Here you go again, Lily Henderson, she thought, shaking her head, *dreaming about your very own picture-perfect country life. How do you know that that is what* he *wants, too?*

Because he said so. Four children, and two dogs. No cats, at least not in the house — they could sleep in the barn with William and catch mice. Of course they would have a large house in the country, perhaps with a veterinary surgery attached so people could …

'Hello there! Can I offer you a lift?'

Lily started as she turned to see Lucy stopping her car a few yards behind her. She had not even heard her coming!

'Oh! Hi, Lucy. No, don't worry, it's not far now, is it, and it's such a beautiful evening. I'll see you next week at the *Dog and Partridge?* Quiz night?'

Lucy gave her the thumbs up and inched her way past her, waving out of the open window as she did. Then she accelerated and sped up the lane, leaving Lily to shake her head and laugh. Picking a last sunflower, she started to run up the lane, her curls flying in the wind.

***

On Sunday morning, Lily got up extra early to get ready for her rendezvous with Joseph. She washed her hair (the paint had come out easily, unlike the hair dye back when she was a child) and splashed her wrists and neck with Coco de Chanel (her mum's obligatory Christmas present and Lily's last reminder of her Oxford days) before pulling on a pair of bootcut jeans. Knowing it would be chilly, she put on her Fair Isle pullover and her new Joules socks with a fox on each foot. They were soft and warm. When she had dried her hair with a towel — she did not want to wake Abi with the hair dryer — she tiptoed down the stairs, made a thermos flask full of coffee and popped the sticky buns she had made the evening before into a greaseproof bag. At quarter to seven, she slipped out of the house, whistling to Theo as she did.

Half an hour later, she was still waiting. Leaving Theo to stand watch by the gate, Lily went back into the house to get her mobile, but there was no message, and no missed call either.

'That's odd — he may be scatter-brained, but he is not unreliable. Hm. What do you think, Theo? Should we have a coffee and a bun to pass the time? Not yet? You would wait until half past seven? Okay. Let's do that then.'

But at half past seven there still was no sign of Joseph,

no message, no phone call. Lily tried calling him, but he did not answer. She texted him but got no reply. Finally, when she was getting cold, and a fine drizzle was beginning to fall, she turned and started to walk back to the house. She was just going to push the door open when she heard the screeching of tyres behind her and spun around — and was surprised to see Lucy's and not Joseph's car stopping outside the gates. Within two seconds, the door was flung open, and Lucy came running towards her. She was crying.

'Lucy! Whatever are *you* doing here at this time of day? What's happened?'

'It's Joseph! Oh, Lily, it's Joseph!' Lucy was out of breath and tears were running down her cheeks as she stopped just inches before Lily, grabbing her shoulders. 'Lily, I'm so sorry —there … there has been an accident —'

'What??'

'An accident! And it's really bad, Lily. There were cows and … oh God, Lily!' She caught Lily, who had begun to sway dangerously, just in time, and spoke hurriedly, and with great urgency. 'Dad sent me, he said you had to know right away. We actually saw the helicopter in the field — you might have seen it, too —, but we had no idea it was carrying *Joseph*!'

Lily stared at her friend. 'What are you talking about, Lucy? What cows? What field? We were going to go for a walk! That's why I'm standing here at this gate — because I've been waiting for him to collect me! He *can't* have been in a field! And what heli —' Then suddenly she remembered. Yes, there had been the sound of a helicopter at around the time she was coming out of the bathroom. She had not given it any notice of course — how could she have known?

'Oh God! Tell me this isn't true! Please!' Covering her eyes with her hands, she began to sob. It had to be a mistake, a terrible, terrible mistake! It had to be someone else, someone who might have had any business to do up there. A farmer, or even another vet, but not Joseph! Surely, this could not be happening to her *again*, could it?

She turned to Lucy, her eyes wide with fear. '*Please* tell me you're wrong. He wasn't even on duty, he —'

Wiping her cheeks with the sleeve of her sweater, Lucy shook her head, then gave an inaudible sigh of relief as she saw Abi emerging from the farmhouse, a look of concern on her face. Lucy put up a hand to signal her to come over. To Lily, she said, 'I'm sorry, Lily, but I'm afraid it is true. They are taking him to Hull Infirmary. Mum told me, and she's had it from Mrs Wilkinson. They were the ones who called the ambulance, obviously. Do you want me to take you there? To Hull?'

CHAPTER THIRTY-NINE

'I'M SORRY, MISS, we can't let you through. At least, I'd have to check with the doctor first. But I believe ...' The woman at the reception checked her clipboard. 'Yes, Mr Hancock is in theatre already. But Mr Hancock's parents are waiting in the cafeteria — perhaps you would like to join them? The cafeteria is not open yet, but there is a vending machine, so at least you can get yourselves a hot drink while you wait.'

'We've got a thermos, thank you. Come on, Lucy, let's go.' Dragging a rather overwhelmed Lucy with her — driving with an incessantly sobbing Lily in the passenger seat had proven a hard task even for someone as naturally positive and cheerful as Lucy — Lily followed the signs for the cafeteria. Huddled together at a table in the far corner, Joseph's parents were nursing tea from plastic cups, and they could hear Mrs Hancock cry even from a distance.

'I'm not sure I can wait this long! Three hours, they said. *Three hours* — and I don't even know if he will live!'

'There now, Peggy, don't cry. Don't cry. Mr Wilkinson found him quickly, the ambulance arrived within half an hour, and he is in good hands now. He's a strong lad, is our Joseph, and a fighter. Remember how you thought you were going to lose him when you were pregnant and tired yourself out and had those sharp pains one night — but you didn't, did you? And then, when he was born with the cord around his neck — but they got that sorted quickly, and he was right as rain when they put him in your arms. He will be alright now, love. He will be alright.'

'Is he talking to her, or is he talking to himself?' Lucy whispered, holding Lily back.

'I don't know …' Lily turned to her friend, tears brimming in her eyes. 'Lucy, I don't know if I should even talk to them now. Look at them, clinging to each other! How do you introduce yourself to your boyfriend's parents if you — if you don't even know you *will* be his girlfriend for much longer? Because if he dies …'

'Shh! They might hear you. And of course he is not going to die. He'll be alright, you heard his dad. They know him, they know how strong he is. He won't die. Don't even think it!'

Spencer was strong, wasn't he? Young and fit and strong. That's what I thought, anyway. But I was wrong, wasn't I? He was not strong enough after all. His heart wasn't …

'Come on. Let's offer them some of your coffee. It's fresh, Abi just made it before we left, and we have your buns, too. They might come in handy later.'

'Lucy, I cannot possibly …'

'Later. I said, later. Come on.' Taking Lily's hand, she led her to the table where Joseph's parents were sitting. 'So sorry to interrupt you but — this is my friend Lily, she — she is your son's girlfriend … Do you mind if we sit with you?'

The next thing Lily knew was that she was being pulled into the fiercest hug she had ever received, and pressed firmly against Mrs Hancock's soft, ample bosom. 'Oh, lass — oh, lass!' she cried. 'I am so glad you've come! Our Joseph told us so much about you! Poor lass! If I had known that this was how we should first meet ... Do call me Peggy.'

Lily mumbled something into the fabric of Mrs Hancock's polyester blouse that smelled of 4711 while she heard Lucy introducing herself to Mr Hancock — Joseph, senior, obviously. Then she pulled back and saw Peggy Hancock's tear-streaked face, and burst into tears herself, and suddenly everyone was crying and nothing else mattered.

***

Two hours later, they were still sitting at the same table, but Lucy, practical as ever, had gone out in search of some food. Although the cafeteria was now open, none of them could bring themselves to eat any of the food on offer, and the buns had all gone. Funny, Lily thought, how you could still eat even when you were in the depths of despair. But maybe it was that same old mantra she had been repeating to herself when Spencer had died: *You've got to eat. Not eating won't help.*

'So how did it happen — do you know?' It had taken Lily all this time to summon up the courage to ask the question that had been burning at the back of her mind ever since Lucy had said Joseph had been attacked by cows.

Joseph's dad sighed. 'Well ... from what we've been told by that farmer's wife ...'

'Mrs Wilkinson,' his wife chipped in, dabbing at her eyes with a cotton handkerchief.

'Yes, Mrs Wilkinson — she said that Joseph had been walking through the field, and his dog was following him. He had been called to look at one of their cows apparently ...'

'But he wasn't *on duty* at all!' Lily cried. 'How come he ...'

'Well now, I dunno, lass, it seems that he was after all. That's what Mrs Wilkinson said, anyway. And then — Peggy, do you remember what she said about the dog? Why was Inigo there? Had he escaped from the boot of his car or something? Anyway, the lead cow first went after the dog, and then Joseph got in the way and ...' The big, strong man faltered, and tears fell from his blue eyes. *Joseph's eyes*, Lily thought and swallowed hard.

'And then they were all over him. Mr Wilkinson was there double quick and managed to stop them soon, but by then ...' He shook his head. 'Good thing Mrs Wilkinson called 999 immediately and then went to rescue Inigo while her husband was looking after our Joseph. The dog's still with the Wilkinsons, isn't he, Peggy?'

His wife nodded, patting Lily's hand. 'He is, yes, and they will look after him until somebody picks him up. Inigo could stay with you, couldn't he, Lily? He knows you. I'm sure that that is what Joseph would want.'

'Of course. We'll pick him up on the way home, won't we, Lily?' Lucy put her arm around Lily's shoulder. Lily just nodded, unable to speak.

'Mr and Mrs Hancock?'

They all looked up to see a doctor standing at their table. He was a tall, wiry man in his early fifties, and looked very serious. Lily bit her lip. She hoped he had not come to tell them ...

'My name is Dr Singh. I'm here to tell you how we have been getting on in theatre. If you would like to follow me?'

***

'Now then,' Dr Singh said, steepling his long, slender fingers as he looked from the notes on his desk to Joseph's parents. 'Being farmers, you will probably know that the risk of getting attacked by a herd of cattle is relatively low. However, if they do attack, it is very often fatal. In your son's case, it was … pretty close, but he was lucky in that the farmer stepped in so quickly and the ambulance arrived so soon. He did suffer some serious injuries, however — will you be alright to hear this, young lady? You do look very pale.'

Lily, who was just wondering how Dr Singh knew that the Hancocks were retired farmers, started as she felt the doctor's gaze on her. 'Sorry?'

'You look very pale — are you sure you want to hear this? I will be giving Mr Hancock's parents here a detailed account of the injuries your boyfriend suffered. You can wait outside if you'd rather.'

Lily shook her head. 'No! No, please — I want to hear it. I need to know …'

Mrs Hancock, who was sitting next to her, gave Lily's hand a reassuring squeeze. There was a worryingly loud rushing sound in her ears, and Mrs Hancock's hand felt clammy on hers, but Lily did not dare pull away for fear of upsetting her.

'Right. So, we are talking about a fractured thighbone, a fractured collarbone, multiple fractures of the right arm, including wrist and elbow, and six broken ribs. One of them punctured his lung, so breathing is difficult to say the least, and very, very painful. That is why he had surgery first thing after being admitted this morning. We stabilized his ribcage by putting in some metal plates. But when he woke up, he was in such agony that we decided to induce a medical coma.'

Lily swallowed. 'What — what does that mean?'

'It means he will be asleep for the next couple of days, and you won't be able to talk to him. You can speak to him of course, and we strongly encourage you to do so, but he won't hear you, or answer. But don't worry, it's for his own safety, and comfort, really. We'll wake him up in a couple of days or so, depending on the progress he's making. And then we'll be able to tell you more. Until then …'

'You mean — you can't tell us whether he's going to live?'

Mrs Hancock was leaning forward in her seat. She had let go of Lily's hand, leaving her to get out a tissue. Slowly, Lily began to pull it apart, while she held her breath and waited for Dr Singh's answer. It was so quiet in the room, you could hear the ripping of the thin cotton.

'I'm afraid I can't make any promises now — we'll have to wait and see how he comes round after the coma — and even then there is always the risk of internal bleedings. The good thing is that he did not suffer any visible head injuries other than severe concussion, and his spinal cord has not been damaged either, so …' He pressed his lips together and Lily realized how difficult this must be for him — because whatever he said, they would always hold him responsible, wouldn't they?

'But he will live? And walk?'

Dr Singh did not answer immediately but studied the medical notes for what seemed to be a very long time. Finally, he lifted his gaze to meet Mrs Hancock's, the notes now gathered in his hands. 'As I said, the spine has not been severely damaged, so that's another good thing … So … if he makes it through the critical stage,' he narrowed his eyes as he looked at them over the rim of his glasses, 'then yes, he will live. I'm sorry I cannot promise you anything until then.'

Mr Hancock nodded and took his wife's hand in his. 'That's alright, doctor, we did not expect to hear much more than that. It's something to hope for though, isn't it? To get us through the next couple of days. We will be able to visit him, won't we? Even if he — if he won't see or hear us.'

Lily shook her head violently as she felt her anxiety level rising. 'What do you mean, critical stage? How long will that be? And what if …'

The doctor gave her a sympathetic smile, but Lily felt sick. What if she had to lose Joseph as well? How would she ever survive that?

'It means that we have to wait until he comes round after the coma. The longer he remains unconscious, the longer it will take him to recover, so we'll try and keep it short. But he is young and fit and strong, so I think his chances are,' he tilted his head, 'quite good.'

Are they? Lily thought bitterly, remembering how she had told herself that Spencer was 'too young and fit and strong' to die. He *had* died though, hadn't he? Because at the end of the day, it didn't matter how young and fit and strong they were …

'Can we see him now?' Mrs Hancock's voice cut through Lily's thoughts, making her start.

'Of course. If you don't have any more questions, I will get a nurse to take you to the ward, and you will be able to come and see him for a few minutes every day. I know it's not much, especially since you live a bit far off but I'm afraid that's all we can allow while he is in ICU.' He took off his glasses and slipped them in the pocket of his coat as he got to his feet. 'Right then, shall we go?'

'You may find it upsetting to see him in this state,' he explained as they walked along the corridor, 'but I assure you, he is as comfortable as he can possibly be, and well looked after.'

Which does not mean that he won't die, Lily thought and tried not to cry as they stood and waited for an elevator. Nobody said anything now, and the silence was unnerving.

***

THEY EMERGED FROM the elevator and stepped onto the brightly lit corridor of ICU. There was a stillness lying over the ward, a hushed silence that made Lily want to hold her breath, for fear of the sound of her heavy breathing disturbing the silence. Everything was quiet except for the squeaking sound of shoes on rubber as they walked down yet another corridor. When they came to an open door, Dr Singh had a quick word with the nurse before he turned to Lily and Joseph's parents. 'Nurse Clarke will take you to him in a minute. She will show you how to disinfect your hands and give you medical masks, caps and gowns before you go in. If you have any more questions, Nurse Clarke will be glad to answer them.'

To Lily, he said, 'Do come and see him as often as you can, Miss, and speak to him — he will know you are there even if he doesn't respond just yet. The same goes for you, of course,' he added, nodding at Joseph's parents. 'And if there are any changes — any at all — we will let you know immediately.' And with a slight nod, he walked away, leaving them to wait for the nurse.

Lily closed her eyes and tried to concentrate on her breathing. She wished she were at home on the farm, drinking tea with Abi, or even chasing the goat out of the flower beds — anywhere but here, in the ICU of the Royal Infirmary in Hull …

Wasn't it only nine months since she'd sat with Spencer in ICU? He had not even survived the first night.

'You may hear alarms and bleeps from the equipment,' the nurse explained while they were getting ready. 'Don't worry about that, it's perfectly normal. Patients who are ventilated in Intensive Care need very close monitoring — that is why Mr Hancock has one nurse looking after him all the time. As I'm sure the doctor will have assured you already, he will never be alone, not for one minute. And, please, don't hesitate to ask if you have any questions. Shall we go?' She smiled encouragingly as she beckoned Joseph's parents to follow her, and Lily stayed behind, waiting until it was her turn. It was the longest five minutes she had ever had to wait.

'Go on then,' Mr Hancock whispered as he passed her on his way out, briefly putting a hand on her shoulder. 'It's not too bad. His face is all clean and good.'

Nervously chewing on her lower lip, Lily took the first hesitant step into the cubicle.

Joseph was lying underneath a starched white sheet that smelled strongly of disinfectant. Everything smelled of disinfectant, and everything was white. It made the place seem even more sterile, still, and lifeless. A series of tubes, wires and cables were attached to the patient, and the bleeping sounds coming from the monitors made Lily want to turn on her heels and run — but her love for him and the need to see him was stronger and gave her the courage to go on. She held her hand close to her heart, as if to guard it from the shock she knew was awaiting her.

'I'm here, Joseph,' she whispered, 'it's me, Lily. Can you hear me?'

I said that before, she thought and swallowed, forcing

herself to go on. *This is different. This is Joseph, not Spencer. He has had an accident, not a heart attack. He will live.*

'You gave us such a fright. But you are going to be alright. You are in good hands here, and I will come and see you as often as I can. I would sit with you for hours if they let me, night and day.' She would, too. She would sleep on the floor if that meant she could be with him.

Placing a tentative hand on the sheets that covered most of his bruised body (was that allowed? The nurse did not stop her however, so she left her hand right there), Lily lifted her eyes and found, much to her relief, that his face had indeed been left without so much as a scratch.

'I miss you, Joseph. I miss you so much,' she whispered. 'Please come back. I need you.' Tears were hanging from her eyelashes as she spoke, and she shook her head, trying to hold them back. 'Please, don't leave me. You mean so much to me, Joseph. So much. I …' She swallowed, but found that she could not bring herself to say the words. *I love you.* Not again. She had spoken those words so carelessly before, believing they would stop a man from dying whom she had never truly loved at all. She had lied — and what was worse, her words had failed. He *had* died. So what was the point in making the same mistake again, even if this time she would be speaking the truth. Words could wait. What he needed now was to feel her hand, hear her voice, see her face when he woke up … oh, if only he would wake up!

'I wish I could stay with you. As I said, I would be quite happy to sleep on the floor, you know, just to be near you. But I will be back as soon as I can, I promise.' She spoke faster now, conscious of the fact that her time was running out. 'Just hold on, my darling. Hold on. You've got lots to live for. Your parents, Inigo, your job … your friends — and me. I miss you so much, Joseph. Please, please get better. I —' Her voice broke. 'I love you …'

With a gentle tap on her shoulder, the nurse beckoned Lily to say goodbye. Stifling a sob, she stepped back and blew him a soft kiss. 'Goodbye,' she whispered, 'goodbye, my darling.'

A sudden memory stirred, causing her heart to burn as if somebody had dropped a fireball right into it, making her hold her sides as she gasped desperately for breath.

Goodbye. Better say goodbye.

She shook her head, faster and faster. 'No! No! No, No, NO!'

'Are you alright, Miss?'

No! Of course I'm not alright! My boyfriend might die yet, no matter what the doctor said, how can I possibly be 'alright'? How will I ever be alright again if he should die, too?

Sobbing violently, Lily pressed a hand over her mouth and nose as she pushed past the nurse, through the door, and past Joseph's parents who must have been waiting for her. She could not bear to look at them.

'Lily! Lily, wait! Please!'

Ignoring their calls, Lily ran down the corridor and to the door which led to the staircase, then down the stairs until she was finally back on the ground floor.

Lucy was leaning against the wall, tapping into her phone, when she saw Lily dashing towards her, sobbing and panting. Putting her phone away quickly, she held out her arms. 'Come here, sweetie,' she said softly, and Lily collapsed into her arms. 'I'll take you home.'

The kind receptionist offered to get a glass of water first. 'For your friend,' she whispered a minute later, handing Lucy a paper cup across the desk. 'Let her drink first and calm down a bit. Unless you want me to call a nurse?'

Lucy shook her head. 'No, thanks, we're alright. Aren't we, Lily?'

'Yes,' Lily whispered as she took the cup from Lucy's hand, and drank thirstily. Then she placed the empty cup on the receptionist's desk. Her hand was shaking. 'Thank you.'

'Okay?' Lucy put an arm around her shoulders, steadying her. 'Ready to go? Or would you rather we waited for Joseph's parents? They're just coming, look.'

Lily would much rather have left at once but as it would have seemed extremely rude to walk out on them a second time, she nodded. 'Okay.'

On approaching Lily and Lucy, Mr Hancock waved with one hand while steadying his wife with the other. Poor Mrs Hancock's face was as white as paper, and Lily's heart went out to her despite her own pain.

'I'm so sorry I just ran past you,' she said quietly, putting a hand on Mrs Hancock's arm. Her voice was coarse from crying, and shaky. 'I shouldn't have done that. It was the shock. I'm sorry.'

Mrs Hancock closed her arms around Lily. 'Oh, lass! Oh, lass …'

Whispering something to Lucy, who nodded gratefully, Mr Hancock left. Lucy followed him, and five minutes later, they were back with two trays full of tea things. There was cake, too, a traybake of some sort which Lily eyed rather suspiciously. But Mr Hancock was adamant. 'You need to eat, ladies — I'm sure our Joseph would agree. You need to be strong for him. Not eating won't help.'

Now where have I heard that before? Lily thought wryly as she took a piece. It was a coffee and walnut cake, and it tasted surprisingly good, even though she did not care much for walnuts.

When they had finished their tea and cake — most of the time none of them were speaking, but that was fine with Lily — , they exchanged phone numbers, and Mr Hancock suggested they come and pick her up tomorrow, so they could go to Hull together. 'No need for both of us to drive, and besides, I think we should support each other as best as we can, don't you agree?'

'Thank you, Mr Hancock, that is kind of you. Although I'm sure Abi wouldn't mind driving me ... but yes, thank you.' Draining her tea cup, Lily got out a tissue to dry her eyes. No matter what she did, or how hard she tried, she just could not seem to stop the tears from falling.

'I'll call you tomorrow morning then, before we leave. Goodbye, Lily. It was so lovely to meet you at last — I wish circumstances had been different but ... well. Goodbye.'

Unable to speak or meet their eyes, Lily nodded her goodbye and gratefully accepted Lucy's arm. Slowly, they made their way towards the door.

But it was not until they stepped out of the hospital and into the bright sunlight that Lily trusted herself to breathe again.

CHAPTER FORTY

'What do I do if he doesn't wake up? What if he — if he dies? I can't bear it, Abi, I know I can't! Whatever will I do without him?'

'Lily, he won't die! You heard what the doctor said. His head is alright, his back is alright, and the rest — what was it? Collarbone, elbow, wrist, some ribs, and a thighbone? That sounds an awful lot, but they can fix that. It just takes time.'

Lily was standing with her back to the Aga in Abi's kitchen, cradling Inigo in her arms while Abi was busy getting a tray with coffee things ready. Of all the days, the builders had chosen today — three days after the accident! — to get started on the barn. Who cared about a stupid barn now? They were not even doing anything exciting, just clearing out the rubble, and preparing the building site. Who knew if Joseph would even live to see the cottages next year? Because no matter how often people kept telling her to stay positive, she knew better, didn't she? She had lost a boyfriend before. She had *been* there.

She put her hands over her eyes and shook her head. 'Yes, but — oh, Abi, I wish he'd wake up! I need him to tell me — that ... that everything's going to be alright ...'

Abi was by her side in seconds, putting an arm around her slender frame. 'There now, don't cry, lass. Everything *will be* alright. Just give it a little time …' Cradling Lily in her arms, Abi kissed her hair and said, 'Tell you what, why don't you let me bring the builders their coffee, and then you and I will go for a nice walk, perhaps stop at Jessie's café for lunch — what do you think? It's such a lovely day.'

'She doesn't allow dogs in. And I can't leave Inigo. He's not used to being on his own.'

Abi tutted. 'Spoilt him rotten, he has. Always taking him on his rounds like he does.'

'Did.'

Abi gave her a stern look. 'No, lass — *does*. Because he will work again, and Inigo will be with him again, in the car, like he used to. Come on now, let's go. Inigo will be fine with Theo.'

For all her brusqueness, Abi was increasingly worried about Lily. She was not sleeping, she was not eating, she was always going on about Joseph dying, and it seemed there was nothing she could do or say to make her niece feel better, except take her to Hull as often as she could, so she could at least see Joseph. And late at night, when Lily had retreated to the sanctuary of her bedroom, Abi would stand at her own window and stare into the darkness, wishing she had the faith to pray. 'Just bring the lad home,' she would say, 'please, God — just bring him home.'

***

IT WAS THE Saturday after the accident, and Lily, unable to go back to sleep after another night of endless tossing and turning and nightmares about angry cows, had got up at seven and taken the dogs out. She was just walking past the church when something made her stop. She stood and listened — there was somebody in there, singing. A young woman's voice, or perhaps a girl's, singing a simple song about a person's heartaches and struggles, and how God knew about all that. The voice was exquisite, crystal clear and full of passion. Whoever it was, she was certain that this girl actually believed what she was singing.

For a moment she thought about going in, but she did not want to leave the dogs outside, and also, she had a feeling the singer might not want to be disturbed. Quite possibly, she had heartaches of her own. Instead, Lily got out her phone and recorded the last few verses, thinking she would ask Beth about the song. Beth knew all sorts of hymns and songs of worship, she would know the title.

Just as Lily was putting her phone back into the pocket of her jeans, the church door opened, and a girl of about sixteen came out. She was wearing a red sweater, jeans, and boots, and had a dreamy, faraway look about her that made Lily smile.

'Hello? That was beautiful — your singing.'

'Thank you.' The girl smiled back, but Lily noticed there were tears hanging from her dark eyelashes. Wrapping a huge mustard coloured scarf around her neck and giving herself a brief hug, as if to keep that aching heart inside warm, the girl gave her a little wave and turned to go. Lily watched her as she walked up the lane towards the abandoned village of Broughton. Before people had settled in Bishops Bridge, they had lived up there, near Broughton Castle, the ruins of which still remained today. Old Broughton's church, also in ruins, was one of Lily's favourite haunts when she felt in need of some solitude. The churchyard was still in use today, and Lily remembered Abi saying there were services held at the old church on Boxing Day and on Easter Monday. In 1428, when the Black Death had come to Broughton, it had killed most of the inhabitants, and driven the surviving dozen down the hill. The village of Bishops Bridge was named after the ancient stone bridge across the stream, and the bishop who had come to bless the new settlement upon its foundation in 1430.

***

'IT'S A SONG by Judy Bailey. It's called *My God Knows* — you can find it on YouTube, I'm sure. Very beautiful song. I love it, too.'

Lily nodded, already tapping in the title while listening to Beth's excited report on their new parish, the vicarage, and the nursery that was now ready to welcome the twins. Matthew's knee was still giving him trouble but at least he was at home after his op, and able to do the odd job. Thinking that she would listen to the song later, when she went to bed, she sat down on the floor with Inigo, ruffling his silky black ears.

'So, when are you going to open that bookshop then?' Beth asked, changing the subject.

'I don't know,' Lily sighed, wishing people would stop pestering her about the blooming bookshop, or the blooming barn. 'The plan was for the sixth of October, but that does not seem likely now, not only because of the accident, but because David won't be able to finish the shelves until then, even if he has help from some retired *Mouseman* joiner he knows. But honestly, Beth, I couldn't care less! Pete asked me the other day — he's the builder who is converting the barn — if I wanted *an extra roof window* in the bathrooms! Seriously! What do I care about windows?'

Beth sighed. 'Oh, Lily. You really love him very much, hm? Poor sweetheart.'

That was all it took to open the flood gates once more, and for the next half hour Beth had to do her best to console her friend over the phone. Lily was not even sure if she wanted to be consoled. She *wanted* to cry, she *wanted* to listen to sad songs that made her cry even more, and watch Winston Churchill's funeral service on YouTube. Stephen had caught her watching that after Spencer's death, and rolled his eyes at her.

'Who in their right mind watches the funeral service of a British PM who died half a century ago? You weren't even born then!'

If her book of *Famous Churchill Quotes* had not been so precious to her (she had bought it in an antique bookshop in Cheltenham when she was a student), she would have thrown it at Stephen's head.

She knew of course that this was different from what she had gone through in the spring —she wasn't grieving now, she was just fretting. Her anxiety had never been worse, despite the fact that there was a very real hope now: Mrs Hancock had told her that they were going to reduce the anaesthetic drugs in order to help Joseph slowly emerge from the coma next week. *Next week.*

'How long will it take until he is fully conscious then?' she had asked anxiously. 'I know it probably won't be like in the movies, where they wiggle their little finger, open their eyes, and sit up in bed chatting within ten minutes?'

'Probably not, no. Doctor Singh said it will take anything

from a few hours to several days, but the chances of a full recovery are much higher than if he had fallen into a coma, and also because the induced coma will have been relatively short. Let's wait and see, shall we? And in the meantime, we keep on visiting, speaking to him, and you read your books to him.'

Lily looked at the book she had bought for him in Thirsk the other day — James Herriot's *Dog Stories*. She knew he loved both, James Herriot, and dogs, so she had thought that would be the perfect choice. Once he was awake and on a regular ward — or better still, able to sit on a bench outside — she might even be able to bring Inigo.

'You miss your master, don't you?' she asked the little dog as she got up from the floor now and placed her mobile on the bedside table, stretching her back. 'So do I. Come on then, let's get you settled for the night, and then I will listen to this song.'

'God *does* know,' Beth had said. 'He knows you're hurting, sweetheart. He knows you love Joseph, and that you need him to wake up and tell you that he loves you, too. And he will, Lily. He will. I will pray for you, as I always do, and God will answer — as He always does.'

***

EVEN THOUGH IT was quite a journey — ninety minutes or more, depending on traffic — Lily went to see Joseph at least every other day. Sometimes she stopped in Hutton-le-Hole and got in with the Hancocks, who were kind enough to take her so she wouldn't have to drive, but most days she went alone. She didn't mind. Even if he did not respond, she needed and treasured this private time with Joseph. She read to him, she told him about the progress they were making on the bookshop (rapidly, thanks to David who took his 'Priority Project' very seriously and came over nearly every day, or never went back to Nidderdale at all) and on the barn (slowly, but as Lily didn't mind whether they would welcome their first guests in June, July or August, or even later, it didn't matter), and about the kindness of the village people who had heard about what happened to 'that nice vet with the bouncy spaniel'.

'Look,' she said when she sat down at the foot of his bed, pulling out a small cross made of smoothly carved olive wood. 'Miss Lavender gave me this. She says it's a comfort cross — the kind you would hold in your hand when you pray, or keep in your pocket. I don't pray myself, but I know she does, and a lot of other people in the village do. My friend Beth and her husband pray for you as well. We must go down and visit them in Devon next year. I have never been to Devon, have you? I would have scones with clotted cream every day! So, um, praying …' She looked down at the cross in her hand, feeling the warm smoothness of its surface. 'I would pray for you now but … I don't quite know how. Do you believe in God, Joseph? I never asked. We never talk about these things, do we? Whyever not until we get trapped in situations like these, where suddenly a miracle seems the only answer?' Gazing out of the window at the dull grey skies, she asked, 'Would God listen to me, do you think? Beth says he would. But being a vicar's wife, of course she would say that. I wish I had her faith!'

Feeling fresh tears welling up in her eyes, Lily remembered how Miss Lavender had placed the little cross in her hand and closed her fingers around it. 'Courage, dear heart,' she had said, 'courage and faith. It will all turn out right.'

Looking back to the still shape of Joseph's bruised body underneath the stark white sheets and listening to the bleeping sounds from the monitor above the bed, Lily was not so sure at all, and she turned her head away, swallowing back the tears.

Later, when she walked slowly across the hospital car park, she felt her energy draining from her like a trickle of water in the desert, and once she was seated behind the wheel of her little car, she pulled the door shut, and cried.

CHAPTER FORTY-ONE

When Joseph first opened his eyes, he did not know where he was, or how on earth he had got there. He looked down at the ill-fitting blue night gown he was wearing for some reason, and at the tube which was attached to a needle that was stuck in his left hand. His right arm was plastered all the way from below his shoulder to his hands, leaving only his fingertips to stick out. He tried to lift it but found that he couldn't. *Bother*, he thought, and licked his lips. They were dry and cracked, and he wished more than anything for a cup of tea, but as he could not even turn his head, never mind press the button at the side of his bed, he decided to give up, and drifted back to sleep.

***

'You have been in an accident, Mr Hancock,' the nurse explained. She had brought tea, but it was weak and lukewarm and presented to him in a hideous beige plastic beaker. He shook his head as the nurse tried to lift it to his mouth.

'What accident? I don't remember ... I don't remember anything.' He didn't either. He could not remember a single thing that would have had him ending up in this dismal hospital room. Speaking was a huge effort, as was breathing. Everything hurt.

'You were attacked by a herd of cows, and taken to Hull Infirmary in a helicopter. And because you have suffered some rather severe injuries and were in terrible pain, doctors thought it best to put you in a coma. You have just woken up, it's perfectly normal that you don't know where you are, and can't remember what happened. Try and get some rest now, Mr Hancock, and I'll come back later with some food. How does that sound?' She tugged at his sheets, checked the monitor one more time, and pulled the curtains around Joseph's cubicle before heading on to the next one.

Bring some proper tea, he wanted to call after her, but decided not to bother. She would not listen. Bother, he thought and closed his eyes. No tea. No Lily. *I might as well go back to sleep*, he thought wearily. And he did.

***

There were cows everywhere. They were standing in a tight circle around him, shoulder to shoulder, and closing in on him — fast. He could feel the heat of their breath that escaped through their nostrils. One of them was pushing towards him, stamping her hooves. It was not a friendly cow like Daisy though, begging for a treat and a tickle behind the ears. None of them were friendly. In fact, they looked hostile and more than ready to attack — next thing he knew he was being tossed in the air, and as the first cow put her hoof down on his chest, he woke up screaming ...

'Noooo!'

And then there was a hand holding his, and another gently stroking his forehead. There was a soft voice that was speaking to him, too, telling him it was alright, he was safe …

Safe.

He opened his eyes, and there was Lily sitting on the edge of his hospital bed, holding his hand. She was smiling down at him, but he could tell she had been crying. There were tears hanging from her long, dark eyelashes.

'Hello, you,' she said softly, curling her fingers around his. 'Long time, no see.'

'Long time indeed,' he answered in a croaky voice that did not sound like his at all. 'What time is it — what day, even? I have no idea … Have I been here long?'

Lily smiled but there was a sadness behind her smile that made his heart ache for her. 'It's the eighth of October. You have been here for just over two weeks.'

Two weeks, he thought. *Crikey. Poor Lily!* He tried to reach out and touch her cheek, but his arm would not obey his foggy brain's order, and he sighed. 'Oh, Lily. I'm sorry, I can't even hold you now. Poor you! You must have been through hell and back these past two weeks.'

She shrugged, and a single tear made its way down her cheek. He wished he could brush it away. Instead, he watched as it dropped onto the sheets.

'It's okay. You're awake now — and I am the first to get to hear your voice, and see you smile! You don't know how much that means to me. Oh, I need to call your parents and tell them you're awake. They will want to come and see you.' She tried to get up, but his fingers closed surprisingly tight around hers.

'Don't go — please, stay. I'm sure the hospital has already called them. But you could get us a decent cup of tea — that would really cheer me up! Especially when it comes in a proper mug and not in one of *those*.' He rolled his eyes at the offending beaker that had been sitting on his bedside table since lunchtime. Needless to say, he had not touched it.

Lily smiled. 'I'll go and get you a cup in a minute. I'm not sure I'm allowed to drink tea in here — look,' she said, indicating the medical mask she was wearing, 'safety first. We don't want to risk any infections now, do we?'

'No,' he sighed, 'of course not. I can only hope they'll transfer me to a regular ward soon. In the meantime, do cheer me up with some village gossip. And tell me about your bookshop — is it open yet? And whatever happened with Mr Nettleton — I hope he has not caused your poor aunt any more trouble?'

Lily was taken aback. 'You remember *all that*? But you don't remember the accident? That's odd. But I suppose it's normal after this trauma … and you did suffer concussion. So, about the bookshop — I hope we will be able to open at the end of October now. I know you still won't be able to be there but … at least we know you're safe now.' She hesitated. 'You are, aren't you? Safe?'

But one look at him told her he was not listening anymore — he had fallen asleep. Smiling, she leaned down to kiss his forehead, whispering 'goodbye'. With a last tender look at his face, she straightened up, took her handbag from the foot of the bed, and left him to sleep.

***

A WEEK LATER, she found Joseph sitting upright in his bed, smiling at her, and another week later, he told her he was to be transferred to the general ward the next day. He had mixed feelings about this transfer though, as it would not give them more but possibly even less privacy.

'There'll be three other guys and all of their visitors to put up with, so I expect the noise level will be distinctively higher, and I'll get less rest ... I can't wait to go home. But I'm afraid I won't be going anywhere for a while yet, not until I can at least sit in a wheelchair — and then it's on to rehab for three to six weeks! I'll be lucky if I get home before Christmas ...' He grimaced in pain as he tried to lift his shoulder. 'They told me it would get better after the surgery, but it still hurts like hell ... sorry. I'm whining. How are you? And how are things at the farm?'

Lily smiled. 'You have every right to whine. And some. All is calm on the farm right now, and yes, Christmas is only nine weeks away, so I have brought you ...' She rummaged in her large shoulder bag and produced a biscuit tin. 'Ta-dah! Mince pies! Homemade, of course. Abi was horrified, but I don't care. Talking of Abi being horrified — do you think I could let you in on a secret?'

'Horrified Abi? Secrets to tell?' He raised his eyebrows several times, making Lily giggle. 'Can things get any more exciting than that for a poor invalid stuck on a Major Trauma Ward?'

***

WHEN LILY LEFT the hospital half an hour later, her mobile pressed to her ear as she waited for Joseph's parents to pick up (they had got into the habit of giving each other short updates after their respective visits), she felt happier and more hopeful than she had in a long time. It was a bright, sunny day, and very warm for October. The leaves were beginning to fall from the trees, and she caught one with her free hand as she walked through the car park. For each leaf you caught you would get a lucky day, wouldn't you? Well, she hoped there would be more than just the one, but it was a start.

And just to be on the safe side, she felt for the little cross in her pocket — because she knew that on Friday she would need all the luck, and all the help she could get.

CHAPTER FORTY-TWO

Friday proved to be the perfect day for the Retrieval of the Picture. It was a grey, drizzly day where a free lunch at the local pub, and a couple of pints into the bargain, was an offer too good to be resisted even by grumpy old Nettleton. So, while Abi was shopping in York with Mrs Talbot, Mr Bell and Mr Wilkinson picked up her unsuspecting neighbour at twelve accordingly, to take him to the *Coach House Inn* at Rosedale Abbey ('safer to take him the extra mile', Mr Bell had winked when he had dropped off his wife at Fern Hill Farm on the way). Lily loved Lucy's grandad. For all that he was well past eighty, his rheumy blue eyes still twinkled with mischief — needless to say he had been the first to agree to Lily's plan.

'That daft old bugger needs some proper dressing down, and no mistake! We're only too happy to help, aren't we, Caroline?'

'Aye, we are that. I'll be watching that lane like a hawk, Lily.'

Lily thought she would much rather she called her in case anyone *should* come, but decided she would simply have to trust the ladies. There was always calm, no-nonsense Mrs Wilkinson, who had promised to bring her phone. She was the only one in the group who actually had one. Trying not to think about how she had used it to call the ambulance for Joseph only five weeks ago, Lily finished her coffee and picked up her keys.

'And you two had better be good!' She wagged her finger at the dogs who were sitting side by side on the kitchen floor, thumping their respective tails, and looking up at her devotedly. 'No chewing, no barking, no sleeping on the sofa, and *under no circumstances* will you let that goat in!' That was a joke of course, but Lily was so nervous, she felt she could do with cheering herself up a bit. Predictably, it didn't work.

***

HAVING MADE SURE Mrs Wilkinson had added her to her contacts as well as called her once to make sure she had got the number right, Lily gave a satisfied nod. 'Okay. Now all you have to do is press *redial* in case you have to alert me. Two rings, remember. But I very much hope not to hear those two rings!'

'Remember, you could always just be a potential buyer who is having a little look around the farm,' Mrs Wilkinson reminded her in a kind attempt to calm her nerves, indicating the *For Sale* sign the estate agent had put up the other week. When Lily had told Joseph about it, she had claimed that 'no one in their right mind would even come to look at, never mind buy that run down old place.'

'As if,' Lily mumbled. Her throat felt like it was lined with sandpaper. Wiping her clammy hands down her jeans, she said as resolutely as she could, 'Right then, here we go.'

On reaching the farmhouse, Lily fumbled for the key she had brought (luckily, Abi still had a spare key for Nettleton's house) and put it in the lock. With trembling fingers, she turned the key — only to find that the door was open.

Now what does that mean, she thought. Did he forget to lock up or is there somebody in the house? There had been no car in the drive, so it could not be Mary. And Mr Nettleton was safely installed at the pub; he would not be back for some time. Still, she suddenly wished Joseph was with her, if only to reassure her. But the new Lily seemed to be of the stubbornly independent kind — the kind that would say *no* even if she meant *yes*. It wasn't long ago that it had been the other way round.

Biting her lip, she went inside and peered cautiously into every room, even the pantry. All was quiet, and there was no one to be seen. Letting out a small sigh of relief, she tiptoed upstairs where she hoped to find Mr Nettleton's bedroom.

She was lucky, it was the second room on the right, next to the bathroom, and the door was ajar. Hesitating only for a split second — to hold her breath, mainly — Lily stepped over the threshold and made straight for the rickety bedside table where she knew Mr Nettleton kept the sketch (because the old fool had been stupid enough to tell Abi, no doubt in an attempt to make her cringe). The bedside table was covered in a thick layer of sticky dust and there were no less than three mugs, no doubt half full of old milky tea, if the stench was anything to go by.

Fighting the urge to retch, Lily quickly opened the top drawer — 'Ha! Gotcha!' she muttered as she retrieved the picture, and pushed the drawer shut as quickly as she could. *Good thing he hasn't lied about where he kept the picture*, she thought and resisted the temptation to look at the sketch here and now. There would be plenty of time for that later, once she was safely back at Fern Hill Farm.

Lily had just made it back to the lane where Abi's friends were waiting when they saw a red Porsche coming up from the village at high speed (Lily was not sure if those cars *could* actually go at a slow speed).

Mrs Wilkinson squinted at the bright headlights. 'Now who can that be, I wonder?'

'I have a feeling your stunt may have been a close one, Lily,' remarked Mrs Bell dryly. 'I'll be buggered if that isn't Mary Mighty Nettleton, and in some foul mood, too!'

Lily looked with big, fearful eyes from Mrs Bell to Mrs Wilkinson and finally to the car which was now turning into the yard with screeching tyres, sending bits of mud flying.

Seconds later the door was flung open, and a furious Mary got out and came stomping down the drive, her eyes narrowing dangerously as she approached the unlikely group. 'What are you doing here, loitering around my father's farm? Does he know you are here?'

Before Lily could even think of something to say, Mrs Bell was quick to retort, 'He doesn't have to, since we are not actually trespassing — we're outside the gate, as you can see, standing on the verge of a public road, even if it's just a track. Which, if you don't mind me saying so, you should not speed along quite so fast. It was a car that nearly killed that goat, you know. The one Miss Lewis was kind enough to save.'

Trust Mrs Bell to always think of some retort or other, thought Lily, suppressing a snigger. Then she looked down at the picture in her hand. What if Mary's sharp eyes spotted it?

It is not hers. It is not even rightfully her father's. Abi just showed it to him, and he snatched it from her and refused to give it back. It is not legally theirs.

And she did not see me coming out of the house, thank God.

She quickly hid the piece of paper behind her back, trying to keep a straight face. It did not help that the air was filled with smoke coming from a bonfire Mr Marston had lit in his adjoining field.

But Mary saw she was hiding something and turned on her heel to fix Lily with a steely glare. 'You!' she hissed, jabbing a finger at her. 'I knew you'd be trouble the first time I saw you! What are you hiding there? Have you been inside the house? That's trespassing, I'll have you know. In fact, it is more than that, it is burglary. Are we dealing with a little criminal here, hey? Come on, show me! If that is the picture my dad was telling me about, I'll …'

Three things happened in quick succession now — first, Mary tried to grab Lily's arm, second, Lily quickly thrust the paper into Mrs Bell's hand, and third, the picture was equally quickly passed on to Mrs Wilkinson who tossed it over the drystone wall and into Mr Marston's bonfire.

Lily turned to Mary, a smug expression on her face. 'I suppose you'll never know now, will you, Mistress Mary? Have a nice day!'

***

ABI HAD TO sit down when she heard about Lily's stunt that evening, suddenly quite pale. 'Lily! I knew you were angry for my sake but — burglary! You could have got yourself into serious trouble!'

Handing her a glass of sherry, Lily shook her head and smiled. 'But I didn't, did I? And anyway, for one thing, the house was not locked, for another, we had a key, and I could have left a pie or something. And last but not least, it was not his picture to keep in the first place, it was yours! Well, now it isn't, obviously. I'm sorry it's lost, Abi. I hope you are not too sad.'

'Sad? Oh, Lord, no! I'm relieved! This wretched picture has been nothing but a curse, so good riddance. It's only money, isn't it, and as we all know, money can't buy you happiness. But I'm glad it ended well, and that none of you got into trouble. I so wish I could have seen that look on Mistress Mary's face though!'

And she laughed until the tears rolled down her cheeks.

CHAPTER FORTY-THREE

THE NEXT MORNING, Lily walked down into the village to discuss the details of the bookshop opening with Miss Lavender. David was already waiting for her when she crossed the old stone bridge, having walked along the other side of the stream, as was her habit. She had acquired quite a few habits since she moved here seven weeks ago — like collecting eggs from the Colbecks on her way home, or stopping for a chat across the hedge with Mr Barnsley, the old schoolmaster, when she passed his house on Church Lane, never mind her donkey walks. Without William — and Inigo — she was sure she would not have survived the ordeal of the last few weeks.

'Hello! You look cheerful this morning — in fact, you look a bit like ...' David cocked his head and squinted, '... like the cat who got the cream! Why is that, I wonder?'

Lily stopped and stared blankly at him. 'Sorry? Cat? Cream? I don't ... oh! Oh, no! How do *you* know?'

He grinned from ear to ear. 'I have been to the farm this morning to lay down my offer. I'm going to buy the place and set up my workshop there — no more trespassing then, do you hear?' Wagging his finger at her in mock reprimand, he then put a hand on her shoulder and nodded approvingly. 'Well done, you. Very well done. Although to be fair, I haven't got a clue what exactly this so-called *burglary* business was about — you can imagine what else Lady Mary had to say on that matter — but it seems to have done the trick. He's going to Cornwall with her today, and won't come back.'

'What?'

Laughing, David put an arm around her shoulder and turned her towards the shop window. 'Look, Lily, all done! You are ready to open your business, and I am going to set up mine here too. That is why I'm buying Wood End Farm — so the *Squirrel of Lofthouse* can become the *Squirrel of Rosedale*, and you and I are going to be neighbours to both sides. Double neighbours, so to speak. Hopefully not double trouble though — do tell that donkey of yours I don't want to be woken up at six in the morning!'

Not sure if she had heard this right, Lily shook her head. '*You* are buying the farm — my, my, who would have thought? Oh dear,' she laughed, 'I sound like Abi now! And as for William, he doesn't wake me quite so early these days. I like to think I ...' Suddenly she frowned. 'Hold on! Why would he wake *you*? Does that mean what I'm thinking it means?'

'Aye, it does. Susanna and I are getting married next summer. After the baby is born.'

The baby? What baby? What else have I been missing here?

But she just nodded as if it was the most natural thing in the world for two people to get back together after twenty years, and get married just months later. *And* have a baby.

***

'Wow!'

Lily gasped when she caught a glimpse of the beautiful shelves inside the shop. Opening the door (it creaked frightfully as she did, and she made a mental note to have it oiled before the opening, as well as washed), she turned to give David a quick hug before stepping inside. The cream shelves looked stunning set against the sage green walls, just like she had hoped they would. Lily could just picture herself standing behind the counter, handing over a gift-wrapped book to a customer. There were tears glistening in her eyes when she said, 'This is beautiful. Thank you, David! Thank you!'

He laughed. 'I'm glad you like it. And now, if you'll excuse me, I've got an appointment with the estate agent in Lofthouse. I'm putting my cottage on the market. And you might want to pop over to Susanna's when you have a moment in between organizing bookshop openings, overseeing barn conversions, and your trips to Hull. She has a question she'd like to ask you.'

***

'So, I'm going to sell postcards and framed prints of Susanna's landscapes, too, and she said she would help Abi and me to find someone who can do prints of Uncle Donald and Aunt Margaret's paintings. We can have some in the cottages, and if our guests like them, we can tell them they are welcome to buy a copy in … Jessie? You aren't listening, are you? What's up?'

Jessie, who was sitting with Lily on a bench by the stream, looked up. 'Sorry? What were you saying?'

'You look like you're miles away — is something

bothering you? Is it about Louisa May?'

'It is, yes. Nothing to worry about but — actually, Lily, I've got a favour to ask.'

'Don't tell me — you are moving to Durham and join Nate at the Coffee Experience? We are not going to be neighbours in business after all?'

Laughing, Jessie said, 'No! No, it's not that. But I was wondering if you would hold the fort for me next Thursday, so Louisa May and I can go to Durham. I know the bookshop opening is on Saturday — I haven't forgotten about that. And I will make a special cake for you, as promised. It's only for the afternoon. I'll pick up Louisa May after school — they finish early on Thursdays — and we'll do some shopping in Durham and then meet Nate for tea. I told her about him and,' she paused for dramatic effect, 'guess what, she's excited to meet him! Nervous, but excited. Believe me, at the rate she's going, she has already found out more about him from the Internet in one week than I have in two months! She even knows he's got a cat.'

'Well,' Lily deadpanned, 'that settles it then — he's not my type. I don't like cats,' and they both collapsed in laughter.

'So will you?' Jessie asked when they had calmed down, looking pleadingly at Lily. 'Hold the fort for me on Thursday?'

Lily's heart went out to Jessie as she realized how much this must mean to her. Her whole life might be about to change, and she could not be happier for her if it did. 'Of course. It's only for a couple of hours, and I know now how to make a perfect latte, don't I? I did a Barista Masterclass in Durham, remember?'

***

'If people seriously think that country life is boring, they don't know the half of it!'

While setting the table for an early lunch, Lily had just told Abi the latest news concerning Wood End Farm, and was now looking out of the window watching the builders as they carried long planks of wood to the barn. They were going to fix the roof today. Pete had said they should be ready to make a start on the interior by the end of November. Looking at the barn now, she found that hard to imagine, but then she wasn't the expert, was she?

'And don't underestimate how long *that* is going to take — internal walls, floors, electrics, tiles — more than enough to keep us busy all through the winter, don't you worry!'

'Aw, I never said that!' Abi came to stand next to her, a tea towel in her hands. 'Although we might end up missing old Nettleton, if only for the …'

'Missing Mr Nettleton? Never!'

'I was only joking. I'm glad David is coming back to live here, and set up his business on the farm. Right — do you want to ask Pete if they are ready for a coffee break?'

'Yes. And then we can set a date for our cottage shopping trip — you know, sofa and coffee table, cushions, curtains, kitchen equipment, and so on. I'm warning you, I've got a long list!'

'Of course — if it makes you happy. Although of what use *I* will be I'm sure I don't know — I don't know anything about modern kitchen equipment and reclining sofas, never mind all that fancy electronic stuff! Do you think a kitchen radio will do? And will they need a video recorder with their TV?'

Lily smiled fondly at her aunt. 'I'm afraid you'll find we have moved on a bit since the days of video recorders, but don't worry, I'll sort that out. I would ask Stephen, but I don't suppose he'd come up here for a shopping trip with his little sister who doesn't know a DVD from a Blu-ray.'

'A what?'

'Oh, never mind. I'll go and take the builders' coffee order, shall I?'

***

LUCKILY, JOSEPH HAD left his phone in his car on the day of the accident, so as soon as he was able to use his left hand again, he and Lily started texting a few times a day, and met for video chats in the evenings. Having now been transferred to the Major Trauma Ward — which was still serious enough, but less frightening than ICU — he had just given Lily an update on the plans for his rehabilitation.

> They offer a place in Devon. You could come, too, and stay with Beth?

Lily smiled, pleased that he remembered Beth's name and the fact that she had moved to Devon, even though he had never met her. He really was very attentive, and a good listener.

> I'd love to, but I can't — I'm opening a bookshop on Saturday, remember?

> Oh yes! I had forgotten about that — joke! Of course not. What about Cumbria then? That's not too far off, is it? I'm afraid the choice is not great a few weeks before Christmas.

A few weeks before Christmas? It's not even November yet!

I know. But I'll be stuck here for a while yet, and I'm to spend at least 4 weeks in rehab. I'll have to learn how to stand on my own feet again, and walk, before I can even think about going back to work (never mind all sorts of other nice things, like taking you dancing). So, what do you think? Cumbria?

Lily sighed. Then she remembered that only six weeks ago she had feared for his very life, and now she was fretting about how long he would be in rehab, learning to walk again. It would take as long as it took, simple as that. The main thing was, he *would* walk again, and he *would* be able to do his job again — a job that she knew he loved so much.

Dancing? Oh yes, please! And I don't mind where you take your lessons, even if it means I have to join you in Cumbria. The Lakes are pretty in winter, I've been told.

Alright, Cumbria it is then. Must go, physiotherapist will arrive any minute. Got to get fit for that ball!

She chortled. Ball? Now you're pushing it. See you tomorrow?

Absolutely. I can't wait, as always xx

Stuffing the phone into her back pocket, Lily whistled to the dogs. 'Come on, boys, walkies! Fancy a paddle in the stream, Inigo? Where's your ball?'

And she laughed as she watched the spaniel getting his red ball out of the basket by the door. It had all started with that red ball, hadn't it?

CHAPTER FORTY-FOUR

'Are you ready?'

Miss Lavender brushed an imaginary speck of dust from the gleaming surface of the counter as she turned to Lily. 'There is quite a little queue outside waiting to be let in at last. Shall I open the door — or do you want to do it?'

Lily straightened the tartan skirt she had bought just before Christmas last year and never worn. *Last Christmas*, she thought. That seemed a lifetime ago now. She had even put her Morris cushions on her armchair by the window in her room now. Actually, she had done that on the morning of her birthday, just before she had set off for Hull to sit with an unconscious Joseph.

And look how far we've come since then, she thought, wiping a stray tear from the corner of her eye. *Look how far we've come.*

'We'll do it together. Come on', she said, offering her arm. Miss Lavender took it, and together they walked to the door, an unlikely pair to any outsider — Miss Lavender with her long white hair put up in a neat bun, held in place with an ivory comb, and Lily with her recently cut brown curls bobbing just above her shoulders as they walked. But Lily knew, and so did Miss Lavender, that they had been kindred spirits right from the start and were fast becoming the best of friends.

'Now?' she asked, and when Miss Lavender gave a slight nod, she turned the key in the lock and opened the door.

The singing started the moment Lily fastened the hook to the ring outside the door to stop it from falling shut. 'For she's a jolly good fellow, for she's a jolly good fellow, for she's a jolly good fellow — and so say all of us!'

Looking up, Lily could see a group of people coming from the other side of the bridge. There was the vicar, who led the singing, and a number of school mums with their children, as well as the various generations of Wilkinsons, Talbots, Bells and Marstons (they had brought Victoria and Edward, too, Lily noticed, and smiled as she waved to them), and many more.

Lily's hand flew to her mouth when she saw the large hand carved wooden sign David and Susanna were holding up together. It read *Bishops Bridge Books*.

'Oh, my God!' she whispered, feeling her throat tighten with emotion and wishing more than ever that Joseph was here to share the moment. But he had texted her this morning to wish her good luck, as had her family and even Beth, who had given birth to her twins on Tuesday. Underneath a picture of the peacefully sleeping babies she had written, *Wishing you lots and lots of 'scope for imagination' in your new bookshop — Lily Anne & Samuel Oliver xx*

She could not believe that Beth had named her daughter after her, as well as after their mutually favourite literary character, Anne of Green Gables (thus the quote about imagination). *If I ever have a daughter, I will call her Diana Elizabeth*, she thought, *and then they can be friends, spending their summer holidays in Devon and Yorkshire.*

'Are you dreaming?'

'Sorry?'

Jessie scrutinised her, then shook her head and laughed. 'You are! Come on, Lily, time to welcome your customers and sell some books — you can do the dreaming later, when you are back at a certain vet's bedside, telling him all about it.'

***

ONCE THEY WERE all gathered inside the little shop, Miss Lavender gave a very short, very charming speech which put a smile on people's faces, offered their first customers a glass of champagne or orange juice from a tray, and let Lily do the talking and the selling. The chocolate fudge cake Jessie had made was an amazing work of art, three storeys high, and decorated with red rose petals and white chocolate hearts. She had kept a large piece for Joseph, thinking she would take it to the hospital with her tomorrow, along with a book, of course. The book was about *Romantic rambles in the North York Moors National Park*, and inside, she had written *Looking forward to many happy hours of walking alongside you next year. Lily x*.

'Lovely sign,' she heard someone remark at some point. 'Hand carved, too. Is that the young Stanton lad that's come home?'

Catching David's eye as she looked up from gift-wrapping a book, she nodded with a smile. Returning her smile, he put an arm around Susanna's waist and whispered something in her ear that made her giggle, and Lily turned her attention back to her customer. 'That's seven pounds fifty then, please.'

Kelly Graham was busy taking pictures and interviewing people — David, among others — and taking notes on her iPad. Lily felt like she was walking on air, and before she knew it, it was two o'clock, and time to close the door after the last customers had gone (most of them had stayed all morning, with intermittent trips to the Bridge Café).

'I say, that went quite well, didn't it?'

Lily turned to see Miss Lavender coming through the connecting door with a tray of tea things which she put down on the counter. Pure Ceylon, of course, loose leaf. No tea bags for Miss Lavender, and no mugs either. Lily smiled. Not for the first time she wondered how a fine lady like Miss Lavender had ever ended up in sleepy little Bishops Bridge.

'It did. To be honest, I did not expect quite so many customers on the first day. I sold more than fifty books!'

'Well done,' Miss Lavender remarked, 'and now — the cash balance. Or would you like me to do it today, so you can go home and put your feet up? Or perhaps you want to go and see Joseph?'

Though touched at Miss Lavender's concern, Lily assured her that she was fine. 'I have so much to learn, there's no point in putting it off. I can go to Hull tomorrow.'

While they were doing the cash balance, Lily took the opportunity to share some of her business ideas with the old lady. 'Because, nice though it is of my friends to drop by and buy a book every now and then, this will never be enough to make this bookshop a profitable business. So, first things first — Christmas! I thought a Christmas story reading afternoon for children would be nice. I could print posters and put them up in the primary school, the village hall, and the church perhaps? And we could have a reading night for adults, too — which could actually kick off a book club. Is there a book club in Bishops Bridge?'

Miss Lavender cocked her head and thought for a moment. 'There used to be one, but I don't think they still meet. Yes, Christmas themed reading nights, why not? I'm sure that would go down a treat with the little ones. As they will be your future customers, I suppose it makes sense to start with them, if you don't mind me saying so. Especially as they would bring their mothers, or grandmothers, and get them to buy books.'

'Yes, that's what I thought. Also, I could make up enticing little book bundles, you know, tie them together with Christmas ribbon, and put them in wicker baskets lined with soft red fleece.' She looked about her. 'There will be fairy lights strung from shelf to shelf, of course, and I will get Jessie to help me decorate the window. And for the new year I was thinking —'

But Miss Lavender put a hand on her arm to stop her. 'All in good time, Lily. All in good time! When we are finished here, I suggest you go home and have a rest. You have done more than enough today.'

'You are right,' Lily said, stretching and putting a hand to the small of her back, rubbing it where it hurt. 'To be honest, I *could* do with some rest before tonight. Jessie has booked a table at the *Red Grouse*, to celebrate ... You wouldn't care to join us, would you, Miss Lavender? It would be an honour.'

'No, dear,' Miss Lavender said, smiling as she poured herself another cup of tea. 'But it's kind of you to ask. Very kind indeed.'

***

Only two more months until Christmas. Two more months and three days until the first anniversary of Spencer's death.

Lily sat at the desk in her room, her open journal in front of her, chewing her pen as she thought about what to write next. It wasn't that there was nothing to write about, but the pages of her faithful old journal were still staring blankly back at her, as if to say, NOW WHERE HAVE YOU BEEN ALL THIS TIME? WHAT HAPPENED TO THE OLD LILY THAT COULD NOT LEAVE THE HOUSE WITHOUT ME AND HER SPECIAL PEN IN HER RADLEY HANDBAG, ALL NEATLY ORGANIZED AND READY TO FACE THE DAY?

She is gone. Left behind when she decided to go to Yorkshire and live on this farm. Because ultimately, no amount of organizing and neatness could prepare her for something as terrible and devastating as the sudden loss of the man she had believed herself to be in love with. And because you cannot organize your way out of this dark valley called grief. The only thing you can do is to go on, until you find yourself standing in the light again, alive. As I am now.

EPILOGUE

Christmas Eve

THE FIRST SNOWFLAKES began to fall when Lily, her parents, and Stephen set out to walk to church late on Christmas Eve. Emily was staying behind with baby Susan, just four weeks old, and Abi had offered to keep her company.

Meanwhile William, the star of this afternoon's nativity play in church, was all tucked up in his warm stable, munching his well-deserved ration of hay. *He has no idea,* Lily thought as she closed the gate behind her and ran after Stephen who had the torch, t*hat he has just kicked off a new tradition in St Peter's of Bishop's Bridge, and that at least half of the village children were now begging their parents to buy them 'a real live donkey!'* She felt a little guilty about that because it had been her who had introduced William to the children during her very successful and highly popular Christmas reading sessions. It was during the last session, a week before Christmas, that she had found the courage to read her own brand-new story about *William, the Donkey that saved Christmas,* after which some of the mothers had approached her and suggested she bring the 'wonder donkey' to church. Once the vicar had agreed that that was 'a truly wonderful idea', Abi had then volunteered to help Lily and get William to church and back for the rehearsals and of course, today. Lily was touched at the magic the little donkey had worked, especially with the children, and with Victoria and Edward Marston, who had also attended the family service with their parents this afternoon. But what touched her the most were all the messages she had received on her phone after the service, and the comments and pictures posted on the Book Shop's Instagram account.

There was another message that had made her burst into tears of happiness while making mince pies this morning.

> Hello and merry Christmas to you from drizzly old Market Deeping! You won't believe it, but it turns out that we will all meet Nate and his family at church this afternoon – his younger brother Jonathan, who was diagnosed with a rare genetic disorder called PURA syndrome (you might want to google that, but I will tell you more when I get back – there is SO much to tell!) shortly after he was born, is taking part in his school's nativity play, and Nate invited us to come along! I'm so excited! Have a very happy Christmas, Lily, and do make the most of every precious moment with Joseph, as well as with all your family. Love, Jessie xx

She had not had time to google that disease, but had made a mental note of doing so tomorrow, when they would all be sitting on the sofa, stuffed with turkey and Abi's brandy-soaked Christmas pudding, quite unable to move. She might even find the time to reply to some of the messages on WhatsApp, Twitter, and Instagram – but if she didn't, it could wait until after Christmas. There were more important things to think about now, like whether Joseph would kiss her in front of her parents, as well as his, or not.

***

When they walked up to the lychgate, Joseph was waiting for her, making her stomach flip and her heart swell with love and happiness. He was wearing a charcoal wool coat and a red stripy scarf and looked quite the dandy, even on crutches.

'Hello, stranger,' she said as she stood on her toes to kiss him, slipping a small packet into his pocket. 'And merry Christmas to you!'

'And a very merry Christmas to you, darling Lily,' he whispered in her ear, dropping a little box into her open handbag without her noticing. And then he kissed her, full on the lips, and for everybody to see, sending the butterflies in her stomach into somersault mode.

Lily enjoyed every minute of the festive service. There was a small but highly talented young choir who began the service by entering the church in a candlelit procession, singing *Once in Royal David's City*. She recognized the girl she had heard singing in the church shortly after Joseph's accident — in fact, she was the one who sang the solo, her crystal clear soprano filling the church. Then the rest of the choir joined in, followed by the congregation, and Lily sang with confidence and heartfelt joy.

'You have the most beautiful voice,' Joseph whispered, squeezing her hand.

'Thank you,' she whispered back, and put her head against his shoulder.

In between the Nine Lessons and a short but surprisingly thought-provoking sermon, they sang all of Lily's favourite carols, *O Come All Ye Faithful*, *In the Bleak Midwinter* and by the time they got to *Hark! The Herald Angels Sing*, she was crying. Instinctively she reached for the heart pendant, then remembered she had taken it off just this morning. It was now lying on its velvet cushion in the box it had come with, and there it would stay, in memory of Spencer and her old life, and nothing else. She did not need to feel it any more. She had everything she needed and wanted in her life right here.

And of course she had the comfort cross – when she had told Beth about how she still carried it around with her everywhere she went, her friend had laughed and said, 'I'll get you to pray yet, Lily Henderson, just you wait!' — to which she had replied, 'Well, I don't know about that, but it's good to know it's always there, in my pocket.'

But now she took it out, held it in her hand and whispered, 'Thank you.'

'What for?'

She was about to close her hand around the little cross as she turned to Joseph, but changed her mind and instead showed it to him. 'I said thank you to God. For saving you. And — well. For everything ...' She swallowed, and he reached out to push a strand of hair from her face, looking at her so tenderly, she thought her heart was going to explode in her chest.

'Oh Lily,' he whispered, pulling her close. And they stood there, leaning against each other in the pew, while everybody came and wished them a happy Christmas. There was lots of hugging and laughing and chatting, but to Lily, everything seemed to happen in slow motion, as she smiled and nodded and thanked people for their good wishes without even realizing that she did any of these things. It was like a dream.

When they stepped out of the church, the snow was still falling against the velvety darkness of the December sky. Joseph took her hand, and she turned to look up at him, her face radiant. Neither of them spoke, but when their eyes locked, they found themselves in a world of their own, where everything else — faces, voices, laughter, and music — blurred and faded into nothingness.

THE END

Acknowledgments

JUST DAYS BEFORE my lovely mum passed away in 2021, she said, 'Anne, why don't you just quit school and do what you love most? Write!' It took me another year to realize that she was right. Thank you, Mum, for never failing to believe in me, especially when I had ceased to believe in myself.

My biggest and most heartfelt thanks goes to my husband Wolfgang. Without your unfailing love and support (and a constant supply of tea and Cadbury Mini Bars whenever I get anxious) I would not be where I am today. I love you so much!

To Lukas and Rachel, for putting up with a writing mother who is so often lost in her world of imagination that it is hard to get her attention at times!

To Linda and Ian, and everyone at Low House Farm, for your kindness and friendship. I will never love a place so well as I love this farm, and Dairy Cottage will always be home to me.

To Geoff, for pointing me in the right direction on that rather fateful walk we took near Burford on Good Friday last year. 'If you don't do this now, you will regret it for the rest of your life!' I did it, didn't I? And I have no regrets whatsoever.

To the wonderful Witney Home Group for your support and prayers throughout the process, and to my super-efficient advance readers: Rebecca, Ali, Deborah, Ruth, Shirley, Geoff, and Dieter. Your help has been invaluable.

To my fellow writers Adoara, Iulia, and Jenny, for their support and encouragement along the way. Isn't it a great comfort to know that we do not have to walk alone?

Thank you, Ken, for creating such a lovely, lovely cover for this one, and I am already looking forward to the next book cover adventure! And thanks to Kate, who really is the most patient and most encouraging typesetter I could have wished for, down to the tiniest little detail! I know I'm a perfectionist, and I wanted it just so – but you understood. Thank you for that!

And last not least, thank you to our most beloved Benny dog who unwittingly modelled for the handsome Hamish :-). As you cannot read, I will just slip you a treat instead. Good dog.

A note on animals and places in this book

When I said that any resemblance to actual *persons* was entirely coincidental, I must admit that there are two equine exceptions – Ronnie and Delilah are my favourite Welsh Mountain Ponies and the pride and joy of their owners at Low House Farm, Carlton in Cleveland, North Yorkshire. (And yes, Ronnie does stick his tongue out if you ask him to!)

In order to find the perfect home for my fictional village of Bishops Bridge, I took the liberty of stretching Rosedale a bit, even dried out the middle part, to make room for some more farms, tracks, pubs, and such like. I hope the people of Rosedale will forgive me, and I will still be welcome to enjoy my walks there, even if I don't bring a donkey.

Jessie's Cinnamon Swirls

500 g strong bread flour
¼ tsp salt
50 g caster sugar
1 sachet of fast action dried yeast
100 g unsalted butter
150 ml warm milk

For the filling:
60 g very soft or melted butter
60 g soft brown sugar mixed with
1 ½ tsp of cinnamon, plus extra sugar and cinnamon for sprinkling

Variety: Add 50 g sultanas, apricots or dried mixed peel to the filling.

STEPS:
1. Mix flour, salt, sugar and yeast, then add warm milk and butter to form a soft but not sticky dough. Knead for at least 5 minutes (either by hand, or use the dough hook of the food processor).
2. On a floured surface, knead the dough for a further

5 minutes, then pop it back into the mixing bowl and cover with clingfilm.
3. Leave to rise in a warm place for at least 45 minutes, or until doubled in size.
4. Roll out the dough into a rectangular shape (about 4-5 mm thick) and brush generously with soft or melted butter, then sprinkle with sugar and cinnamon.
5. Roll up into a long sausage, turn over so the edge is underneath, and cut into pieces of about 1.5 cm, depending on how many you want, and how thick you like them. You should get about 12.
6. Cover loosely with clingfilm and leave for another 15 minutes or so, until slightly risen.
7. In the meantime, grease a baking tray or a large, square cake tin, and preheat the oven to 190°C.
8. Place cinnamon swirls into the tin or onto the tray, cut side down, and sprinkle with a little extra sugar and cinnamon. Bake for about 20 minutes, or until well risen and golden brown.

JESSIE'S TIPP:

For extra indulgence, you can brush the warm buns with butter or apricot jam, and / or give them an extra dusting of cinnamon.

About the Author

MEET ANNE WHORLTON

Anne has published four novels in German under her real name of Anke Weidinger. In 2022, after eighteen years of teaching, she made the life-changing decision to leave the classroom behind, and began to write in English. Anne now spends as much time as possible in her writing retreat on the North York Moors, where her stories are set. When she is not writing, you will find her roaming the Moors with her faithful Lassie dog, or spending precious time with her husband. Anne loves baking, reading, and singing, and has not yet given up on the idea of one day owning a donkey.

You can find Anne on Instagram @bishops_bridge_books and Facebook @AnneWhorlton, or visit www.annewhorlton.com.

Reading Group Questions

1. Did you enjoy reading *In Lily's Books*? What would be the one scene that you would always remember from this book? Why?

2. A key feature of the novel is the setting, which includes Oxford as well as Yorkshire. How does the setting contribute to the story?

3. What were the recurring themes or motifs throughout the book? Do any of them resonate emotionally with you?

4. Which character did you like best or feel the most sympathy for? Do you have a quote connected with this character?

5. With most of the book being set in the country, there are a lot of animal characters, too. What different roles do they play, and which of them would you give the most credit for Lily's healing?

6. When talking about her book barn idea, Lily says, 'So I need to come up with a Plan B. Probably a Plan C and D as well, just to be on the safe side.' How does this quote describe Lily's character?

7. Which of Lily's decisions are the bravest, considering her character and disposition?

8. Was there a moment when you disagreed with Lily's decisions or actions? What would you have done differently?

9. *You deserve to be happy. Even if that stupid nagging voice in your head keeps whispering you don't, you know you do. Don't listen to the lies inside your head. You did that before, and you know where that got you.*
These are Lily's thoughts when she is on the brink of starting her new life in Yorkshire. Why does Lily find it so hard to trust people, and herself?

10. What do you think the pendant and the cross symbolize in this story?

11. Can you imagine why the author would have chosen the title *In Lily's Books*?

12. What three words would you use to describe the novel to a friend?

Printed in Poland
by Amazon Fulfillment
Poland Sp. z o.o., Wrocław